T0064605

Modern Infidel:
Filet of Soul

A Novel by

R. Thomas Risk

authorHOUSE®

AuthorHouse™
1663 Liberty Drive
Bloomington, IN 47403
www.authorhouse.com
Phone: 833-262-8899

Published by AuthorHouse 06/03/2021

ISBN: 978-1-4969-0010-4 (sc)
ISBN: 978-1-4969-0013-5 (hc)
ISBN: 978-1-4969-0006-7 (e)

Library of Congress Control Number: 2014906033

Print information available on the last page.

Other Books by R. Thomas Risk

Where We Find Ourselves: Portrait of a Modern Infidel
(AuthorHouse 2010)

On Christmas Day, 6-year-old Randolph runs into the family room and cries, "Daddy!" Two men – William and Cyrus – answer his call. In his quest to unravel the mystery of two fathers, which leads to a reunion with his birth mother and the exposure of grim secrets William tried to bury half a century ago, Randolph rediscovers himself. Thirty-three years after that ominous Christmas Day, as William tries to atone from his deathbed for a lifetime of deceit, Randolph realizes that he has solved a far greater question: *Does God exist*? The practical and political implications of his answer will astonish you.

In this autobiographical tale of betrayal and liberation, R. Thomas Risk enlists the analytical skills of a lawyer, the savvy of an investigator and the eloquence of an award-winning poet to forever change your perception of society's sacred institutions – the most insidious of which are Religion, Celebrity and National Politics.

CONTENTS

This book is dedicated to

Mary Larson

Of a precious few people may it be said that the world we know has been vastly improved by their sojourn here. You, Mary Larson, are one.

Acknowledgements

The subtitle to Chapter Thirteen is derived from Mark Twain's incisive observation: "Under certain circumstances, profanity provides a relief denied even to prayer."

The line "Fear in a handful of dust" was borrowed from T.S. Eliot's classic *The Wasteland.*

Overture

Don't Feed the Cannibals

"Just keep the perimeter intact. I don't want any citizens up there, and we don't need any pictures on tonight's news."

Captain Chick Barceno Villanueva, a 24-year detective with the city police, smooths his prodigious mustache as he addresses a milling clump of young uniforms, one of whom raises his hat to capture Villanueva's attention.

"It's a massacre up there, Cap. Gotta be gang related."

"Garver, you think everything is gang related. You think the pajamas I sleep in are gang related."

"I'm just saying …."

"I counted fourteen bodies. Somebody say we have an eyewitness? Unger, make yourself known, son."

"Yeah, Cap – one Eldra Frye, the babe at the front desk. Says she watched the whole thing. But she's hysterical – claims one perp did all that. I don't think she's reliable."

"You and Garver are making my gastroenterologist rich."

"Huh, Cap? You think there's a Cuban connection?"

"Shut up, Garver. Even an unreliable witness can give you probative evidence. The Razor of Occam, gentlemen. The most simple explanation is the most preferred. I will interview this Eldra Frye now. Where is she?"

At Unger's nod, the austere detective lumbers up the steps to a nearby EMT trailer. Jostling a serpentine path through the fitful hive of first responders, he clomps the length of the trailer to find a tremulous Eldra cowering in the floor next to the oxygen tank that inspirits her nasal tube. Chanting underbreath, she works a rosary strand in each frenetic hand. He takes a seat on the floor across from her – no small feat for a man of his girth.

"*Dios te salve, Maria.* I am afraid that is all I remember."

"Hail Mary, full of grace. Our Lord is with thee. Blessed art thou among women, and blessed is the fruit of thy womb, Jesus. Holy Mary, Mother of God, pray for us sinners, now and at the hour of our death. Amen."

"My wife, she often prays. Me, not so much."

"Hail Mary, full of grace. Our Lord is with thee. Blessed art thou among women …"

"Ms. Frye?"

"Holy Mary, Mother of God, pray for us sinners …"

"Ms. Eldra Frye?"

"… at the hour of our death. Amen."

"What troubles you, my dear?"

"Azrael."

"Who is this Azrael?"

"I saw him."

"Yes, but who –"

"He wore the hooded cape, he … swung that merciless axe."

"Good, Eldra, good. What color was this cape?"

"Dim. Foreboding. Like the dirt at the bottom of a grave."

"You're doing fine. Describe for me this weapon of his."

"It had a knotty wooden shaft, half as long as the one my grandfather used on the ranch, and a leather strap that ran its length. The head … I've never seen anything like it."

"What was unique about it?"

"The shaft extended an inch or so beyond it. The blade was slimmer … more rounded, like the waning crescent of the moon. And the heel protruded and tapered like a dibber."

"I am not familiar with the word ... *dibber*?"

"A round, wooden stick that narrows to a point. I use one to plant bulbs in my garden."

"You draw the picture in my mind of an eighteenth century tomahawk. Are you telling me one man with a Native American artifact is responsible for the slaughter I have just surveyed?"

"That was no man. It was … a machine. It gave no quarter, even when the boy fell to his knees and pled. Yet it spared me."

"Was there any gunfire?"

"No. Just that heartless axe. Like a pendulum, it would not stop or slow down. And with its other hand it used … a thresher sort of thing … like a folding knife whose blade was only partway open."

"A scythe?"

"Yes. But smaller, and with that same brutal crescent shape."

"Did this Azrael say anything to you?"

"When it was over. *You need not fear me. I have not come for you.* And this is how I know it was Azrael. The solid brick wall at the far end of the room retreated from its path."

"Eldra, I must know. Who is Azrael?"

"The angel of death. It made me its outrider. Don't you see? The iniquities of the ages are forgathering in this place, at this time. What happened today was an augury – retribution is nigh. As it is written in Isaiah 13:6: *Howl ye; for the day of the Lord is at hand; it shall come as a destruction from the Almighty.* And if you're on the wrong side of Jesus, Detective, you're fucked."

With a fatherly pat on the hand, Villanueva leaves Eldra Frye to her prayers. When he ambles out to the courtyard he is accosted by Unger, who is so eager that even when he stands still he plods in place like a Labrador puppy.

"What do we do now, Cap? Want me to take Frye in? Need a note taker at the scene? My instructor at the academy said I was a variable proxy at note taking."

Lamenting the fact that generations of rampant steroid abuse have rendered today's typical rookie ten IQ points dumber for every ounce of muscle he boasts over his predecessor, Villanueva removes the boy's hat and thwacks his prematurely bald dome (another side effect of the steroid misuse) with his gold nugget wedding ring.

"The phrase is *veritable prodigy*, genius. Does it not unsettle you in the slightest that I enjoy a better command of my second language than you do your native tongue?"

"Oh, I'm not an Indian that I know of, Cap."

"Do you even own a book?"

"Why yes, sir. As a matter of fact, I have two: the *New American Standard Bible* and the service manual for this baby right here."

Unger pats his semiautomatic sidearm. Villanueva nods toward the yellow tape in dismay.

"That is why you will do nothing but traffic patrol and crowd control until the day I retire. Stand right there and do not stray from that spot, even if you catch fire."

As his blithe subordinate waggles away, Villanueva paws at his cell phone. Some minds work best pictographically, like that of the sculptor or cartographer. Writers, on the other hand, are oriented toward letters. Villanueva's analytical gift comes alive only when he hears the spoken word. Thus, while his colleagues scribble on notepads, he records his thoughts and observations remotely on an old fashioned *Dictaphone*, which his secretary transcribes at day's end.

"Scene summary, 21 January. Fourteen deceased males in administrative offices, each of whom exhibited multiple cuts and blunt force trauma. No evidence of break-in. No reports of gunplay. No identifications as yet. The only eyewitness is Eldra Frye, a thirty-two-year-old receptionist with a high school education. The balance of the staff consists of eleven male accountants. At precisely 11:45 every morning, they all leave together for a two-hour lunch, and Ms. Frye locks the front door behind her. Today, she forgot to turn the *Out to Lunch* sign. Her employer, whom she has never seen in person, is very particular about that sign. So she walked three blocks and a half back to the establishment. When she entered to turn the sign, she saw a man in a dark brown raincoat in the midst of a furious rampage with an unusual combination of weapons: a Sioux tomahawk and a knife known as a khukuri – a Nepalese fighting blade approximately one foot in length and offset at roughly a thirty-five degree angle. This curvature is conducive to the slashing and chopping motions because, when held with its edge toward one's adversary, the wrist need not bend to deliver an effective strike. Ms. Frye knew none of the men he was attacking, and she understood not why they were there or how they even got in. After the last victim had fallen, the assailant told her he was not there to kill her, but that he needed her as a cautionary witness to others unknown. He then exited the office through the rear wall, which is opened by the means of an electronic sensor beneath the linoleum.

"Only two kinds of perpetrators leave alive an identifying witness: madmen and revenge killers. I know my share of street fighters and veterans of war. But I know no man capable of meting out such carnage as this which I saw today. I saw a skull split down its midsection, crown to sternum. I saw a disarticulated forearm wedged in the ceiling fan. Though Ms. Frye insists this was the work of the one man, I can not overlook the fact that she is given to delusion. It is, therefore, my opinion that the man she saw had at least six accomplices who had exited the room before her arrival. I deduce that our offenders are both mentally unsound and pursuing some sort of a vendetta. And they are quite cunning. Not only did they obtain entry undetected, but they sprang with such intensity and agility that, even though some of their targets possessed at least one illegal firearm, none had the time or the mental presence to even draw his weapon, let alone discharge it. Ms. Frye confirms that, in the midst of the mayhem, the last remaining attacker had such command over his environment as to briefly interrogate one of the victims even as he slew another.

"It is a shame I must arrest these hellhounds, for their skills would be quite availing at the academy. Persephone, please omit my closing personal comments from the report, thank you."

DON'T DO DRUGS ... FOR RECREATION, THAT IS.
DO DO DRUGS IF THEY HAVE BEEN PRESCRIBED BY
A MEDICARE OR MEDICAID APPROVED PHYSICIAN
FOR ADD, ADHD OR ANY OTHER CONDITION THAT
TENDS TO MAKE YOU UNCOOPERATIVE WITH PUBLIC
TEACHERS AND OTHER GOVERNMENT AUTHORITIES.

*This public service announcement is brought to
you by the Food and Drug Administration.*

Chapter One

Cosmic Cellmates

October 14, 2020

"God save us from the puritans."

Freddie can no more see the face of the smartly dressed passerby who uttered this paradox than he can grasp its simple irony. Nor does he attach any significance to the bulky cigar the man brandishes as he talks to the guards at the gated end of the alley. Freddie cares for nothing beyond the fact that this is the last time a prison van will carry him from a penitentiary to the side entrance of a downtown courthouse. This is the last time he will suffer the indignity of having to wear ill fitting jumpsuits and being trussed up in chains like a roasting hog before he can venture beyond the razor wire, the last time he'll be ordered to duck his head through the doorway to that filthy elevator, the last time he'll have to be respectful to that deputy Sheriff who stands too close and smells like toe-jam. After … well, more days than he can count, this is the last time Freddie will have to stand next to that wormy public defender who shakes hands like a twink.

"Next on the docket?"

This is not the same judge who sentenced Freddie. But he looks every bit as angry at being saddled with his present task.

"State v. Freddie Herzog." The judge peers over his granny-glasses at Freddie in patent distaste, "aka Slinky Sam," then drops his gaze again to the slip of paper his clerk just passed to him. "On August 7, 2006, Mr. Herzog … I have a date of offense but no offense. What did this man do? Where is his file?"

The bailiff whispers in the judge's ear.

"Do you mean to tell me the court clerk has had this docket for two weeks but can't do me the simple courtesy of producing the man's file?"

The judge yanks his glasses off and gestures with his coffee cup.

"Attorneys approach."

The prosecutor scurries to the bench, Freddie's effeminate defender close on his heels.

"Gentlemen, all I have on this guy is a five-by-eight slip of paper from the Sheriff. I'm trying to make a record here. What crime did this man commit?"

The attorneys trade blank glances, then the prosecutor frantically thumbs through a legal pad and says something inaudible to the judge.

"Well, I have to tell the both of you, this is one hell of a way to start the day. Do we even know the man I am about to cut loose is the same man the jury sent up? Do I look illiterate to you? Of course the name on the Sheriff's inventory matches the one on the federal writ. But it's the surname *Herzog* that takes me aback. The man sitting at your table in chains is most definitely of Latin descent. How can I be so sure? Look at my nameplate, counselor. I think I'm qualified to assess whether or not this man is a Latino. Neither of you brought a file? Enough, I'm going to get to the bottom of this right now. Step away."

As the attorneys saunter back to their respective tables, the judge stretches his neck and drums the bench with an impatient ink pen.

"Will the prisoner please stand?"

At the nod of his epicene mouthpiece, Freddie climbs upright.

"Sir, is your name Freddie Herzog?"

"Yes, that it is, your honor."

"For what infraction are you serving time?"

"Man, I don't know nothing about Algeria."

"Algeria?"

"That math class with them infractions and rations and whatnot."

"What is your mother's maiden name?"

"Mary Magdalena Areces Galaviz, your honor. I ain't seen her since …"

"Your father?"

"Well, Judge, I don't think she know. But she got a marryin' license say Mary Magdalena Areces Galaviz Herzog, so I guess *mi padre* be a Hebe."

Freddie's laughter finds no purchase. Hearing the same remonstrative sputter from his attorney that his mother used to make, he does his best to be conciliatory. "And, uh, I mean that with all dual aspect, your honor." A cadaverous hand pulls him down to ear level as his effete representative whispers frantically. "Sorry, your honor, my mouth over here say that's dual respect. Yeah, with all dual respect."

"That's enough, Mr. Herzog."

"Sure, Judge. I'm just saying –"

The judge's gavel rattles the courtroom like a gunshot.

"Shut your mouth, Mr. Herzog. No, no, keep standing; just do so quietly. Now then. For whatever crime of which you were indicted, on December 18, 2009 a jury of your peers handed down a sentence … which was obviously far longer than your actual tenure in our justice system's various facilities; hence, the endearing catchphrase *early release*. Pursuant to the federal *Criminal Rehabilitation and Reform Act*, that sentence was commuted to time served. You are free, sir, to reenter society without restriction. The deputy will now take you to processing, where you will be provided with a new suit of clothes, a prepaid cell phone with five thousand minutes of talk time and, because what little information I have indicates you were on death row, a debit card with a balance of $10,000 to compensate you for the cruel and unusual punishment the State has inflicted upon you."

Less than one hour later (the fastest he has ever been processed), Freddie smooths the coat sleeve of the hand-tailored worsted wool suit for which he was fitted last Friday. Though he always hated wearing ties, he figures he can find an alternative use for this one, so he tucks it securely into his pocket. With one last look in the mirror, Freddie nods to the attendant who then summons the deputies under whose escort Freddie will, for the first time in his thirty-four years of life, walk out the *front* door of a courthouse.

No sooner does he emerge into the invigorating autumn air than Freddie discovers his gun-toting contingent is a mere formality. At the base of the courthouse steps mills a crowd which erupts into applause at his appearance. Scraggly college students, who have camped nearby in anticipation of this event, wave banners on which they've painted the threadbare cliché *Free at Last*. Men bounce toddlers on their shoulders while their enraptured wives throw open palms skyward and shout *Thank you, Jesus!* A delirious woman haphazardly clad as Mother Earth releases a white dove from a cage containing ten – one for each inmate who will be released today. Feeling a tug at his trousers, Freddie stoops to accept a purple rose from a girl no older than the boy who once gave him something so much more memorable. He then wades into the crowd, where he is conveyed so effortlessly by handshakes and hugs and shoulder claps that he emerges on the other side of the street feeling as though he hasn't made one footfall. But like a vagarious wind, when the next early releasee fills the juridical doorway, all of the well-wishers abruptly turn their backs and forget Freddie ever existed.

All, that is, but one. As Freddie straightens his jacket and ambles toward a café, he fails to notice the immaculate man standing in the dim of a store entrance.

"An historical day, Mr. Herzog, is it not?"

Freddie turns to spy the man he overheard on his way into the courthouse, his face obscured by smoke from his newly lit cigar.

"An unaccountable millionaire signs a piece of paper fifteen hundred miles away and, as a direct result, your life is restored to you and your slate wiped clean. In the United States of America, no less. How does one comprehend such a thing? I call that phenomenal. I call that stupendous. I call that historical."

Freddie doesn't know what to make of his new acquaintance. Middle-aged and just beginning to bald, at first glance he seems an easy enough mark – the skittish sort of fop who might surrender his money and jewelry if a street kid did nothing more than scowl at him. But there is something in the way he punctuated that last word with his cigar that gives Freddie pause. And when the mist clears, with it vanishes any inkling that this man is a sucker. Freddie knows that facial expression – the corners of the mouth upturned ever so subtly, not quite enough to form a smile, and the unrelenting eyes as round and fixed as those of a stalking cat. He's seen that look on the street. He saw it in the pen. And he has always paid it wary respect.

"Yeah, man, that there's what it is – hysterical."

As Freddie shuffles away, the man jaws his cigar and retrieves a PDA from beneath his arm. Before Freddie has taken five steps, he has arrived at the corner deli. Reaching for the door, he hears a new effusion of accolades. He gazes back to see the fickle mob cast the day's second parolee onto the sidewalk, where he encounters the same mysterious greeting as Freddie:

"An historical day, Mr. Versace, is it not?"

As Freddie acquires the nearest vacant barstool, the courthouse door coughs up Peter Mott. Peering in bewilderment at the fanfare, Peter stumbles into the throng only to clear a path for the Sheriff's contingent that just acquired the steps behind him. Still in shock when he is spat out at the other end, Peter yelps in fright when the well groomed cigar toter clasps his shoulder and spins him round.

"Who the hell are you?"

Peter gropes for words as the man fingers his PDA.

"You are not on my list. Your name, sir, I must have your name."

"Puh …"

"Starts with a P, very good, continue."

"Peter, um, Peter Mott."

"Is that Mott with two Ts?"

"Yes, but why –"

"Move it along, Mr. Mott, we are on a tight schedule today. Go on, beat it."

Sauntering past the same establishment in which Freddie succumbs to a steaming mocha java, Peter gropes for his cell phone. The voice of his administrative assistant lends him comfort.

"Mira, it happened again."

"Oh, thank goodness it's you, Mr. Mott. I've been calling all morning. Where are you?"

Peter surveys his environs in no less wonderment than that experienced by Neil Armstrong on July 20, 1969.

"Downtown. I just left the courthouse. I never go to the courthouse. Unless … oh, dear God, do you think I was arrested?"

"You? I'm sorry, Mr. Mott, I don't mean to laugh. No, no, no. This is the monthly release day, remember?"

"The prayer vigil?"

"Yes, Mr. Mott."

Peter checks the date on his phone.

"But that was yesterday, Mira."

"That's good news!"

"How is that good news?"

"It means you only lost one day this time."

"Mira."

"Yes, Mr. Mott?"

"When I say I just left the courthouse, I mean I was very recently *inside* it."

"Well, there could be … one, two, three … I can think of a dozen very good reasons you may have entered that structure, none of which have to do with being arrested."

"But that doesn't mean I wasn't."

"Now that is just silly, Mr. Mott. You are no more dangerous than my sister's poodle Honeypea."

Peter loses himself in the latest of many reflections on how honey and peas bear not the slightest relevance to each other.

"Mr. Mott, don't hang up – you're going to be late if you don't find Jesus!"

"My driver is from South America. His name is pronounced Jesús."

"But the pun just doesn't work that way."

"Mira."

"Yes, Mr. Mott?"

"You said I was going to be late. Late for what?"

"Your lunch date with Julia Bross. I just texted Jesús, and he's parked on Hudson just around the corner from the court building."

"Nice catching up to you again, Mr. Mott."

An attentive Jesús guides Peter into the open back door of a nondescript sedan.

"Mira, you've got to cancel that luncheon. I've been wearing the same clothes for two days, I haven't brushed my teeth … my shorts have bunched up in the strangest spot … people, Mira, I'm not big on people today."

"Now don't you fret, Mr. Mott. I've restocked your emergency bag as I always do."

"I have an emergency bag?"

The *emergency bag* is a suitcase that contains Peter's toiletries and two changes of clothes – one casual and the other formal. Mira inaugurated its use the same day she hired Jesús, just hours after Peter's first blackout.

"It's in the trunk, and I reserved you a table at the Hyatt where I also booked you a room so you can be as fresh as a puppy's breath."

"Please cancel the luncheon. I'm not in the mood."

"I will not cancel, Mr. Mott, and I don't care how mad you get."

"How's this for mad? You're fired."

"The hell I am! Ms. Bross is a very nice lady, and I won't have you standing her up."

"Well, I'm not going. Jesús, take me to my office."

"Jesús has his instructions, Mr. Mott. You're going to the Hyatt."

"I pay the man's wages. You hear that, Jesús?"

"No, Mr. Mott. Your corporate trust writes his checks, but he works for me."

"Are you kidnapping me in my own car? By proxy?"

"It's not your car, Mr. Mott. It belongs to your subchapter S. Now you just stop being a fusspot right now and pretend you're the old Peter Mott we all grew to know and love because, if you aren't nice to that sweet girl, I'll be very disappointed in you."

Resigned to his fate, Peter falls back against the headrest and stares out the window. As the car circles the block to exit the one-way street, the realization that thanks to him Mother Earth will come up one dove short distracts Peter just long enough to steal a restorative dream from the muddle that has been his life of late. He drifts back to December 25, 1997. The aroma of the cinnamon and spice tea that had been steeping all night suffused the little house he shared with Deanna, who shivered in giddy anticipation as they watched five-year-old Millie open for her little brother Dylan his very first Christmas present.

"Mr. Mott? Mr. Mott?"

Wiping a tear from his cheek, Peter climbs out of the car and follows his driver into the hotel as though he were walking to his own execution. When the concierge extends the key card toward Peter, Jesús snatches it and leads Peter by the arm into the awaiting elevator.

"Jesús, I'm a grown man. I don't need a nursemaid."

"My mission is to deliver you to Ms. Bross. Ms. Mira was very explicit. According to Ms. Mira, there are seven escape routes between here and there, and it is my job to deter you from those avenues. Here we are, Mr. Mott, Room 302."

"You're not going to bathe me, are you?"

On the main floor, the hostess shows Julia Bross to her table. Julia's most striking attribute is not the penetrating Caribbean green of her eyes; it is that she is thoroughly at ease with herself. Hence, she commands every situation with such finesse that both friend and foe succumb to her will, thinking every step of the way that it is she who is yielding to them.

"Good morning, ma'am. I'll be serving you today –"

"What's your name, Hon?"

"Christopher, ma'am."

"*Ma'am* … Aren't you just a doll? I'll tell you what, Christopher. Don't worry yourself with the menu spiel; I already know what my guest and I will have. Meanwhile, if you'll bring me a glass of house merlot and make sure I never see the bottom of that glass, I'll be your newest best friend."

As her blushing waiter scurries to the bar, Peter ambles to the hostess perch like a scolded schoolboy. Seizing on the hostess' momentary preoccupation elsewhere, he turns away on the hope that his dogged driver has left his post. Jesús scarcely has time to grin at his venerable boss before Julia takes his charge in hand.

"Jesús, you're my hero. Thanks for getting him here."

"Always my pleasure, Ms. Bross."

She guides a reluctant Peter past the stand to a corner table.

"And for the gentleman?"

Startled by the waiter's question, Peter knocks his bread plate to the floor. Before Christopher can react, Julia has retrieved it for him and straightened the tablecloth.

"You mean me?"

"To drink, sir?"

"I … I don't …"

"Don't be silly, of course you do. Sweetie, bring him a whiskey soda, and go easy on the whiskey … let's say half a shot. He's a lightweight."

Peter fidgets in his chair, sets his forearms tentatively on the table, lifts them, plants his elbows in their stead and clasps his hands, but is uncomfortable with that and finally folds his arms in his lap. All the while, he stares at the sugar tray in the middle of the table as Julia studies him over a museful sip of wine. When Christopher brings Peter's drink, with but a glance and a gesture she entices the young man to put the food order on indefinite hold and slink away in silence. She then picks up the sugar tray and casually flings it to the floor, never once averting her stare from her increasingly agitated lunch companion. Peter tries to recover the tray, but she grabs his arm and maneuvers him back into his chair. When his gaze lands on the pepper well, she knocks it over. Peter can take no more.

"Julia, why did you call me?"

"I hear you're looking for more commercial lots, and I've got some killer interest rates."

Peter finally makes eye contact, but for only a fleeting moment as his budding smile fades. "Why did you call me?"

"I wanted to tell you to your face that, in my opinion, she's the epitomal bitch for doing what she did to you."

"Don't say that about Deanna."

"A true lady does not walk away at a time like that."

"You don't know her, Julia. That's not fair."

"I don't have to know her, Peter. I know you."

"You don't know everything that happened."

Julia sets the drinks aside and takes Peter's hands.

"I've known you since I was four. Remember how I couldn't pronounce my Ts because of that speech impediment, so I called you PeMo? When they took my tonsils out, you spent the whole afternoon bringing me shaved ice from that parlor two blocks away. Don't forget, I was the one who set you up with Father Kinion's daughter and, had I not, you might still be a virgin today."

"That doesn't mean –"

"I *know* you. Remember the last time we saw each other? It was at your wedding. Your consulting firm was growing faster than the national debt, Peter, and your eyes glistened because your future was a voluptuous tramp who would give you everything she had just for the asking. And what have you become? Some sort of New Age pimp."

"I am an ordained minister and interfaith facilitator."

"The Peter I grew up with subdued and dissected every convention that got in his way. Now you're nothing more than a purveyor of stale tradition."

"Somebody told me I was meeting an old friend, here."

Peter tries to extricate himself, but Julia tightens her grip and pulls him closer.

"Name one person in your life who has been a more loyal friend than I – just one – and I'll leave you alone."

When he was in kindergarten, a teacher called Peter down for shuffling his feet on the carpet and shocking a girl. This marked the first time he had ever been rebuffed by any adult other than his parents. He wanted desperately to escape the teacher's disapproving stare, but at the age of five he had nowhere to go. No less fervent is his urge to flee Julia's inquest. Alas, his troth to her prevails.

"Peter, look at me."

Julia's employees and associates know her only as a cunning businesswoman. One CFO remarked after she had bought out his natural gas company, *Though she is the most barbarous shrew I've ever had the misfortune to know, I still have wet dreams about that infernal woman.* But when Peter engages her, all he sees is the gawky neighborhood kid who snuck into his room on stormy nights to watch old *Laurel & Hardy* movies which the networks played to keep viewers entertained between severe weather alerts.

"Why did you come here?"

"I want my PeMo back. He's in there somewhere. But he can't get out unless you talk about it. Talk to me, Peter."

The agony in his expression is almost more than she can abide. He draws a deep breath, but all his strength dissipates with its egress. He closes his eyes in defeat.

"I can't."

"You can't, or you won't?"

At the sound of his therapist's voice, Peter plants his feet and grips the arms of the gray leather chair like an aviophobe who just awoke in an airplane at thirty thousand feet.

"What the devil are you doing now?"

"It just happened again. How long have I been here?"

"You sat in that chair not half an hour ago." Dr. Kelner removes his reading glasses with deliberate care, leans forward with intense concentration. "Have you lost time again, Peter?"

"I just sat down to have lunch with Julia. She was asking me questions and holding my hands … it was seconds ago!"

Dr. Kelner checks his notes.

"It was two and a half hours ago."

"Is that what we've been talking about?"

"You talked, I scribbled notes like mad trying to keep up. And all the while you were rehashing it for me in real time, apparently reliving it as though your psyche were a DVR. I really wish you would consent to a CT scan."

"What was the last thing she and I discussed?"

"She wanted you to talk about the same thing you have most obstreperously avoided discussing with me since our sessions began."

"Which I can't."

"Or –"

"Won't, yeah. And that really irks you, doesn't it?"

"Peter, these sessions are for you, not me. I can offer guidance, but in the end it's your money. Now that I've sufficiently patronized you to satisfy my licensing board's rules of ethics, yes, your continued refusal to broach the subject which we both know lies at the root of your blackouts chaps my hide no end. Now that you are awake, as it were, I suppose you'll want to mesmerize me with another of your erratic dreams?"

"That would make me happy, Doc'."

The sullen doctor drops his notepad on the endtable, marches to the credenza to retrieve the carafe of coffee, tops off his and Peter's cups, returns the urn to its cradle and reclaims the notepad.

"Proceed."

"I'm standing in a field. It's cold and windy, but there's no breeze."

"Peter, you can't have it both ways. Either there's wind or –"

"It's blowing in the distance, but it's calm where I am."

"Are you standing next to a rock, a tent, what?"

"No, I'm exposed on all sides."

The doctor rubs his bushy forehead as if to hold a migraine at bay.

"There is wind or there is no wind. Are you in a protective bubble?"

"No, no bubble."

"Peter, there is either wind or no wind."

"It's a dream, Doc'. Why can't it be both?"

Dr. Kelner springs to his feet.

"I'll tell you why. Because I'm watching you slip farther and farther away from reality. It is my job to stop that process. It is my job to bring you back from unreality, and I must take a stand against this wind-but-no-wind nonsense! Now is there wind or isn't there?"

Peter stands defiantly and squares off with his bulky-sweatered benefactor.

"There's both."

With a grunt, the doctor slumps into his chair. Peter stiffly regains his own.

"Fine, Peter. Fine. We've ten minutes. Continue."

"In the distance I hear a rumbling noise. It grows louder and louder. I look in its direction and I see four horses. One is white, one is … two are black and one brown and … they're all changing color like barber poles. Is that significant?"

"If I tell you it is, will you agree to the CT scan?"

"As they come nearer, one is black, one brown, another yellow and the last white."

"What do their riders look like?"

"They don't have any."

"Peter, you are depicting the Four Horsemen of the Apocalypse. Horse*men.* You of all people should be familiar with that imagery."

"I see the same horses three or more times a week, Doc', and I'm telling you they're running free."

"Go on."

"They're galloping right toward me, but I can't move because the wind is hitting me from all sides."

The doctor issues a heavy sigh.

"So the wind-no-wind is now multidirectional?"

Peter grimaces.

"Yes."

"But there's no vortex, no thunderstorm?"

"No."

"Mhm."

"Just before they trample me, they veer off and pass within inches. And I see that they have words branded on their hindquarters. The first says WE."

"So this is a French horse?"

"No, w-e."

"Is the wind also hitting you from above and below?"

"I don't know about … how could it possibly hit me from below if I'm standing on the ground?"

"I see. You acknowledge the laws of physics only when they suit you."

"May we get past the wind, please?"

"If you insist. So the first horse has the word WE tattooed on its ass."

"Yes. And the second horse reads DON'T STOP."

"We don't … stop. And the third?"

"I don't know what it says."

"Why not?"

"Because they always disappear before it passes within view."

"What the hell am I supposed to do with that?"

"Excuse me, Doc'?"

"Expecting me to interpret an incomplete dream is like asking a guitarist to play with only one hand. Peter, I'm not a clairvoyant. If you insist on monopolizing my time with these psychedelic romps of yours, at least do me the courtesy of bringing me the complete package."

Dr. Kelner sets his coffee down, but before he can initiate his watch-tapping gesture Peter has acquired his coat.

"You know, you sure are snippety for a mental health professional."

Dr. Kelner extends a warm hand.

"And you're rather recalcitrant for a man who never knows when he'll lose consciousness or where he'll be when he regains it."

"Good coffee."

"I'm of a mind to spike it with thiopental sodium next week."

"That would be cheating, wouldn't it?"

Peter trundles down Dr. Kelner's front walkway into the open door of his car. As Jesús drives him away, the stylish man with the cigar watches from the city park across the street. Next to him stands a taller, younger man who holds the hand of a prim little girl with a fuchsia bow in her hair.

PLEASE DISREGARD THE BOXHEIM PAPERS.

This public service announcement is brought to you by the Committee to Reelect the Active President.

Chapter Two

Pigtail Diplomacy

As Peter's Town Car glides away, the three observers resume their stroll through the park. The taller man turns to his companion.

"So, Ani, who is this guy?"

"An enigma, Jarry."

"I think the polite term is *African American*."

Ani elbows Jarry.

"E-nig-ma. Conundrum. Puzzle."

The little girl chimes in, "Mystery."

Ani jabs Jarry again and grins at the girl.

"That is very good, Lissy. Peter Mott is a mystery. Ten were scheduled for release, but eleven walked out that door."

"You want me to check him out?"

"No. No, I will work him myself for now. This particular assignment intrigues me."

"He looks familiar."

"Yes, reminiscent of Albert Brooks."

"That pro golfer with the crooked nose?"

"No, the actor with a smile that could melt Leona Helmsley. At any rate, what I want you to do –"

A skateboarder trying to pass them loses control and, as he tumbles to the ground, his board flies into Melissa's path and trips her. Ani catches her before she hits the asphalt and scoops her up in his arms. As Jarry lumbers toward the skateboarder to remind him this area is restricted to pedestrians, it becomes apparent that Jarry knows a few choice synonyms of his own. Noticing the green bandana tied around the kid's arm, Ani canvasses the surroundings and, on a basketball court fifty feet away, he pinpoints the leader among the kid's fellow gang members – not because Ani has ever met any of them before, but because he has always had a knack for identifying and dividing his enemy. Jarry and the skateboarder are now shoving each other, and the gang is taking notice.

Ani yanks Jarry away and stuffs Melissa into his arms.

"You see to your daughter. You, come with me."

Without even turning to look at the skateboarder, Ani seizes him by the ear and marches him toward the approaching horde. Many at least a head taller than Ani, the agitated pack encircles him, taunting him with cabalistic hand gestures and profanity that even Jarry doesn't know. In little time the threats and catcalls subside. When the mob parts, Ani emerges unscathed. He and the leader stroll abreast toward Jarry and Melissa, the leader dragging his subordinate by a handful of sweatshirt. At Ani's nod, Jarry sets Melissa down on her feet. The leader turns a wrathful stare onto his confederate, who steps forward and kneels with all the reverence a sixteen-year-old banger can muster.

"Little girl, I 'pologize. I shouldn't o' been on this road." Sheepishly he starts to rise, but the leader smacks the back of his head. On his knee again, he removes his gold necklace and drapes it around her neck. "I hope I didn't cause you no hurt, little girl. I'll be looking out for you here on." Before he can ponder whether he has sufficiently atoned for his transgression, the leader wrenches him away by the scruff of his neck and shoves him toward the basketball court.

The leader turns a respectful brow to Ani.

"So, Mr. Stearns, sir. We cool?"

Ani nods. The leader and his retinue fade into the periphery. Ani squats in front of Melissa.

"Are you hurt anywhere?"

"I'm okay."

Ani gently removes the necklace.

"May I disinfect this overnight and return it to you tomorrow?"

"I don't like it anyway. It's too heavy."

"Well, dear, it is a gift. It is a token of recompense. If you refuse to wear it, at least when you come to the park, that boy's … associate will think you did not accept his apology, and life will become very unpleasant for him. But I know a jeweler. With this much gold, he can cut you a necklace to size and fashion two bracelets with the excess. How does that sound?"

Melissa responds with an eager grin.

"Then we have a deal. Excuse me for just one minute, dear, so I can talk to your father. Wait for me on the bench over there?"

Melissa skips to a concrete picnic table while Ani stands and straightens his tie. When she is out of earshot, he drums his kid brother on the chest and pulls him close.

"What is the matter with you, Jarry? You have a little girl to watch after, she depends on you for everything, and you start kicking some punk's ass in front of his innercity posse? You have to be smarter than that, do you understand me?"

Jarry raises his palms to his temples and clenches his eyelids. He does this every time Ani lends him a bite-sized epiphany on how life works.

"I'm sorry, Ani. I was mad."

"What have I told you? Life does not forgive if you lose your temper. Use it; never let it use you. You must go now to make your four o'clock. Lissy and I will meet you at the bistro on Tonawa at 8:30."

"Got it. I'm sorry, Ani."

"You are my brother. You do not apologize to me. I only ask that you focus on the task at hand. Will you do that?"

"Sure, Ani, sure. I can focus. I will."

"Come here."

Jarry leans down so Ani can send him on his way with a kiss to the forehead. Ani pulls a thermos of hot apple cider from his overcoat and joins Melissa at the bench. As he pours, Melissa clutches his forearm in her teacup hands and rests her head on his elbow.

"Daddy isn't very smart, is he?"

Ani holds the steaming lid toward her, but she declines with a scrunched nose. He sets it and the thermos aside, drapes his arm around her.

"*Smart* is a relative term, honey. There are corporate CEOs and Ph.D.s who have not the first idea how to change a lawnmower spark plug. Your father loves you."

"You're very smart, Uncle Ani."

"Like I said, smart is relative."

"Most people don't say anything when they talk. When *you* talk, you make me think. Why's everybody call you Ani?"

"*Does*, darling. Why *does* everybody call me Ani. Contractions tend to defile the language, and language used poorly will, in turn, cause mental decay. You should, therefore, use elisions as seldom as possible. Your father coined the nickname *Ani* when he was just an infant. It was his truncated version of Anthony."

"Why did that man apologize and give me his chain? What did you say to his boss?"

"I told him that you are a very precious young lady, and that I would be grateful to him if he would treat you as such."

"The boarder looked nervous enough, but his boss looked scared."

Ani retrieves his half-smoked cigar and lights it, then gives his niece's shoulders a squeeze.

"That is what happens to men in the presence of beauty such as yours. Get used to it, kid."

Melissa punches him in the thigh.

"I am six years old, you know. I'm not naïve. That boss guy was afraid of you, not me. When Daddy says things to grownups, he has to repeat himself a lot. You don't. Why?"

Ani empties and refills the thermos cup, then holds it gingerly beneath Melissa's nose.

"The sun is setting. Come on and take a few sips. This will keep you warm."

Melissa obliges.

"As men go, I am not the largest. Though I was far from scrawny as a boy, my musculature was by no means above average. Still, no matter how great my opponents in size or number, the only fight I ever lost was my first – for which I later evened the score. In fact, nobody raised a hand to me beyond the age of fifteen. But I was no bully – I took advantage of no one. I once asked my football coach why the other kids were so deferential to me. 'Ani,' he said, 'it is not because you are a mean person. It is because of the intensity with which you respond to every challenge. They see that you are resolved to do anything, to endure any hardship necessary to the accomplishment of your task. Though commonplace in times past, this quality is a stranger to the modern era. They defer to you, Ani, because your mere countenance exposes their weakness.' Take another sip, honey. I fear that my reputation robbed my younger brother of opportunities to prove his mettle to himself. In any event, that is the difference you discern between him and me. It makes him no less a man, no less a father."

Melissa takes the cup and immerses herself in a long gulp of froth.

"It's okay, Uncle Ani. I know Daddy loves me. But I worry about him because he's just not very bright."

Ani tosses his cigar and turns Melissa to face him.

"You listen to me, Lissy. It is not your job to worry about Jarry. That responsibility is mine alone. His, in turn, is to you. And that is where it ends. Your heart is bigger than his and mine together, but it is far more fragile. You let me take care of that lummox; you take care of yourself."

Melissa sets aside the cup, grabs Ani around the middle and squeezes him as hard as she can.

"You're my hero, Uncle Ani."

He tousles her hair.

"We have discussed this. Hero worship is the basest form of self-contempt. Love me if you like … trust me only so far as I have earned it. But do not surrender yourself to a preconceived notion – of me or anyone."

DON'T DRINK AND DRIVE, OR TEXT AND DRIVE, OR TALK AND DRIVE, AND TURN YOUR RADIO OFF, AND KEEP YOUR HANDS AT TEN AND TWO AT ALL TIMES WHILE DRIVING 7 MPH BELOW THE POSTED LIMIT ... IN FACT, DON'T EVEN THINK WHILE YOU DRIVE BECAUSE GOVERNMENT STUDIES HAVE DETERMINED THAT, IN 99.87% OF TRAFFIC ACCIDENTS, THE AT-FAULT DRIVER WAS THINKING ABOUT SOMETHING AT OR NEAR THE TIME OF IMPACT.

This public service announcement is brought to you by the National Highway Traffic Safety Administration.

Chapter Three

United States of Appeasement - Side One

The only thing extravagant about Ani's corner office is its location. From his desk he can muse at the bustle of the Riverwalk to the west, and he can gaze at the air traffic to the south. But the opposite view through those picture windows is contrastively austere. The leather furniture in his conference nook is comfortable but not ornate. His desk is presentable and substantial, but not ostentatiously so. Other than the diplomas and awards that hang above his credenza, the wood-paneled walls are bare. A federal tax auditor once asked Ani why he did not display pictures of his loved ones.

"My family is nobody's business but mine. And *nobody* includes you, smartass."

The Stearns Law Firm occupies a renovated warehouse within walking distance of the county courthouse in the capital city. Employing an average of eighteen lawyers and twice as many support staffers, it is a comparatively modest sized venture, and its clientele varies with the talents and interests of its service providers. As a young associate in the last century, Ani deduced that the traditional partnership track is too often antagonistic to the interests of the clients; thus, Ani offers no operational control in his firm. Nonetheless, so coveted is a position there that ten years ago he opened a satellite office next to his favorite delicatessen to manage the steady influx of résumés. Ani's hiring criteria are deceptively simple. As he summed it up for his Human Resources manager:

"Any monkey can read a book and regurgitate it for a test, and your typical A-student in the post-graduate milieu is little more than a kissass. The obsequious and the pathologically dishonest are cut from the same cloth. So the CVs of the Law Review and the Phi Beta Kappa and the Order of the Coif nerds all go straight to the shredder. I want independent thinkers with unshakable moral codes. Nine times out of ten, the kid in the middle of the class is the upstart who has the balls to challenge his professor's worldview despite the academic fallout. That is the kind of lawyer who will stand up to a judge and defy an appellate panel when the right thing must be done. These are the scrappers I want on my crew."

No less elementary is Ani's business model. Each new hire is dubbed Junior Associate and given a base salary. Five years later, the Junior Associate is given a choice: accept the pay scale of an Associate or clear out his office. Though the Associate's base salary is half that of his younger counterpart, unlike the Junior Associate he keeps as a bonus a pretax percentage of every penny he earns for the firm. As the Associate brings in more and more business, his profit percentage increases (and his base salary proportionately dwindles) until he ascends the status of Senior Associate. With this incentive scheme, Ani has built a dynamic income source for himself and an incomparably diverse legal resource for both corporations and individuals. The mandatory wallpaper on every computer monitor bears the same aphorism as the plaque on every attorney's wall: *Truth is the one constant that keeps chaos at bay in the legal forum. To forsake it is the basest repudiation, not only of one's client and colleagues, but of the countless forebears who toiled and sacrificed over these many generations to dignify our profession.*

The spartanism of Ani's office is by no means indicative of his attitude toward his employees. Once every few months, Ani makes it a point to have a casual tête-à-tête with each attorney, paralegal and assistant in the building. Some last ten minutes, others as long as two hours. While he places no stock in the supernal fables of his youth, Ani does not discount the innate human bent for altruism which undergirds the mythology of Christmas. He uses the holiday to impress upon his staff that human benevolence transcends ritual and dogma. Thus, an ancillary agenda for his frequent confabs is to determine the one thing that would most improve each employee's quality of life. His gifts run the gamut from paying off medical bills to providing nutrition advisors, from permanently relocating stalkers and abusive exes to arranging and personally moderating reunions with estranged relatives. He often refers to his staff as his second family. To be sure, he is known to a great many of their children as *Uncle Anthony* or *Grandpa Stearns.*

Faithful as he is to them all, he expects no less loyalty in turn. If one of his attorneys is alleged to have abused a client's trust, he does not turn a blind eye and hope the bar association is too busy to care (as it usually is). Nor does he leave it to his malpractice insurer to buy the client off. He investigates the matter himself. If he finds the accusation baseless, he meets privately with the complainer, explaining to him in graphic detail how ferociously he will defend the good name of his associate. And he proceeds to do just that, if necessary. If the attorney is in the wrong, he calls everyone concerned to a meeting and hashes out a resolution. A negotiated settlement might entail the culpable attorney paying the legal fees of an attorney of the client's choice to cure an innocent mistake. In the case of a more egregious ethical violation, Ani will make good with the client himself, then he will give the attorney two options: work for however long it takes to repay the debt or quit. In the former scenario, the attorney will be forgiven. Since Ani founded the firm over twenty years ago, only four attorneys – all Junior Associates – have been handed the ultimatum. Though Ani never divulged the broader ramifications of the latter alternative, the first three chose the reimbursement option and today, years after paying off their obligations, they count among his most trusted Senior Associates. The quitter suffered the same fate as if he had willfully mistreated a colleague or stolen from the firm: though no physical harm befell him, his sullied reputation so resoundingly preceded him after his separation that he could hardly find work as a menial laborer – let alone a lawyer – in any U.S. State or territory.

Ani's philanthropy is not restricted to his immediate and appurtenant relations. He bears an uncommon sense of responsibility to society at large. The city park Melissa so enjoys, singlehandedly ramrodded through City Hall by Ani, is the only public park in the greater metro area which is safe enough for children and unarmed adults to frequent. Thanks to an aggressive early intervention program Ani helped the Sheriff develop, the gang he tangled with yesterday will not be seen again in that park until next spring – in the employ of a private landscaping outfit. But Ani's sense of obligation to his community is not restricted to convenient efforts which find their fruition in water fountains and afterschool programs. Unlike the vast majority of the fellow citizens whose existence he labors to elevate, Ani acknowledges the harsh reality that devotion exacts a heavy price – that intimacy often demands the unspeakable. It is this enhanced, holistic awareness of civic duty that compelled Ani to incorporate into his practice an alternative client service.

Like the typical law school graduate at the bottom of an ominous totem pole, Ani was forced to cut his forensic teeth representing various relatives and friends of law firm partners in criminal and divorce matters. It was not long before he noticed that the judges assigned to the domestic section were a notably sullen sort. And he understood why when he attended his very first Victim Protective Order docket. Midst a sea of elderly who had been robbed and generally maltreated by their own children, minors who had been beaten by their stepparents and wives suffering sundry abuses from their husbands, the futility of the entire protective order scheme was typified by an exchange between Judge Yamane and twenty-six-year-old Gaia Tosten.

Gaia had packed her meager belongings and toddler son into her car and was exiting the apartment complex when her impetuous boyfriend of seven months came home unexpectedly. He followed her to her mother's house, where she had scarce time to deposit the toddler on the front porch and bang on the door before he seized her by the hair and threw her facedown onto the driveway. Demanding that she return home immediately, he kicked her indiscriminately until a neighbor, hearing her mother's screams, chased him away with a baseball bat and a cranky German Shepherd.

Beneath the softball sized cement burn on her left cheek, Gaia's expression resembled that of the countless complainants who had preceded her to the bench – hollow yet hopeful, as if she were summoning every last ounce of strength to issue a final plea for rescue before surrendering to her apparent fate.

"Here you are, Ms. Tosten."

The judge extended a piece of paper.

"You file this with the clerk, and make sure they give you enough copies to file one with the Sheriff."

"Thank you, judge. And how soon will the Sheriff arrest him?"

"Don't misunderstand, Ms. Tosten. This is not an arrest warrant. This is a court order that forbids him to get within five hundred feet of you or your boy pending trial or other final disposition of the assault and battery complaint. The Sheriff will not pick him up or contact him at all unless he violates this order."

"But how will he know?"

"You need to give a copy to him, too."

"Judge, he reads this and it'll just make him madder."

"I am bound by procedure, Ms. Tosten."

"But he's out on bond and he knows where I live. I can't go to work because he's already been to the salon telling my boss and my clients that I'd better drop the charges or he'll make me wish I were never born. How will this piece of paper stop him from killing me?"

"Mr. Stearns, you don't look busy at the moment. Why don't you show this nice young lady where she needs to go? Next on the docket, please."

Standing no taller than five feet, Gaia could not have weighed more than ninety pounds. As Ani guided this wisp of a woman to the outer hall, she collapsed against the wall, slid to the floor and hugged her knees tightly as if to make herself invisible.

"Where am I supposed to go?"

At that moment, Ani identified more clearly than ever what his Constitutional Law professor had called *the bastard child of due process* – because judges are not given the discretion to deny a defendant notice and opportunity to be heard under even these circumstances, the very order issued to protect a victim in Gaia's shoes often becomes the catalyst that hastens her demise. Though he knew it placed his career and freedom in jeopardy, Ani embarked upon the only available moral pathway. He wrapped his suitcoat about her shoulders and sat on the floor beside her.

"Ms. Tosten, tell me about this guy. What are his habits? Whom or what does he treasure?"

Six hours later, Ani marched into The Woodshed – one of a dozen identical strip joints that skirt the State fairgrounds – wearing the same suit he had donned before sunup and carrying a brown paper bag. He had no trouble spotting Gaia's boyfriend, whose nickname *Izzy* was tattooed on his left forearm. Clad in a wife-beater shirt that boasted more beer drinking than working out, along with the distressed jeans and facial piercings that were just coming into vogue with the day's youth, he played pool at the far table, cocking his head unnaturally to keep his own cigarette smoke from irritating his eyes. After Izzy missed his shot and sidled to a barstool, Ani strode up to him, plucked the cigarette from his lips and snuffed it out on the back of his own hand.

"What's up your ass, college boy?"

"My name is Anthony Wayne Stearns, and I have a message for you."

"Yeah? What's in the bag?"

"We will discuss it outside."

While Izzy scrabbled for words, Ani strode out the side exit. Izzy and two friends chugged their beers and bustled to a narrow alley, where they found him casually draping his coat over a stack of empty kegs.

"Now you wanna hook it up? For what?"

Shirt sleeves rolled evenly, Ani retrieved the bag and grinned ever so slightly as he advanced.

"Here is my message. Gaia Tosten is off limits to you. She is out of bounds, verboten, forbidden. The same goes for her son, her parents, her friends, her associates, her pets and her houseplants. Am I understood?"

Lighting another cigarette, Izzy chuckled and slapped one of his pals in the stomach.

"What that bitch say to put you up to this? Go home. She knows she don't get rid of me."

As another round of juvenile laughter erupted, Ani stepped closer and shook the paper sack.

"Let us find out what is inside, shall we?"

Ani opened the tote and yanked out the carcass of Izzy's prize cockatoo, whose neck he had wrung just half an hour past. Izzy yelped and turned away, but Ani advanced. Reaching into the bag again, Ani produced a *Polaroid* picture of Izzy's thirteen-year-old sister which he had snapped three hours earlier as she boarded her school bus. As Izzy and his friends hastened a disjointed retreat, Ani maneuvered Izzy into an alcove and thrust the dead cockatoo into his timorous face.

"I am the new fish in your little pond, badass. There is nowhere I will not go to hurt you. And so long as you are a threat to Gaia, you will not be rid of me. How many pieces of you shall I destroy?"

"She … she your girl, man. I'm out, I'm a rumor."

Ani flung the bird into a puddle of muck. Izzy winced at the sound.

"My advice to you, Izzy, is to take a vacation very far away, and very soon."

Days later, Izzy skipped his arraignment. As the bondsman hauled him two hundred forty-six miles back to the county jail, Izzy ranted the entire way about a lunatic who had killed his parrot. Judge Yamane summoned Ani to his chambers and asked him if there were any truth to the outlandish yarn.

"Well, Judge –"

"Why is it you never call me *Your Honor*?"

"I don't know where you've been or what you've done off the bench, Judge. How can I possibly vouch for your character?"

"So, how about this kid's story?"

"Justice is a fickle mistress, is she not?"

"Fickle, yes. Mr. Stearns, I realize they're working you like a dog over there at Dobbins, Carroll and Carroll, but I have a keen radar for aptitude, and I think you have a knack for domestic relations law. I'd like to see your face on this floor more often."

As Ani's inaugural year as an attorney progressed, his referral rate steadily climbed. Though forbidden to recommend any particular attorney over another, Judge Yamane and his colleagues had little trouble circumventing that rule. Whenever a dire situation presented itself, they would advise the victim to get an attorney, then ask the bailiff to provide a random list of one hundred or so names printed in a tediously small font. As an afterthought, the bailiff would *find* Ani's business card in a purse, drawer or pocket and *inadvertently* tender it along with the official list. By the end of the following year, Ani had amassed a sufficient client base to hang his own shingle. Because virtually every client he signed was in need of his underground assistance as well as his legal services, his stint as a sole practitioner lasted only twenty-eight days before he was constrained to expand. So long as Ani's *creative negotiations* only occasionally strayed into physical violence, the district judges were pleased. And these happy district judges proved powerful allies a generation later, when the tug-o-war between federal and State authority escalated.

Like alcoholism, the pursuit of political power is a progressive disease. As history has proven over and again, in the statecraft arena, what starts as a means to an end quickly becomes an end in itself. The corruption takes hold the very moment a campaigner discovers that he can, with nothing more than a lofty sales pitch, attain a position of influence over the poor saps who constitute the historically unparalleled economic machine called the United States of America. Thereafter, it takes very little time for him to realize that the survival instinct will motivate the poor saps to keep that machine churning regardless of whether he keeps those promises. It is at this pivotal juncture that polity ceases to be a fiduciary mission and degenerates into a grand game of one-upmanship in which (a) the incumbent's sole objective is to defeat the bum gunning for his seat by any and all necessary means and (b) laws, constitutions, manifestos and charters are useful only to the extent to which they further that objective.

As his second term drew to a close, the nation's first nonwhite (well, by a slight margin, anyway) President devised a plan that would secure him more time in office: enter an executive order which would (a) declare a state of national economic emergency (b) suspend House and Senate elections indefinitely and (c) abrogate the four-year limit on Presidential terms. Such an order would freeze the federal government in place until the *economic crisis* had ended. Though the bitter-enders on his staff were overjoyed at the prospect, some of his closest advisors dreaded the fallout.

To gauge public reaction, they saddled the First Vice President of the First Mostly Nonwhite President with the task of leaking the plan so that, if popular opinion turned sour, his boss could assert plausible deniability by disavowing the "rumor" as a cocktail-hour joke dropped by a man whose penchant for verbal blunders had been the stuff of legend for decades on end. The first of a series of leaks was scheduled for the Friday of Labor Day weekend. That Wednesday, as the First Mostly Nonwhite President briefed cabinet heads on the high points of his scheme, his press secretary scurried in and demanded an immediate adjournment. He then whisked the First Mostly Nonwhite President to the Roosevelt Room, where he was impatiently expected by the Joint Chiefs of Staff. Without awaiting permission or even bothering to greet him, the Commandant of the Marine Corps and the Chief of the National Guard Bureau lit into their Commander in Chief as though he were a truant schoolboy. The barrage of threats and epithets flew so fast that the secretary could just make out the phrases *Kent State* and *May 4, 1970* before the door was slammed in his face.

Not fifteen minutes later, the Chairman led his comrades from the chamber without asking leave. The First Mostly Nonwhite President called feebly, "General, this is mutiny, isn't it?"

When the Chairman turned back, the secretary stood dumbfounded in his path. Tucking his cover precisely underarm, the Chairman removed the secretary's horn-rimmed spectacles and crushed them beneath his patent leather bootheel.

"Clear the road, little man."

The secretary sidled away. The Chairman stepped just inside the doorway.

"I say this, Mister President, with the last grain of respect I can muster. I am appalled that a man of your resources knows so little about history, about loyalty. Don't you know by now that the secret to maintaining unlimited power is to cloak it in the illusion of democracy? What defeated King George III had less to do with bullets and military strategy than with his arrogance: he made the mistake of openly asserting his dictatorial power in the Age of Enlightenment. This executive order of yours pushes the charade beyond its breaking point – it is a powder keg that will singlehandedly dismantle the facade of evenhanded governance that we and our distinguished predecessors have striven to build and to preserve since 1792! If you light its fuse – and my colleagues are in full agreement on this – you're on your own. Should you force our hands with it, I wish you luck finding someone foolhardy enough to try and arrest us."

Like little Opie having just been chastised by Sheriff Taylor, the First Mostly Nonwhite President brooded in his chair for an excruciating two full minutes, his hands palm-up in his lap. He then handed his legal size, blue leather pouch to the secretary.

"Get rid of this like it never happened."

As though he were smuggling a newborn baby, the secretary slunk from the meeting room with the satchel that contained the only complete copy of Executive Order 13775. But in the moiling cesspit of megalomania that is called Washington, D.C., secrets never die.

On November 8, 2016, the country's first she-male executive (who, per Presidential decree disseminated on November 9, 2016, will be referred to hereafter as the First *Female* President despite an overabundance of contrary evidence) edged out her Republican opponent by a smattering of votes – a fact which spoke far less about the popularity of her nemesis than it did about the dismal turnout at the polls. Though he abhorred her for being his most venomous political enemy eight years past, the First Mostly Nonwhite President saw an opportunity to exploit the First Female President in his crusade against that which he had been groomed since toddlerhood to think more odious than she: a competitively capitalist society. In his successor, he saw the fruition of his party's quest for a political dynasty, which he summed up in an aside to one of his aides just before signing the United Nations *Enlightened Society Treaty* on November 11: "You thought this glib black man got away with a lot of sneaky stuff thanks to his minority status? Wait 'til you see non-leftists of all colors and creeds try and say *No* to that vindictive battleaxe of a white woman."

Though the First Mostly Nonwhite President was no stranger to the thuggery it takes to advance to upper echelons of politics, ultimately he remained just an affable parasite who, though drunk on power and loath to see the festivities end, had no stomach for personal, face-to-face conflict. Thus, when he smugly assured the nation that the treaty was merely a token demonstration of international goodwill, even he could not comprehend the destructive force it would have in the talons of an unmitigated misanthrope such as his successor, who zeroed in like a shark to bloody water. The First Female President had lusted after limitless power ever since she had hitched herself to the coattails of her libertine husband, who preceded her to that coveted office by two decades. Now that it was in her clutches, she was determined to never let it go. So she devised a three-prong plan to pave the way for the implementation of her own perversion of Executive Order 13775, the first two of which were laws sold to the American public as necessary to facilitate compliance with the UN pact.

Though she and her fellow party loyalists had been relentless in their efforts to distort the gun control debate by littering their every public statement on the issue with the catchphrases *sport hunting* and *home protection*, her pollsters informed her that a mulish minority of middle-aged citizens refused to denounce what their history books had taught them – that the sole impetus behind the Second Amendment to the Constitution was to provide the taxpayers a safeguard against the tyranny of a renegade centralized government. To overcome this principal obstacle in her all consuming ambition to capture the helm of a one-party government for the indulgence of her every autoerotic whim, she proposed and shepherded the passage of the *Safer Community Initiative*. Modeled after the National Socialists' *Weapons Law* of 1938, the Initiative repealed all State laws authorizing non law enforcement individuals to carry a concealed handgun in public; restricts firearm ownership to a single twenty-two caliber revolver and no more than five rounds of ammunition per household; requires all game hunters and competitive marksmen to (a) undergo a yearlong training course to obtain a special license and (b) store all "special use weapons" (anything beyond a .22 revolver) and corresponding ammunition in a government armory when not in use. The law further requires that all home-protection weapons be inspected annually, prescribing stiff monetary penalties and jail time for the owner of any weapon not certified in writing as safe by the Department for the Preservation of Public Order. Thanks to the snail's pace for which federal bureaucracies are notorious, this last requisite has rendered a full 86% of residences weaponless at any one time.

Ani and his staff were exempted from this law. Having suspected this turn of events two years earlier, Judge Yamane had made Ani and every last person on his payroll Special Court Officers, licensed to own, carry and store wherever they liked whatever weapons they deemed necessary "to protect and preserve every citizen's right of judicial redress."

Inherent in any remedial law is the cavalier denial of a timeless truth which, in this instance, is: *Laws do not deter the lawless.* As any dimwitted five-year-old might have predicted, the federal armories quickly became popular burglary targets. As home and business invasions skyrocketed, the police found themselves increasingly outmanned and outgunned. Taking advantage of a loophole in the Initiative, State and local law enforcement began deputizing civilians at a dizzying pace. Thanks to the inherent inefficiency of bureaucracy, however, as many miscreants obtained badges as law-abiding citizens. To curtail the resultant bloodshed, State agencies turned to the private sector for help. At Judge Yamane's recommendation, Ani and a select cadre of other business leaders were commissioned to amass a network of intelligence gatherers who quickly eliminated the criminal element from the deputized ranks. Ani proved so resourceful in this endeavor that prominent functionaries made special note of him when the task force was dissolved.

The second law was the *Criminal Rehabilitation and Reform Act.* Not only did this law abolish both the death penalty and the life sentence; it preempted all existing federal and State sentencing guidelines, drastically reducing jail terms for all offenses on a retroactive basis and pardoning all deathrow inmates. Finally, it voided all State restrictions on voting for ex-convicts, parolees and inmates alike. Though its preamble was generously adorned with lofty human rights rhetoric, even the dullest of spectators saw the ulterior motive behind the ruse – by claiming a larger illegitimate voting bloc for her party than could have been realized by the various foiled immigration stratagems of her forerunner, the First Female President was maneuvering to achieve a lock on reelection. Then, while her U.S. Attorneys diverted the attention of State governments with lawsuits over their defiance of *The Safer Community Initiative*, she could invoke the very executive order which the First Mostly Nonwhite

President had failed to bring off without alienating the Joint Chiefs, because any dissent offered by a confused and disarmed citizenry would not escalate to a point that would necessitate military intervention; instead, it would be easily put down by the IRS Police, whose ranks had surreptitiously increased fivefold over the last decade.

Within mere months of the CRRA's implementation, the national murder rate quadrupled. Desperate to find an alternative to flooding society with the vilest of offenders, local public safety officials turned again to Ani. The immediate solution was apparent to everyone – a bloodthirsty animal that can not be controlled must be killed – so Ani reenlisted his old network, which he dubbed *The Utility Committee*. Among the released felons, this team targets only the forcible victimizers – those who have both inflicted bodily harm on innocent people and overtly threatened to do so. But they do not proceed on the unquestioned edict of the referring agency alone. The committee conducts what appellate courts call a *de novo review* of each case – rather than accept the conclusion of a judge or jury, it assesses every last piece of evidence introduced at the trial, including evidence declared inadmissible for any reason. Only upon a unanimous vote of guilt beyond a reasonable doubt does the committee advocate adverse action against a subject. The team then votes on which particular member is best suited to the task, and makes a written recommendation to Ani. Only when Ani grants his imprimatur does the team proceed to eliminate its subject. On the rare occasion Ani overrides his committee, it is usually because Ani has determined a particular job warrants his own expertise.

Ani's task is complicated by the fact that, in order to mitigate retaliation by victims or their families, the CRRA mandates that (a) all criminal records be sealed from public view and (b) the released felons be relocated to a town in another State a minimum of five hundred miles from the location in which they committed their crimes. This entails the temporary transfer of jurisdiction from State to federal courts. As a result, records often get lost or intermingled. Untangling these little snafus requires Ani's committee to enlist the tacit aid of multiple agencies throughout the country.

While the client's only concern is to rid society of predators, Ani is very particular with regard to how that is done. He and his committee have immersed themselves in medical and psychological treatises that evaluate and quantify the various levels and attributes of pain associated with a vast array of traumata. But the team does not craft a punishment to "fit" its underlying crime; Ani insists that the penalties exceed the original offenses to account for willfulness. As he once explained to a skeptical cabinet member during a closed multistate session of governors and senior executives:

"You are no doubt familiar with The Social Contract, first articulated by Plato. Quite simply, it offers as a model of society the barter system. If I want something of yours, for it I trade you something of comparable value. I restrain myself from striking and maiming you during a disagreement, because it is my hope that someone bigger and meaner than I would exercise the same composure in relation to me. Now let us suppose, madam, that a big, scary man breaks into your home and presses a knife against your throat, assuring you that you will die unless you hand over your jewelry and cash. By forcibly divesting you of your valuables in this manner, the thief has repudiated The Social Contract which constitutes the very fabric of civil society. The unprovoked knife attack is his declaration that the rules no longer apply to him.

"Now let us say that your husband, neighbor or girlfriend subdues the assailant. What will you do with him? Suppose you say to him, 'We have decided to stick you in a cubicle and feed and entertain you for a certain number of months or years and, when we release you, we expect you to be nice to everyone in return.' This numbskull has just breached an ethical code he has been taught to abide by since birth. How do you rationally expect him to honor yours?"

"Mr. Stearns, I understand the need to eliminate such an element from society. But how do you condone torture? That just seems cruel."

"Let us return to our hypothetical. He could have come to your door, knocked politely and humbly asked for your help. He did not. He chose to place you in fear of impending death. Have you ever faced death, madam? Have you ever been in a situation in which you perceived that one wrong move could end your life?"

"No."

"But I am sure you can imagine the terror. Were you to die one minute from now, think of all you would lose. Consider the hundred seemingly trivial plans you have within the next twenty-four hours. Dinner and cocktails at your favorite club once this monkey show has ended. An early evening stroll with your Shar-Pei. A visit with your son who is home from college for spring break. Finishing the last chapter of that thriller you have been reading for a month. All of it gone. No power to forestall its end. No more control over anything, including yourself."

"Mr. Stearns …"

"You now have only twenty seconds, madam."

"Mr. Stearns, really …"

"Fifteen. What do you do? Whom do you call?"

"Okay, your time is up …"

"Ten, madam."

"Will somebody please kill his mike?"

"Five seconds. No more Facebook, no more Sunday brunches, no opportunity to respond to those coquettish texts from that twenty-seven-year-old waiter at the concourse café you have been flirting with since June. All of your plans unfinished."

"Next item on the …"

"BAM! Dead! Nothingness – everything and everyone gone. How does it feel, madam?"

"Mr. Stearns, I see your point."

"What right did he have to threaten you in that manner? And how can anyone possibly erase the fearfulness of that episode? No, madam, you do not see my point, not yet. I will exit this chamber momentarily, but first I suggest you reevaluate the meaning of a quaint term known as *justice*. Without the remotest provocation, he took something irreplaceable from you. It is only fair that you take at least twice that from him. That, madam, is *deterrence*."

The irony of Ani's undertaking is that, even though he is acting at the behest of State officials, he must be especially cunning in the way he disposes of the bodies. This is because the federal law installed in every jurisdiction a Compliance Bureau consisting of FBI personnel (working through specially commissioned State police liaisons) and UN auditors, which conducts random inspections of prisons and morgues. Because those who prey upon society typically live an underground existence, however, the mere disappearance of a felon goes largely unnoticed. To exploit this reality, Ani has partnered with mortuaries throughout the State to offer free estate planning reviews and consultations to the families of the deceased. Though Ani's firm reaps a modest profit from these meetings, their main purpose is to provide a mechanism through which the State can reimburse both Ani and the funeral director for the real job at hand – to furtively dispose of bodies by either interring them beneath freshly dug burial vaults and gravesites, or cremating them. Because chance is a whimsical creature, Ani is not satisfied in the former scenario to just dump a body into a hole. He takes care to plant the DNA of another doomed criminal to account for the remote event in which the corpse ever resurfaces. Because the patsy must remain alive for some days or weeks after the decease of his *victim*, contact must be made with some targets twice or more to (a) obtain that DNA and (b) assure that they harm no innocent bystanders in the interim. This requires patience and finesse – two qualities Ani has been trying to instill in his brother Jarold since he was born.

"For the last time, Jarry, we will discuss this in my office."

As the Stearns brothers exit the elevator and stroll down the hall, they engage in handshakes and shoulder slaps and congratulatory greetings more befitting of a postgame locker room than a business office. This is the typical mood of the firm: whether he won a case, lost it or simply stepped out for lunch, everyone on staff is welcomed back with the warmest of regards. So seamless was the transfer that, when Ani ushers his brother through his office door, Jarry is astonished to see a passel of telephone messages in a hand that was empty just seconds ago. Once that door has closed, Ani tosses open Jarry's suitcoat and flicks his tie.

"What the hell are you wearing?"

Jarry inventories himself as if accused of leaving his fly open.

"What? After putting a percentage of that bonus you gave me into Melissa's trust fund, *like you told me to*, I treated myself to a little something they call men's furnishment."

"Furnishings, Jarry."

Ani offloads an armful of files into his chair and leans against his desk as Jarry fidgets.

"What have I told you? Dress nice; do not dress stupid. There is a vast middle ground between niggardliness and extravagance."

"Ani, I wish you wouldn't use those racial slurs. I saw a guy get worked over pretty good for using that one."

"Which one is that?"

"You know ... the one that rhymes with chigger."

"Jarry, there is nothing remotely racist about the term *niggardly*. Its root word n-y-g-g is of fourteenth century Scandinavian origin. It means miserly, tightfisted, so stingy that you only shop at secondhand stores."

"Boy, words sure are tricky!"

"It boggles the mind how much senseless violence and general animosity could be averted if everyone consulted a dictionary for mere seconds a day. But let us revisit your manner of dress. The well tailored, moderately priced suit and tie tell your friends and associates that you respect yourself; therefore, you respect them. When you swagger around in a $5,000 showpiece, your friends and associates shun you like a prima donna while your enemies decide you have something they would prefer to take rather than trade for."

"But Ani, look at the supple way this baby hangs."

"I am not telling you to return the suit. Save it for a special occasion. But you should always buy your business attire off the rack, because professionalism consists in words and mannerisms, not regalia. Now, having said that ..." Ani straightens his brother's tie and snaps his lapels in line, then pats his cheek and beams, "you look damned handsome in that suit."

Ani retrieves his files and leads Jarry to the conference nook, where fresh coffee and carob coated raisins await.

"By the way, you did very nice work on that Crowley job."

"Thanks, Ani. I was proud of that one."

"See? I told you things would come more smoothly with practice. Here are the court files for the next Utility meeting."

"Only ten? No luck on Mott?"

"You have a keen eye, kiddo. This man has me perplexed. Nobody claims to have a shred of paper on him. Everybody else strutted out of that box like a heavyweight title holder. But this Mott fellow had an unsteady gait, and he was visibly disoriented. Maybe he is just some schmuck who never hurt anybody in his life, doing a hitch for drug possession, who got loaded up by mistake. He could just as easily be a Compliance Bureau plant, in which case we could be sent to a firing squad by the very body that outlawed capital punishment."

Jarry pitches a wary glance at the office door, then hunches closer to his brother.

"Could he be a drizzler?"

"Drizella, you mean."

Thanks to the CRRA's inordinate abbreviation of criminal sentences, so overburdened have court dockets become with repetitious trivial crimes that they have neither the resources nor the incentive to prosecute the major ones. Their solution was to add the thorniest of clauses to their tacit contract with Ani and his crew. In the event authorities identify an accomplice weeks or years after the principal actor was convicted, rather than arrest him they arrange a surreptitious way of placing him in Ani's path for investigation and possible elimination. Because such an arrangement is so repugnant to bedrock due process precepts, Ani is forced to fly blind in this scenario. He is given no advance notice, and prosecutorial files are withheld from him. He is forced to reconstruct the case with nothing to rely on but his own intuition and persuasive skills. Because such an assignment is as toilsome as it is fraught with peril, Ani christened it *Drizella* after the dingy haired, ugly stepsister of Cinderella. The only assurance Ani was given before receiving the unspoken charter to form his committee was that his attention would be drawn to the Drizella under circumstances sufficiently unique to dispel any notion of coincidence.

"We can not rule out that contingency, Jarry. Mott is a very delicate problem. Speaking of problems …."

Ani taps his index finger on the Herzog file. Jarry opens it to find the same obscure slip of paper that so confounded the judge.

"Start making the usual calls about this one. Meanwhile, I will shake some bushes regarding our elusive Mr. Mott. With these assignments, we navigate a dark and treacherous alley, so we must be vigilant. Make sure you call me fifteen minutes before your meeting."

DON'T WEAR EXCESSIVELY BRIGHT COLORS OR UPBEAT PRINTS LEST YOU DISTRESS THE MELANCHOLY OR DRIVE THE DEPRESSED TO SUICIDE.

This public service announcement is brought to you by the First Female President and First First Lady to Become President and Only Former First Lady to Become the First Female President's Council on Mental Health.

Chapter Four

United States of Appeasement – Flipside

Approaching the entrance to the Hyatt, Julia overhears something peculiar as she passes by a spotless luxury sedan. She turns to see a genteelly clad gentleman embroiled in a rather intense exchange with a taller, far bulkier man. Curious to a fault, Julia approaches and taps the shorter man's elbow.

"I beg your pardon, but did I just hear you ask this man why a body is in his trunk?"

When the gentleman turns, she is stirred by his engaging smile.

"What a tragedy that would be – as winsome a creature as you happening upon such a scene. As an aficionado of linguistics, I can understand how a looker-on might misinterpret homonyms such as *Bonnie* and *drunk*, which is something I hoped to not advertise about the poor girl. I apologize, madam, that my voice carried."

As Julia pauses to process this information, the gentleman straightens his tie and folds his hands.

"Of course, if it adds an element of intrigue to your day, I will be flattered to have you think me a paid killer."

In a burst of *joke's on me* realization, she jostles his shoulder.

"Paid killer! Aren't you just adorable? I'm sorry I intruded, and rest assured that Bonnie's secret is safe with me."

"A very pleasant day to you, madam."

When Julia enters the hotel, she finds Peter much the same as when they first met here for lunch two months ago, but with one encouraging difference. Though he stands at the entrance to the dining room looking as lost as a refugee, conspicuously absent tonight is his faithful driver. She gives him a prankish hug from behind, takes his arm and guides him inside.

"Where's Jesús?"

"Waiting in the car."

"Mira loosened your leash? I'm proud of you!"

When the hostess stops at a floor table and places the menus, Julia picks them right back up and deposits them in the girl's startled arms.

"Honey, I gave my assistant explicit instructions to reserve us a booth. In fact, I specified that corner booth right there, which is now occupied by a couple so grossly obese they should have been refused admittance! How do I know my assistant did what I told him to do? Because I've been paying him very well to do just that for eight years."

"But, ma'am, this is the table our manager –"

"Don't *but ma'am* me! Point me to the muttonhead you call a manager."

"He's, he's the redhead … over there at the bar."

Julia raises a forbidding finger. "Neither of you move a muscle."

Peter and the hostess gaze like sightseers as Julia marches to the bar, squares off with the manager, punctuates every third word with a poke to his chest, and with a slap on the shoulder sends him scurrying to the corner booth, whence he unceremoniously banishes its porcine patrons to a floor table. Her eyes still fixed on the same redheaded manager who is himself an intolerant taskmaster to his underlings, the waitress nearly drops the menus at the sound of Julia's voice.

"Get a move on, honey, I'm starving, and if I don't see a cooked meal soon I'll hack myself a steak out of your mammoth hind end!"

Once they are seated, Julia grabs Peter's hands. "How are you?"

"I'm afraid if I give you the wrong answer you'll carve me like a turkey." Peter's grin broadens her own. "I see you haven't changed. Truest friend, bloodiest enemy and nothing in between."

"Life's too short to live it in the middle, Peter. You told me that when I was fourteen, remember?"

Julia's favorite waiter Christopher brings the drinks they no longer have to order when they dine here. Without averting her eyes, she hands her open menu to him and points out the evening's desired fare. Taking Peter's hand again, her smile anneals ever so slightly, like that of a difficult child's longsuffering mother.

"Peter, how are you?"

"Would you mind asking an easier question?"

"That's fair enough. Tell me how one of the brightest rising stars in business finance became a preacher."

"Interfaith facilitator."

"Do you stand at a pulpit and tell people how to live their lives?"

"I graciously borrow a position of influence to advise people on points of morality."

"You're a preacher, Peter."

"But that's a small part of what I do."

"So what do you do, exactly? Start at the beginning."

"After Deanna left, nothing mattered. We had built a cozy little life in McMinnville. We were just two hours from the coast, and it seemed there was a vineyard everywhere we turned. But this is home. So I sold the company. I sold the houses and the boats and everything else that reminded me of that selfish existence. I decided I wanted to be a giver and not a taker, and one day I found myself filling out an application to a seminary. A few years later, I was an ordained minister with my own church."

As the first course arrives, then the next, Peter entertains Julia with the significant events of his recent life. In 2015, the First Mostly Nonwhite President signed the *United Nations Multifaith Reconciliation Treaty* which requires that (a) every church incorporate services for each of the twelve major religions or (b) any church of a single ideology be built in close proximity to structures devoted to the other eleven. Though touted by the White House as a sterling example of American compassion, nontraditional media cited numerous credible sources averring that the First Mostly Nonwhite President had acceded to this pact solely to avert the threat of a jihadist attack to rival that of September 11, 2001. As a record number of existing churches were forced to close their doors, Peter saw the perfect opportunity to engineer a new alliance among Christianity and its sister faiths. Enlisting the capital he had amassed in his previous career, Peter acquired forty commercial lots adjacent to his church and transformed them into an interfaith conglomerate dubbed *The Miracle Mile.*

Next, he forged contractual relationships with each of the eleven churches required for his own to remain viable and dogmatically exclusive. He then secured third-party funding for, and oversaw the construction of, a house of worship suitable to the cultural origins of each non-Christian tradition. Surrounded by landscaping to secure their privacy, the sanctuaries cover the tract in an oval pattern at whose center Peter constructed a doctrinally neutral building where the head of each worship center meets with his counterparts once a week.

What set Peter's church apart was the fact that it was the first in known history to operate openly as a for-profit organization. Then, in response to a lawsuit filed by a faction of Muslim imams, Congress passed the *Equality of Contributions Act* of 2017, which imposed on traditional churches a federal property tax, redistributing that revenue to the less popular churches to offset any imbalance in private tithing.

Long reviled by the general religious community as a pariah, Peter was promptly hailed as a trendsetter after his nonprofit colleagues received their first tax bills.

Savoring a pensive sip of merlot, Julia sets her glass down, straightens her back against the seat cushion and crosses her right leg over her left. This is the negotiation posture that has sent countless business moguls sauntering away in bewilderment like shamed schoolboys. Though Peter has never encountered her in a business setting, he knows his old friend's mannerisms. But rather than evoke fear, they invigorate him.

"Before you even say it, Julia, you and I both know – and history bears this out – that churches have never been strangers to the accumulation and consolidation of power and wealth. That doesn't cheapen the spiritual quest. All I did was to end the hypocrisy."

"And I applaud that. What mystifies me is your conversion all those years ago. I'll be the last to find fault with your personal convictions, but let's be honest. As agnostics go, you were the most strident opponent of organized religion I've ever known. Now you're spreading it faster than a venereal disease. Something changed you, Peter, drastically and fundamentally. You know what it is, and I know what it is."

As Peter's heart sinks, so do his eyes and cheeks.

"Julia, please."

"I'm tired of tiptoeing around the grumpy gorilla you have in tow every time I see you."

"Julia …"

"What happened between you and Deanna?"

"This is not the place to go into that."

"Then where *is* the right place? Your church? Your car? You won't come to my home, and I can't come to yours because, Peter, you don't have one!"

"I do, too, have a –"

"No, Peter. No. A sitting room with a convertible couch and kitchenette that adjoin your office do not qualify as a home."

Thirty feet away, Christopher loads fresh drinks on his tray. Just as he turns toward their table, Julia trains her finger on him without breaking her stare at Peter. Christopher obediently sets the tray back on the bar and attends to other matters. Julia slides next to Peter, drapes her arm across his shoulder and takes his hand.

"What happened with you and Deanna?"

"Julia –"

"Don't run from me, Peter."

"I can't –"

"You can."

"No, I can't remember it all. And what little I do I can't bear. What I saw … what I did."

"You have to try."

"Why? Why do I have to do anything? Mira, Dr. Kelner, now you … I'm in a safe place, but everybody tells me I have to leave it. You, of all people … please stop trying to drag me outside."

"Peter, your haven has become a dungeon. These blackouts –"

"Dr. K calls them waking dreams."

Julia squeezes his hand and pulls him closer, but she fears she has lost another skirmish with Peter's pain as she watches his chin fall to his chest, hears the timber of his voice regress to juvenescence.

"Waking dreams, not nightmares."

"These *waking nightmares* are taking you over. You hardly ever eat, you sleep like a fugitive, you wouldn't be able to function without Mira and Jesús. Peter, you have lost control of every aspect of your life. I'm watching my oldest friend deteriorate like a crack addict, and I'm doing what I can, but I can't put you back together by myself. I need your help."

As he withdraws further into his emotive cavern, he closes his eyes and shakes his head almost imperceptibly.

"Tell me what you recall."

"Stop."

"I don't care what you did or said; I'm just asking you to talk to me."

"No."

"Peter, come on."

"Don't."

"Why did Deanna leave you?"

Unable to abide his own skin anymore, let alone her prodding, Peter bursts from his seat and buries his face in his hands to try and stave the panic.

"Stop pushing me! There can be wind and no wind because none of it is real! Don't you people see that? They're just dreams and figments and fantasies, and I may not know from day to day where I am or how I got here, but I know I'm still me, and that's all I need to know!"

Startled to hear his words reverberate so, Peter listens for the familiar sounds of whispering restaurantgoers and bustling waitpersons … the faintest tinkle of a sterling utensil on china. But he gleans nothing but stiff silence. Peeling wary hands from his eyes, he finds himself standing at the lectern in his church's sanctuary, dressed in the suit he reserves exclusively for the Christmas Eve service.

When he lifts his head further, he sees that his stunned congregation heard every word of his outburst. Visitors and sporadic attendees are sneaking away in the outer aisles. Little Krissy Canaught is weeping in her mother's lap. Old Man Harlen has been sitting in the front row ever since this church was built, always in the same position with his back straight, feet planted on the floor and both hands on his upright cane. Though he remains in that posture tonight, his cane trembles in sync with his quavering jaw.

Before Peter can begin to delve into his fragmented psyche for the right apology, Mira acquires the stage with a ruffled assistant pastor close behind. While the assistant lingers to straighten his shirt and tie, Mira pulls Peter aside and addresses his flock.

"All you guests of ours, and the regular membership who have become such dear friends, as many of you know, our pastor has been under tremendous emotional strain of late. We're working feverishly with his doctors to find the underlying cause. On behalf of the pastor, the staff and the deacons, I ask your forgiveness for what you just witnessed, which was obviously a bad reaction to medication. Please keep Pastor Mott in your prayers."

As the stand-in fumbles with his scripture, Mira shuttles Peter off the stage via the quickest possible route – not through the side door but through the choir entrance which leads, not to the ground floor where Peter's office is, but up a flight of steep stairs to the second floor. As they climb, Peter emerges from his stupor.

"Mira, you just lied to our members during the most sacred observance of their year."

"I did not. Watch your step, Mr. Mott, and slow down. If you take a header down these steps, I will not be able to pick you up."

"Doctors?"

"Though he dabbles in psychological counseling, Kelner's sole certification is as an M.D. And, as you know, I have a Ph.D. in Sociology."

"I'm not on any medication."

"Do you know that for a fact?"

"Do you know something I don't?"

"I chose my words carefully, Mr. Mott. The private elevator is just around here."

"I have a private elevator?"

"I used the word *obviously* because it is my personal impression you must be on something to be acting this way. That little qualifier turned a declaration of fact into a hypothesis, so nobody got lied to just now."

"When did I get a private elevator?"

"Installation began the same day I packed you an emergency bag and hired Jesús. Now you just relax right there, Mr. Mott."

Easing Peter into his recliner, Mira loosens his tie, props up his feet, removes his shoes and deposits them in the nearby armoire. She then retrieves from the hotplate the cup of cocoa she always prepares for him during evening services. On her way out, she takes her customary pause to ask if there is anything else she can get him.

"Thank you, I have everything I need."

"Don't you sit there all night brooding. Get some rest."

"Mira?"

"Yes, Mr. Mott?"

"That dinner with Julia was three days ago?"

"It was."

"The blackouts are getting longer."

"They are."

"I'm scared, Mira."

"We all are, Mr. Mott."

As Mira plods to her office down the hall, Ani emerges from the back pew at service's end, fingering his PDA and conversing with a portly fellow.

"That Mott delivers a mighty impassioned sermon. You have been coming here … three years? So what is his story?"

DON'T WEAR HEELS TALLER THAN 1/4 INCH SO THAT YOU DON'T OPPRESS PEOPLE SHORTER THAN YOU. IF YOU ARE EXCESSIVELY TALL, SLOUCH AS MUCH AS POSSIBLE WHEN IN PUBLIC.

This public service announcement is brought to you by the First First Gentleman and First Ex-President to Serve as First Gentleman and Only Ex-President to Service as First First Gentleman's Anti-Bullying Commission.

Chapter Five

The Delicate Politics of Homicide

Before resuming their discussion, the brothers pause to devote their full attention to Julia as she glides away and disappears into the hotel entrance. Their motivation has nothing to do with lust – they are merely paying solemn respect to the indescribable beauty a self-aware woman radiates. No less reverent are they than the soldier who salutes his country's flag. But every observance must have its end, and Ani wastes no time in returning to the matter at hand once Jarry has joined him in the seclusion of his car.

"Admit it, Jarry. There is a body in your trunk."

"Don't worry about it, Ani."

"We do not transport human remains in our vehicles. Do you comprehend the far reaching consequences of your getting caught? We are not two-bit hoods desperate to pick up any odd job for a fix. We are private contractors for our State government performing a clandestine service to protect our neighbors. If our secret gets exposed, not only do we face execution, but so does everyone who cooperates with and assists us. And need I remind you of the countless innocent people who stand to suffer if we are prevented from performing this task?"

"Don't worry, Ani, it's not a contract job."

Ani grips the steering wheel with both hands and draws a self-centering breath.

"Jarry, when do you possibly have time to freelance? No, do not answer that, it is none of my business. Just tell me who and why."

"You remember Lynetta Braynard, the girl I took to a couple dances in school?"

"She had the twin brother with the funny elbow, sure."

"The guy I done –"

"*Did*, Jarry."

"The guy back there is her live-in boyfriend. Every time he got drunk, she got a beating, worse each time. And he got sauced pretty regular, let me tell you. She kept leaving, but he'd always find her. It had to be done, Ani."

"What had to be done, Jarry? Who did what to whom?"

"I killed the boyfriend."

"Do not leave this car. Do not call anyone. Do not answer your phone. Just sit here."

There is a singular panic that, if we're lucky, we experience only once or twice in our lives. It usually attacks when a bedrock assumption about the world and people which we've carried with us since birth appears to be in doubt, and the threat of losing that reality changes our perception of everything around us as starkly and thoroughly as if an alabaster lens had been removed from our field of vision. Imagine going to work or school tomorrow and returning to the same place you have called *home* for decades, only to find that utter strangers have moved in, remodeled and sold every possession you once called your own. It is this sort of unease that compels Ani to bolt from the car. Pacing the sidewalk like a madman, he folds clenched fists beneath his arms – not to stay warm but to suppress the nausea that beckons from his core – and mutters underbreath: *Jarold Bertrand Stearns is not a killer. He is not!*

Ani's mind drifts to a spring day when he was eleven. He and Jarry were riding their bicycles to school. It had stormed the night before. As the sun peeked over the horizon, the dew sparkled on the turning leaves, washing the surroundings with the nostalgic sepia tone of the pictures of long dead relatives their mother kept in a foot locker in the attic. Jarry stopped without warning and ran to the base of a tree. Ani doubled back to find Jarry kneeling in the mud. A baby bird had fallen in the night. The wind had slammed it against the trunk on its way down. Terrified and unable to lift its head, the chick cried out for its mother through a broken beak. A tarantula approached. Jarry picked it up and hurled it across the street. Ani knelt beside him.

"We can't save him, Jarry. Look at him."

"I know."

"You plan to sit here all day tossing spiders and snakes?"

"If I have to."

"He's in pain, Jarry. He's scared. You know the best thing you can do for him."

"I know."

Jarry stood and raised his foot over the ailing chick. Again. Again. Again. Unable to perform the deed, he turned away in disgrace. Ani ended the tiny creature's distress with a compassionate, decisive stomp. As he held his grieving little brother, Ani knew his role had forever changed.

Ever since that day, Ani has strode a gauzy line between insulating Jarry from and enuring him to the world's untold cruelties. The pathway has had its share of pitfalls. A mere two years later, the brothers were walking to Tower Theatre for a Sunday matinee when five older boys confronted them in an alley and demanded their movie money. Jarry would not embark upon his tremendous growth spurt for three more years, and Ani had not yet earned his fearsome reputation. Undaunted, Ani stepped in front of his brother and told his elders that if they wanted money they should get jobs and earn it. The last thing Ani saw before losing consciousness was the business end of a sawed-off hockey stick flying toward his temple. When he came to, he found Jarry had been beaten so mercilessly that his left ear was barely visible amidst swollen tissue and brain matter. Despite blurry vision and a faltering gait, Ani managed to carry his brother the entire five blocks home.

That night, their father came into Ani's hospital room and sat beside him on the bed. Franklin Stearns was not a fun dad. So foreign to him was the concept of play that the boys learned to catch and throw balls from their mother. A Korean War veteran, Franklin owned and oversaw a thriving construction company. Amiable and gregarious, he spent most of his leisure time either drinking coffee in a neighbor's garage or volunteering at school functions. Though Franklin did not deny his sons exposure to television, he never once entered a room where *the babble box* was on, preferring to sit alone in his study poring over political and philosophical essays. The most common adjective used to describe the man was *solid.* As a disciplinarian, he was firm but fair. What he denied the boys in the way of recreational and athletic grooming he more than compensated for with wisdom and compassion.

"How are you, Ani?"

"Don't worry about me. How's Jarry?"

"They operated a very long time. He will walk and talk again, but the doctor fears he has permanently lost some of his higher functions. Who did this? I'll be paying them and their parents a visit tomorrow."

Though the scarred and sinewy hand on his shoulder comforted him as always, Ani's shame would not let him accept his father's offer.

"You know their names, don't you?"

"Yes, sir."

"I gather you would rather handle this yourself?"

"I let Jarry down, Dad. It's my debt, not yours."

"Fair enough. How many?"

"Five."

"How big?"

"Average, I guess, for juniors in high school."

"Whoever did the most talking, he's the one you take out first. And you never want to confront multiple opponents with empty hands. I'll take you to the jobsite tomorrow and show you some tools. Just promise your old man one thing. Your mother can't know about this. If she finds out, it's both our asses."

For the next two weeks, father and son would sneak to the basement in the wee morning hours, where Franklin would teach Ani a hodgepodge of his Army training and the stray Tae Kwon Do technique he had picked up during his time in Korea. His aim was not to prepare the boy for formal competition by any stretch of the imagination – rather, it was to familiarize Ani with the vulnerable areas of human anatomy and how best to cripple them. After their last training session, he imparted the following counsel:

"A street fight is not a fair fight. People lose fights, not because they're unwilling to withstand punishment, but because they don't have the grit to deliver effective punishment. If you remember only one thing, make it this: Only the dirtiest sumbitch walks away."

The very afternoon his mother brought Jarry home from the hospital, Ani stalked his assailants through the downtown shopping district until they ducked on the far side of a dumpster in an alley to drink a fifth of ouzo they had swiped from an unlocked car. Careful not to be detected until he was ready, Ani crept down the near side. Ditching his heavy winter coat behind a stack of pallets, he strapped to his right forearm the roofer's axe whose shaft his father had sawed off to accommodate his size and strength. In his left hand, he held an awl whose smooth, wooden grip Franklin had replaced with a four-fingered knife hilt. With one last gulp of rousing fall air, Ani marched to the dumpster's far side and confronted the leader.

"I came for my brother's money."

The leader had unwittingly made himself an easy target by crouching against the wall. No sooner did he open his mouth to laugh than Ani dislocated his jaw with the blunt of the axe. With a parting stab to the neck from the awl, Ani turned his attention to the biggest of the gang. After he had brought two to their knees, he was tackled from behind. Like a beachgoer caught in the undertow, Ani gnashed and flounced, unsure which way was up and desperate for air, his father's voice intoning: *When they get you down, and they will, don't stop moving. Your edge over them is that you know nothing is sacred in combat. They think that once they get you down and bloody your nose, you'll whimper and plead like every other schmuck. When they hurt you, that is the time to strike hardest. Warfare is about calculation and patience, not brawn.*

In time, Ani sensed he was the only combatant still squirming and jabbing and kicking. Like emerging from a dark theater, his focus widened by increments as he peered warily about. Three lay unconscious, one had fled and the last floundered between Ani's legs in a fetal position, half his ear missing, chanting,

"Please stop … please … please stop …."

Tasting warm, salty steel, Ani presumed his jaw was injured. But there was no pain when he prodded it. He cautiously reached inside and retrieved the other half of the boy's ear. Though the film heroes of his tender years were always equipped with a trenchant parting line, Ani saw no need for such cheap melodrama. Without a word, he stood to retrieve his weapons. As he crouched to fish his father's axe from beneath the dumpster, shooting pains in his lower back indicated that someone had temporarily divested him of the awl during the melee. Secreting the implements in his winter coat, Ani limped two blocks to another alley, where his father waited with a nurse who was dating a member of his framing crew. As she gingerly washed Ani down with hydrogen peroxide on the tailgate of the pickup, Franklin took his shoulders into his weathered grasp.

"Anthony Wayne Stearns, no man could be prouder of his son than I am today. I wish you could have seen how fast that little momma's boy was running!"

Franklin then removed the axe and awl from Ani's jacket. Those tools were never seen again. The story he told Ani's mother was that Ani had been attacked by a dog. Though she knew better, Mrs. Stearns played along with the farce because she was gratified by its underlying sentiment.

"Well, I trust the two of you made damned sure that dog won't harm anyone else."

Jarry's body eventually healed, but he never regained his full mental acuity. Inevitably, he grew to emulate his elder brother. When Ani formed the Utility Committee, he brought Jarry in initially as a researcher and coordinator. Keenly aware that his brother would not be satisfied with purely administrative tasks, he then carved out a special mission to get him in the field. Perhaps twenty percent of their assignments do not call for measures as drastic as execution – they respond quite nicely to good, old fashioned intimidation. With his bulky frame and dullard carriage, Jarry has proved quite effective in this role. Ani never dreamt Jarry would grow capable of homicide. He doesn't want to believe it. Still, though the very thought curdles his bowel, he must ascertain the truth. He furtively opens the trunk, examines the corpse, shuts the lid with care, reenters the car and leans close to Jarry.

"Let us make no mistake about this. What happened at Lynetta's house?"

"I knocked on the door, he answered, I told him to leave town, he refused, I killed him."

"When did this happen?"

"This afternoon. Two-thirty, three o'clock."

"How did you kill him?"

"I don't know, we were scuffling. Maybe he hit his head."

"Maybe he hit his head?"

"Yeah, there was a lot of sharp corners around. In fact, that coffee table –"

"Jarry, the man in your trunk was strangled to death, apparently with an electrical cord."

"Oh that. I forgot that part."

"You forgot?"

"It was a pretty rough fight. A lot was going on."

"Yet you have not a scratch on you."

"Yeah, lucky, huh?"

"Jarry."

"What?"

"What happened at Lynetta's house?"

"What do you mean? I just told you."

"Tell me again. When did this happen?"

"Three o'clock, latest."

"Rigor has already begun to dissipate, Jarry. That man has been dead at least twelve hours."

"Rigor schmigor, I told you –"

Ani grips the nape of Jarry's neck and gives it a loving tug.

"Jarry, you do not have to lie to me."

"I did go over there."

"That is rather obvious."

"The door was half open. Lynetta, she had bruises all over. Her clothes torn all to hell. She was sitting in a corner of the bathroom holding one of those study lamps, cocked like she was in a batter's box, and staring at him."

"They fought, and she got the upper hand."

"Yeah, she'd been sitting there since last night, afraid he would get up and come at her again."

"She is a tough kid. It must have taken a girl her size some four minutes to kill him with that cord."

"Anyways, I felt bad for her. You know cops and D.A.s – she didn't need them poking around and twisting facts. So I told her I'd take care of it."

Ani squeezes his brother's shoulder. "Your heart is in the right place, Jarry, as always. But taking responsibility for this man's death is more problematic than you may imagine. Our special arrangement with the government prohibits us from handling private sector jobs."

"What do they care?"

"That is not my point. It is a simple matter of professional courtesy. Though the knuckleheads in the Compliance Bureau are unaware of what we do, it is no secret to the private syndicates. On the street, you and I and everyone on the Utility Committee are marked as government men. Because renegades and psychotics are unwelcome in both camps, the syndicates respect and even support us in our endeavor, but only so long as we do not interfere with their activities or jeopardize their sources of income."

"I didn't take her money, Ani. I went over there as her friend."

"They do not care whether you made a profit; they only care that you prevented them from doing so. Your best course of action was to refer the disposal job to a private outfit. We could have paid their fee from our operating fund on her behalf. The result would have been the same, and you would have built goodwill with the private sector. Now I must pull Connie and Eldon off our contract jobs to protect you until I can make amends."

"I can handle myself."

"No, Jarry. They will not send some high school punk to rough you up. They will send a pack of their nastiest Pit Bulls to make an example of you. This is not negotiable. Whenever I am not with you, Connie and Eldon will be."

"At least give me two dudes."

"Have you seen what Connie can do with a four-inch blade and how fast she can do it?"

"No."

"Trust me – if this thing has to be resolved in the street, you will want Connie at your side. What more do we know about Mr. Herzog?"

"What *don't* we know?"

With a sportive grin, Jarry retrieves a briefcase from his back seat, producing from within a weighty manila folder from Yamhill County, Oregon. Ani accepts it with the anticipation and reverence of a twelve-year-old birthday honoree.

"You found the court file?"

"Yeah, it was misfiled under one of the victim's names."

"Jarry, you are one gifted investigator. It is a privilege having you on my crew."

Ani grabs his PDA to check his notes.

"Well, that was a short dinner date."

Jarry follows Ani's gaze to the hotel's revolving door, where an agitated Peter Mott bolts from the exit and scurries to his awaiting car with his hands over his ears. Just as he collapses into the back seat, Julia emerges. Though Jesús holds open the front passenger door for her, she shakes her head, summons her own driver and saunters out of view.

"I tell you, Jarry, our friend Peter Mott is running from something quite repugnant."

NEVER RUN IN PUBLIC, EVEN IN AN EMERGENCY, AND ALWAYS WALK AT A SLOW, MEASURED PACE SO THAT YOU DON'T OFFEND THE HANDICAPPED, THE ATHLETICALLY CHALLENGED OR THE CHRONICALLY INDOLENT.

This public service announcement is brought to you by the U.S. Department of Labor and Leisure.

Chapter Six

Saviour Syndrome

Just as she turns the corner toward her office, Mira spies a clump of well-wishers milling about her door. But Mira – the softspoken intermediary who has yet to meet the parishioner or government agent she can't manipulate with her South Carolina allure, the PR crackerjack who is never at a loss for the perfect words to avert disaster – is fresh out of platitudes. Before they catch sight of her, she backtracks and ducks into an empty classroom which is lit only by the amber glare of the *Adeste Fideles* sign above the nativity scene just outside the window. Locking the door, she sits on a preschool writing desk. She gazes at the artwork on the bulletin board in pursuit of solace, but the looming storm will not be denied, and the crayoned Christmas cards perform a ghoulish dance in the prism of her tears.

Two doors down, Peter drifts into a syrupy twilight, where he is menaced yet again by the thunder of converging hooves. So violent is the clamor that the very soil on which Peter stands begins to crumble away. As he struggles to maintain a foothold, the horses pass by and, just before he tumbles into the abyss, he deciphers the word on each of the last two horse's rumps: "FOR" and "SHIT."

Peter falls into ever darkening pockets of mist until he lands facedown on damp cement. Retaking wary feet, he can see nothing but haphazard heaps of scrap metal in the eerie light that emanates from what sounds like a rotary saw in the distance. As he picks his way through the maze of jagged wrought iron and warped metal conduits, the acrid odor of burning flesh batters him to his knees. Desperate for untainted air, he presses on even though the sound and light grow more intense with his every footfall. He finally reaches a clearing, where he finds a tall, scraggy old man dressed in a grungy-gray jumpsuit who points a knobby index finger at a globe of Earth which floats in front of him. Deducing that the source of the shrill noise is the lightning that spews from that fingertip, Peter summons every last cranny of his diaphragm to ask:

"Who are you?!"

Though Peter could not hear his own voice over the din, the old man drops his finger and turns to face him. At once, the clangor falls quiet and the air loses its stench. As he peers up at fathomless, verdigris eyes, Peter wishes he had remained silent. From beneath a jungly mass of reddish yellow hair, a roughhewn face grimaces at him for a moment that drags like a freight train. The old man takes one step closer, then another, each punctuated by the echo of a hammer strike on an iron door. Peter wants to retreat, but a stone wall has materialized behind him. As the old man converges, Peter feels a coldness wash over him – the same spiteful chill that emanates from a sorority girl's every pore when she discovers your father isn't rich – and he realizes that the source of the foetid odor is the old man's breath. Nose to nose with Peter now, the old man issues a disapproving grunt.

Afraid of what might happen next, Peter shuts his eyes.

He falls backwards onto something soft. Hearing a coquettish titter, he opens his eyes to find himself lying on a red velvet couch in a wood paneled office which smells of *North Sea* pipe tobacco. A lovesome young woman licks the sweat from his cheek. Dressed in a black hostess frock, whose bone-tight skirt just kisses the top of her fishnetted thighs, and a lace bodice opened in a V from her navel, she speaks to him with a sultry, Austrian air.

"You like me better this way? Perhaps a drink? A drink and a schnitzel, and then off with my clothes and you can pin me down with your big, strong arms and have your way with me as your ancestors have wanted to stick it to me for millennia!"

Peter squirms out of her embrace. But she pursues on hands and knees with a saucy grin and, no matter how far he scurries, he can't seem to find the end of this couch. With a wink, the voluptuous temptress waves her hand.

The frock melts away.

Peter surrenders.

As she enfolds him, this oratorical wizard who is quite practiced at analogy can divine no worldly equivalent to her finesse. As she nimbly dances above him, her every stroke elicits a feeling he has never known and is loath to forget – an effusion of orgiastic release mixed with the craving for more, each eruption slightly more intense than the last. He reaches for her. She pulls him closer. She giggles again, then stiffens and closes her azure eyes … no doubt, Peter figures, to revel in her own climax. And there is no mistaking the telltale clinching of the brow and guttural moan.

But Peter soon finds these gestures signify, not a culmination, but a prelude. When she opens her eyes again they have turned blood red.

And, though he can still feel her hands on his face, something equally prehensile clamps around his nether protrusion. Writhing and laughing in the throe of an uncanny sexual paroxysm, she squeezes ever tighter until Peter lusts for any reprieve, even death. Just when he thinks he can bear no more pain, she redoubles her grip. Barely able to breathe, Peter begs:

"Please … tell me … who … you are!"

Peter now sits in an elementary schoolroom. There are no other students. At the head of the room, the teacher has written a jumble of indecipherable words and symbols. The only sound is that of the eraser he meticulously, tediously brushes across the blackboard from right to left, top to bottom. When he is finished, he places the eraser precisely in the middle of the tray, claps the dust from his palms and suitcoat, and turns to face his class of one. From his disheveled hair to his striking mustache to his skinny tie and lapels that are inexplicably stylish again after half a century, the teacher reminds Peter of the British comedic actor John Cleese, fresh from a 1970 *Monty Python* set. The teacher folds his hands at his waist, looks to the floor, throws his head toward the ceiling, looks back at the floor, raises his head again, drops his chin to stare Peter straight in the eye, then takes a deep breath through minacious nostrils.

"Now then."

The teacher begins to pace stiffly and slowly. As he patrols from left to right, Peter's full name scrawls itself on the chalkboard behind him. When he stops, it disappears. As he troops right to left, Peter's name reappears in reverse. Left to right, right to left, left to right.

"Mr. Mott."

The slate becomes a mirror. Though Peter neither moves nor utters a sound, his reflection pounds an invisible podium and retorts, "That's *Reverend* Mott, if you don't mind!"

The teacher stops and turns to face, not the derelict reflection, but Peter himself.

"*Reverend* Mott, is it? My, aren't we all impressed?"

The mirror now reflects everyone Peter has ever met in his life, each occupying one of the ocean of student desks behind him.

"Surely someone deserving of such high regard can enlighten the class on the etymology of the modern English word *reverend*."

Everyone behind Peter's reflection scoots forward to hear his answer, but the shadow is as dumbstruck as its host.

The teacher resumes his tedious pacing.

"Perhaps, Mr. Mott, you are confused by my delivery. When I make a statement, I require silence, a complete and utter void of physical motion. When I ask a question without addressing it to any one individual, that is called a rhetorical question and I don't expect an answer, it's as though I were making a statement. But when I ask a question of you, you and you alone, I want that little mouse in your head to run the treadmill that turns the flywheels of your little brain, and I want that brain to formulate words and sail them to your mouth on the river dopamine so that it will say something halfway intelligent in response to my question. It's called communication. I can count only a handful who are any good at it, but there are modern human beings who can do it. Now. We have a lot to cover today. May I please have an answer to my query?"

The mirror now reflects with unnerving accuracy the blustery November day when nine-year-old Petie was one word shy of winning his class spelling bee, but blew it on the final syllable.

"No? Right then. Conjugate the Latin verb *revereri*." Left to right, right to left. "Take your time." Left to right. "I understand brilliance must not be hurried." Right to left. "*Revereri*: to revere? No? Perhaps something less difficult. The noun *reverendus*, gerund of *revereri*, recite the cases of the first declension, if you please. No rush. Cases, Mott – Nominative, Genitive, Dative, Accusative, Ablative."

The mirror reverts to the image of Peter and his horde of classmates. Peter now wears a 10-foot tall Dunce hat. The teacher approaches with a pretentiously formal gait and stops just inches from Peter.

"You disappoint me, Mr. Mott. Class dismissed."

The room spins beneath the screams and pitter-patter of feet and books slamming shut as though two thousand first-graders have just been excused for recess. Peter clutches his chair as tightly as he can, but the commotion throws him clear, and he somersaults through a red sky and splashes down in a huge black metal pot full of water and allspice and carrots. Though the water is boiling, he feels no pain. The teacher appears overhead, his face painted for war beneath a porcupine headband. Other headhunters gather round and peer curiously as the teacher chops onions and tosses them into the cauldron. Testing the air with his cavernous nose, the teacher sizes up the nearest headhunter and throws him into the stew with Peter, where he turns into a ladle from which the teacher samples his concoction.

"By George, we're almost there!"

A headhunter makes unintelligible noises. Annoyed, the teacher turns to him.

"Well, speak up, man!"

The headhunter mutters again.

"Ah, very good. Do tell her I'm coming, old chap."

He turns again to the pot and takes another sip of broth.

"There's just something off about this recipe. Too much … too much ...."

At the wave of his hand, a gargantuan iron lid begins to close over Peter. Before it falls to, the teacher gives him a wink.

"You just simmer there a bit more, Mr. Mott. I shan't be long."

Just as the lid closes, the veil is lifted from the birdcage in which Peter now finds himself perched. He peers out into a cozy den with a fire blazing beneath a black marble mantle, on whose either side looms a high-back chair upholstered in red velvet. He can not see the occupants because the chairs face the fireplace.

"So, I walked up to the premiere ... no, they called him an emperor. Or was it a president? I forget."

"Pharaoh, you silly boy, pharaoh."

"Oh, what's the difference? Anyway, I walked up to the bloke and I said, 'Hey, Ram-baby, you'd better clear out the dustbin in your parlor tonight, because there's some kind of bacterium growing in there that I haven't seen for ages and it'll take your bleeding lung out if you don't kill it where it breeds.' The stupid man thinks I'm giving him a poser."

"I think you mean parable, dear."

"What's geometry got to do with it?"

"Just go on with your story."

"So the poor, scared devil jumps up and leaves the party. That very night, the lunatic sends his soldiers on a bleeding rampage to kill every firstborn son in that little province, *including his own*! When I heard the official cover story – that Dad had done it – I got my ass out of there because I knew Dad would blame me. When I pop in on them twelve hundred years later, they're calling themselves Romans. The simpletons are forming committees and boasting that they're the conquerors of the world, and it sounds so damned comical to me that I decide to hang about for a while, make like I'm one of them and see what sort of fun I can have. Remember now, I'm on holiday, right? Sightseeing and what have you? I don't want to stand out, so I put on the clothes of a drifter, a layabout ..."

"A what?"

"A layabout, Mum. You called them beggars in your time."

"Layabout? That's cute. Lay-a-bout. Poetic, don't you think?"

"There's nothing poetic about it; I'm simply trying to educate you in the ways of the universe. You've got to keep up with the fads. If you don't, well, look what's happened to Dad."

"I'll tell you something about your father. Oh! Son, look over there. What is that?"

The man who rises and turns to study Peter is the spitting image of another *Pythoner*, Eric Idle. At his side emerges the most impressive woman Peter has ever seen. Her beauty does not shout at him like the boisterous bulges of the Austrian proprietress. This woman's charm whispers to him. It taunts him. It eludes him. From her left leg which peeps out from the folds of her dress, to her statuesque hand which rests on the hearth, to the beguiling way she cocks her head and throws her raven hair from her cheek – her every feature exudes a charm that transcends the sum of her physical parts.

"What are you up to this time, Jesepi?"

She sashays toward Peter with a teasing grin.

"Why do you always jump to the conclusion that it's me? I've never seen that simian before."

She stops half a hormone from Peter, considers him head to toe.

"I'll take it up with your father, then. Do finish your story, Jeson. What happened next?"

"Anyway, the Roman leaders' baser ambitions soon tainted their understanding of their historically proper administrative role. As always happens with centralized governments, no sooner did they stumble upon power than they forgot that it was nothing but luck which had won them that power, and they devoted their every waking moment, not to the betterment of their society but to the maintenance of that power. And the common people began spoiling for a revolt. They wanted blood on the *iter*, I tell you!"

"I've heard about the Romans. Where did I ...? Of course, that was the century your father was recuperating from his breakdown. But, please, more about your holiday."

"I'm sitting on the shore of a little pond they called Jordan, talking to this hot piece of humanity ... what was her name ... Mary ... Magpie or something. I'd been drinking with some of the local peasants the night before, and I guess my tongue had gotten away from me. I couldn't get five seconds of privacy with this sumptuous dish, because people would flock around us and ask me questions like I was their rabbi or something. In fact, that's what one of them called me.

"This prawn, who was obviously a bureaucrat – I could tell because his robes clashed – walked up without a bleeding invitation, sat down next to the girl and asked me, 'Rabbi, is it proper for us to pay taxes?'

"I said, 'Taxes? What are taxes?' I had never heard the term before. So he explained that a tax is what the government charges you to be a citizen. He seemed to understand it perfectly until I told him my interpretation. 'Sounds like ransom to me, chum. If you don't pay it, your king sends his goons to divest you of your appendages, am I right?' The bloke says I'm right. So I say, 'Listen, mate, do what you want. You know the consequences. If you like what the old sot is doing for you, pay him a reasonable fee. If you don't like it, depose the bastard. Raise yourself an army and crack his potted skull. What's so bleeding difficult about this proposition?'

"The man's face turns as milky-white as this chick's breasts, which I've been trying desperately for hours to coax out of her gown. But he won't leave! He just sits there gawking like a retarded chimpanzee. So I say, 'Show me the goods you pay this tribute with.' And he digs in his purse and produces a flat, oblong piece of silver with a man's head on it. I say, 'Whose likeness is this?' And the old frog says, 'Everybody knows,' and I say, 'Not everybody knows, you bastard, because I obviously don't,' and he heaves his chin like I offended him and says, 'That's the head of Caesar!' I've had about all I can stand from this weasel, so I say, 'Well, if this Caesar fellow's head is on it, then it must belong to him, so give the damned thing back you stupid man.'

"Imagine! The fool is asking me if he should pay a tax and I find out he's paying the silly thing with something he obviously stole from this Caesar person and, before I know it, I've got crowds of revolutionaries following me and throwing gifts at my feet and asking me for gratuities like I'm some sort of prince ... what's so bleeding funny?"

"You, my dear boy!"

"What? Let's have out with it, what do you find so humorous?"

"Money, Jessecht! Money!"

"What in bloody hell is money?"

"I'll tell you all about it later. Do go on. What did the man do?"

"Well, he stood up without another word and shuffled away."

"What happened with Mary?"

"Over the months that passed, I managed to outrun most of the hero junkies, but there were these twelve insufferable sycophants I couldn't shake. Layabouts, every last bleeding one. All they wanted to do was keep me awake all night, plying me with booze and asking me about Dad. *What's he like? What does he think about the Code of Hamurabi? Where does he stand on requital for robbery and murder? Which gladiator does he like in this weekend's games, and what odds would he give?* I got so sick of those piddling rodents that I left them out on the pond in a storm one night. Scared the shit of them! When the storm had passed, I came back to the boat, and they made a big stink about the fact that I was walking on the water. Can you believe that? I mean, water is fine when you're in the mood for a drenching, but the human body has billions of sensory receptors on its surface that can get to be a real pain in the ass –"

The woman, who has been fidgeting like a cat in a cage, points at the lamp on the endtable by the couch. The lamp disappears and reappears across the room just before it smashes itself on her son's forehead. He bolts to his chair and crouches behind it.

"What did I say?!"

"You can not get to the point, the way you let these tangents carry you away at their whim! It is a simple task, Jesep. I asked you about Mary. All you have to do is tell me about Mary. Can you do that?"

"I'm coming to it! I just wanted to give you the context in which it happened."

She points her finger at an empty space between the chairs and a credenza. A gilded day bed materializes from thin air and, the instant it appears, she appears supine on top of it, her forearm draped over her eyes.

"Finish your story, then."

He sidles over and sits on the floor beside her.

"So I had the twelve parasites over for this big dinner and got them all drunk. When they passed out, I finally got Mary alone in a garden called Gethsemane."

She bolts upright, cradles his face in her hands.

"Oh, sweet Jesus, I'm so proud of you! You taught that dear woman how to revive her soul through sex!"

"Well ... I started to. I was almost there, but then Judas brought some soldiers to the garden and ... well ...."

"Don't tell me you got killed again."

"*Killed* is such a harsh term. I prefer the word *relocated*."

"When will you learn, Jeso? You've been drawn and quartered, forced to drink hemlock, burned at the stake. What did these Romans do to you?"

"They ... sort of ... crucified me."

"Why didn't you stop them?"

"Oh, it's going to sound stupid."

"Tell your mother, dear."

"Okay, it's like this. I know that, as a species, they're a primitive mob of noetic mangoes. But there's something lovable about the humans. Dad has said it himself. I want them to like me, that's all."

"Oh, my dear child. Let us keep this little crucifixion a secret. There's no telling what your father would do to them if he found out."

He pushes her away, turns toward the fire and hangs his head. "It's a bit late for that."

She stands and folds her magnificent arms across her chest.

"Why did you tell him?"

"I didn't have a choice."

"Your father can not make you do anything, you whimpering weed."

"That's easy for you to say, because he's got needs only you can fulfill!"

"Enough!"

The boy's mouth stops in mid-gape when she plants her finger in front of him like a cork on the bottle of his ravings.

"What did your father do?"

"What *did* he do? He's still doing it! He began his bleeding vendetta by killing a quarter of the population of a little settlement called London. Infected a horde of rodents with what their historians call *bubonic plague*. Four centuries later ... well, you remember this. When those pioneers who had settled in North America took the advice

I gave that Roman? Told their British king to piss off and formed their own government?"

"Wasn't that an exciting time?"

"When did you look in on them last?"

"I've been busy with other things, son, you know that. There was talk about writing a manifesto, but that's the last I heard."

"The manifesto became known as the United States Constitution. It was a fine piece of work. Their idea was to develop a commonwealth of sovereign States, with a tripartite balance of power consisting of a legislature, an executive branch and a watchdog which they called the judiciary, thereby virtually eliminating any avenue toward despotism. The State governments were given exclusive power over their citizens. The national government was to be little more than an affable brute who organized the State militias to prevent invasions from foreign powers. I was damned proud as I watched them develop it.

"Then Dad stepped in and spoiled the whole thing. As his second act of recompense for my crucifixion, he persuaded them to add five words to their constitution. In Article I, Section 8, they had given their congress the power to regulate commerce with foreign nations and the indigenous race with whom they were negotiating for expansion. Well, it was more of a slaughter followed by forced assimilation, but that's beside the point for now. The regulation of foreign trade was a reasonable provision, I think you would agree. But, after days of vicious debate and occasional brawls, the nitwits inserted into that once noble document the phrase, *and among the several States.*

"It's come to be known as the Interstate Commerce Clause. Believe you me – that manifesto had barred every conceivable door to tyranny. But Dad's five tiny words opened them all up again. The country has fifty States carved out of an area the better part of four million square miles, populated by some four hundred million people who can barely wipe their noses without violating the federal code."

"*Federal*? I don't know that word."

"It's a ludicrous euphemism for the word *royal*. A handful of humans who are separated into two political parties run the whole scam from a tiny district on the east coast.

"Now in their third century of existence as a unified country, their founders' grand blueprint for a true republic has been perverted into a treasure map for hundreds of petty kings and queens called *senators* and *representatives.* They spend so much of their time bickering over partisan dogma and laundering payola that they can't even manage their own little district, let alone the country. They've used the interstate commerce clause to suck the States dry of their power and resources, and they've got their bumbling paws into everything. With one hand, they tax up to half of every honest citizen's income. With the other, they stick a tidy sum into their own pockets, then piss away the rest on a growing population of layabouts. Bloody pirates!"

"Why don't they throw the bums out?"

"It's too big for that. The *federales* have infiltrated every State, setting up their own agencies in office buildings, and every year they hire thousands of new converts over to their side. It's like a bleeding virus the way the federal parasite spreads. If you don't pay their annual tribute, they seize your property and throw you behind the very bars that you paid them to build. There's Dad's revenge for you."

The woman stamps her exquisite foot. The universe trembles beneath her rage.

"I have had all I will take of you and your father manipulating our corporeal children for your amusement! I will deal with your father soon enough. Before he gets here, Jisoh, you will tell me about any more *accidents* you've had with the humans."

The boy retreats to the mantle.

"Um ... I sort of became an idol of theirs. Between my arrest and the time they nailed me to that clothesline post, I wrote some letters to Judas. I wrote a lot of letters, actually. I wrote to Judas because he was the only one of those morons who ever understood me. I have it on good authority that his group of twelve started calling themselves *apostles* after my crucifixion. One night, after Judas fell asleep, five of his cohorts killed him and stole all my letters. The nickname they had given me one night when we were getting smashed was *Christo*, meaning *anointed one* and *healer.* Within a short time after I had gone, they started calling themselves … *Christians.*

"Millions worship me now. They've rearranged my words, in some instances completely bastardized my message, and published my letters under their own names. They've divided their calendars into B.C. and A.D., and the turning point is my birthday, even though they're off by nine years and one hundred sixty-seven days … which is further complicated by the fact that I was never actually *born* in the human sense. And they market little icons. The most popular is an emaciated statuette of me hanging on a cross. They've gone completely insane with it. Supposedly, I'm the embodiment of a new peace treaty between them and Dad. They've built extravagant cathedrals in their communities where they congregate and sing songs about me. The entire world has embraced the madness, and they all have their own individualized doctrines.

"For instance, when the *Christians* first experienced Dad, he was having one of his more lucid days, so they named him *Yahweh* to reflect a benevolent dictator who stood by his covenants. When they later witnessed his forgetful anger, it so frightened them that they deluded themselves into thinking this homicidal lunatic wasn't their beloved *Yahweh* at all, but must be a demented uncle or something of the sort, so they added to their worldview a fictitious character called *Satan.* Over time, their poor little imaginations went haywire, and they dreamed up various entities to fill the gulf between the ideals of pure good and pure evil, calling them *angels* or *demons* according to where they fell on the spectrum.

"Some six hundred years after the *Christian* tradition began to spread, a desert nomad with a knack for storytelling conjured up a bloke named Muhammad, who was supposed to be an incarnation of yours truly. This pretended prophet founded a competing doctrine called *Islam*, but he wasn't all that imaginative in doing so. For *Yahweh* he substituted *Allah*; for *Satan*, *Shaytān*. *Angels* became *malaks* while *demons* translated into *jinns*. Apparently, the Islamic fablers had no grasp of the concept *plagiarism*.

"Anyway, over the next fourteen centuries, the Christian and Muslim cosmologies grew to become the top two by world population percentage. But in the process there was some animosity and a bit of ... bloodletting, I'm afraid."

Though she stands ten feet away from him, when she makes a slapping gesture with her open hand, the boy's head snaps aside and he yelps in pain.

"A *bit*?"

"Oh ... um ... I ... I sort of stopped counting at eight hundred million."

Her next long-distance strike sends him tumbling into the fire.

"You ignorant little ass!"

Impervious to the flames, he huddles in a far corner of the firebox for fear of another blow from his matriarch.

"All I tried to do was tell one human being what I was all about! All I tried to do was save him from the absurd and stunted path his kind were on and, before I knew it, they'd murdered my only human confidante and turned me into a cursed messiah!"

Leaving the boy to weep alone, the woman struts toward Peter and evaluates him some more.

"So your words got twisted. You're surprised? Until you infected them with ideas they wouldn't be ready to hear for another thousand years, your father had stood aloof from them, an ill tempered beast who wouldn't show himself even in the darkness. That is the way we wanted it. As I have told you time and again, unearned knowledge breeds evil. Our children must evolve in their own time. They must make their mistakes. Their progeny must use those mistakes as stepping stones across the river to their rebirth. Your father is not avenging your humiliation on that hill. He is pulling the puppet-strings of the humans to teach you a lesson you should have learned long ago."

As the woman's gaze intensifies, Peter hears a loud crash, then the teacher enters the den clad in diving fins, a Scottish kilt, a fluted tuxedo shirt with ruffles and a Panama hat. The woman folds her arms and turns to him.

"Lucifano!"

"Yes, dear?"

His shoes change to moccasins, his kilt into dungarees, and a dashiki completes his new ensemble, but for only seconds before they transform into a red seersucker suit crowned by a World War II aviator's hat. The woman cups his face in her palms.

"Focus, darling. Focus."

His wardrobe finally settles on a white wetsuit, purple tuxedo tails and a cowboy hat as she slowly averts his head. The sight of Peter gives him a start.

"Well, if it isn't Mr. Mott! I say, Ethano, that was awfully industrious of you to snare this elusive little varmint. I thought I'd lost him for good in the Yucatan."

She pulls his gaze back in her direction and enunciates slowly, deliberately, as though she were talking to an autistic child.

"Darling, that is no way to treat a guest. You should set a table and feed him."

"But of course. Straight away." Her tender kiss sends him on his way … for only three bounds until he turns back. "I'm sorry, dear. *Feed* him?"

"He's a temporal creature, my darling. He must be refueled periodically."

"Right, dear, right. Um … refueled with what?"

"Organic matter."

"Right! Carbon needs more carbon. Oh, dear. I wasn't supposed to cook him, was I?"

"No, my precious one, you were supposed to cook *for* him."

The teacher grins voraciously and claps his hands.

"And cook I shall! Mr. Mott, please consider us your host and hostess. Dinner is served!"

DON'T LAUGH OVERLY LOUD, OR FOR LONGER THAN TWO SECONDS, IN PUBLIC; YOU MIGHT DISHEARTEN THE MELANCHOLY OR DRIVE THE DEPRESSED TO SUICIDE.

This public service announcement is brought to you by the First Female President and First First Lady to Become President and Only Former First Lady to Become the First Female President's Council on Mental Health, and the First First Gentleman and First Ex-President to Serve as First Gentleman and Only Ex-President to Service as First First Gentleman's Anti-Bullying Commission.

Chapter Seven

Regaining Unconsciousness

At the snap of the host's finger, the birdcage vanishes and Peter finds himself lying prone on a bed of sticky lettuce. A fork three times his size scoops him up, and a mammoth set of incisors bears down upon him. Just before he is bitten in half, an immense hand swats at the fork. Peter vaults through the air and plunges into a sea of molten gravy, only to be plucked out again by a colossal spoon which raises him to another massive mouth but, rather than eat him, this one blows a gentle mist to cool him. An elephantine napkin then envelops him and, when it is removed, he finds himself sitting at an unadorned, oaken dining table with the host to his left and the hostess to his right. Thankfully, he is now of comparable size.

Peter can tell by the manner in which he eats that the host is now as coherent as his new *country gentleman* attire. And this impression is vindicated when the man speaks.

"I must apologize for trying to eat you just now. And for that little incident with the crock … and, well, I suppose for the classroom ridicule. But in my defense it is quite galling to see how little of your Latin education you have retained. Have you no shame, man?"

"Luciete! Temper, darling." The hostess pats Peter's hand and pulls him round to face her. "Peter, my dear, what troubles you?"

As he gropes for words, Peter's gaze falls upon his supper plate, which contains not only the identical fare his mother served on his most venerated of Thanksgivings but the exact amount and dimension of each portion.

"You're not real. None of this can be real."

"Are you telling me, Peter, that you trust your own present senses less than you do a motley collection of stories written by forty different authors over a span of five centuries, the latest of which was penned sixteen hundred years ago? You must be positively famished after your journey. Do eat something, dear."

"I'm … not hungry."

"You uncouth little bastard!" The host backhands Peter into a roiling sea, where briny murk fills his lungs as the waves bat him to and fro like a cat toy until a great white shark hits him from the depths like a racing locomotive but, just before the gargantuan fish crushes him, an oversize albatross plucks Peter from its jaws and drops him gently onto a chaise lounge that sits next to a glassy swimming pool on the uppermost deck of a cruise ship which sails through outer space.

Each now clad in safari togs, the host and hostess reappear, sitting in bamboo fan chairs beneath a cellophane umbrella. The hostess sips a pink cocktail through a straw made of cobra skin while the stoic host grimaces at Peter from behind mirrored sunglasses. Her kick to the shin breaks his sullen silence.

"I *apologize* for the shark." The bottom-of-the-glass gurgling of her straw elicits yet another expiatory ejaculation. "*And* for the insult."

As he resumes his brooding stare, the hostess flings her drink aside. The glass becomes a field rat which the cobra, now alive, devours before she snatches the cobra by the tail, whereupon it transforms into an emery board which proceeds to manicure her already splendrous nails.

"My dear Peter, let us cut the crap. You know who I am. I'm sure you have many questions. If you'll indulge me while he simmers down, I'll try to answer them. But I must begin by asking one of you. Aside from that dreadful little incident fourteen of your years ago, what single thought has haunted you since your birth?"

Though still frightened and angered by the host, Peter is so captivated by the hostess that he dares trust her as implicitly as he does Mira.

"Why am I here? Why do I have arms and legs and a brain? Why do I hope for better things? Does the ability to contemplate my own existence prove I have an eternal soul, or does positing an immortal spirit underscore my own vanity? Why, not do I have this existence, but do I exist at all? Why *must* I exist? My ego insists, something has got to be. But reason rejoins, nothing *had* to be. And time is running whether I know it or not, so the choice is exist and then cease to exist or never have existed at all. Having been alive for a single moment, how can I comprehend nonexistence? It's a riddle that makes me want to escape, but I don't know what from or where to."

"I get the same fits of panic. You and I, Peter, are on the same journey."

"I don't understand."

"Your ancestors have called me many things. You have called me *God.* That name assumes more than I can deliver."

"But you … he … are the beginning and the end. Exodus 3:14 – *I am who am.*"

The host stabs a menacing finger at Peter's chest.

"Don't go citing that rubbish in my presence, you filthy little mongrel!"

The hostess eases her fuming counterpart backward.

"Think about that concept, Peter. Your beginning was clearly defined. When you were born, there were larger versions of you at beck and call, nurturing you and making nonsensical noises in your ear. A wealth of history preceded you, occupying you in your formative years with the story of humankind. My birth, if you can call it a birth, was to find myself conscious at the snap of a finger I did not hear. I was born alone, into nothingness. You, Peter, were born *from* nothingness. You know the comfort of an origin. Yet I know no father, no mother. You, my child, have watched others like you cease to function and you call it death. I've no concept of what my own death might be. Often I yearn for sleep. The best I have done is to learn to forget. Imagine my loneliness, Peter. And his. Perhaps that is the purest bond he and I share. For aeons, we had each other, which was far better than the alternative. But something was lacking.

"So we created you as an experiment. We wanted to figure out what we came from. So we gathered pieces of the universe around us and breathed life into the simplest glob of goo we could devise and sat back to watch what would happen. We proceeded to devise different designs of increasing complexity, at each step learning more about our own anatomy. Your species, Peter, represents our latest effort … regrettably not our finest, however.

"You see, we can imitate physical forms and forces, but we haven't the first clue how to imbue another creature with that which we ourselves can not poke and prod and dissect: the thought process itself, or consciousness. So we gave you all of our fundamental faculties and hoped for the best. What neither of us counted on was that, as we watched your race grow, your successes and blunders would awaken in us memories of a childhood which we still can not fully reclaim. And, dear Peter, I wish I could recount for you our wonderment when, some thirty million years ago, we realized that each of you had developed a unique personality. It was then that you became dearer to us than mere laboratory subjects.

"Alas, caring for so many individuals at once soon took its toll. When we saw you repeat your mistakes *ad nauseam*, it was frightening to think how long it must have taken us to evolve. I responded with sadness; he with anger."

At her tacit invitation, the host begrudgingly enters the conversation.

"Once I even obliterated everything from the face of the planet. Nothing survived, not even a microbe. When Athene found out about it, she made me put everything back – even the five imbeciles who had pissed me off to begin with."

The hostess covers his mouth and flashes the conciliatory mug of a mother whose child has spoken out of turn. "Elvis tends to digress. Now then. As I have already told you, your ancestors started out with no knowledge."

Peter can not deny his curiosity.

"Elvis? That's your name?"

"What of it, worm waste?"

"Yes, Peter, that is one of my favorite names for my illustrious companion. Anyway, your progenitors had the hardware, if you will, but no software. A clean slate."

The host smirks.

"That's *tabula rasa* in Latin, you malodorous little cretin."

"So, the first human beings knew nothing but what they could see, touch, hear, et cetera. As you evolved, you built your conceptual world upon that physical foundation. Still, as you know from reading your horribly inept history lessons, in time you grew dissatisfied with what you saw in front of your faces. From the day every human is born, his bedrock goal is to discover a cogent explanation of himself. I call it the *Primeval Why*. He seeks out elders and notables from the past, hoping they will lend him that magic nugget of truth. When he inevitably fails to find the answer, he looks ever outward. So it was natural for you to hypothesize invisible powers beyond your familiar dimensions. Then our bungling son paid you a visit. The advice he gave was flawless. But you were not mature enough to understand its fullest meaning. As a result, the *Primeval Why* was perverted on a worldwide scale.

"Inevitably, a group of sexually deviant men wanted the same power held by the kings, but they had neither the balls nor the brains to stand up and seize it. So they manufactured myths about how the world was created, wrote voluminous storybooks and claimed that they, exclusively, had the ear of Elvis. They turned the spiritual quest into an alternative political machine. They twisted the *Primeval Why* into an institution, with corporate executive officers and treasuries and branch offices and market competitors and front line soldiers fighting for the biggest piece of the power-pie by enslaving as many confused and overworked people as they could in whatever way they could.

"Had Jeshua kept his bungling nose out of your affairs, the religious frolic would have died out within five hundred years. His goal, though he didn't realize it until decades after he was crucified, was to destroy that institution, to remind every man and woman that the spiritual search is an individual quest. But all he succeeded in doing was to fan the flames of zealotry. Not only did the church grow stronger thanks to him, but it found new life, a new cause. The Board of Directors – the priests – quickly added a new silent partner to their rolls – Jesus Christ of Nazareth. His self-proclaimed disciples – social outcasts looking for a way to weasel their way into the priesthood – wrote self-serving stories about their supposed experiences with him. To what end? A fast-food religious franchise. The existential mystery has been ground into powder, diluted with charts and timetables on glossy pamphlets, stuffed into five-pound bags and stacked in rows on a grocery store shelf, then injected like Jonestown Kool-Aid into a mindless herd of Sundayschool sheep, who stumble away from the sanctuary in emotional poverty while Joel Osteen skips off the stage to buy another yacht with his spoils!"

Though his face appears resigned, Elvis' voice bears a hint of mockery when he adds, "And thanks to Ms. Cosmic Packrat, there's no point in my stepping in to correct the situation because, if she doesn't agree with my reason for killing any of you vermin, she'll stick whomever I've eliminated right back into the gene pool."

Athene pats Elvis' knee.

"But the tide is beginning to turn. Fearless thinkers with a keen sense of integrity are, as we speak, reclaiming the *Primeval Why* from the charlatans and the moralistic meddlers. I suspect an awakening is afoot. And none too soon, Peter, because I must confess that my own patience with the lot of you is nigh its end."

Peter can no longer contain himself. Thrusting his palms toward her like a traffic cop, he shakes his head.

"No, no, no! The events depicted in The Bible may not be historically accurate, but they communicate deeper truths. They contrast right to wrong, a distinction without which civilization can not thrive."

Though equally nettled by Peter's comment, Athene keeps a firm grip on Elvis to hold him at bay.

"Peter, the peril that inheres in the ability to reflect and imagine is that the unpracticed often lose sight of the boundary between what is and what isn't. Right and wrong are artificial concepts. In what you call nature, which is unadulterated by human machinations, there are no such polar values. The only universal law, if there is such a thing, arises from the instinct for self-preservation. Elvis and I have learned to take care in what we do to each other. If I hit him in anger, I can not fault him for striking back. If I lie to him, I invite him to deceive me. Simply put, what I do to him I also do to myself. Hence, we scrutinate our intentions carefully before we act. It's a simple concept. We were not taught it. We had no king to make us do it. It is a principal which quite naturally presented itself when we chose friendship over reciprocal annihilation. Your species discovered the same ethic millennia before the so-called *golden rule* appeared in any doctrinal text."

Peter stands and kicks his chair away, leveling a defiant finger at his hostess.

"I don't know whether I'm dreaming or having a psychotic meltdown, but I do know this. Whoever … whatever you are, the both of you are insane if you expect me to believe anyone who espouses amorality is anything but evil. Matthew 16:23 – 'Get thee behind me, Satan. Thou art an offence unto me, for thou savourest not the things that be of God, but those that be of men!'"

Athene throws confounded arms skyward. Elvis stands and levels his ill-boding finger. As Athene and Elvis merge into one being, Peter again feels the agony of the Austrian barkeep's orgasm. Then everything vanishes.

Most of us equate nothingness with the colors black or white. But nothingness has no color, no shape. No solid underfoot, no clouds or stars overhead. Imagine being suspended in an ocean transparent as glass and without a current, with no gravity pulling you down and no gasses holding you afloat. No form or shade for as far as you can see. An infinite transparency. An emptiness that eats you alive. With no atmosphere to push against, there is no movement. And with nothing of external substance to latch onto, inner thought falls mute. Peter finds this *non*place far more terrifying than the groin pain of recent past. Then he hears the resounding voice of Elvis.

"I did not conjure up morality; you did. You, Mr. Human Race, chiseled a cleft down the middle of your personality and assigned converse values to either side. Now you propose to cut me in half without even asking my permission. You've replaced personal responsibility with policemen and judges and senators. You should have evolved far beyond that by now. Laws and rah-rah fight songs and political platforms are the fruits of cowardice – that despicable stain of self-contempt which underlies every religious pursuit. The same faintheartedness of which you reek, *Reverend* Peter Shroyer Mott. You ask my forgiveness, you indoctrinate a rabble of groupies with a manmade bastardization of what I am, because you want me to expunge your responsibility for the atrocities that befell your little ones all those years ago. But neither I nor your caricature of me can forestall the penance that awaits you. Don't come crying to me for proof of what I say, you vapid little termite – dredge the depths of your own feeble brain and work out your own goddamned salvation!"

"They … they really don't."

"Yes, the last two horses have finally passed within view. We've covered that. I don't know what it means any more than …."

Dr. Kelner, who has been taking notes at a furious pace, stops in mid scribble.

"Has it happened again, Peter? Are you conscious now?"

Dr. Kelner was seven when he took his first ride on a Ferris wheel. When it stopped rotating near the top of its arc, the chair rocked from the momentum. He wrapped his arms round the safety bar and fixed his eyes on the rivets that held the seat to the main structure, focusing all his mental energy on the intent that they remain secure. At that moment, nothing in the world was more sacred to him than that rusted metal chair to which he clung for dear life. Peter is now clasping the office chair with the same white-knuckle grip. Scrambling to his side, Dr. Kelner checks Peter's pulse.

"Peter, I know it's the tritest of clichés, but I want you to lie down on the couch. Come on. There, now close your eyes."

"Don't leave me, Doc'!"

"I'm not going anywhere. We need to depress your heart rate before you have a stroke." Dr. Kelner begins massaging Peter's carotid artery. "Now stop ranting for a moment and breathe."

"I don't care what drugs you have to pump into me. Don't let them take me back there. I can't go back there. I can't go back. Don't let them, Doc'. They don't stop for shit!"

Dr. Kelner rushes to his credenza and returns moments later with a rubber tourniquet and a syringe.

"Peter, I'm injecting a very light dose of a sedative called diazepam. You'll feel better in no time."

As Peter's breathing slows to normal, Dr. Kelner slaps a digital blood pressure cuff on him and drags his chair closer to the couch. Keeping a watchful eye on the readout, he gropes on the floor for his notebook and pen. Just as he settles into his chair, Peter drifts into the first peaceful sleep he's had in the better part of seventy-two hours. Dr. Kelner tiptoes to his desk and phones the receptionist.

"Rana, before you go to lunch, would you please cancel my afternoon appointments? What's that? Kaiser's Deli, eh? Oh, a Reuben would just hit the spot. Would you mind bringing two? You're a saint, my dear."

Poring over the pages of notes he took as Peter relived his latest dream, he meanders to, not the duplex file cabinet where he stores patient files, but the bottom drawer of his desk in which he keeps a timeworn, leather backed notebook under lock and key. It is in this notebook that he starts writing on a fresh page.

> In just three months, a fast growing number of my clients report that they have been visited by recurring dreams having to do with the supernatural. These visions cut across cultural, social and political lines, each with imagery and lore appropriate to that person's formative traditions. Though these cold data suggest an epidemic psychogenic response, commonly referred to as mass hysteria, that diagnosis entails a common external catalyst which I simply can't find among these cases.
>
> Of particular note is Peter Mott for two reasons. First, his dreams are the most vivid. Second, his are the most debilitating because they have progressed to the point that

they present as waking hallucinations during which he is incognizant of the real world even though he is functioning in it. The vast majority of us are fortunate in that our brains manage to dispel, or at least dilute, nightmares before we fully awaken. Were these visions allowed to occupy our conscious reality, we would all descend into psychosis. Something has either defeated or altogether destroyed this safeguard in Peter. Though he exhibits a remarkable awareness of what is happening to him, his condition nonetheless bears many hallmarks of schizophrenia. Not only is he plagued by disturbing visions; it appears as though his conscious and autonomic psyches intrude upon each other so regularly that perhaps they are irretrievably merging. He also exhibits marked contradictory behavior. On the one hand, he is an ordained minister who preaches the conventional Christian gospel. On the other, he just spent eighty-five minutes ranting in a fashion the typical congregationalist would condemn as the obscenest heresy.

For example, he portrays God as a bipolar personality with homicidal tendencies, sexual identity confusion and an Oedipus complex, who also suffers from stage four dementia. If I recall my younger days in the Catholic church, the concept of hell was a state of unmet needs. But Peter insists just the opposite. To paraphrase:

"Since the age of two, I thought that once I saw the face of God he would give me the answer to the mystery of life. But if God embodies the end of the quest for knowledge, how stifling and stagnant would heaven be? No, it is the striving, the incomplete condition, that gives life its flavor. It follows that hell is the place without hunger, without questions, without ambition, and for God to exist he must be imperfect, because perfection is tantamount to death."

He ricocheted from that thought onto a tangent about epistemology which, if memory serves, is the study of knowledge itself. I seem to recollect a discussion in college about whether my perception of a yellow pencil matches my classmate's. When Peter took a breath, I tried to break his train of thought by asking about the stale pop-philosophy theory that our universe is merely a dream in some greater being's mind. This so animated him that he almost came out of his chair. Paraphrasing again:

"For that matter, am I your dream? Are you mine? Who cares? Look around you, Doc'. The clock on your wall, the car you drove to the office this morning, the road you drove it on, the appliances that refrigerate your food and cook your meals – each of these concrete pieces of reality we take for granted today were once only dreams. If I can turn imagination into reality, why can't I dream my way out of, or through, death? And if I can't, time is relative anyway, so how does one measure eternity? Why not make that last second of consciousness extraordinary? Better yet, why restrict ourselves to preconceived notions? If something does, indeed, exist beyond this realm, why not make our last moment of lucidity one of open-minded and eager acceptance for whatever may come?"

These are scandalous hypotheses for an orthodox minister to ponder, let alone vocalize. And as his grasp on reality continues to deteriorate, I worry not merely for his mental state but for his professional and bodily welfare. Fundamentalists, after all, are notorious for maiming and killing over the slightest derogation from groupspeak. It is my opinion that Peter's precipitous lifechange and his latest delusional ravings are characteristic of a man who suffers from a veritable mountain of guilt. I presume the historical record needs no further documentation of the peculiar association between criminal offenders and evangelicals. But I can only speculate about the catastrophic events of 2006, because the man refuses to speak about them.

YOU SHOULD PRESUME THAT ANY INGESTIBLE OR LEISURE ACTIVITY IS BAD FOR YOU UNLESS AND UNTIL IT HAS BEEN CERTIFIED AS SAFE AFTER EXHAUSTIVE TESTING BY THE FEDERAL GOVERNMENT.

This public service announcement is brought to you by the Food and Drug Administration.

Chapter Eight

Shoats Aloft

"Mark my words. He's either Jesus come again or the antichrist."

"This just reeks of fraud. Everybody knows third parties are a joke."

"Hell in a handbasket, that's all I can say."

Julia's offices occupy the northeast quadrant of floors twenty-five and -six of Leadership Tower, a thirty-story office building downtown. Every morning, she steals away to the ground floor delicatessen, orders a chai spice hot tea, sits at a table near the deli exit and downloads the morning news to her smart phone. Passersby think it curious that she would not opt for a table farther away from the commotion and chatter to enjoy a midmorning refresher. But Julia doesn't care so much for the news as she does for the reactions of her fellow tenants to it, and she chose this little table carefully. Though there is more spacious seating near the entrance, she finds that people going in are preoccupied with personal greetings and what to order. It is only after they have dispensed with such trivia that they are free to discuss current events.

Though the Presidential election is nearly two months past, its bewildering outcome remains the primary topic of discussion. On November 3, in an unprecedented upset, Libertarian candidate Altus Carsen Olm sailed to victory over his Democrat and Republican opponents despite the fact that his party membership boasts no more than a fifth of the total electorate. As an added insult, every incumbent in Congress, regardless of party alliance, was ousted by a freshman of either Libertarian or Independent affiliation. So stunned are the media that Olm remains the centerpiece of the morning news telecasts:

Hostess: Once again, we return to a story that's even more sensational than the revelation of the Boxheim Papers. President-elect Altus Olm, a Libertarian underdog, scored an astounding 100% of the vote last November. Olm has come to be known as the anti-President because he ran a campaign that defied just about every rule in the book. The first in over a century with facial hair, Mr. Olm is the only U.S. President other than Chester Arthur to wear mutton chops.

Host: But a far more serious obstacle, and one nobody we talked to thought he could possibly overcome, was his criminal conviction for assault and battery. Just eleven years ago, President-elect Olm pled guilty and was sentenced to three years in Angola, which he served in full. Most people don't know, and I was surprised to find out, that Article II, Clause IV of the Constitution, which lists the threshold criteria for President, does not prohibit convicted criminals from running for the nation's highest office.

Hostess: A good example is labor leader Eugene V. Debs, who in 1920 ran for President while serving a ten-year sentence for, of all things, sedition.

Host: But it's the story behind Olm's conviction that voters we polled found so endearing.

Hostess: As we all know by now, thanks to a bold and quirky marketing campaign that recast plumbers and electricians as male underwear models, breathing new life into the service industry, Altus Olm grew his one-truck, two-employee handyman venture into a national home service empire.

Host: And he soon learned that success doesn't insulate you from trouble. After a nasty breakup, the former boyfriend of Olm's stepdaughter spread a false rumor that she had HIV. Olm confronted the young man at an outdoor benefit concert and demanded a public retraction. The young man, Braden Scorria, refused.

Hostess: Stories conflict about what happened next. Some say Scorria threw a bottle at Olm, while others insist he only made an obscene gesture. At any rate, fisticuffs ensued. It was by no means a pretty fight, as neither is known to have had any formal training. And, by all accounts, there was no clear winner until the very end.

Host: You can tell from this mugshot that Olm definitely took his fair share of punishment. A Beauregard Parish official described the altercation as a classic case of mutual combat in which each side dealt the other a "proper and thorough beating." At one point, two onlookers tried to pile on Scorria, but Olm pushed them away.

Hostess: Scarcely one minute into the fight, both were so winded and bruised that they could barely walk straight. Olm landed one final punch that sent Scorria to the ground so hard he broke his … I can never pronounce the scientific term, and it looks dirty to me, so let's just call it his tailbone. At that point, Scorria dropped his hands and apologized.

Host: Olm then picked Scorria up and carried him to a medical tent, where he called authorities and turned himself in. At his arraignment, he waived his right to counsel and pled guilty to "taking it upon myself to defend my little girl's honor by the only method that would teach that boy a lasting lesson, a method I knew was unavailable in these hallowed halls."

Hostess: Because Olm had a spotless record, the judge was inclined to give him probation, but Olm convinced him otherwise, saying: "Though we may wish the world were different, we're bound by current realities. I provoked that fight, Judge, and I'm not the least bit remorseful; therefore, you have no discretion to be lenient on me."

Host: While in jail he put his stepdaughter in charge, and she did such a fine job that she continues to run his operations today.

Hostess: Now, as you know, the Democrats and Republicans – referred to by Olm as *The Big Two* – have come under increasing fire in recent years for their unwillingness to give third-party candidates a podium at their Presidential debates. Olm was similarly frozen out.

Host: But that didn't stop him from staging his own debates against various Big Two subordinates, many of those contests garnering more primetime viewership than those of his opponents. And he ended every closing statement by calling both the incumbent and the Republican nominee cowards.

Hostess: Though neither accepted his challenge, the *First Female President*, Preston – I *know* you read the White House directive – did tap the noted Senator Lester Jefferson Booker to debate Olm in her stead. And the commentators all agree that, hands down, the most memorable event of the entire campaign season was the now infamous exchange between Olm and Booker.

Host: Senator Booker, of course, is the First Female President's most trusted economic advisor, having earned a Ph.D. in the field from Harvard.

Hostess: Tempers flared toward the end of the debate, and Booker made some ... well ... controversial statements.

Host: Controversial statements, Sherry? How about downright offensive?

Hostess: The White House Spokesman was quick to defend the senator, saying at a press conference the next morning: "Hardly anyone realizes the pressure shouldered by a candidate's staff behind the scenes. Senator Booker simply can't be held responsible for your misinterpretation of what admittedly are inartful comments, because he suffers from what our staff psychiatrists have diagnosed as *campaign fatigue syndrome*."

Host: Booker was not alone. As Election Day neared, *campaign fatigue* became the excuse of the hour for both the First Female President and her Republican opponent, who just couldn't seem to keep their feet out of their mouths.

Hostess: In fact, it is a widely held belief that the First Female President singlehandedly squandered what was said to be a virtual lock on reelection when she answered a casual question from the pool of reporters that accompanied her to a fundraiser.

Host: When asked why she was so confident she would win reelection, the First Female President replied: "You constitutionalists are such babes in the woods. In all of the major precincts, we have far more dead voters on the active rolls than live ones." A subsequent investigation proved that statement no mean exaggeration with reference to both the Democrats and the Republicans, and immediate reforms paved the way for perhaps the first fair election since 1796.

Hostess: The debate between Booker and Olm was moderated by psychologist Donald Kellogg, who hosts the Emmy award winning daytime talk show, Dr. Don.

Host: Let's watch.

Kellogg: Experts and pundits agree that the state of the economy is one of limbo, where we vacillate between moderate growth and recession bordering on depression, and that this limbo state has plagued us for over ten years. How does the deficit crisis relate to our stagnant fiscal state, and how will you pull us out of it? Senator?

Booker: Microeconomic decisions will often lead to inefficient macroeconomic outcomes which require extraordinary government intervention entailing both monetary action and fiscal policy to stabilize output over the business cycle. When fixed investment decreases, interest rates decline at a greater rate than savings, and spending becomes virtually stagnant.

The resultant inelasticity of supply and demand vis-à-vis loanable funds requires drastic action by the Fed to close the savings/investments gap. Now, when interest rates fall too far, we encounter the liquidity trap, and that brings on the paradox of irresponsible spending and unwarranted saving on the part of bondholders. This is why we need countercyclical fiscal policies, such as deficit spending, stimulus programs, redistribution of capital and, of course, long overdue tax increases on the top 42% earning sector.

Olm: Do you understand a single word you just said, sir? I certainly don't.

Booker: Hold on right there. I work my fingers to the death for my folks in Illinois, and those nice people elected me to a sacred office, and I consider it a slight, Mr. Olm, that you do not address me by the title whereby I have striven mightily.

Olm: From the day I was born, my mother and father called their parents *sir* and *ma'am*, a tradition that goes back generations on both sides of the family. I was taught to call, not just my parents, but my elders and colleagues and everyone in a public forum by the same titles. When I asked why, my father told me it is because *sir* and *ma'am* connote the highest forms of respect. But as you wish, *Senator.*

Booker: Thank you.

Olm: The truth is that the only crisis in the minds of you and your cronies is that you don't control a hundred percent of our economy.

Booker: And from where did you acquire *your* doctorate in economics, *Mr.* Olm?

Olm: That's the problem with you people. You have an exceptional talent, I'll give you that. But what is that talent? It's the ability to ingest and regurgitate bookish terms that require speech therapy to just articulate. And you presume that your vomiting skills grant you some supreme level of credibility, but all your advanced education has done is to fill your head with a vocabulary you're not wise enough to use for meaningful communication. Let me give you a quick primer, *Senator*, in effective communication. I'll translate what you just said so everyone in the audience can understand it, not because I'm smarter than them, but because I have a team of advisors who have translated your hogwash into terms the rest of us can grasp. According to you, too much saving and not enough spending is bad for an economy and, when that situation occurs, the government should raise taxes and use that increased revenue, not to pay its mounting debts, but to flood the market with empty wealth.

Booker: What is this *empty wealth* you're throwing around?

Olm: Crucial to any economy is valuation of currency. A dollar is only as valuable as the goods or services it represents. The most basic economics principle is that money does not enter a market except in exchange for a good or a service.

Booker: In an ideal world, that's right.

Olm: So if the Fed threw open its doors and started handing out cash to all comers, the value of that cash would plummet because it would not be backed by goods or services.

Booker: Well, that's not the most sophisticated way of putting it, but I will accept your terminology.

Olm: And that is what you recommend here, tonight. Stimulus spending manipulates the economy by injecting money into the market in exchange for either unnecessary services or none at all.

Booker: Yes, but only in extraordinary circumstances such as these.

Olm: Can we agree that true capital is created only through private industry?

Kellogg: Um, Mr. Olm, that topic is not on the agenda.

Booker: No we absolutely can not. Why, the federal workforce is some thirty-one million strong.

Olm: Don't duck my question, *Senator*. Federal employees are paid solely by the federal government, whose only capital consists of taxes collected from the private sector.

Booker: And a substantial portion of that tax revenue is derived from federal employees.

Kellogg: Gentlemen, we're getting off program.

Olm: Do you think the American public is that gullible? If you pay someone from your front pocket but withhold fifteen percent of that pay and transfer it to your back pocket, you have earned nothing. You may as well have just paid that employee fifteen percent less from your front pocket.

Booker: I'll concede that, but then you must concede that those federal workers provide valuable services for their salaries.

Olm: Services, yes. Assuming purely for the sake of argument that those services are valuable and necessary, which I don't concede for a second, at the federal employee stage the capital is largely neutral, because in many cases the delicatessen owner and the commodities trader could just as easily contract with a private outfit for those services. Do you agree?

Kellogg: Actually, the synergistic relationship between commerce and taxes is a subject I had slated for later –

Booker: Shut up, Don. Yes, Mr. Olm, at that point the government is simply a middleman, or broker, if you will.

Olm: So how do you justify straying into the negative capital zone where you raise taxes on the top forty-two percent and redistribute that capital among the fifty-two-point-three percent who are on one of countless forms of government assistance in exchange for no services of any conceivable kind?

Booker: Easily. And I'll boil it down to your level, Mr. Olm. Money must be spent to promote economic growth. Unearned wealth gets spent more freely than wealth you sweat for. And everybody knows that the man at the low end of the economic spectrum will spend anything and everything he gets his mitts on, right? That's why he's where he is. So the quickest way to stimulate the economy is to get as much money as you can out of the hands of the wealthy, who tend to hoard it, and into the hands of the poor, the underprivileged and the disenfranchised, who you can always count on to blow it. And you have to do it *outside* the market. That's money in motion, my friend. And that's the sort of stimulation that will set an economy on fire.

Kellogg: Ladies and gentlemen, please take your seats and stop throwing things. Having covered far more heated debates than this for many seasons, I can assure you that what Senator Booker meant to say –

Booker: You can just pipe down, you little pop-psych pipsqueak! They heard what I said. I don't need a damned go-between; I went to Harvard!

Olm: I regret, *Senator*, that I gave you the wrong advice. You were better off sticking to a script whose jargon nobody who matters could decipher. In the late 1950s, the percentage of the U.S. population taking a federal handout was only twelve. It took half a century for that ratio to climb to twenty-one-point-eight. And here we are at fifty-two-point-three percent in only eight years. You have just told the electorate why. When I announced my candidacy, I warned my fellow citizens to beware the party that postures as the champion of the poor and the downtrodden, because that party will only stay in power if the ranks of the poor and downtrodden are maintained. You, *Senator*, have just advocated cultivating an impoverished underclass by feeding them a steady stream of unearned, empty wealth to keep them locked in a vicious cycle of feast and famine, guaranteeing they will remain exactly where you'll need them come next election cycle.

Kellogg: Here's what I propose. I think our fine audience would like a breather, and I know I –

Olm: If my wife and I are walking down the street one night and we're accosted by a knife-wielding thug who demands my wallet, I would hazard a guess, *Senator*, that your advice would be to hand over my wallet.

Booker: Well, of course, Mr. Olm.

Olm: What if I just lost my job and emptied my bank account to stay one step ahead of my creditors, and every last dime I have is in that wallet?

Booker: I fail to see the relevance of this line of inquiry, but I always endorse the sanctity of life. Give the crazy man what he wants and live to see another day. After all, it's only dollars and cents.

Olm: *Give the crazy man what he wants.* Ladies and gentlemen, I give you the President's righthand man on economic policy. Be it a mugger on the street or a federal government that wants to tax you into the poorhouse, it's only dollars and cents to Mr. Booker. Here is where you and I are worlds apart, *Senator.* This five dollar bill I just pulled out of my pocket is only a piece of paper to you. To me it's a reward for my hard work. It represents my time and energy which, once expended to earn it, are forever gone. You see taxation as strictly a monetary proposition; I see it as a threat to the dignity of myself and everyone I hold dear. And it is basic human dignity that spurs me to fight the tax collector as vehemently as I would that thief.

Booker: That is the craziest analogy … you need to get some more schooling, friend, read some history ….

Kellogg: I may have lost a page. Have we moved to gun control?

Olm: I've got plenty history for you. In *McCulloch v. State of Maryland*, a case decided in 1819, Chief Justice John Marshall said: "An unlimited power to tax involves, necessarily, a power to destroy." The key issue is not how to reduce the deficit or shore up Medicare – these are trifling details that distract the voter from the underlying philosophical battle between the proponents of free enterprise and those of socialism. You start every fiscal debate with the presumption that confiscatory taxation is a fundamental fact of life, and the only permissible area of contention is how high rates should be. What I and a staggering percentage of Americans want to discuss is whether there should be an income tax at all. Like I said moments ago, at stake here is not mere dollars and cents but dignity. And I submit to you that any form of a pre-consumption tax fundamentally debases the individual taxpayer.

Booker: You don't need schooling; you need your head looked at. Maybe Kellogg has some room for you on his sofa. No government in history has ever been able to sustain itself without some form of taxation.

Olm: The key phrase, *Senator*, is *some form*. This network does not have enough time for me to read a list of the various hidden federal tax schemes that are operational today. Yet the Big Two have, for over a half century, rejected a far more evenhanded system than the income tax – the national sales tax. Why is that?

Booker: Now I see why the real candidates don't want to waste their time debating you, Mr. Olm. You don't understand the first thing ... you can't expect our federal government to function at the mercy of a fluctuating economy!

Olm: Why are you so afraid to have your spending power directly tied to the economic wellbeing of the taxpayer?

Booker: Because it's not just about spending power! My colleagues and I at the Capitol are there because the voters recognize, election after election, that we are best equipped to make the hard choices. The single teenage mother of four doesn't have the time or the brainpower to determine that *Big Gulps* and *E-cigarettes* are bad for her and her children! The day laborer with a hot temper and a liking for booze doesn't have the wherewithal to understand why he can't be trusted with a loaded handgun, and the redneck boot-scooting hillbilly is by no means sophisticated enough to comprehend the idea that prejudice against African Americans isn't voluntary – it's congenital, inborn to all you Brady Boys and Betty Crockers – which is why you'll always need caretakers like me to crack the whip of affirmative action and redistributive justice! Why, we intellectuals have a grave responsibility to steer the rank-and-file in the right directions. You have a child, so you know – at least I hope you know – that you don't let a toddler play alone outside. And you can't reason with a child the way you can an adult, so you have to lead by force and fear. All a tax really is, is an act of compassion for those who don't know any better, a fence around their yard, a locking panel on their playpen. Freedom ain't all it's cracked up to be, my naïve little plumber friend. We are the gatekeepers, saving all you common folk from yourselves. Just where do you get the sauce to stand there and tell me you know better?

Olm: Every time you people go off-script, I get the urge to goosestep and shout *Seig Heil*.

Kellogg: I'm told we're overdue for a commercial break, so –

Booker: You cut away, Kellogg, and I'll stick this lectern in your uppity ass! Olm, this is the second time you've done that, and I can not let it pass without comment. Where do you get off in this day and age pointing at me, an African American, and saying *you people*?

Olm: That's another problem with you people. When you start losing the argument, you accuse your opponent of some hotbutton infraction like racism to divert everyone's attention from the fact that your position doesn't make a lick of sense. By *you people* I refer to elitists. I despise elitists, *Senator*.

Booker: Listen to yourself. This government was conceived to usher in the age of nonviolent transfer of political power and civil debate. *Civil* debate, Mr. Olm!

Olm: You confuse civility with complaisance. If I lose this election, your boss need not hold her breath waiting for a concession call, because it won't come. I will fight that fascist to the last vote!

Booker: And, I dare ask, what if you win?

Olm: If I get my hands on the power of the Presidency, *Senator*, I'm going to burn it all down.

Booker: Say what?

Olm: You heard me. *Burn it down.*

Booker: You and what rebel army?

Olm: They're right there, *Senator*, in the studio gallery beyond your teleprompter, in the restaurants and the offices and the living rooms at the other end of the audiovisual feed. You're surprised that your dig about a rebel army didn't get any laughs? I'm not, because an uprising is exactly what I taste in the air. And I am the last conciliator that stands between you and that throng. President Thomas Jefferson is often quoted: "The tree of liberty must be refreshed from time to time with the blood of patriots and tyrants." If I lose this election, *Senator*, I predict blood will stain your highest offices and the finest china on which you dine, and when the dust settles your epitaph will read *Sic Semper Tyrannis*!

What keenly intrigues Julia today is that not one deli customer will admit to voting for Olm. As she overhears patrons grouse and moan about the Booker debate, the only way she can reconcile their disgust with the unmistakable election results is to conclude that virtually every tenant in this building is a nonvoter.

"I'll tell you right now. He'd better keep his hands off my husband's disability checks."

"Disability? I thought he was an aerobics trainer."

"He served his country with distinction; he's an Iraq war veteran."

"Veteran of what? He was in the Air Force band. He spent his entire *tour* in San Diego, and his *injury* was carpal tunnel syndrome."

"You try lugging a tenor trombone around for four hours a day."

"He's a closet tax-and-spend liberal, like all the rest of them. Just you wait and see."

"I hear he eats nothing but shortbread cookies and raw horse meat."

Julia's amusement is interrupted when she catches sight of a familiar figure by the arboretum. As he nears, she recognizes the nice gentleman from their chance meeting some weeks ago at the Hyatt. And he notices her.

“Well if it is not the charming lady who asks perfect strangers if they carry corpses in their motorcars.”

She welcomes his outstretched hand.

“Julia Bross.”

“A pleasure, Ms. Bross. Anthony Stearns.”

“Of the Stearns Law Firm.”

“Have we represented you?”

“Let’s just say our interests have aligned on occasion.”

“I see. May I?”

As Ani seats himself, Julia marvels at how smoothly this man adapts to his environment … almost disturbingly so.

“So what is it you do, Ms. Bross?”

“To tell you that would be to give away my mystery.”

“You will not provoke me into guessing, madam. I am a man of facts and intuition.”

Intrigued, Julia sits forward.

“Mr. Stearns, are you flirting with me?”

Ani remains perfectly poised with his right leg crossed serenely over his left, his dominant hand holding an unlit cigar.

“Perhaps I am making friendly conversation with a new acquaintance.”

“Or you’re investigating me.”

“Flirting, trading platonic pleasantries, researching … is there a substantive difference among these activities?”

“All right, Mr. Stearns …”

“Anthony, please.”

“*Mr.* Stearns, dazzle me with your instinctual prowess.”

“You do not run a company so much as you are your company. Like me, you are a generous but exacting employer. You remain loyal to friends and associates even when doing so works to your detriment. You are a tough, oftentimes relentless woman. Am I correct thus far?”

“So much so that I wouldn’t be surprised to learn you’ve checked me out already.”

“Now, there you go speculating again. One misses the day when a gentleman was not required to fend off irrelative accusations when all he wanted to do was make a lady’s acquaintance.”

“That day never existed, and you know it.”

“If that is the meaning I assign to it, how is that not my reality?”

"The rational person can't simply divorce perception from objective reality. If we can't agree on commonality of experience, there's no point in trying to cooperate or even communicate."

"From infancy to the age of twelve, every time a little boy asks his mother for food or comfort she kicks him in the stomach. Ten years later, he meets a nice girl. Do they fall in love and stroll off into the sunset, arms interlaced? Or does he sabotage that promising relationship because he is only comfortable being maltreated? I submit that his trauma-based perception trumps your objective reality."

"So you *are* flirting with me."

"Is that your perception?"

"You're twice my age!"

Ani twirls his cigar like a baton, then taps it on the table.

"Now whose subjectivity is beclouding reality?"

"A lady might take grave offense to that remark."

"I prefer a woman."

She doesn't yet believe this man's intentions are romantic, but the possibility most definitely intrigues her.

"So tell me, old man, does your plumbing still function?"

"My stamina is inversely proportional to the botulin and/or silicone content of my partner."

"There's nothing here I wasn't born with."

"Then I would foresee no issues in that department."

"I never had children, and I never will."

"A pity, that."

"Why?"

"It saddens me that those who are best equipped for the responsibility refuse to assume it while the ignorant and the malicious continue to infest our planet with more of their kind."

"Why do you talk that way?"

"I have long believed the overuse of contractions is a symptom of indolence."

"The alternative sounds snobbish to me. Anyway, my tubes are tied."

"That is a shame."

"A man your age wanting to sire a child ... doesn't that strike you as chauvinistic and selfish?"

"I never said I wanted a child."

"Why else would a man pursuing a woman be disappointed about a tubal ligation?"

"I was merely offering a practical observation. It is a shame you wasted the time and resources on an invasive procedure in light of the fact that menopause is, as we speak, solving your problem quite unobtrusively."

Julia senses the playfulness of this encounter has come to an abrupt end.

"*Mr*. Stearns, am I a desirable object or am I a target?"

As Ani responds, she takes a deliberately slow sip of tea – a technique she learned from her father when she was only thirteen. *When you feel anxiety in the air and you think it may overwhelm you, refocus your attention and that of your opponent. Redirect that energy onto an object between you – a notepad, a cigarette, a glass of water – just long enough to reclaim it for yourself. A pause of five seconds is all you need. Three'll do in a pinch.*

"As I was saying, Ms. Bross –"

"You didn't run into me by accident today. This tells me you have an agenda. So when do we stop sniffing each other's asses and bare our teeth?"

With a smile, Ani stacks his hands in his lap.

"If I may finish the thought I tried to express before your false assumption took us on this little detour, you are a formidable force in the business arena. Yet you reserve a tender, dare I say vulnerable, place in your heart for one Peter Mott."

Though Julia maintains her boardroom posture, it takes all her effort to repress the shocks of compassion and anger and terror that assault her stomach in one steely pulse after another.

"And what is your interest in Reverend Mott?"

"*Reverend* Mott. That honorific is intriguing in itself, is it not? Why would a man of letters, a discerning man of considerable means, surrender his skepticism to traditional mythology overnight? Were I given to the gaming hobby, I would put my money on a move in the opposite direction every time."

"Ask him."

"I am unable to do that as yet. It is a matter of timing, you see."

"And what makes you think I can answer your question or, for that matter, why I even care to?"

Ani considers the cigar in his lap, then raises his brow ever so apologetically.

"Two lunches and five dinners at the Hyatt."

Another gastric jolt pulsates. She chooses to flow with it, because its underlying emotion is pure anger. She bolts forward.

"Who's digging into my friend and why?"

"I am sorry, madam, but I can not tell you that."

"Confidentiality prohibits your revealing client communications, not client identity."

"But I am neither pursuing nor threatening legal action against you, Ms. Bross. Like I said, this is just a friendly conversation."

Ani ends his sentence with another smile and a gentle pat on the back of Julia's hand. She brushes his hand aside, stomps to her feet and levels a stern forefinger at the bridge of his nose.

"You work for Deanna, don't you? You've been hiding under a rock, watching and waiting for the right time to pounce. You see Peter faltering, so you figure you can extort another windfall from him because that little cunt blew everything he gave her in the divorce. He may be floundering right now, but he is the best friend I ever had, and I have a hotline to my own law firm full of bulldogs, so do not, Mr. Stearns, *do not* underestimate my devotion to those I hold dear!"

Ani takes his feet, clutches her accusatory hand in his and kisses it before she can react.

"Thank you, Ms. Bross."

Stunned by his gesture, Julia holds her hand in midair even after he withdraws his.

"What the hell for?"

"For the priceless insight you have granted me today. And for permitting me to spend time in the company of a woman who boasts such aplomb as I have not known since my dear Maura died. I know you care deeply for your friend, but I would admonish that there is an imperceptible line between proximity and solitude."

This time her finger finds his chest, and with sinew that takes them both asudden.

"Is that a threat?"

Ani steps back ever so gingerly, folds reverent hands at his waist.

"No, madam. Please consider it free advice, along with this. You appear to be a woman of diverse interests, so I will use an analogy I think you can appreciate. A man's past is not unlike the *Staphylococcus aureus* bacterium, a frequent colonist of human skin. So long as it remains on the epidermis, the outermost layer, it is harmless. But all it takes is an untreated cut, or an unsanitary hypodermic needle, to grant that microscopic germ access to your bloodstream and, before you know it, you have a killer in your midst. It would be a shame for you, Ms. Bross, to be in the peripheral field of fire when *Reverend* Mott's past comes calling."

Just a nanosecond before her open hand connects to his face, Julia sees in Ani's eyes that he knows it is coming. Yet he neither blocks nor evades it.

"I am truly sorry to have upset you, Ms. Bross."

"Walk away, Stearns!"

In public discussions, it is recommended that you preface your every opinion with a glowing endorsement of any and all opposing stances so as to not offend, or in any way marginalize, your adversaries or their supporters.

This public service announcement is brought to you by the First Female President and First First Lady to Become President and Only Former First Lady to Become the First Female President's Committee for Equal Time and Fair Play.

Chapter Nine

Shoestring Epiphany

Though she carries the same surname as James Butler Bonham, Mira is the progeny of Thomas "Gamecock" Sumter who, upon his death in 1832, was the last surviving general officer of the American Revolution. A distinguished fighter in his own right, James Bonham endured heavy Mexican fire to become the last man to enter the doomed Alamo in 1836, where he perished alongside Jim Bowie and Davy Crockett. Mira ruined a perfect score on her eleventh grade history final when she confused Crockett with Daniel Boone, who had died sixteen years earlier – a fact of which her teacher has reminded her ever since by sending her a coonskin cap for her birthday (contrary to popular myth, Boone was partial to wide-brimmed felt or beaver hats). But the gift is by no means a sadistic gesture, as her grin testifies when she opens the Federal Express envelope from Mount Pleasant, South Carolina, on this thirty-fifth commemoration of her nativity.

She treats this latest installment with uncommon reverence. Smoothing the tail and picking every trace of lint from the fur, she carefully hangs it alongside its predecessors on an expandable coat rack mounted beside the fireplace in her downtown loft apartment. This is certainly not the only gift she receives on this occasion. Nor does she foster a general affinity for such headwear. In fact, had she received this hat in the last decade, she'd have tossed it into a spare drawer or shoebox amidst other marginally sentimental trinkets. But life was kinder, and she far less heedful, in those times.

When Mira was a junior at the College of Charleston, she and her best friend Polly skipped their evening study group to unwind at the Blind Tiger Pub on Broad Street, indulging in margaritas and Pierogies, and rating male patrons by which monetary denomination they would stick in their g-strings at a ladies' club. Just two tables away sat a raucous group of young men with shaven heads, guzzling beer and jostling each other in the sophomoric fashion of fraternity boys. A basketball game unfolded on a plasma screen behind the nearby barfront. When one of the teams sank a three-pointer, the celebration of the man on the corner in the blue flannel shirt caused a passing waitress to drop a tray of food. None of them paid the frantic girl a second thought as she scrambled to clear away the mess while steadying the single dish she had managed to salvage.

From somewhere behind Mira, a lanky young man with ruddy forearms strode into view. He sported the same distinctive gold ring Mira had seen on other gentlemen with a crewcut like his. Pulling a handkerchief from his shirt pocket, he helped the waitress shovel the spoiled appetizers onto her tray. As she scurried to the kitchen, he approached the group and slapped the flannelled offender on the back of the head. All six chairs at the table toppled as their brawny occupants sprang to the ready. Mira and Polly clutched their purses, preparing to bolt for the powder room once the inevitable brawl erupted.

But once they caught sight of the interloper, the belligerents averted deferential eyes and quietly retrieved their chairs. Each, that is, except for the man in the blue flannel shirt who, prompted this time by a stern finger to the forehead and a louring schoolmaster glare, ambled toward the kitchen to make amends with the waitress.

Mira elbowed Polly. "Where's the closest ATM? Baby needs some twenties."

When Polly's laughter drew the attention of the modernday food industry paladin, he marched to their table and, producing yet another fresh hankie, wiped from Mira's chin a speck of sweet potato casserole – fallout from the waitress' recent mishap. When she thanked him, the swaggering mover of men stumbled and stammered like a schoolboy in the throes of his first crush. His name was Cortland Massey, and his distinctive ring signified that he was a First Class Cadet in his senior year at The Citadel. The rabble he had just upbraided were freshmen – hence their shorn pates.

"So don't you go and think my confronting those men was any act of valor. It was my rank talking, not my might. It's often scary what folks with the right bars and patches can get the naïve and the downright ignorant to do. But that's none of your concern, ma'am, and I do hope that little ruckus hasn't spoiled your evening."

At Mira's insistence, Cortland joined them for a final round of drinks before he had to meet curfew. Though an avid beer aficionado, he adhered to the promise he had made to his grandfather to imbibe nothing but water and coffee until graduation. When the waiter brought Mira and Polly their tab, Cortland placed a gentle but resolute hand over it.

"Ma'am, I would be honored to pay for your meal."

Having noted that his shoes were worse for wear than even hers, Mira proceeded to fish for her pocketbook.

"That's awfully sweet, but these days women pay their own way."

"Beg your pardon, Ms. Bonham, but a lady of your caliber … well, that just wouldn't be right."

Mira acquiesced.

Cortland consulted the check. He rummaged in his wallet. He consulted the check again.

"I'm … rather embarrassed to … I can just cover the ticket. If you would be so kind as to tip this hardworking young man –"

So enchanted was Mira by this gentleman whose every movement bespoke gallantry and poise, she'd have agreed to pay every tab in the bar even though she had only $846 to her name.

"Give me that damned thing before puppies and cotton candy start falling from the sky!"

Polly paid the tab and tip.

Mira scribbled her email address on a coaster.

Cortland kissed her hand.

When he proposed to her four months later, Mira, a child of strict Southern tradition, was prepared to forsake school and career to transform herself into her preconception of the quintessential military wife. But Cortland would have none of that.

"As I live and breathe, Mira, you'll always have first dibs on my paycheck in the good times and my last penny in the bad. But no wife of mine is going to be an invalid or a dependent. There's no dignity in that kind of life, and I'd sooner gouge out my own eyes than to have you squander your potential for anyone, let alone the likes of me."

Therefore, though they were both eager to start a family, they agreed to defer that ambition until Mira had established herself in the working world.

Despite Cortland's modesty, Mira soon deduced that he enjoyed an extraordinary power of persuasion over military and civilian brass alike. Though ordered to begin OCS at Quantico just six weeks after their wedding, he convinced the Base Commander to grant him a twelve-month deferral so he could stay in Virginia and support Mira while she earned her last twenty-two credits for her baccalaureate degree. And midway through her final semester, she began receiving job interview requests from top echelon marketing firms to which she had not even sent a résumé. Christmas 2007 saw Cortland secure his commission as Second Lieutenant, while Mira accepted an advertising position whose starting salary, to her amazement, exceeded Cortland's pay grade by a factor of almost three.

During the Battle of Sangin in 2010, twenty-five American soldiers were killed. One of those casualties was Captain Cortland Massey of the Third Battalion Fifth Marines.

An executive in the firm by now, Mira did not have to ask her bosses for indefinite leave. With the enthusiastic support of her husband, a private sector psychologist who served Walter Reed Medical Center as an independent consultant, Polly moved in with her on the day of Cortland's funeral. Accustomed to Mira's notorious impatience with process, she intended to stay only one or two weeks to usher her through the five Kübler-Ross stages. But as one month dragged into three, she fretted that Mira, having altogether bypassed the first three phases – Denial, Anger and Bargaining – had sunk to a depth of depression from which she might never rebound. The only personal hygiene she engaged in was the bath and tooth brushing Polly would give her every three to five days when she grew tired of waiting for Mira to take these tasks upon herself. Polly had to leave bowls of dry cereal and nuts in strategic places throughout the house because she could not cajole a cooked meal down her friend's throat. If she didn't force Mira to sit on a toilet at regular intervals, her only remaining option was to truss her up in an adult diaper – a tactic to which the exigencies of her own family life had forced her to resort on occasion.

One night, after Mira had fallen asleep crouched in a kitchen corner gazing vacantly at a two-year-old picture of Cortland and her posing in leis and grass skirts, Polly phoned her husband.

"She's an old-world girl, Elian. Try as he did, that poor man couldn't keep her from losing her identity in him."

"I know the woman, too. She deserves more credit than you give."

"I'm not talking about her, damn it! I can't take much more of this. I'm not a nurse."

"But you *were* talking about her! Never mind. I am no more the magician than you are the nurse. If we place her in an inpatient setting, that will only facilitate her infirmity and prolong it."

"I can't just sit here and watch her deteriorate."

"What is the one thing she most needs to understand?"

"You, the psychologist, are asking me?"

"I, the man who knows Mira only by happenstance, am asking the woman who is her best friend."

"That she needs to pull her head out of a dead man's ass before it gets stuck there."

"So how do you tell her that without alienating her forever?"

"You're the damned therapist!"

"Who is the one person she would listen to right now more than anyone else?"

"He's dead, dear."

"Don't be so sure."

"Are you telling me –"

"And keep in mind as you consider my last comment that I remain the only Guatemalan in modern history who is not a practicing Catholic. So you need don't bother ribbing me about the angels and the spirits and the hobbling goblins."

"So how do I get a dead guy to talk?"

"Everything he ever said to her is coursing through her memory. What you must do is capture a piece of his phraseology and redirect it."

"She confided in me about everything. I wouldn't know where to start."

"Focus on the significant moments … the benchmarks … the high points. Something Cortland said to her that expressed who he was in his marrow. If I may?"

"I wish to hell you would."

"We all have idiosyncratic mannerisms, characteristic ways of speaking, what do you call … slogans … catch … something catch … catch*phrases*."

"Oh, baby, baby, I got it!"

"That's my smart girl."

"What do I do with it?"

"She floats for now in the dusky stratum, where the words are not really words. It all seeps up from inside her in a droning whisper. You need to assault a sensory apparatus – her ears, her hands, her eyesight."

"I think I follow you. Like using a loud noise to snap a puppy out of bad behavior."

"I could not have picked a better affinity."

"You mean –"

"Analogy, thank you. Because the humans and the canines, we all learn the same way."

"Elian, that is a cold and cynical thing to say."

"This is the hazard of my trade, as I am surrounded here by the fucking psychiatrists so thoroughly engrossed in their own grandiose delusions that they long ago lost whatever driblet of insight and empathy they once had. But that is not your concern, for you have the present problem of Mira."

Inspired, Polly snuck away to buy permanent markers and *Post-It* notes. When Mira stirred the next morning, the first thing she saw was a note stuck to a cabinet door Polly had positioned just millimeters from her nose. It read:

NO WIFE OF MINE

Turning aside, she found another note bearing the same message on the wastecan. Everywhere she looked, from the refrigerator to the coffee maker to the stepstool, another pastel square displayed an identical sentiment. As she crawled on hands and knees, unsteady from weeks of sporadic, involuntary use, the epigram NO WIFE OF MINE accosted her from the endtable and the couch and every drawer of the sideboard and every inch of the hallway wall; every surface of the bathroom, too, where she pulled herself to her feet to escape the iterative bywords that stung her like blowdarts. At the top of her climb she encountered the mirror she had painstakingly avoided for one hundred four days. There, a withered zombie stared blankly back at her, its eyes so distended by its sunken cheeks that they overwhelmed its face like those of the Martians depicted on mid-twentieth century celluloid.

NO WIFE OF MINE

The outside world crashed in upon her with the abruptness of a flying two-by-four to the jaw. At once, the fecal odor from yesterday's diaper joined forces with the fusty stench emanating from her bearded armpits, and no sooner did she vomit in the sink than she felt the waxy remnants of week-old pecans that coated her teeth like errant caulk. Issuing a guttural scream that would put Janet Leigh to shame, Mira grabbed a toothbrush and flung herself into the shower. She spent the next hour scouring her mouth with soapsuds, shedding garments like burning embers and scrubbing herself pink with the loofa, blubbering barely intelligible variations of *Why did you have to be a soldier* and *Please don't leave me, you sonofabitch.* When her ventral convulsions finally subsided, she found herself balled up in the fetal position on the linoleum, clutching a bathrobe with her arms and knees the same way she had enwrapped her husband so many times when he had fallen asleep beside her on the couch after a grueling day on base.

Then, emanating from somewhere in the bowels of her psyche, a wisp of serenity dried her tears. Venturing out of the bathroom with the wariness of a spelunker, she discovered that her home had become a mausoleum. Pictures and mementos of her life with Cortland blanketed the walls, littered the shelves, dangled from the rafters. Unwilling to relinquish, not just the man she loved but the emotional shrine she had built around the very idea of him, she had entombed herself in his relics long before his demise.

As Polly's doting Elian distracted her from her friend's plight with Chablis and a DVD of *The Wizard of Oz* eleven miles away, Mira embarked upon a rampage, collecting every last trace of her life with Cortland and laying it to rest in a trunk. Just before the lid fell to, she paused to gaze at the image of two ebullient Masseys emerging from a canopy of crossed swords. The photograph was snapped mere moments after he had whispered to her his secret vow: *I will prove my love to you every day, precious Mira, by never asking you to shoulder my inner burdens.*

"I understand now. Goodbye, my darling Cortland."

She then lugged the trunk into the garage and set it beneath the attic. When she reached to pull down the ladder, she found a gift bag that had been tied to the cord. From inside it she retrieved one of her old coonskin caps and a note from Polly.

> Hey, spindly chick. If you're still alive, think of this little bauble as a touching ground to who you once were, a stepping stone to who you can become. If you're dead or about to be, blame Elian.

For the next few days, Mira obsessed over that cap with the same unbending devotion a dog pays to its only toy, never letting it out of her sight and jealously guarding its welfare lest the only possession she holds dear be taken away. She eventually salvaged its companions from their nook-and-cranny exile. Over the years, each new addition to the collection has been for Mira a symbol of continuity, a bridge between her pre- and post-Cortland lives.

Cortland's next of kin, suffused with Old Virginia wealth, wanted desperately to take her in. Other Massey relatives offered to set her up on their sweeping Texas homestead. But the coonskin cap made her mindful of why she had been so soundly attracted to a man who had defied the same outstretched hands: like him, in the fashion of the heroes of her childhood history primers, she wanted to live and die on her own merit. Though she could not explain it to even herself, she felt drawn to the Heartland. So she packed her things, shook from her pumps the dust of the divisive cesspit of the greater D.C. environs and headed west to resume her studies in Sociology. Having cashed out all her government and private benefits, she knew she could live comfortably on savings for two years. But just months after she had affixed the permanent coonskin cap display adjacent her new hearth, she met a man whose vision spun her life in a direction she had never dared dream.

A frequenter of personal empowerment seminars, Mira attended a program at the downtown Hyatt titled "In the World and of the World: The New Alliance between Business and Faith" by Peter Shroyer Mott, M.B.A., M.Div. Opening with the passage from Luke 16:9-11 – "I tell you, use worldly wealth to gain friends for yourselves, so that when it is gone, you will be welcomed into eternal dwellings. Whoever can be trusted with very little can also be trusted with much, and whoever is dishonest with very little will also be dishonest with much. So if you have not been trustworthy in handling worldly wealth, who will trust you with true riches?" – Mott interwove Mosaic Law with the teachings of Jesus, primarily from Matthew 25, to endorse an idea that would have sounded insane in the mouth of any other speaker – the profit-sharing, commercial enterprise church model. His closing appeal: *True devotion need not cower under cover of a 501(c)(3) refuge. If we would hold ourselves out as righteous, we must pull our own weight in the community. How do we prove to the world the strength of our faith if we're not willing to test our convictions in the marketplace?*

Stirred by both his thesis and his energy, Mira decided she must meet this incisive thinker. She knew she would never get close to him in this packed auditorium, so she lay in wait for him just outside the ground-floor exit. Ninety minutes later, he emerged from the elevator with two stalwart hangers-on, and she could tell from his stride that he was anxious to shed them. She pounced from the cover of a pillar, entering the lobby through the revolving door just as he approached it, grabbed his arm and ushered him out through the same door, intoning,

"There you are! And it's about time, we are so late for the annual deacon's summit."

As she hustled him down the steps, Mott appeared more amused than apprehensive.

"There's no such summit I'm aware of. Who are you?"

"There's always a summit somewhere, Mr. Mott. Where's your car?"

"Why?"

"Because if you don't play along, those annoying salesmen will catch up to us and you'll be stuck talking to them all afternoon."

"Maybe I need to talk to them. People aren't exactly burning up my phone line to set up symposia. I've got a message to deliver."

"Don't you know anything about publicity? Car, car, where's your car?"

"I took the bus."

"Tell me you did *not* take a city bus to a speaking engagement!"

"I don't stand on pretense."

"We'll take mine."

"To where?"

"Anywhere but here. No, not the passenger seat, here, sit in the back like I'm your chauffeur."

With the brusqueness of a secret service agent, she shoved him into the rear seat of her Hyundai Elantra and scurried around to the driver side.

"I know it's not a limo, Mr. Mott, but everybody has to start somewhere."

"Who are you, and why are you kidnapping me?"

"Don't be silly, Mr. Mott. I'm Mira Bonham, no relation."

"To whom?"

"Never mind. I think there's a deli somewhere on Park … hot damn, there it is, and there's an open meter right in front if I can just … hang on back there … got it! Oh, honk your wrinkly little tushie off, you old spinster, I got it fair and square! You okay back there, Mr. Mott?"

Unable to see him in the rearview, Mira peered over the edge of the backrest to find him prone across the seat with his arms over his head.

"It's all right, Mr. Mott, we got the spot!"

"Ms. Bonham?"

"Yes, Mr. Mott? And call me Mira, please."

"If you aren't kidnapping me, what are you doing?"

"I'm helping you."

"With what?"

"Marketing, silly."

"Marketing is for showmen and hustlers. I don't know what you think you heard in that convention hall, but my program is not a gimmick. I sincerely believe Christ can use my background in finance to make salvation accessible to millions by delivering his message in a language that has until now been condemned by the Christian establishment."

"I believe you, Mr. Mott. But innovation does not sell itself. The first rule of public relations is to be accessible but appear unavailable. Give your prospects just enough to whet their appetite, but leave them hungry for more. Here's all you need to know about me. I'm the craftiest little promoter since P.T. Barnum, and you need me, sir. I hear this place sells a BMT sub that'll make you sell your soul to the devil himself. My treat, come on!"

A little more coaxing drew him out of the car and into the restaurant, where Mira took charge of the agenda, ordering and paying for the food, staking out a table in the alcove to give them privacy, overruling his milkshake order in favor of raspberry tea, and interrogating him about the minutest detail of his marketing plan … which was particularly arduous because he had none.

"Mr. Mott, you have advanced degrees in divinity *and* business administration – have you never heard the old adage about practicing what you preach? You haven't written a book or even an article, you haven't built a website, and this print ad you run once a week is just pitiful. You need a platform, a bully-pulpit. Oh, my sweet Jesus, Mr. Mott, that's it! You're spinning your wheels in the wrong venue. If you want to get this mission off the ground, you should quit lecturing and start preaching! We need to get you a church. What's the denomination of the seminary you attended?"

"Southern Baptist."

"Oh, my. And here I thought all the cavemen had died out long ago."

Peter paused in mid-bite and glared.

"Forgive that, I didn't grow up around here. But you must know, Mr. Mott, that your thesis is far too sophisticated for those knuckledraggers. They'll never give you a church. We'll have to start with some fundraising, forge some charitable affiliations …."

As if stirred from a trance, the pall fell from Peter's visage. He leaned forward and peered at his loquacious lunch companion with earnest curiosity.

"Mira, is it?"

"Morning news radio is a very fertile – Yes, Mr. Mott?"

"What is a church, anyway, but a structure where likeminded people convene to share and strengthen their beliefs?"

"I'm on your wavelength, Mr. Mott, but in today's climate a tent in an abandoned parking lot does not instill credibility. At the very least, we need to raise enough capital to rent a vacant storefront or office for a year. And location is a key factor. You don't want to preach self-reliance as an article of faith in a community where scheming to collect government benefits is considered a career in itself. That's a surefire way to get yourself popped in the butt by a pawn shop .32."

"What if money were no object? What do you suppose it would cost to buy a zoned lot and build a church?"

"A damn sight more than I've got. How about you?"

"I'll need an assistant, somebody young and feisty and energetic like you, and … and a coach, someone to keep me focused. I'm sold on your outreach skills. How are you with budgets, salaries, federal/State withholding, that sort of thing?"

Unsure whether to question his integrity or his sanity, Mira studied him with no less scrutiny than she had leveled at her fifth grade Comparative Religion teacher when she informed the class that Jesus was not a Christian but a Jew. She then took a large bite of her neglected sandwich and sputtered through the prosciutto and provolone.

"Let's just take two steps back, *James Pierpont*. How am I supposed to believe that a man who takes a public bus to give a speech has the funds to pay me what I'm worth, let alone build a church from the ground up?"

"Is this skepticism I hear from my forcible abductor? Trust is not a one-way street, Mira. Why are you attacking that sandwich like a stray dog?"

"It may just be my last."

"Why?"

"Because I believe you."

By lunch's end, Peter had hired her at the salary she had left behind in Virginia. As a show of good faith, he escorted her to his bank two blocks away and paid her six months in advance. Before that term had expired, ground was broken for the construction of Vanguard Cathedral.

With Mira as his rainmaker, Peter was free to expand his research beyond the confines of conventional scripture and, as a result, generate sermons and Sunday school lessons with deeper insight than his seminary indoctrination had allowed. As the years progressed, Peter proved to Mira that he did, after all, subscribe to harmony of word and deed. He restructured youth camps and summer Bible schools and adult retreats, so adroitly interweaving spiritual studies with classical education and progressive pursuits that the headmasters of two prestigious private schools harangued him until he instituted an internship program for their junior faculty members. In very little time, the ever expanding services of Vanguard Cathedral were in such demand that Mira was forced to abandon outreach altogether. In fact, she, her growing staff and Peter were all so busy that it was not until after the completion of *The Miracle Mile* that she discovered Peter had no home *but* the church.

It was then, too, that Peter changed. His first blackout lasted for only a matter of seconds. He repeated a verse during the Easter service. He did this so often for emphasis that no one in the congregation noticed. But to Mira, who was intimately in tune with Peter's cadence and mannerisms, he might as well have dropped his trousers and set fire to the podium.

DON'T WEAR MORE THAN TWO PIECES OF MODEST JEWELRY IN PUBLIC, AND AVOID OSTENTATIOUS HAIRSTYLES, SO THAT YOU DON'T OFFEND THE PLAIN AND THE UGLY, OR INTRUDE UPON THE PROVINCE OF THE GLITTERATI.

This public service announcement is brought to you by the First Daughter to Serve under a Female President and Only First Daughter to Serve under the First Female President's Respectful Couture & Coiffure Initiative.

Chapter Ten

Ante Up

In the 1940s, the term *hepcat* referred to an enthusiast of big band jazz. The hepcat strode on the cutting edge of mainstream society – he always had money in his pocket for good food and booze, he knew the classiest joints, he spoke the nightlife lingo and he did everything with a distinctive aura of *au courant*. The lazy American palate morphed the term into *hipster* during the 1950s, and it fell out of vogue during the turbulent 60s and 70s when the deviation *hippie* took center stage. In the 90s, careless social commentators misapplied the mothballed cognomen *hipster* to describe its antithesis: an acutely narcissistic conclave of adolescents and twenty-somethings who, thanks in large part to overindulgent parents, failed to grasp the ubiquitous truism that nothing in life is free. Suffering the delusion that being a shiftless burden upon society is a prerequisite to attaining the status of *cool*, today these lavishly spoiled brats adopt anything and everything that might be considered counterculture, from androgynous and comically asymmetrical haircuts to clothing that even a homeless person would shun. Their musical idols, ironically badged *alternative*, babble lyrics even more nonsensical than their *psychedelic rock* predecessors. As with any generation who never had to earn the toys and trinkets that adorned their formative years, the typical hipster assuages his misplaced guilt by supporting pie-in-the-sky social policies.

Though they are considered antagonists, the hipster bears many similarities to the *yipster*. Known as *yuppies* in the 1980s, the yipster segment of society consists of professionals in their twenties and thirties with moderate incomes, basking in the titian glow of the corporate carrot, who, like the hipsters (a) pretend to be far more refined than they really are and (b) devote an unhealthy majority of their time and energy to striking poses rather than actually living. The yipster frequents certain sporting events and restaurants for the same reason the hipster follows his fellow sleepwalkers to the grunge concert – not necessarily because he appreciates the fare, but because it is the current rage for *everyone who's anyone* in his clique – thus, in each competitive realm of existence, rebellion is unmasked as just another sham permutation of conformity.

To add cosmopolitanism to his pretentious social résumé, the American yipster takes special care to be seen often at establishments with European names. No one knows this better than the owner of Ennis Pub, LaRhonda Willis, who turned her ailing Soul Food Boutique into an urban goldmine by emblazoning on her front door a title she had picked at random from a book of Irish male baby names, and breathing new marketability into her artery choking fried food by redubbing *Porgies and Fries* as *Fish-n-Chips*.

Thanks to her success, LaRhonda is spending the last few hours of December 31, not at her corner booth handing out grandmotherly advice to the regulars, but in a downtown law office hashing out the details of her third franchise contract. Were she at the pub tonight, she might take watchful notice of her newest patron. Feeling ten feet tall from the ice he just smoked at the switching yard, Freddie Herzog takes a stool and flips the bartender a hundred dollar bill – all that remains of the ten-grand he was given by the State in October. He's been living large in a condemned building, frittering away his modest windfall on gold neckchains, beltless bluejeans so oversized that he has to hold them up with one hand wherever he walks, crack whores and whatever drug is readily available on the streets.

Ennis Pub is not Freddie's scene. He is here tonight, not for the company, but to troll for a suitable victim from whom he might score some sorely needed cash … and in whose apertures he might satisfy the insipient urge no street strange can assuage. And this place is a predator's smorgasbord – everywhere Freddie turns he spies someone who fits his profile to a tee: an unescorted, lily white female aged thirteen to seventeen, no taller than 5'6" so she'll be easy to dominate, who likes to show off her curves and is ignorant of the barbarity that lies without the boundaries of her strawberry-margarita-designer-jeans-Acura-MDX world. As the bourbon oozes down his throat like melting caramel, he pinpoints his prime candidate.

Though Chrissa Hendley turned sixteen last month, her naturally curly blond hair and high forehead lend her a fetching prepubescent air, and her *Invisalign* braces are but icing on the cake. Genetics shortchanged her in the breast department, but her hips (her "business end" in Freddie's parlance) boast more than enough girth to accommodate what Freddie has in mind for her. Standing only 5'2," a full foot shorter than he, Freddie should be able to subdue her without marring her succulent skin. And Freddie was always a sucker for a cleft chin. As he watches her flit about the dance floor and play video poker, one bourbon turns into four.

He could not care less that Chrissa is so lovesick over seventeen-year-old Science Club Prexy Stuart Levy that she hopes she'll muster the courage to surrender her virginity to him on his birthday two weeks hence. Nor would Freddie be moved in the least by the knowledge that the city mayor plans to name a dog park after Chrissa this coming spring in recognition of her tireless volunteer work at the local animal shelter. To Freddie, Chrissa is not a human being. She is an oppressive force, a succubus who provokes him by flaunting her carefree life of privilege. She is both an object of his hatred for the world at large and the instrument by which he means to express that animus. The longer he fixates on her, the more convinced he becomes that little Chrissa is the only receptacle in the universe which can contain his angst. And when it is over he will kill, not Chrissa, but the shame he has disgorged into her.

At 10:15, Chrissa kisses her friends farewell, dons her rabbit fur jacket and announces she is off to greet the New Year with Stuart and his parents at a private club. She strolls past an adjoining bar to the end of the building, where she turns into a breezeway at the end of which she must negotiate a flight of dilapidated concrete steps, at whose base she must traverse another short alleyway, then climb a flight of metal stairs to the covered parking lot. There is a shorter route which bypasses the steps, but it is unprotected from the sleet and blustering north wind. Besides, Chrissa has been admonished since toddlerhood to avoid blind corners and dumpsters, from which unsavory types can spring. Having kept pace ten steps behind her, Freddie takes the detour with the aim of intercepting her as she summits the final stairway. Clearing the garbage bins, he stops short of the parking lot. Unzipping his pants so that his now throbbing penis will hold them up, he pulls a bowie knife from a sheath strapped to his naked thigh. He rests his back against the wall on whose other side he can hear Chrissa trundle up the metal steps.

Clunk ... clunk ... clunk ...

She has only four more to climb. Every cell in Freddie's body pulsates to the rhythm of his slowing heartbeat as he strokes his penis with the dull edge of the blade.

Clunk ... clunk ... clunk ...

Just once, he would like to forestall ejaculation until he has mounted his prey, but he is powerless to contain himself and, as his viscid intentions coagulate on his boots, he is left with only resentment.

Abashed, he raises the knife in his right hand while turning just slightly to ready his left for her neck.

Clunk.

At the sight of Chrissa's doll-like foot, Freddie summons a lifetime of unmet aspirations and lunges.

But his intended assault transmutes into a retreat as a gloved hand clamps over his mouth from behind and another wrings his right arm like a green twig until his knife falls to the pavement. A chopping pain in his left calf drops him to his knees as his assailant wraps him in a vicelike chokehold. Adrift in a billowing haze of oxygen deprival, he watches helplessly as scrumptious Chrissa wends away to live her charmed and wide-eyed little life, unaware that Freddie Herzog ever existed.

Freddie's next sensation is the pungent odor of bleach tempered by a hint of rose and lilac. He opens his eyes beneath a glaring cloverleaf light fixture. Unable to raise his hands to block the beams, he turns his head. To his right, a deep-basin stainless steel sink with gooseneck spigots and hand sprayers covers the fifteen-foot wall. He appears to be strapped at the wrists, waist and ankles to a metal frame … perhaps a table akin to the one on his left, at the foot of which someone is draping a man's necktie over a silver coat tree that has only two oddly configured hooks and stands on wheels. When the figure turns, Freddie recognizes the same well dressed cigar smoker who asked him that baffling question on the day of his release.

"Ah, you are awake. So nice of you to join me."

Leisurely, the man begins to roll his shirt sleeves precisely three times apiece.

"Freddie Herzog, also known as Slinky Sam. I am Anthony Wayne Stearns. I am here to kill you."

"What I care who you are?"

The man named Stearns retrieves plastic coveralls from a satchel on the table beside him.

"I say it for my benefit, Mr. Herzog, not yours."

"Why?"

"It keeps me honest."

"How so, honest?"

"It is a final test of my resolve."

"So … you ain't sure you want me dead?"

All limbs inserted and fabric smoothed, the man named Stearns zips the suit from crotch to neck, then covers his perforated wingtips with plastic footies which cinch just below the knee.

"You pose the wrong question, Mr. Herzog. As a general principle, I do not want anybody to die. But such sentiments are not germane to this equation. The simple facts are these."

The man named Stearns walks deliberately to Freddie's tableside.

"On the seventh of August, year twenty-aught-six, you raped, anally and orally sodomized, and strangled to death fourteen-year-old Millie Renee Mott in front of her nine-year-old brother, Dylan Paul, whom your accomplice detained at knifepoint. You then anally and orally sodomized the boy and stabbed him to death, fleeing the scene with the $20 bill Millie's mother had given her for pizza and Dylan's genitals, which you had severed while he still breathed. For these offenses, you were sentenced to die by lethal injection."

The man named Stearns turns back toward the satchel on the table.

"That there is a fact. And it's another fact, yeah. They done let me out. Opened them doors and –"

Freddie is stunned by, not so much the brain-concussing backhand to his jaw, but the swiftness with which the man named Stearns pivots and delivers it. Returning to the satchel, the man named Stearns methodically retrieves a cattle prod, a scalpel, a miniature reciprocating saw, a speculum, a cleaver, a rubber mallet, a leather pouch with an assortment of drug vials and syringes, and seven one-liter bags, four of which contain a clear liquid and the balance of which bear something thicker with a crimson hue.

"As I was saying, your sentence was vacated and your record expunged because of certain extenuating political realities over which neither you nor the court had any control. But you see, Mr. Herzog, when political organs create a vacuum, practical agencies such as I step in to fill the gap. I am the fine print, as it were, in the order of release you were handed October last."

Freddie's pulse begins to race, not because the cloud of crack and bourbon has dissipated, and not because he necessarily appreciates the gravity of his predicament. His heart pounds because someone else is in complete control of him.

"Now, now, wait a damn minute, man! I got contributional rights!"

The man named Stearns shuts Freddie's mouth with two thicknesses of duck tape, then methodically dons surgical gloves and affixes a face shield to his forehead.

"You renounced your *constitutional* rights the moment you accosted those innocent children. And I will pay a visit to your accomplice in due time. Nonetheless, you are responsible, Freddie, for Millie and Dylan. And right now you have to pay in kind, wound for wound, violation for violation, three times over."

The man named Stearns retrieves the cattle prod and tests its charge.

"I do hope you savored that last bourbon, because this will take some time."

DON'T USE MULTISYLLABIC WORDS, OR WORDS THAT SOUND FOREIGN, IN PUBLIC LEST YOU OFFEND THE IDIOTS AND THE IDLERS.

This public service announcement is brought to you by Professor Ryan A. Gardner, the First Bushleague-Language Tsar and the Only Bushleague-Language Tsar to be So Named by the First Female President and First First Lady to Become President and Only Former First Lady to Become the First Female President.

Chapter Eleven

Generation Gaffe

New Year's Day – 6:10 a.m.

Ani's frugality is not confined to his business persona – he lives in a modest ranch style house at the end of a meandering gravel path in a sparsely populated, unassuming neighborhood tucked so snugly midst an industrial district that it can not be detected from a main road. The house itself, characteristic of many in *Tornado Alley*, is built into the broad side of a berm, invisible to any visitor traveling the roughhewn byway which terminates at a dilapidated, corrugated metal outbuilding. But thrift is not the sole motive for Ani's reclusive abode. The ruthless barrage of ever increasing federal taxation schemes these last eight years has so decimated the middle class that America has regressed to the brutal *have vs. have not* climate of centuries past. So volatile is this state of society that those who have managed to eke their way out of the lower class must hide their largesse and be prepared to defend it upon a moment's notice. Thus, a storm cellar conceals his front door. The back door, patio and windows look west onto an untamed wooded acreage with a creek. His home security system consists of two Rottweilers named Mojo and Bindi, a pugilistic housecat named Tarbaby and a variety of some seventy-five weapons secreted beneath furniture, within yard implements and behind trap doors.

Not unlike the typical human being, who so instinctually empathizes with the discomfort of others that he vicariously shares their physical and emotional distress, Ani finds opprobrious the willful infliction of pain on living creatures. Hence, the five hours he just spent dispatching the late Freddie Herzog took a tremendous toll upon him. In truth, Freddie's ordeal lasted only three hours. Because all intentions and motivations cease at death, Ani always takes extra time to devote earnest reverence to the corpse of his late target, washing and wrapping it in a dignified manner before depositing it in the designated receptacle for the mortician. With this ritual, Ani pays homage to the innocence with which even the most deranged of brigands first entered the world.

To revitalize his spirit, Ani has developed a meditative ritual he follows every morning after a Utility job. He pours a steaming cup of hot apple cider from a pot that has been simmering on his stovetop since last evening and cradles that cup as he traverses to the back patio, where his animals enjoy breakfast while Ani retrieves a half-smoked cigar from the ashtray. Ani never finishes his last cigar of the day, because he revels in the stale aroma of a spent cigar as much as he enjoys the bouquet of one freshly cut. Like a dusty violin case, the muted pungency of yesterday's diversion whisks him back to the 1960 Plymouth Belvedere, in whose front seat he and Jarry spent many a Sunday morning accompanying their father on donut runs to one of the half dozen children's homes in the greater metro area. Born during the Great Depression, six-year-old Franklin Stearns lost his own father to suicide. Destitute and with no extended family to assist her, his mother relinquished him to an orphanage, where he remained a ward of the State until an oilfield foreman and a social worker adopted him at the age of eleven. Though the care he received in the interim was far from exemplary, Franklin never lost sight of the alternatives – life on the street or untimely death – so he was abidingly grateful for the food and shelter. He told his boys on their inaugural journey:

"We're not rich; neither are we poor. This morning, I require your company, because I want to show you that hope and sincerity are usually found in the humblest surroundings. After today, you don't have to accompany me unless you want to and, if you don't, I will not hold your decision against you."

The Stearns brothers never missed a trip thereafter. They forged many friendships on these outings. In fact, upwards of thirty percent of Ani's present office staff were once boarded by such institutions.

As he gazes at the slats of sunrise that pierce the treetops, he eventually loses himself in memories of Melissa. This reminiscence lasts anywhere from ten minutes to two hours. At reverie's end, he refills his cup, lifts Tarbaby onto her favorite perch – his right shoulder – and escorts the dogs along the bank of the creek. He then returns to the porch and, as WWII era swing lilts from the overhead speakers, he sketches plans for his next birdhouse. He builds them from freshly fallen tree branches he has trained Mojo and Bindi to retrieve during their daily explorations, and he fashions them after structures which were meaningful to him as a boy, sparing no detail – from the round windows of his favorite hoagie shop to the wraparound front porch of his grandfather's farmhouse.

12:35 p.m.

Abuelita Rosa's is the only riverfront restaurant that survived the downtown renovation project without being forced to surrender its own distinctive building and become a tenant in one of the undistinguished brick structures that snake to either side of it. Boasting the most diverse selection of Tex-Mex cuisine within two hundred fifty miles, it is one of the few such establishments which do not depend upon a massive volume of customers to turn a sizeable profit – it serves dinner by reservation only, even on weekends and holidays.

When you walk through the front door, you are greeted by one of the owner's three daughters. The entire staff speaks impeccable English, albeit with a native Spanish accent, and every waitress wears a freshly cut azalea in her hair whose color changes according to season and event. The hallway to the left of the hostess stand leads to a large array of booths of varying shapes and capacities for semiformal and family dining, while that to the right branches into a series of private rooms. If you count among the majority of Abuelita Rosa's patrons, you proceed straight ahead, where you will find floor tables for casual dining. Should you partake of so many refreshments that you find yourself in need of relief, you may avail yourself of either of the sex-appropriate restrooms by taking the hallway that extends from the left end of the bar and turning right. If you turn left, you will encounter a metal door marked "Private ‹› Storage." This door is accessible only by means of a magnetic lock which is controlled exclusively by the bartender. Under no circumstance will you be permitted beyond this door … unless, of course, you are a member of Anthony Stearns' Utility Committee.

So seldom does Ani himself appear for committee gatherings that the bartender did not even notice him today until, after bumping his forehead on the door, Ani caught his stare and spat a few aphonic epithets in his direction. Ten feet down the spiral stairway, Ani has greater success with this door, which opens into a spacious room whose walls are lined with a fully stocked bar and a fresh buffet. To the uninitiated observer, this scene would be more depictive of a banquet than a business meeting. In the room's center sprawls an oval table with nineteen plush chairs, eighteen of which are already occupied by jovial partakers. Ani steps behind the bar and fills a mug with the brown ale which, though it is only brewed seasonally in an obscure hamlet of Belgium, is always on tap for these meetings. He then walks the perimeter of the table, exchanging handshakes, chuckles and heartfelt greetings with everyone before acquiring his seat at its head.

"Please, do not stop eating on my account. You are busy people with many commitments. In fact, I will not be staying long. I have only a quick … offering, shall we say, before Jarry takes over." Ani gestures toward his brother, who sits to his right eating a chili relleno, nestled safely between Eldon and Connie.

Eldon Welge is a high school English teacher. An Olympic medalist in the sport, he also coaches wrestling. It is no mere coincidence that he graduated from the same high school as all of his colleagues at this table, save Connie. Recognizing that trust is the most problematic element of human interaction, Ani thought it prudent to populate a group of this nature with people who share a common history.

Connie Plachette, a freelance CPA, is a former client of Ani's. Eleven years ago, she was in the midst of a seemingly amicable divorce when her husband's behavior turned ever more erratic and belligerent until, one evening, he forced her into the attic at the point of a fire poker and locked her in until dawn. The very next day, she hired Ani to impress upon her soon-to-be-ex the importance of playing nice and disappearing from her life as quickly as possible. Ani planned to pay the husband a personal visit that very evening but, when Connie returned to her home that morning she found that he had only pretended to go to work. No sooner did she drop her keys on the kitchen table than he lunged at her with a carving knife, cleaving her right cheek clean in two. Groping for an implement of self-defense, Connie laid hold a paring knife and, before she knew it, her assailant lay choking on the floor with a punctured trachea, as well as severed femoral and carotid arteries.

So precise were her cuts that Connie, who in her thirty-six years of life had never so much as raised her voice in anger, was charged with second degree murder. So ashamed was Ani that he had not anticipated the timing of the husband's attack that he refunded her money and pledged to defend her free of charge. Edilberto Agbayani – a master of the Filipino martial art known as *Eskrima*, who testified for the State as an expert on knife-fighting – handily perceived Connie's natural talent with edged weaponry. As he exited the courtroom after testifying at the preliminary hearing, he slipped his business card into Ani's case file. Connie later spent fifteen months studying under Sr. Agbayani at his estate in Puerto Princesa.

Standing only 5'5" and not especially muscular, Connie's appearance is commensurate with her vocation. She keeps her waist-length hair tied and pinned in a bun and, though her eyesight is 20/20, she likes to wear horn-rimmed glasses in business settings. Fetching as she is in a dress and heels, she always wears long pants and flat shoes because "a girl's gotta move." Though her facial scar is not distracting, it is visible, and she refuses to cover it with makeup. Not only does it serve her as both a reminder of human vulnerability and a badge of honor on the street; she sees it as an adornment that distinguishes her from the crowd no differently than a beauty or birth mark. When the Lieutenant Governor solicited his services in the wake of the *Criminal Rehabilitation and Reform Act*, Connie was the first person Ani approached in assembling his crew.

"As you all surely anticipated, our business is now concluded with Mr. Herzog. Because the details of his offense so complemented your skill set, I wish to apologize, Rita, for taking that job away from you on such short notice. Let us please suffice it to say that with Mr. Herzog comes … baggage with which I deem it best you remain unburdened. My decision did not reflect the slightest lack of confidence in your abilities, my dear friend."

Next to Connie sits Rita Baynes, a redheaded over-the-road trucker who boasts having a special man in every major Midwestern city. Surprisingly graceful for a woman of 6'4", she sports a tattoo of Pinocchio on her left breast. Exceptionally versed in chemistry, in her travels she has amassed an elaborate collection of pills, powders and creams. She raises her glass of iced tea with a smile.

"Ani, you couldn't offend me if you tried. Besides, you freed up my Friday night for Mr. Tucumcari!"

Connie raises her wine glass and shares a decadent laugh with her friend while the other women on the Committee clap and cheer. Ani and his male associates grin and wince at once, unsure whether to celebrate Mr. Tucumcari's fortune or to pity him for the long recovery path upon which he has only just embarked.

"Then I will consider myself absolved. Thank you, all, for your tireless assistance in these matters. You know the drill, but discretion is never a cliché. Shred, shred, shred those documents."

As Ani yields his chair to Jarry, Connie grabs his arm. Thanks to nerve damage from her ex-husband's attack, Connie has had to retrain her muscles to prevent her head from cocking when she utters certain vowel sounds. She loses this discipline under stress.

"Ani, a moment?"

Ever attentive to his most treasured committee member, Ani ushers her to the empty bar and tops off her glass.

"Connie, within the hour I will be able to relieve you of Jarry-sitting duty. Most rational people I know would be dancing a jig at that news. What troubles you, kiddo?"

"Who's the Drizella?"

"Well, though similar stories appear in literature as early as the ninth common century, in the seventeenth a Frenchman named Perrault penned the version of *Cinderella* that has become part of the core childhood curriculum in perhaps every developed country. The basic theme –"

No sooner has the foot of Connie's glass found its coaster than she has yanked Ani's tie taut against the edge of a stiletto she seems to have drawn from thin air.

"Where in hell do you stash those things?!"

"Who is Freddie's baggage?"

"You know this is the tie Lissy gave me for my fifty-third birthday?"

"The one you've worn every New Year's Day since."

"In fact, you helped her pick it out."

"And I'll cut it if you patronize me once more."

The quickness with which Connie can produce a blade is rivaled only by the alacrity with which her compatriot can span the chasm between playfulness and reprimand.

"Well, what am I supposed to do, Connie, when you treat what we do here with all the decorum of a pom-pom girl at a sleepover? I was very explicit with each of you before you signed onto this committee – the more delicate the job, the fewer of you need to know its details, and every ultimate decision is mine alone. This is not a legitimate concern we are engaged in, where the consequence of failure is a monetary fine. If errors are made, everyone remotely involved gets a bullet to the head. While I trust you implicitly, I withhold many things from you so you will have plausible deniability. In short, Freddie's baggage is none of your business and you damned well know that."

"Well, now you're just insulting me." Ani's ire turns bewilderment as she withdraws the knife and, with a motherly air, smooths his tie back in place. "I can deal with insults; it just makes me crazy to be talked down to. You know I wouldn't ordinarily ask. But if this has anything to do with Peter Mott, Julia Bross made it my business when she asked me to look into you. *Me*, investigating *you*! I know schizophrenics with more sensible lives."

Among the various ventures Julia has resurrected is a life, accident and health insurance company. When she dove into the books in search of the company's ills, she noticed an alarming dearth of fraudulent claims. Human nature dictates that, no matter how many policyholders get caught and prosecuted, a certain element of the insurance buying population still thinks it can get away with filing a false claim. Therefore, such claims constitute fifteen to twenty percent of the typical insurance carrier's annual losses. When she saw consistent reports of less than ten percent, Julia knew claims investigators were in collusion with policyholders, but she couldn't figure out how they had succeeded. She vented her frustration to Connie, who was then one of thirteen junior accountants in the CPA firm which handled Julia's payroll and tax matters. When Connie asked to review the books, Julia acceded only because she was a close personal friend of the firm's owner. She granted her an access code to her office for that evening. The next day, Connie emailed Julia an encrypted report detailing names, dates, locations and strategies accounting for every penny of the company's mysterious multimillion dollar hemorrhage. Julia marched into Connie's cubicle that very afternoon, helped her pack her things and placed her on retainer as an independent auditor. Since then, she has proven herself an invaluable asset to Julia, not only as a forensic accountant but a particularly tenacious gumshoe – the investigator who keeps the investigators on the straight and narrow.

"Well then, I suppose you will need this." Ani produces a microdrive from his inner coat pocket. "Here you will find everything I have on Mott, including the raw footage of his police interviews of August 7 through 9 of 2006, and the complete record of his trial. Do not deviate from full disclosure, Connie. And do not worry. You may think it counterintuitive but, as a matter of fact, I invited this little probe." As Connie gropes for adequate words to express her consternation, Ani grins again and delivers the old joke that never fails to elicit a smile: "You can trust me; I am a lawyer."

With a wink of the eye, Ani kisses her hand and slips out the door. Upstairs, he has a brief chat with the flustered bartender, leaving him in brighter spirits with another joke and a fatherly pat on the back.

On his way to the exit, he makes his customary stop at the hostess stand to bestow upon each of the owner's daughters a kiss to the forehead, a strict warning against running with the wrong crowd and an exquisite piece of jewelry.

While Ani is successful, he is not necessarily affluent. In fact, federal legislation has cast society into such disarray that the conventional indicators of wealth have become obsolete. Taking a lesson from Adolph Hitler's *blitzkrieg*, or *lightning attack*, the First Female President knew that overwhelming the taxpayers with multiple laws in one fell swoop would diminish their ability to mount a successful legal challenge to any one of them. She also knew from her study of history that the only way monocrats can secure unlimited political power is to promote a collectivist mentality among the commoners, maligning individualism at every turn. So, as her henchmen prepared to ram down the congressional throat the *Criminal Rehabilitation and Reform Act* and the *Safer Community Initiative*, she fine-tuned the last prong of her plan to usurp totalitarian rule – the *Social Security Act* of 2017. Touted by her army of newstalk propagandists as the only way to bring FDR's chronically molested pension fund back into the black, with two key provisions buried amidst a rat's nest of amendments to existing statutes and regulations, the new law:

- Raised the social security withholding levy by eleven percent across the board;
- Imposed a one-time, thirty-five percent tax on all existing retirement accounts; and
- Rescinded tax credits on all future private sector retirement contributions.

Before the law was even passed (by unanimous bipartisan vote), even the least sophisticated retirement investors foresaw the wholesale nationalization of their nest eggs. Only a daring few investors were willing to risk the impending civil and criminal penalties that could result from "fiscal expatriation" of their future income, so the vast majority moved their funds out of the country ahead of the deadline. In a desperate ploy to hide assets from a voracious IRS, scores of people destroyed their credit/debit cards and converted their bank accounts to cash, reviving the heretofore thought obsolete days of stashing wads of *long green* beneath one's floorboard or mattress. The First Female President struck back by ordering the Federal Reserve to conduct seizures of old currency and hoard the new. Overnight, the ancient barter system was reborn for personal transactions, turning trinkets, textiles and comestibles into legal tender on streets and in offices alike.

No sooner has Ani emerged from the eatery than the valet rushes to help him tuck his scarf into his overcoat.

"Your car, Señor Stearns?"

Having grown up in the halcyon days of Detroit, when thoroughbreds such as the Stingray, the Charger and the 442 lent a distinctive sense of pride to the process of car buying, a quick perusal of Abuelita Rosa's parking lot saddens Ani. As an immediate result of the controversial automotive bailouts of 2008-10, the safety and reliability of production vehicles began to falter. Then, in 2016 – the fiftieth anniversary of the *Motor Vehicle Safety Act* which had created his position – the Secretary of the National Highway Traffic Safety Administration passed a regulation declaring the Federal Motor Vehicle Safety Standards to be *maximum* criteria. This seemingly insignificant semantic change sealed the fate of the American motorist by immunizing car manufacturers from liability for defects. The crux lay in the method of FMVSS compliance: because the NHTSA had scarcely the manpower to independently inspect every new vehicle that came off the assembly lines, it had always relied on the manufacturers themselves to certify in a one-sentence memo that their vehicles passed safety requirements. So long as the FMVSS were considered *minimum* benchmarks, victims of unsafe vehicles could hold manufacturers responsible (and, thus, ensure that safety defects would be remedied in successive models) by filing civil lawsuits. By making FMVSS a ceiling rather than a floor, and leaving the self-certification system unaltered, the Secretary essentially made every manufacturer's unverified avowal that its vehicle complies therewith an ironclad defense in civil court. As the safety of motorcars thereafter plunged, consumer interest in older vehicles revived and the used parts/service industry was resurrected. And in no time, all the true classics were gobbled up. As a result, it is a rarity to see any car on the road that is not at least fifteen years old.

"Thank you, Lucio, but it is a fine afternoon for a … *paseo*?"

"Ah, a stroll. Very good, sir."

Society has become so polarized that, in your average neighborhood, frontporch paradise gives way to backyard squalor. It is an everyday occurrence for entire families to vanish merely because they parked in the wrong lot. Lucio and the eight young men under his supervision are not conventional valets. Each (a) has been both mentally and physically trained in the latest urban combat techniques at a ten-week boot camp which the Utility Committee founded four years ago in anticipation of the United Nations *Enlightened Society Treaty* and (b) holds a commission as a reservist for the Sheriff's office, which excepts him from the restrictions of the *Safer Community Initiative*. Though Abuelita Rosa's adamantly discourages its patrons from venturing afoot beyond the aegis of Lucio and his crew, Lucio understands more than most why Ani and his team move about the sidewalks and alleyways with impunity – it was Lucio's father whose ear was mangled by thirteen-year-old Ani in reprisal for Jarry.

Ani tucks a pack of Lucio's favorite imported cigarillos into his vest pocket. "*Prospero Año Nuevo*. I shall not be too long, my friend."

With a gracious pat on the shoulder from Lucio, Ani proceeds north from Abuelita Rosa's for two blocks, then turns into a cobbled courtyard surrounded by more modest restaurants and pubs. He ascends the flagstone steps to a cozy burger joint just two doors west of Ennis Pub called Custard's Last Stand. After a brief conversation with the bartender, Ani follows one of the bustling waiters into the kitchen, meanders his way to the back and boards a freight elevator that carries him to the third floor and opens onto a long, dimly lit hallway with no perceptible doors or windows in either direction. Ten paces to the right, Ani flips a seemingly defunct light switch three times. A gap slowly opens in a false wall behind him, leading to an unlit alcove from which he can survey the greater surroundings undetected.

Ani can barely contain his amusement at the fact that no more than fifteen feet ahead of him hangs a glass door that faces the very courtyard from which he entered this building so many twists and turns past. On the adjacent picture window are stenciled the words "Shipping « Receiving » Accounting." The interstice between the false wall and the door is strewn with a dozen identical, gray metal office desks, each occupied by a harried and constipated looking gentleman in dingy suitpants, white half-sleeve dress shirt and remissly knotted tie. A buzzer sounds. In near perfect unison, the staffers leave their desks and file out the front door. The receptionist in the front lobby flips a "Gone to Lunch" sign, pulls opaque shades to obscure the glass, retrieves her purse and locks the door behind her.

With a curious grin, Ani hangs his overcoat on a nearby coat tree, strides to the far end of the room, turns to face the wall he just accessed and folds his hands cordially behind his back. Momentarily, the passage swings to, and through it shuffle the other attendees of this impromptu convention. As the men file in, Ani's contemporaries greet him with either a handshake or a hug while the three of the younger generation move the desks and chairs together in the center of the room to form a makeshift roundtable. The last man to enter is not only the meeting's chair; he is both the ringleader of this bunch and a voting shareholder in a nationwide consortium of similarly situated concerns. A tree stump of a man, Bart Milland walks as much with his arms and torso as he does his legs.

"Ani, Ani, my old collaborator, it's been too long!"

The childhood pals embrace. When they part, Bart takes Ani's hands in his and gives them a hearty shake.

"How's that fiery little lady of yours?"

"Not good, Bart. Not good at all."

"What's wrong?"

"Maura died six years ago. Imagine being dead for that long, Bart. How would you feel?"

Ever since they sabotaged their second grade teacher's toiletry kit, Bart has been at Ani's emotional mercy, never knowing where the demarcation lay between gravity and tomfoolery. But Ani was never sadistic – no sooner does a ripple of panic sweep across his schoolyard chum's brow than he grins and pats Bart on the cheek.

"I am not offended. How could you have possibly known? It is good to see you."

Relieved, Bart throws his arm around Ani's shoulder. "Come grab a chair, and let's get this confab started."

As the assemblage convenes, a lack of seating forces the younger men to stand awkwardly behind their fathers. Though Bart all but forces the chair to his immediate right upon him, Ani gives it to Bart's elder brother Arnold. Though he is built identically to Bart, all but the most casual acquaintances speak of Arnold as if he dwarfs his brother. Known in certain circles by the anonym The Dean, Arnold rarely speaks in groups of three or more. When he does converse, he formulates his thoughts so methodically that many listeners find the silence between his utterances unnerving. Content to let his garrulous brother be the public face of their joint venture, Arnold's stolid countenance unveils him to the savvy observer as the sole decisionmaker and final arbiter of disputes. Behind Arnold lurks a hulk whose bejeweled eyebrows and slapdash comportment manifest the impertinence of a nineteen-year-old – Arnold's only son, Lindell.

As Ani deftly takes the chair opposite Arnold, Bart raps a stapler as though it were a gavel.

"Gentlemen, join me in welcoming to our weekly get-together a man who needs no introduction to many of us here. Anthony Stearns and I were friends before Nixon went to China. Back in the day, I was a pretty handsome guy. Now and then, a girl's big brother wouldn't share her attraction to me, so he and his boys would decide to teach me a lesson. I could always count on Anthony Stearns to come to my aid. Why, I could walk the meanest streets on the east side unmolested because everybody knew this man was my friend."

Detecting Ani's growing discomfort, another friend from bygone days calls out from the opposite end of the powwow.

"Enough with this *cosa nostra* cowcrap, Bart. You're an architect, born in Omaha, and you've never even been to Canada, let alone Europe. We know the man. We know he's kicked a lot of ass in his time. We've all kicked our share of ass over the years. That's why we're in this room, for crying out loud."

Bart raps his stapler again, and gestures with it toward the fidgeting youths.

"Merrell, some of us don't share that history. I'm educating the lads."

"Educating? You can't educate these dummies. Nobody can educate these dummies, because they've got Nintendo circuit boards for brains. Don't you know that, Bart? Oh no, you don't because you were smart enough to never have a kid."

This quip draws a chuckle from The Dean himself. Taking advantage of the cover of laughter, Lindell elbows his closest confederate.

"Old man don't look so tough to me."

The room falls quiet but for the affected giggles of the three youths. Merrell, who has just jawed a cigar, stops midway through his lighting ritual.

"What's that you said, Milland?"

As his cohorts slink away from him, Lindell clears his throat to buy a hiccup of time in which to decide between adopting a conciliatory attitude and yielding to the testosterone-induced obstinacy in which he has been awash since the age of fourteen. In his perception, Ani is no more than an interloper in the fiefdom that is ruled by his father and uncle. *How can that dude Merrell be mad at me? I'm like a prince in this crowd. I'll bet he's just egging me on. And Pop ain't moving a muscle. Yeah, they're daring me to stand up to this old fool.* He locks eyes with Ani.

"I said that old man don't look so tough to me."

Merrell slams his lighter down. Ani raises a halting hand, glances momentarily at Arnold, who has not broken his own stare at Ani since this meeting began, then returns his attention to his pubescent detractor.

"Merrell, relax. Lindell is at an awkward age. He is still in search of that near imperceptible boundary between humor and disrespect. I trust the latter was not his intent, was it, son?"

Arnold smooths his tie and straightens his jacket. Lindell folds his overfed arms and raises a defiant chin.

"I ain't your son. And that's Mr. Milland to you, old man."

Bart reaches for his stapler. Ani stops him with but a sideways glance, then casually acquires his feet. As he approaches Lindell, all but the youths detect the subtle transformation in his air from sport to predacity.

No stranger to altercations, trash talk stopped fazing Lindell when he was in elementary school because he quickly gathered that behind every boast and threat is uncertainty. From the playground to the pool hall, the primary objective of the typical swaggerer is to bluff the other guy into backing down. More often than not, the dodge works because each dueling blusterer would prefer not to spoil his good time with cuts and bruises and broken bones. But there is no indecision in this old man. And his silence is more unnerving than the brashest bombast Lindell has ever heard. His every movement, fluid and precise as though he were gliding and not walking, fuels an intensity of focus in his eyes … eyes which neither blink nor stray from Lindell's as each measured footfall hastens the inevitable. Arnold was fond of taking Lindell to the local zoo when he was a toddler. Lindell once saw a Bengal tiger being transferred from a holding cage into his new habitat. Before the handlers released him, he paced from one end of the pen to the other, his desire to tear into their flesh swelling with every stride. The tiger's stare was both terrifying and hypnotic. Though he stands an inch or so shorter than Lindell, the visage of Anthony Stearns is no less daunting.

Toe to toe now, Lindell drops his meaty hands to his side. Ani removes his suitcoat and drapes it atop his overcoat, then unbuttons and rolls his sleeves exactly three folds, his eyes never straying from Lindell as he folds his hands in front of his belt and speaks in a deliberate, businesslike tone.

"It is your move, Mr. Milland."

The old man's eyes remain fixed, their gaze intensifying, as though penetrating Lindell's nethermost emotional veils.

The scope of insurmountable challenges a young man will answer knows no end. But even the most foolhardy of daredevils will retreat from a loaded and leveled shotgun. Lindell needs no deliberation to decide he would prefer the shame of turning tail in front of his peers to lighting this codger's fuse. Training a wary eye on his elder opponent, Lindell steps back and bows his head. When Ani reclaims his chair, Arnold nods his approval and turns to Bart.

"May we proceed now?"

His cigar finally lit, Merrell slaps his desk.

"Hear, hear! We're not making money sitting here playing with our giggle sticks. Why don't you give our guest the floor so we can get out of here?"

With the spastic, accommodating nod of a used car salesman, Bart complies. Ani stands, not because he worries his voice will not carry, but out of fundamental respect.

"Gentlemen, I am very much obliged to you for meeting with me today. In his masterpiece *Man and People*, philosopher José Ortega y Gasset reminded us how vital to society is, not only a division of labor, but a commitment on each citizen's part to both preserve and observe the boundaries between vocations. You and I perform essential services for the greater community in a sociopolitical climate we never envisaged when we were children. Though my task is indistinguishable from yours as a practical matter, we nevertheless operate in separate realms. My contract is with the government; yours are with private entities. Though I enjoy tacit State approval, like you I must be scrupulous lest my activities be exposed to certain regulatory bodies. And, like you, I stand to pay the ultimate penalty should the delicate balance among my endeavors be upset by an unanticipated … meddler.

"My brother has trespassed upon your exclusive province, gentlemen. His intentions are immaterial. Still, damage has been done, and I will not insult you by trying to excuse his actions. To atone for his offense, my accountant this morning opened an endowment fund with a sum that represents the going market value of the job he wrongfully appropriated, plus thirty percent for each of you. Before the close of business today, that money will be distributed to fictitious scholarship recipients, each bearing a notable resemblance to one of you. Your accountants assure mine that they will have no trouble converting those awards into legitimate income. My heartfelt congratulations, all – you are now enrolled in *Madame Rosalee's School of Modern Dance and Classical Comportment*."

Amid the raucous laughter and applause, Lindell makes a crack to one of his sidekicks about Merrell in a tutu. The levity is pierced by a savage smacking sound and a thud. With celerity that took his own brother aback, Arnold has burst from his chair, traversed ten feet and backhanded Lindell so hard that the 240-pound mixed martial arts competitor spun half a turn and collapsed into the wall.

"Get out."

The other youths help a foundering Lindell to his feet and lumber under his weight to the far end, where they shuffle out of sight into the covert hallway. As he reacquires his chair, Arnold gestures for Ani to be seated.

"Please excuse the moron of a son which fate has cursed me with. His mother won't let me kill him, but she's great in the sack, so I'm a prisoner of my own cravings."

This plaint spawns only sporadic laughter, and nothing more than a barely perceptible grin from Ani, because everyone in the room understands Arnold is not jesting.

"Ani, you are indeed a gentleman, inspiringly so. And your act of recompense is both generous and fair. But I must ask myself, 'Why does Jarold Stearns not have the courtesy to extend his own apology?' Though your sense of honor has long been proved to me, I question his."

"Let us not kid each other, Arnie. You stopped caring about ideals such as honor in seventh grade when you accepted $34.17 from Sara Craddock to break the hand that Xavier Stosse had stuck up her skirt. My brother's ethics are of no concern to you provided he does not irreparably interfere with your livelihood. As for a personal act of contrition, mutual respect among us aside, if you sincerely think I would let my brother get within a mile of any of the cutthroats in this room before his debt was paid to your satisfaction, you, my friend, are drinking either too much or too little."

Agitator to a fault, Merrell does not deny himself the impish chuckle his associates have bitten their tongues to contain.

"It is not my ambition that you share a Jacuzzi with him in the buff. I simply ask that you cancel any plans you have to harm him over this little indiscretion."

Annoyed by Merrell's incessant guffaws, Arnold appropriates his brother's stapler. The snickering subsides, but the Cheshire grin only broadens.

Arnold strokes his bald head the way other men knead their chin when deep in thought … even moreso when he engages Ani who, over decades of painstaking self-discipline, has rid himself of all unconscious nervous tics.

"Ani, my friend, words don't come to me as handily as they do you. Sometimes I misspeak. I was merely expressing my personal feelings. I don't like your brother. I never did. But, as you have said, my chief motivator is a commercial one."

Arnold retakes his feet. Ani rises in turn.

"For me and my associates, I give you my word that no hurt will come to Jarold on account of this Lynetta Braynard."

The cagey adversaries share a cordial handshake. Arnold reclaims his seat and caresses his dome. Ani remains standing.

"Gentlemen, I will leave you to discuss other matters. Thank you for your time and understanding."

With another bearhug from Bart, and a comradely nod from Merrell, Ani retrieves his outerwear and exits the way he came. As has been his unconscious habit since he was a boy, he takes mental note of seemingly incidental things such as how long it takes the false wall to close behind him, the volume of the intermittent noises emanating from the hallway to the left, how long it takes the elevator to descend to the main floor, the ethnicity and age range of the kitchen and wait staff, the resistance and weight of the revolving door, and the height and number of steps leading to the front door of the meeting room he just vacated, where Arnold pounds his brother's stapler to curb the carping and grumbling that began before Ani had even boarded the elevator.

"My decision is final. You fellas can bitch about it as long as you want. I'm getting a drink. I don't want any company."

WHEN CONVERSING IN PUBLIC, STOP BETWEEN SENTENCES OR THOUGHTS AND TRANSLATE YOUR PREVIOUS STATEMENTS INTO SPANISH SO AS TO NOT OFFEND ANY UNDOCUMENTED-IMMIGRANT EAVESDROPPERS.

This public service announcement is brought to you by the Secretary of the European & Native American Reeducation Board.

Chapter Twelve

Psycho Soufflé

When the last of the unladen horses passes by, Peter hears a commotion behind him. He turns to see a rustic settlement. From the prevalent stench of domesticated animals to the wooden homes with pyramidal roofs, he reckons he has happened upon a late Middle Ages hamlet. To the west, he spies an oak tree on a rocky outcrop from whose lowest branch dangles a human body.

This must be Massachusetts Bay Colony!

Just ten paces ahead of him looms a woman who has been tied to a stake atop a bed of dry grass and twigs. The black cap lying at her feet, as well as the red paragon bodice looped and bordered in silken multicolor threads, dispel any doubt that today is June 10, 1692 – the date on which Puritan settlers executed Bridget Bishop, their first patsy in what history calls the Salem Witch Trials.

The witch hunt was by no means an invention of seventeenth-century American colonists. Condemnation of alleged sorcery is documented as long ago as the eighteenth century BCE in the Code of Hammurabi. And the classical Roman Empire certainly slaughtered its share of victims. Thereafter, the societal obsession for punishing necromancy appeared to wane as luminaries such as Charlemagne, St. Augustine of Hippo and Pope Gregory VII ridiculed the practice as superstitious folly. But the witch paranoia found its resurgence in 1484, when Pope Innocent VIII commissioned two depraved Inquisitors, Heinrich Kramer and Jacob Sprenger, to provide him with a comprehensive report on witchcraft. Two years later, their publication *Malleus Maleficarum* ("Hammer of the Witches") provoked a new papal edict: Christians must hunt down and kill witches. One of the methods the book prescribed for unmasking a witch was to strip her and examine her for bodily imperfections such as moles or "unseemly protrusions." A century later, the accuser's burden of proof was altogether tossed out the window when, in his book *On the Demon-Mania of Sorcerers*, Jean Bodin endorsed the testimony of children against their parents, as well as the use of techniques such as entrapment and undisciplined torture to obtain confessions. The new craze swept across Germany and Denmark, then erupted in Scotland and England. Though the last execution in Europe was ten years past, the witch hysteria breathed its final historical gasp on May 27, 1692, when Governor William Phipps established a Special Court of Oyer and Terminer ("to hear and decide") for Suffolk, Essex and Middlesex counties.

Bridget Bishop was born Bridget Playfair in 1640. Known for her eccentricities and her flair for "taletelling," Bridget operated a tavern in her home on the outskirts of the village. Unusually attractive for both the times and her age, she dressed provocatively and was flirtatious with her male patronage – qualities which made her an easy target for jealous townswomen, as well as her own customers such as Richard Coman, Samuel Shattuck and John Cook, who were only too happy to reclaim the good graces of their prudish wives by blaming their carousals and sexual dalliances and general shortcomings on the contrived black magic spells of Bridget (a copout which comedian Flip Wilson would, three centuries later, parody with his stock phrase "The devil made me do it."). The only "objective" evidence found on Bridget's person was a blemish – most likely a run-of-the-mill cyst – which "shriveled when pricked."

Peter approaches Bridget. No sooner does he feel the weight of a firebrand in his right hand than he hears the taunts and jeers of frenzied villagers who encircle both him and the condemned. From their ranks, a portly man wearing a soiled white robe reads the official warrant:

> To George Corwin Gent^m high Sheriffe of the County of Essex. Greeting.
>
> Whereas Bridgett Bishop als Oliver the wife of Edward Bishop of Salem in the County of Essex, Sawyer, at a speciall court of Oyer and Terminer held at Salem the second Day of this instant month of June for the Countyes of Essex' Middlesex' and Suffolk before William Stoughton esquire and his Associate Justices of the said Court was Indicted and arraigned upon five severall Indictments for useing practiceing and exercising on the nyneteenth day of April last past and divers other dayes and time before and after certain acts of Witchcraft in and upon the bodyes of Abigail Williams Ann puttnam Junior Mercy Lewis Mary Walcott and Elizabeth Hubbard of Salem Village Singlewomen whereby their bodyes were hurt afflicted pined, consumed Wasted and tormented

> contrary to the forme of the Statute in that Case made and provided.
>
> To which Indictment the said Bridgett Bishop pleaded not guilty and for tryall thereof put herselfe upon God and her Country whereupon she was found guilty of the felonys and witchcrafts whereof she stood Indicted and sentence of Death accordingly passed against her as the Law, directs.
>
> Execution where of yet remains to be done.

Drawing nigh the bedraggled scapegoat on the pyre, Peter calls out her name. As though roused from a stupor, the woman slowly raises her head. But this is not the likeness of Bridget Bishop. By every account Peter has read, Bridget was not this shapely. Nor does this woman's brow display the faintest hint of stress.

"Athene?"

"How delightful to see you again, my boy. But do mind your script in front of the townsfolk, and call me Bridget."

Though he realizes he can learn nothing from images that emanate from his own sketchy memory of a story he read in elementary school, Peter is nevertheless fascinated by the scene. To take it all in, he begins to circumnavigate the pyre. As he paces, Athene rotates with him. The rotund prelate, whom Peter supposes to be Reverend Samuel Parris, continues:

> And this shall be your sufficient Warrant. Given under my hand and seal at Boston the Eighth day of June in the fourth yeer of the Reigne of our Sovereigne Lord and Lady William and Mary now King and Queen over England &c Annoq Dom 1692.
>
> Wm. Stoughton
> June 10th 1692

Ignoring Parris as he passes, Peter addresses Athene underbreath: "But Bridget Bishop was hanged, not burned. What are you doing there?"

"How should I know? This is your dream, not mine."

Peter spins on his heel and thrusts the firebrand at her stomach.

"Aha! You admit this is *my* dream, and if it's my dream you are no god and you have no power over me, so I refuse to play this sadistic game!"

He slings the firebrand aside, and it hits Parris in the head.

"Take care what you say and do in front of the rubes, dearest Peter, because pain is real regardless of your conscious state."

Reverend Parris brandishes the firebrand in one hand, a tattered copy of *Malleus Maleficarum* in the other.

"Sheriff Corwin! What is the meaning of this?"

Before Peter can answer, Athene lets loose a bone chilling cackle and spits at the bovine magistrate.

"'Twas I seized the sheriff's burning sticks and cast them away! How wouldst thou harm the devil with her own form of play?"

Peter turns again to Athene.

"Mind *my* script? Bridget never confessed, and only pompous playwrights speak in rhyme."

"I hardly see how that's relevant here, my dear boy."

By now, Parris has waddled to Peter's side.

"See here, Sheriff. You have your warrant. The Lord's Holy Word is quite clear in the book of Exodus, chapter twenty-two verse eighteen: 'Thou shalt not suffer a witch to live.' There was to be one burning today, but we can abide two."

"Psst … holy man!"

Parris turns to witness Athene's garments fall away. As his eyes dilate, she blows him a kiss.

"Come closer, and let mommy cure all that ails you."

Parris approaches her, hopelessly transfixed, until she transforms herself into a hag with festering boils. She then expels a stream of fire at him and cackles as he topples over backwards, then crawls to the cover of the receding crowd.

"Like the pig said, *Sheriff*, there will be a burning today. So step to, let's have done with it."

Though he never felt the exchange, the firebrand is again in Peter's grasp. He chunks it away. This time, it lands in the haystack just outside Increase Mather's barn. The crowd disperses to battle the ensuing conflagration. Peter storms the pyre and tries to release Athene, but the ropes ravel themselves the instant he has untied them.

"You must burn me, Sheriff, for I have kissed Satan's arse. I am a heretic. I bewitched the Bly sow. I set the black man upon young Susanna Sheldon. And, yes, 'twas I despoiled the virgin lad William Stacy." She shuts her eyes, her tongue caressing her upper lip in a spasm of wanton relish. "And such a flavorful young man he was!"

"Stop it! You were convicted of a crime that was logically impossible to prove because you were an assertive and self-sufficient woman in a society that epitomized priggishness and bigotry!"

Another firebrand appears. Peter drops it. It floats across the town square and deposits itself beneath the eave of the church. Flanked now by fire and billowy smoke, an exasperated Peter squares off with the toying goddess.

"Burn me, Sheriff!"

"You did nothing wrong, and these people are existential ... *re*tards!"

"But you are judging my accusers and me according to twenty-first century values. Morality can not be divorced from the unique culture in which it was devised. Thus, mores are neither universal nor transcendent. You must burn me!"

"No!"

"If you refuse to burn me in this specific place and time, you are immoral."

"I can't turn a blind eye to the lessons history has taught me."

"So which is the chicken, Peter, and which the egg? Does morality dictate human behavior, or does societal caprice reinvent morality with each new generation?"

"*All* morality is of divine origin!"

"Is it, now? I know for a fact that you and Deanna copulated twenty-seven times before you were even engaged to be married; yet her family did not stone her to death at the door of her father's house as instructed three thousand years ago in the book of Deuteronomy. She and you engaged in one hundred forty-three spousal acts of sex; yet you conceived only two children. Four millennia ago, your most ancient scripture told of poor Onan who was killed for employing contraception. Fully twelve percent of your very own congregation, Peter, is of a homosexual persuasion. But according to crusty old Moses, such a practice is an abomination. Either there is a divine mandate, or the man reputed to have the most finely tuned ear for the voice of the Big Boss was lying. It's your move, *Reverend*."

"I'm not falling for that trick. You ignore the fact that your own son spoke in parables so that the full breadth of his truths could be realized as each successive culture became wiser than the last. God's word was simplistic, pedestrian back then because he was talking to societal infants."

"Is that so? According to the same *holy* scribe, in the same time period, the following laws were handed down to the same generation by the same Grand Dictator: 'Thou shalt have no other gods before me; Thou shalt not take the name of the Lord thy God in vain; Remember the sabbath day, to keep it holy; Thou shalt not kill; Thou shalt not commit adultery; Thou shalt not bear false witness against thy neighbour; Thou shalt not covet thy neighbour's house, thou shalt not covet thy neighbour's wife, nor his manservant, nor his maidservant, nor his ox, nor his ass, nor any thing that is thy neighbour's.' You yourself, Peter Mott, preach these commandments verbatim to your supposedly far more sophisticated flock no less than five times a year."

"Some concepts … are … easier to understand."

"Let us return to that little missive about not killing, shall we? My son allegedly exhorted his followers: 'But I say unto you that you resist not evil, but whosoever shall smite you on your right cheek, turn to him the other also'; and 'Love your enemies, bless them that curse you, do good to them that hate you, and pray for them who despitefully use you and persecute you.' And we must not forget that bombastic little busybody, the manic prattler formerly known as Saul: 'Vengeance is mine; I will repay, saith the Lord.'

"But in the same geographical hotbed of religious prankery, Muhammad decreed: 'Paradise is for him who holds the reins of his horse to strive in Allah's cause, with his hair unkempt and feet covered with dust'; 'My livelihood is under the shade of my spear, and he who disobeys my orders will be humiliated by paying Jizya'; 'I have been ordered to fight with the people 'til they say, *None has the right to be worshiped but Allah*'; 'Fight those who believe not in God nor the last day, nor hold that forbidden which hath been forbidden by God and His Apostle, nor acknowledge the religion of truth, until they pay the jizya with willing submission and feel themselves subdued. The Jews call Uzair a son of

God, and the Christians call Christ the Son of God ... God's curse be on them; how they are deluded away from the truth!'

"Which god is real, Peter? Yahweh, the neutered psycho-killer in this hemisphere, or Allah, the rabid psycho-killer in the other? Who wins the pedagogical title fight? Answer me, halfwit!"

With a thousand voices chattering in his head, Peter thrashes in a sea of concordances and commentators, but he must finally admit that the colors with which the busiest minds of history have painted the *Primordial Why* have shed not the faintest light upon its answer. He is left with only suppositions and contradictions and silence.

The smoke has cleared. The villagers again converge on their Sheriff and his quarry. As Peter eyes each in turn, Athene chants from the pyre.

"My addled executioner has no answer to the simplest of questions."

Reverend Parris' meaty jowls are, once again, in Peter's face.

"The witch presses a most probative question, Sheriff. Are you of a self-effacing mind? Or will you accede to your duty this day?!"

Peter cares less for his slumbrous comfort than he does for this vamp who chides him in the throes of a sentence she'll never serve. *This is my dream, and it is only a dream, and I will not condone the idiocy of my ancestors!* He takes his corpulent antagonist by the alb and dunks him in a nearby horse trough, then kicks him to the dirt and turns on the villagers.

"She is not a witch! There are no witches! If you people weren't so afraid of ... pleasure, you'd know that!"

Cotton Mather strikes Peter on the temple with a horseshoe, and the rabble converge. As they immerse his head in the trough, he hears Athene midst his own guttural gulps.

"Now, Peter! Now you must confront your demon, whose name you know so well, and lift yourself, if you can, from the morass of your own ambivalent mind!"

Peter aspirates slimy water, hears the familiar thunder of hooves. The last of the riderless horses kicks him free.

WE DON'T STOP FOR SHIT

He tumbles through muck, landing on a gravel path that reeks of sewage in a deserted, open field, a line of trees to his right and a brook to his left. Having just found his feet, he dives to the dirt again as a black

1963 Cadillac Coupe de Ville roars from the treeline, stopping in a fury of dust and rock just inches from his nose. The driver door creaks open. A crimson crocodile cowboy boot with gilt toecap steps down from behind it. Above it emerge black leather pants and a black leather duster that compliment a crimson pleated shirt, topped off with a black Stetson cowboy hat, beneath which grimace the hard-chiseled features of …

"Johnny Cash?"

"Don't flatter me, son; it'll do you no damned good."

"But you're the spitting image –"

The spectre in black points a weathered finger at Peter's throat, causing it to seize.

"Name's Death, son. And I'm too pretty to resemble any human. Now, you pissant mortal, would you like to breathe again?"

"Yes … please …"

"Follow me. Time, like you, is short."

Cash marches toward the trees. Peter reluctantly follows. They walk for what seems half an hour, an hour, then two. But the trees are no closer than when they started. Weary, Peter slows his pace.

"Where are we going?"

Cash stops, but does not turn away from the trees.

"We're already there. Turn around."

Peter pivots to find a freshly dug grave at his feet. Now clad in dirt-caked work boots, bluejeans speckled with grass and manure, torn double-ply shirt and shearling coat, Cash glowers at him from the opposite side.

"Step to, son."

"You expect me to jump in there? Voluntarily? Go back to hell, or heaven, or a Bahamian beach inside a submarine … wherever Elvis and the other maniacs are playing. I've had enough of this –"

Without moving a muscle, Cash disappears from the far side of the grave and instantaneously materializes just millimeters from Peter's nose. Again, Peter finds himself gasping for air.

"Don't you ever, *ever*, speak that name in my presence! Sure, he may have been a teenybop-pop star for a time, but I never forsook the purity of my craft. And you can't ignore longevity. But I digress. I was not asking."

An invisible hand seizes Peter by his shirt collar, another by his belt, and they hurl him headlong into the pit. Though he has no sensation of depth or speed, he figures he must be falling far and fast when he looks back to see a graveside Cash recede at a dizzying rate. Nor does he detect an impact when he alights on a solid footing. He now stands atop a glassy surface that emits a rich, purplish light. Only this violet underglow sets Peter apart from the sea of pitch all around him as he walks without purpose on feet unshod.

He hears a woman bellow. Her voice is familiar. A stainless steel door that didn't exist seconds ago now yields to an operating room, where a doctor sits at a stool peering neath the green gown of a woman in stirrups as nurses mill around on the periphery. A man in light blue scrubs stands beside her, wiping her forehead. Closer now, he can see that the woman is Deanna and the man himself, twenty-eight years past. A flush of exuberance overtakes him as he realizes he is about to relive the birth of his darling Millie.

Now he *is* his younger self.

"You're doing great, Dee. Short breath, short breath, deep breath, relax."

The doctor orders her to push again. Peter cups her clammy shoulders in his hands, but she wags a frantic finger.

"No, honey, no, I want you to be the first person she sees."

"You'll be all right?"

"I've got it, go, go, go!"

Giddy, Peter hurries to his station at the doctor's side.

"Her head should be coming any second now. There … there … I can feel …"

What the doctor removes from the labia resembles not Peter's remotest expectations.

"Doctor … is this normal?"

The room falls dark except for one overhead light. The doctor and nurses vanish. A tall, black-hooded silhouette obstructs Peter's view of Deanna. He reaches to push it aside, but his hands find only empty space. Sensing a balmy wetness, Peter looks down to see that his pants are drenched in blood. The shadow turns to face him. From beneath the hood, Cash peers down at him, then lifts his gaze, fixing it upon something just over Peter's right shoulder. Peter follows those penetrant eyes to the lifeless body of fourteen-year-old Millie. Lying naked on an autopsy table, she has not yet been cleaned. Burn marks like snakebites, roughly the diameter of an automotive cigarette lighter, bespeckle her left breast and inner thighs like buckshot spray. Her hands that once so nimbly frolicked about the piano keys bear the countless slashing wounds which bespeak her struggle. The greenish blue of the handprint on her neck and the bruises on her battered face is augmented by the pallor of her anemic skin.

Retching and convulsing, Peter is helpless to resist the invisible hand which presses him closer. Millie's head turns in the block. She opens bewildered eyes and, though her lips are mangled and only one front tooth remains in place, her diction is flawless.

"Why, Daddy? How did I fail you? What did Dylan do to deserve this?"

Peter follows her gaze to her right hand, in whose palm rests the mangled member of his son.

"What have you done, Daddy?"

***

It was 3:20 a.m. when Mira mounted the latest addition to her coonskin cap collection. She suffers neither nighttime nor morning insomnia; she has simply adjusted her schedule to follow the chaotic pattern of her boss' waking nightmares. Noticing three days ago the particular strain of aloofness which usually heralds an episode, Mira has taken to rising every morning at 2:45 so that she can be alert and available by the time Peter reemerges – his awakenings have occurred as early as 4:00 a.m.

She arrives at the church at 3:58. Though her office is closer to the sanctuary on the east side of the building, she hates fighting with its gargantuan, leaded glass doors, preferring instead to enter at the north end. Plodding the long hallway, past the classrooms and the kitchen and the special events parlor, she hears an intermittent tapping noise. Wondering if it might be a water pipe, she turns west toward the utility closet, but the sound fades. She doubles back. It grows louder as she nears the sanctuary. By the time she has reached the side entrance, the tapping has grown into a clunk, interspersed with a wailing sound.

Behind the choir loft stands a massive wooden cross, 40 feet tall with crossmembers that span half that length. Mira follows the clamor up the steps to find Peter kneeling at the cross' base, pounding his forehead against it and weeping and howling.

"Mister … Peter!"

She bounds to the top of the loft two steps at a time and tackles him, her momentum tumbling them both into an amplifier stand next to the organ. Bracing her back against the organ's skirting, she cradles his torso and enfolds his legs in hers. Her own tears commingle with his as she kisses his wound, rocking him to the rhythm of her own tormented screams which she directs, not at the heavens but at Peter.

"Stop it! Stop it! He breaks his back for you! Leave him be!"

IF YOU ARE RELATIVELY SKINNY OR PHYSICALLY FIT, WEAR BAGGY AND BULKY CLOTHING IN PUBLIC SO THAT YOU DON'T OFFEND THOSE WITH A CORPULENCE DISABILITY.

This public service announcement is brought to you by the First First Gentleman and First Ex-President to Serve as First Gentleman and Only Ex-President to Service as First First Gentleman's Campaign to Perpetuate the Delusion that the First Black (Well, Not Completely, But Moreso than Her Husband) First Lady Is Relevant and to Deemphasize the First Mostly Black First Lady's Posterior Immensity.

Chapter Thirteen

Relief Denied Even to Prayer

January 18 – 6:35 a.m.

Noble is an underspoken town. Occupying just thirteen square miles, the only reason passers through notice it is because the oldest of its only two stoplights marks the point at which Highway 77 abruptly bottlenecks from five lanes into two and the speed limit plummets to a comatose 25 mph.

At the southeast corner of Main and Chestnut, the morning crew at Tiffany's begins preparing breakfast every weekday at 5:05. But the enspiriting aroma of bacon, eggs and pancakes did not greet the adjoining neighborhood today and, though opening time has long elapsed, the walls strewn with glossies of Audrey Hepburn remain dark and the parking spaces out front deserted. Across Chestnut, Dave's Small Engine Repair keeps somewhat saner hours. Just the same, the owner and his daughter can often be heard in the back room tinkering with lawnmowers as early as 6:00. But no wrenches are ratcheting this Monday, no spark plugs sputtering. Eerily silent, too, are the post office and convenience store which bookend downtown proper. It appears to Charlie Gauge, the Sheriff's Deputy who stands aside his patrol car peering from one end of town to the other and scratching his head, that every Noble resident has gone on strike.

8:24 a.m.

Julia Bross' personal office is a mystery to all but her closest friends and select employees. She prefers to conduct business meetings in her well-appointed conference room one floor below. This arrangement works nicely because most visitors would scarcely know what to do once they had breached her doorway. In lieu of the stereotypical power-desk and leather chair, her computer screens and peripherals sit atop a waist-high, mahogany shelf that spans the south wall, where she stands while she works. To either side of her hang plasma televisions, three devoted to the domestic, European and Asian stock tickers and the last dedicated to world news. Against the fully windowed wall at the north end stands an unplugged *TreadClimber* which serves as a coat tree, and the hanging beads on the west wall lead to a full bath with shower, Jacuzzi tub, dressing area and walk-in closet. The only remaining furniture is the occasional, haphazardly positioned beanbag chair – usually flung against the east wall because, on the rare occasions Julia sits, she prefers to do so cross-legged on the floor.

Julia's work attire in this inner sanctum consists of a cotton t-shirt and either threadbare painter's pants or cutoff sweats. Whenever she has to conduct a video conference, she need only don the silk kerchief and linen blazer that hang from the valet just two steps out of frame. Always barefoot when not in the conference room, her most reliable stress-relieving technique is to pivot the ball of her right foot on the short-pile carpet as if she were extinguishing a cigarette.

Having just emerged from the lavatory with her hair in a towel and a toothbrush in her jaw, she heeds an urgent text from her aunt by switching on the morning news.

Host: Continuing our coverage of the developing tragedy in Oklahoma, the city of Noble boasts a population of 7,243 according to the last census. Early estimates are that fully one half of the residents are deceased.

Hostess: This just in, Preston – that number has been increased to 4,500 as emergency responders comb the residential areas.

Host: One of those responders is Dorla Vourney, an Emergency Medical Technician from the neighboring town of Purcell.

Vourney: *Sue-real.* Ain't no other way to describe it. Whole families just drifted off while they was asleep. Others expired on the couch or at the eatin' table. Critters, too. The few survivors we seen live out in the rural areas. They didn't hear nothing. In fact, one gentleman said last evening was *quawter* than ever' other.

Julia berates in a froth of toothpaste, "How is it that you east coast pricks always manage to find the only person within fifty miles who sounds like a hillbilly?!"

Hostess: Ms. Vourney mentioned family pets. One thing that appears certain right now is that anything or anyone who was inside a house didn't make it through the night, but dogs and horses and stray cats outside survived.

Host: Strange happenings, indeed, Sherry. While authorities will not venture a guess as to the cause of this massive loss of life, the odds of so many people spontaneously meeting the same fate at the same time are astronomical, which makes the cryptic message published last Friday all the more ominous.

Hostess: In a press release issued from Gujranwala, Pakistan, Muhannad ibn Saheim, one of the eighty detainees released from Guantanamo in 2015, and the man now widely recognized as the leader of Al Qaeda, warned the United States of an impending attack, quote – which will make the incident of 9/11/01 look like the amusement of a child – end quote.

Host: He proceeded to identify the exact date it would occur, which is today, and the time of day – before dawn. "You can not stop it, because you will not see it, and you will not even hear it."

Hostess: He closes the communiqué: "In the name of Allah, death to the kuffar," that last word, of course, referring to non-Muslims.

On the rare occasion when she accepts a guest in this office, Julia grants them a four-minute window of access by incorporating their thumbprint into a logarithm that updates every fifteen seconds. This has far less to do with security than with the random way her mind works – so easily is she distracted by new tangents of thought that she relies almost entirely on her personal assistants and meeting attendees to keep her punctual. At 9:12, Connie triggers the magnetic lock on the office door to find Julia standing motionless in the center of the room, stark naked but for the terry-turban on her head, gawking at the overhead news as though she were watching the mythical Second Coming, a pasty spearmint trail snaking from the corner of her mouth to just shy of her left nipple.

"Jule … Julie?"

Julia jabs the toothbrush at her like a conductor's wand, never averting her eyes from the broadcast.

"No, nu'uh, shoosh!"

Connie edges in far enough to let the door fall to, kicks off her shoes, then warily joins her friend and employer at mid-office.

Host:	And now, live from the Rose Garden, the First Female President of the United States.
Hostess:	That is definitely not her.
Host:	Correction, this is the First Mostly Nonwhite President of the United States.
Hostess:	Sour grapes over the election results?
Host:	Or she's afraid she'll say something completely off the wall and contrary to her party's talking points, like she and her running mate did so often during the campaign.
Hostess:	Let's listen.

First Mostly Nonwhite U.S. President

Good morning. People in small towns all across America are the backbone of this country. They get up early every morning, run the kids off to school, and go to the field and work from sunshine to sundark to provide the stables of life for the rest of us. This is why they've been called the sod of the earth.

Last night, one such town was devastated. We don't have an official count, so I won't guess on how many souls were lost. But I know that the American people stand united in holding the families of these self-sanitizing farmers and merchants in our thoughts and prayers.

Now there has been some speculation as to what caused this travesty, but I urge everyone to be patient and not rush to judgment until the experts have a chance to get in there and … do what they do. Above all, let's not go jumping to the occlusion that this was a terrorist attack. In a world of tsunamis and hurricanes and earthquakes … that's just crazy talk. And if we go hypotheticalizing about terrorism, then we start pointing accusatating fingers here at home. Some might take incoming President Olm to task for the unmutilated disrespect he heaps on the sacred institutions of this land. Others would have to rehash all the failed foreign and economic policies of the Bush administration that my successor, *the First Shemale President*, is still struggling to impair as she packs up to leave office. To borrow an old saying, from scripture I think, terrorism is in the eye of the freeholder.

Since our founding, the United States has been a nation that respects all faiths. We reject all efforts to criticize the religious prejudices of others. And during my eight years in office, I spent every awake moment building bridges to forage the new beginning I promised between the west and the Muslamic world – my legacy to all you nice little folks down there who work your little hineys off so smart people like me can live tall on the log. So I call on the new President to hear my call to embrace our brothers and sisters across the water, because in this time of crisis, fingerpointing must give way to placating.

Thank you. May God bless the memoir of those we lost and may God bless the United States of America.

Connie disappears through the beads and reappears with a moist towel and a kimono. Draping the kimono around Julia's shoulders, she wipes her face with one hand while she terminates the newsfeed with the other.

"Uppish patrician."

Julia turns, her face aglaze with the incredulity of a loyal dog that just got kicked by its master.

"Mothers … fathers … sons and daughters and kittens … unfulfilled dreams and unfinished class projects … no opportunity to make tomorrow's kiss better than yesterday's …." A derelict tear resurrects the hygienic trail, diverting it toward her right breast. "Who's going to feed all the little lambs now?"

As impregnable as she is in the boardroom, Julia Bross regresses to preadolescence when faced with the brutality human beings inflict upon each other beyond the bounds of climate-controlled, right-angled cubicles. Though Connie commiserates, she considers it her moral duty to withstand the urge to pitch a sorority-sister pity party.

"The man should check his facts. Farming comprises only point-zero-three percent of that town's economy."

"Does it matter?"

"Everything matters."

"So many people, Connie. How do we make sense?"

Kimono tied and skin wiped, Julia gropes for the beanbag chair Connie has positioned below her. Connie grabs two more, sits in one and props her feet beside Julia's on the other.

"Moms, pops, babies and puppies die. Tomorrow is just a broken promise. There's no right or wrong in it. But what do I know? I'm just an amateur philosopher."

"How can you be so flippant about forty-five hundred deaths?"

"Why are forty-five hundred any worse than one?"

"I hate this kimono."

"Next time, dress yourself before you go catatonic."

Convulsed by a pang of unwanted laughter, Julia hops to her feet and retreats through the dangling beads to find more suitable attire. Connie takes the opportunity to plug the minidrive Ani gave her into the hub beneath Julia's center monitor. She then retrieves the remote, and retasks the monitors and plasma screens so that the drive's contents are splashed across seven portals of information.

"Hey, Con."

"Burnie."

Only two people enjoy unlimited access to Julia's mercantile hideout: Connie and Julia's top assistant Burnice, who ducks into the office long enough to set a tray with a carafe of hot tea and cups on a small table. As he departs, Connie strolls to the opposite wall to gaze down upon the pixel-like people who fritter about like forager bees. Lost in their vertiginous patterns, she doesn't notice Julia's return until she has filled the cups and joined her.

"Why are you here?"

Connie gestures toward the closest monitor.

"My report on Messrs. Stearns and Mott."

Julia tosses her head and fidgets with the disappointment of a kindergartner who asked for a birthday pony but received a stuffed giraffe.

"Oh, you know I hate raw data!"

Connie pats her shoulder.

"I'll give you the overview and you can rummage later for details."

Julia follows her confidant back to the beanbags but, unlike Connie, she assumes her favorite position on the floor, bunching the beanbag in her lap as an armrest.

"First, Jule, tell me everything you know about what happened to Mott in Oregon."

"He and Deanna had always dreamed of living there. I can't recall exactly when they made the move … I spent a lot of time abroad in those years. Anyway, some freak murdered their children. Next I heard, Deanna had left and Peter had moved back home."

"You didn't follow the trial?"

"Of the killer?"

"No, Mott."

"What? Peter? No, Connie, don't kid about a thing like that."

"The man they convicted, Herzog, it took the police eleven days to track down. Mott was arrested that very night. When they sifted through all the physical evidence, they determined Herzog was the main actor. But, Julie, the same evidence pointed to an accomplice."

Julia senses that familiar, fuzzy pang in her abdomen. Her initial impulse is to fling the hot tea in Connie's face, but holding that cup steady somehow keeps a lid on her panic.

"How dare you sit there and tell me something like that? I know Peter Mott."

"And I *knew* my husband."

"Get out! And take that … memory thing with you. I don't want to hear any more."

Keenly aware that Julia is focusing all her faculties on the stability of her teacup, Connie deposits her own, takes to her knees, sweeps the beanbags aside and crawls to within inches of her friend's quavering nostrils.

"What did you tell me the day you hired me? 'Connie, I too often find myself adrift in my emotions, clinging to my presuppositions. I need someone to throw the facts in my face, to tell me the truth when I least want to hear it.'"

She then takes Julia's hands and jerks them upward, dousing her own face in chai. Retrieving a napkin from the tea tray, she calmly dabs her chin.

"That was a freebie. You want me out of here? Throw me out. Otherwise, sit there, shut up and let me do my job."

Holding her stare, Julia scrunches her nose like a schoolgirl who's being teased. Connie reclaims her beanbag.

"Now there's truth and there's overkill. I'll save you the grisly particulars. But understand that the children were not just killed; they were sexually assaulted and mutilated. Mott's story was that he was taking Millie and Dylan out that night for pizza and a movie. Approaching that age where every little girl wants to seize the slightest opportunity for independence, Millie begged him the entire way to let her take Dylan inside, order and pay for the pizza, then text him to come in and join them. Ten minutes passed, then fifteen, but no text came. Mott went inside to find the children missing. He drove to the theatre down the street, but couldn't find them there. He drove all over the city, then the surrounding areas, until he found their bodies in the rock quarry. He gathered them up and laid them in the back seat. A patrolman stopped him for excessive speed. But here is where Mott's rendition departs from the evidence. The crime scene experts have a way of differentiating premortem blood from postmortem. Two samples of Dylan's blood proved that he and his sister were taken to the quarry, alive, in Mott's car. And, at the scene of the murders, there is a stream of Millie's parimortem blood –"

"Perry who?"

"Parimortem. Blood that was spilled at the time of death. There is a stream that extends from her body's final place of rest to the edge of a tire track that matches Mott's front left tire. Samples from its hub and the car's front quarter panel demonstrate that the car was sitting there when her throat was slashed. So was an adult human male, evidenced by a distinct void in the blood spatter on the same quarter panel."

Julia's body flinches the way it does sometimes when she is falling asleep. Groping for control over the moment, she pulls the beanbag to her chin and buries her face in it.

"Though Mott claimed there was a phantom accomplice, the only identifiable DNA was Herzog's, which was found both outside and inside each of the children. Of course, Mott was covered in their blood, and his DNA was all over them – facts which are, standing alone, inconclusive. But the trooper stopped him traveling toward his home, in the opposite direction from the hospital. And the cops soon learned that Mott and Herzog knew each other prior to that night. They'd had dealings that summer when Mott was involved in a community outreach program affiliated with the halfway house Herzog had been paroled to from a two-year stint for heroin trafficking."

Without raising her head from the beanbag, Julia flutters her hands for Connie to pause, then she uncoils and plods to the north wall to scour the building tops in search of diversionary solace.

"You mentioned a trial? He was obviously acquitted."

"They were prosecuted separately, Mott first. The defense tactic was to blame the inconsistencies of Mott's story on the trauma of finding his children in such a horrific state. But what tipped the scales in Mott's favor, I think, was that his lawyer attacked the prosecutor herself. Years earlier, she had convicted a dentist of killing his wife. The single piece of circumstantial evidence she had hung her hat on was that this husband of twenty-four years, who had discovered his wife in the bathtub with a gaping abdominal wound, didn't have a trace of her blood on him. Mott's lawyer turned her logic against her, asserting that Mott, the devoted father, was so distraught that he cared nothing for his Belvest suitpants and Armani shirt in his frantic quest to rush his children home to the safety of their mother's arms."

"But he *was* acquitted."

"So was O.J. And within days of his acquittal, Mott sold everything, moved seventeen hundred miles, found Jesus and reinvented himself."

Julia turns to Connie, falls back against the glass and clasps herself with both arms.

"Do you think he was guilty?"

"We're all guilty, Julie, of something or other."

"I just can't believe he was capable."

"You realize who you're talking to, right? Like you, I was raised on frilly dresses and playhouses. I relied on the beneficence of others, I believed I had a fairy-godmother, until the man I had pinned all my aspirations to tried to lop my head off. I sure as hell discovered some latent skills that day."

On her sixteenth birthday, Julia's father did two things she will forever remember. He presented her with the brand new, baby blue Volkswagen Bug she had coveted since fifth grade. Then, without a word, he kissed her on the forehead, lumbered to his El Camino and motored away. Her mother explained matter-of-factly that she and her father didn't love each other anymore.

"So you just stop that sniveling and clean up these dishes. I promised the ladies at Rotary I'd bring leftover cake tonight, and I will not be late or made a fool of."

There was idle talk of an SEC probe, federal indictments and some fracas in Nevada that left a casino owner with only nine fingers. Whatever the truth of these allegations, Julia never saw or heard from her father again. From that day until she parted with it nearly a decade later, that shiny new car was both an escape and a prison cell – though it rescued her from the tedium of her mother's regimented life, it served as a constant reminder of her father's desertion. In similar fashion, though she is cerebrally intrigued with these newest truths about her childhood pal, she hates herself for having pursued them. She closes her eyes and sinks to the floor, imagining … wishing that the window were a magic portal to blissful ignorance.

Connie kneels at her side.

"Jule, this is the terror of justice, the thin ice on which vengeance treads. The facts can pile up all livelong day. But in the end you assign your own meaning to each colorless datum, bringing to bear your own history with its successes and failures and dreams and dreads. I'm not judging your friend. I'm simply explaining Mr. Stearns' interest in him."

The mere mention of that name jars Julia from her daze.

"So what is that … goon's business? And don't you dare tell me he's just a lawyer."

5:15 p.m.

Across Main Street from Tiffany's, a wrought iron park bench squats beneath a street lamp. A rather large, pleasant looking man dressed meticulously in a handmade Italian suit has sat patiently there since very early this morning. He has watched Sheriff units come and go. He has watched city police stretch yellow tape from tree to fence to stair railing. He has watched rescue trucks meander into and out of alleyways. He has watched one coroner's truck arrive, then pull away to make room for a larger one. He has watched lookieloos drive as close as they could for a wanton thrill. He has watched television crews descend upon this little municipality like scavengers on the Serengeti. He has watched dazed next of kin being corralled into the fairgrounds carnival tent that has been turned into a makeshift command headquarters. He has watched Assistant Medical Examiner Bo Mizener crawl beneath a fire engine to weep.

He continues to watch as Captain Soos coaxes Bo out of hiding with coffee and a candy bar. He reveals no trepidation when Bo meets his gaze, turns to Soos and asks, "How long's he been sitting there?"

"Don't know. He was in that very spot when I came on scene pretty near eight o'clock."

Nor does he flee when the men approach him.

Still, he watches.

But he does not see.

"Looks like a wallet in his breast pocket."

"Jarold Bertrand Stearns."

"I'll take this to the tent."

"Huh uh, the Sheriff's doing notifications."

"Okay, then. Need help loading him up?"

"Nah, I'll get a gurney."

"Hang in there, Bo. There's an end to all this. Dead can't breed more dead, you know."

"You sure about that?"

IF ATTACKED, EVEN WITHOUT PROVOCATION, ONLY RESPOND IN KIND. UNDER NO CIRCUMSTANCE SHOULD YOU RETALIATE WITH GREATER FORCE. THIS WILL GIVE YOUR ASSAILANT TIME TO RETHINK HIS OR HER MOTIVATIONS, AND YOU AN OPPORTUNITY TO WIN OVER HIS OR HER HEART AND MIND, SO THAT THE TWO OF YOU MAY USE THIS TEACHABLE MOMENT TO BECOME FRIENDS.

This public service announcement is brought to you by the First Female President and First First Lady to Become President and Only Former First Lady to Become the First Female President's Task Force on Equality of Outcome.

Chapter Fourteen

That Which Transcends

Julia sits open-legged on her office floor like a forsaken Raggedy Ann doll, casting a faraway gaze at the closest monitor which bears the image of a rose colored grave marker:

Maura Vevina Casey Stearns
January 2, 1975 to April 8, 2014
Pleasant Dreams, My Beloved –
May We Meet Again Some Sunny Day

Before leaving six hours ago, Connie spent the balance of the morning divulging every significant event of Anthony Wayne Stearns' double life, from that Sunday in 1978 when he squared accounts over the merciless beating of Jarold to his elaborate execution of Freddie Herzog just over two weeks past. Connie had to chase after Julia more than once to steady her as she gagged in the sink.

But it was not the violence and gore that vexed Julia so. With each new anecdote about Stearns' exploits, Connie systematically dismantled the world as Julia had perceived it from the moment she first respired. Even as she imagined her very own father fleeing authorities, Julia took consolation from her bedrock assumption that laws and courts and clean-shaven men with badges and guns were all that was necessary to hold tragedy at bay on the periphery of her life. But today she was constrained to accept the fact that no less than five of her employees, as well as her very own cousin, owed their lives directly and solely to the illicit methods of Stearns.

Then Julia heard a tale of such grace, had Connie not spun it, she'd have thought it depicted any man in history *but* Stearns.

Maura Casey was the Assistant District Attorney who conducted the preliminary hearing against Connie in *State v. Plachette* in the summer of 2009. She had barely begun her direct examination of Sr. Agbayani when her boss stormed into the courtroom, whispered to her "Follow my lead and don't say a word," then announced to a befuddled judge: "The State hereby dismisses both counts of the indictment, with prejudice to their refiling, and with my heartfelt apology to Ms. Plachette."

He then discharged Sr. Agbayani most unceremoniously and vanished as quickly as he had entered, leaving Maura alone to pack up her notes and evidence. As she strained to see through the tears of anger and humiliation welling up in her eyes, it was her opponent who stepped forward to assist her. Stacking three banker's boxes onto her dolly, he hoisted the fourth upon his shoulder and escorted her to the elevator, advising colleagues and laity to await the next car. As the doors fell to, Ani mercifully broke the tomblike silence.

"Ms. Casey, I hope you will not confuse the brusqueness of your employer with the remotest lack of confidence in your skills. I have known the man for half of your lifetime, and I can assure you he would not have given you first-chair responsibilities if he did not trust you implicitly."

"Respectfully, Mr. Stearns, your client diced her husband like a master chef. I'm in no mood for your sympathy."

"Who lay in wait for whom, Ms. Casey, and who struck the first blow?"

"I can stomach one fatal wound. I can even grant her the benefit of the doubt for two. But three? There's a difference between self-defense and reprisal."

"And I would ask you to consider, Ms. Casey, that the latter is often an integral component of the former. But this argument is moot, is it not?"

One floor shy of their destination, the elevator stopped. The jarring of the brake loosed a stream of tears from Maura's saturated lids. Pressing a handkerchief into her hand, Ani stepped into the doorway to block the Chief District Judge and two probate magistrates from entering.

"If you don't mind, gentlemen, the lady needs some privacy."

Relieved of her emotional gust, Maura reclaimed poise enough to ask this man what virtually everyone in the courthouse wanted to know by now.

"What just happened in there? Prelims are only formalities in which the prosecution's burden of proof is next to nil. This one would have been a cakewalk with my evidence."

"That was my doing. You see, I learned years ago that a criminal defendant almost always loses at trial. Among the factors stacked against him are a jaded, overburdened judge and societal prejudice. I win my criminal cases, not in the courtroom, but outside of it."

"So how did you win this one?"

"Now, now, Ms. Casey, to divulge such privileged information would jeopardize my relationship with your employer, thus abridging the rights of my future clients. Worse yet, I suspect it would besmirch my reputation in the eyes of a fetching young prosecutor to whom I have taken quite a shine."

"Don't flatter yourself."

When the car finally alit at her stop, Maura seized the box from Ani's shoulder. Straining beneath its weight, she wrested the handcart from his grasp and lumbered through the doorway. When the well snagged her heel, she stumbled. Ani lurched forward, but she recovered and barked over her shoulder without breaking stride.

"Stay!"

Later that afternoon, Ani was regaling a contingent of his senior associates with the story of this plucky new junior prosecutor with curly hair and pouting lips reminiscent of actress Bernadette Peters, when a courier handed him an envelope addressed to The Head Scofflaw. Inside he found Maura's business card on whose reverse she had penned: *You may treat me to dinner, but take heed – I don't fool around with smartasses or dilettantes.*

Ani parlayed that dinner date into another and, as the weeks segued into months, the cagey litigators grew deeply fond of each other. What enamoured Ani so was that Maura, though some years his junior, exhibited discernment far beyond women of his generation. Unable to deny her intellectual curiosity about Ani's alternative interpretation of *legal services*, she engaged him often in rambling debates on the subject. Just the same, she guarded the integrity of her office by insisting that he never tell her the specifics of his extrajudicial undertakings. She didn't like this wink-of-the-eye arrangement any more than he but, a staunch adherent to the axiom that knowledge alone can not rise to the level of wisdom until it is infused with intestinal fortitude, she understood the practical reality that what is beneficial to society is not always socially acceptable.

Though each disdained the ritual as a throwback to a barbarous era in which women were regarded as chattel, it was their shared sense of pragmatism which motivated them to marry. Because his vocation so often strayed beyond the law, Ani strove to portray conventionality whenever possible. And, as her star rose through the pecking order of county politics, Maura availed herself of as many anachronistic customs as she could abide. But they would only bend so far for appearances. Therefore, the consummation of their partnership unfolded in three phases. The first order of business was to meet with the same Chief Judge to whom Ani had denied elevator access two years earlier, who incorporated by reference into their marriage license the mutual prenuptial agreement they had prepared. They then stole away to Belize with their closest friends and family, where two weeks of sun, surf and Mayan ruins culminated in a festive dinner at which the newlyweds recited personally crafted letters of commitment to each other. They saved the public reception for their return.

On their very first date they had unreservedly agreed that, far more often than not, procreation is a rash and selfish act. Still, Maura fostered what at first glance might smell of an antiquated value. She not only adored children; she considered it the duty of every critical-thinking couple to raise at least one child for the betterment of society. To her, this aspiration surpassed concepts such as old-fashioned and new. So thoroughly did Ani agree with her that he unilaterally submitted to a fertility test months before matrimony was ever discussed, and they wasted no time in dispensing with their respective prophylaxes once their union had been legitimized.

The spring of 2013 imparted reward for their efforts, only to renege weeks later with a miscarriage. But it was not long before Maura conceived again, and the wider her belly grew in the ensuing months the greater the workload Ani delegated to his lawfirm associates and committee members so that he could finish the baby's nursery before the onset of the third trimester, by which time, to Maura's astonishment and delight, Ani had so completely rearranged his other commitments that he was at her disposal every hour of every day.

Seven weeks shy of her due date, Maura underwent a spate of contractions followed by excessive vaginal bleeding. The obstetrician diagnosed *placenta previa* – a condition in which the placenta blocks the birth canal. Because babies born to mothers with this affection tend to be underweight, Maura insisted on carrying her child to full term despite the risk that she herself could die at any time from sudden and excessive blood loss. The malady often corrects itself as gestation progresses, but Maura's did not. Finally, at week thirty-four of her pregnancy, the doctor admonished that postponing the delivery any further would imperil the life of her fetus. She and Ani took up residence in a hospital suite on April 7, 2014 to prepare for the next morning's cesarean section.

Toward dusk, a client of Ani's brought them dinner from his bistro. As Ani cleared away the dishes, they laughed at shared memories and discussed candidates for their little one's name. Shortly after sundown, Maura drifted to sleep. Stirring a few hours later, her first sensation was the lack of warmth on her shoulder where Ani's hand had lain so many nights before. Unable to find him in the easy chair next to her bed, she cast a panicked gaze around the room until, in the sitting area ten feet beyond the toes she hadn't seen since December, she spied Ani embracing his younger brother. Jarry sputtered unintelligibly between glottal groans as Ani caressed his nape and told him in a lullaby tone not to worry. Secure in the knowledge that her man was near, she nodded back into dreamland, only to be roused in the dark of night by a lingering kiss on her cheek. Ani was again by her side, smiling more ponderingly than he had on their first lunch date as he spoke to her with the most delicate candor.

"Thank you."

She nestled closer to him, his caress on her cheek eliciting from her smile that depth of playfulness which arises only from unqualified trust.

"What on Earth for?"

"For trying to do the right thing by me."

Her grin fell sallow, not because her secret had been bared, but because of the anguish to which its utterance had needlessly subjected Ani. She wanted to comfort him, to tell him she regretted with her every living fiber what had happened. But to reassure a man of such self-subsistence would only obstruct his path toward recuperation no differently than unearthing a corpse one has already mourned and buried. Because two of the three lives he most cherished lay in the bed next to him, she deemed it most productive to turn the conversation to the third, despite the fact that doing so evoked her own shame for having so imprudently expected someone of Jarry's blunt sensibilities to hide the truth from the elder brother he so adulated.

"Oh, that poor man. He is more a child than he seems."

"And he blundered in here convinced that your ailment was somehow his fault."

Some have likened the male ego to Rocky Marciano with a glass jaw. So interwoven is a man's sexuality with every facet of his being that history is strewn with monarchs and warriors and magnates who have been ruined by the single misdeed of a woman.

Ani had discerned an odd aloofness in Jarry the previous July, but he did not pry because nothing in Jarry's personal or business life seemed amiss. And the last thing Ani would have suspected was a sexual tryst with his own wife. When Jarry had confessed earlier that night, comforting his distraught brother took precedence over self-indulgence, leaving Ani meager minutes between Jarry's departure and Maura's arousal to sort through his indignity and disesteem. As his father had counseled decades before on the occasion of his first heartbreak, Ani bridled the tumult of his emotions by immersing himself in the pertinent facts.

Simple mathematics told him the rendezvous took place within mere days of the miscarriage, during the two-week period he was in El Paso. *How dare she?* Women can become acutely depressed following spontaneous abortions, and Maura had always been highly sensitive to hormonal changes. *Were it any other man!* Given the nature of his business, she was quite aware of the possibility that he might not return from El Paso. *Where did I fail her?* And she knew from the custody case he handled in 2011 that women enjoy a heightened level of fertility immediately after miscarriage. *How can I fault her for anything she might have done in that frame of mind? And how can I blame any man with half a genital for yielding to the seductive rampage that must have taken her over?* Jarry need not have assured him it had happened only once, because Ani knew Maura could never feel trapped by their marriage – thanks to their mutual prenuptial agreement, theirs would be the least complicated divorce in juristic history. And, because of a commonsensical outlook they shared on matters of the heart, it would no doubt be the most amicable.

Though his mother took special care to expose Ani to classical literature, thanks to his father he read every poem and story with a probing eye. Unlike his schoolmates, Ani was not satisfied to sit passively and let the author entertain him. Ani derived a deeper satisfaction from peering behind plot and cadence in an effort to surmise why the author said what he said in a particular way. When he was in seventh grade, an instructor loaned Ani a copy of the play "Twelfth Night." Already familiar with such authors as Twain, Faulkner, Conrad and Steinbeck, it took little time for Ani to deduce what many conscientious students of the communicative process had long since concluded – that Shakespeare was a shopworn hack – especially when he happened upon such drivel as: "If music be the food of love, play on." To Ani, this image embodied a crippling form of self-delusion regarding both music and love which had by now overcome his every peer.

That summer, Ani attended his first and last rock concert. Ani was no less attuned than his compatriots to the rock-n-roll explosion of the 1960s and 70s, but he regarded these live events as a waste of money and time. Why, he reasoned, should he pay an extortionate ticket price to stand on vomit, rum and urine in an arena full of stoned pseudo hippies and listen to a clumsy, distorted rendition of the same songs that had been painstakingly produced and flawlessly captured on the album he already owned? But his pals convinced him The Who was worth the trouble, so he reluctantly accompanied them. He was prepared for the green-gray haze of pot smoke that loomed like soup in the ambient air. He took in stride the occasional elbow to the rib as he and his friends fought their way through the gate. He even stomached a chilidog that stank of rancid cabbage. But what took him by utter surprise was how this crowd of presumably intelligent people deified the buffoons cavorting like monkeys on stage. Ani watched countless young girls shriek and swoon at a mere wink of the eye from Roger Daltrey. He witnessed two grown men pummel a third who had aired the innocent opinion that Carlos Santana was a better guitarist than Peter Townshend. This was no cultural event; it was a churchcamp crusade, a Hitlerian pageant. On cue, some seven thousand people clapped, cheered, sang and convulsed at the bidding of four puppeteers who would be motoring to the next venue come morning, counting their percentage of the proceeds, while their fans nursed hangovers and their groupies suffered suicidal fits. The overarching depravity this spectacle typified in Ani's mind was that millions of teenagers and adults the world over derived profound life lessons from counterfeit ballads whose mindless lyrics were scrawled on rolling papers during bouts of drug-induced euphoria by people who, when stripped of their costumes and amplifiers and shiny instruments, were just a clutch of art school nerds who hovered but a tiptoe this side of psychopathy, and the size and potency of whose arsenal of useful knowledge about life barely approached that possessed by the common garden slug.

Ani left the concert a mere twenty minutes after it had begun, disgusted at the apparent reality that, because music is essentially regressive, because music in and of itself is antagonistic to intellect, logic, reason ... all higher brain functions, the musician is as susceptible to its guileful allure as the listener – confusing his own pubescent angst with philosophical insight and mistaking sexual experimentation for existential achievement. His suspicion was confirmed thirty-four years later when he read Townshend's autobiography *Who I Am*, which portrayed an aimless, narcissistic hedonist who, despite having shamelessly exploited capitalism to live his life like a spoiled brat, had the audacity to posture as a socialist in his royalty-subsidized old age.

A trait shared by the concertgoers of Ani's youth was an unhealthy reliance upon emotion, which rendered them deaf and blind to reality. Similarly handicapped were those who professed to be in love, suffering the misconception that *true love* is a mischievous magical force that besets its victims no less suddenly and forcefully than the anaphylactic shock that ensues after a wasp sting. Franklin Stearns spared Ani this fallacy, reminding him often since the tender age of three: "Only schmucks and conmen *fall* in love; real men *decide* to love."

As musical composition consisted in fantasy, so did the mainstream expression of love. When psychoanalysis became trendy some seventy years past, scores of individuals were taught to become slaves to their own unrestrained and capricious emotions in a headlong quest for that ever elusive catharsis, which inevitably led to the pervasive attitude that nothing was off limits in the quest for self-actualization. From this *anything goes* era of bongos and nudism and acid trips sprang the notion that the ideal love relationship was one in which each participant could say anything that crossed his mind with impunity because, after all, *honesty is the foundation of love, and one's unchecked feelings are truth.* As Ivan Petrovich Pavlov's work with orphans had been bastardized by Madison Avenue, society's predilection for lockstep faddism and silver-screen idolatry rapidly displaced the intuitive dynamic of old, forever obliterating the line between coaching and indoctrination and finding its apotheosis in such snake-oil decoctions as *Cure Stress Device* – a portable, rechargeable brainwashing mechanism that purveyed stale banalities, peddled by a vainglorious religious fundamentalist named Roy Masters under the guise of psychotherapy which, like any overused crutch, systematically divested its user of his unique, innate coping skills. As Ani watched friends and extended family members destroy what once promised to be mutually nurturing partnerships because the reigning wisdom had added outright cruelty to the acceptable self-expression penumbra, he appreciated ever more the wisdom his mother often imparted (usually when she was angry at his father): "There is a singular virtue in holding one's tongue."

Maura saw her own share of secular idolatry during Journey's reunion tour. Nor was her generation immune from self-indulgent, pop psychology fads such as *the inner child* concept exploited through the literary gimmick known as *the male movement* by authors such as Robert Bly and Sam Keen. As a prosecutor, she saw countless acts of spousal abuse and general domestic violence perpetrated in the name of love.

By the time they met, Ani and Maura had developed an exceptionally utilitarian view of interpersonal devotion. Each had concluded that a committed relationship does not bestow upon a loved one carte blanche to make the object of his affection an indiscriminate dumping ground for every vagrant emotional impulse. They had discerned that it is not always good to trot one's innermost feelings out into the open. They both understood the subtle maxim that true love is having the self-restraint to keep a lid on fleeting perturbations the sharing of which will only hurt the other; thus, love is far more an intentional and compassionate act of will than a fleeting and self-absorbed feeling. And, though every selfless act leaves an indelible imprint on its recipient, its giver greets each new day with a clean slate.

By agreeing from the outset of their friendship that each would take full responsibility for their own thoughts, actions and reactions, they closed all avenues toward jealousy and recrimination. It was precisely because they had made this partnership so easy to dissolve that every day each awoke and chose to stay forged a bond of permanency unknown to conventional marriage. Thus, when Ani's inner battle drew to a close, he was left with but one solitary fact that outshone all others: though she could have gone anywhere with anyone else at any time she wished, she had remained with him.

"You were to never know, Anthony."

"I applaud that decision. For you to have told me would have been selfish and sadistic. Is it not ironic, though, that Jarry's betrayal of your confidence afforded me a rare and welcome reminder that I am the man you choose to love?"

"And you will ever be that man. Did he ask you about paternity?"

"No. I suspect he is too bound up in guilt right now for much else to occupy his mind."

"I don't begrudge you or him the right to know. But as far as I'm concerned, she's ours. So long as I live, Anthony Wayne Stearns, she and the rest of the world will know you as her father, and this is not subject to negotiation."

"I would not dare challenge you on that point. Help me sit you up now."

"Stop fussing, I'm not sore."

As he had done every night for the last four months, Ani crawled into bed behind her and commenced to work her neck, shoulders and back.

"This is a preemptive massage. The looser you go in, the sooner you will recover from the carnage those blade-wielding baboons inflict upon you tomorrow."

"But if I don't recover –"

Though he summoned a lifetime of self-mastery to keep his strokes uniform, and though she could not see his swelling eyes, she could feel his dismay in the tortured breath he drew.

"Banish that thought, Maura. I will not hear of it."

"Anthony, you know my chances. Were there ever a time for a man like you to run from reality, this isn't it. I want you to make me a promise."

A HOME SHOULD BE NO LARGER THAN 600 SQUARE FEET PER ADULT OCCUPANT AND 300 FOR EACH MINOR.

This public service announcement is brought to you by the Department of Housing and Urban Redevelopment.

Chapter Fifteen

For the Love of Melissa

January 20

Born into a world in which the telex and the mimeograph were cutting edge technology, whose only telephones were tethered to walls and dialed with a finger-wheel, whose black-and-white televisions received only six channels that had to be changed manually, and for which the thermal paper facsimile machine was celebrated as a communications milestone, Ani embraced the digital revolution with zeal. Still, a steadfast observer of boundaries, he is chary about what he allows to invade his home. For instance, though *bluetooth* technology has advanced to the point where not even an earpiece is required for hands-free operation in the home, Ani still uses a handheld landline of whose speaker function he rarely avails himself. His reasoning is that where the hands go the mind will follow; hence, the act of holding the receiver trains one's focus upon the conversation at hand.

"You and I both know he had it coming. Fine, Ossie, if it will shut you up, I will give you the real reason. I am tired. Tired of protecting a herd of ignorant sheep. Tired of juggling three separate books of account to keep the feds from robbing me blind. And I have had enough of your incessant mother-henning. Yeah? Same to you!"

Ani slams the receiver with such force that he topples the endtable. Not yet ready to confront Jarry's death, he switches on the television for diversion, then bends down to facilitate Tarbaby's leap onto his shoulder and repairs to the patio in eager anticipation of last night's half-smoked cigar. He need not bother finding a news channel because every last outlet is tuned to the same live event:

Host: As we await the inauguration of Altus Carsen Olm, our nation's 46th President –

Hostess: Or 45th, depending on how you look at it.

Host: You raise an interesting point. Democrat Grover Cleveland introduced the numerical confusion when, in 1893, he became the only President in history to be elected to a second nonconsecutive term.

Hostess: Cleveland had served from 1885 to 1889, but lost his reelection bid to Republican Benjamin Harrison, only to stage a comeback in 1893.

Host: So, while Cleveland became the 24th President in 1893, he was only the 23rd individual to fill the office. Sherry?

Hostess: New information continues to pour in about the tragedy in Noble, Oklahoma. Officials have confirmed now that everyone died of carbon monoxide poisoning. The terrorists, posing as HVAC technicians and city inspectors, tampered with the exhaust pipes of water heaters and furnaces, splicing a line that rerouted the fumes and created a backdraft. The opening of the deadly valve was triggered by an electromagnetic pulse sent from the city's power station.

Host: This plan was conceived and implemented over a period of seven years. Sources who wish to remain anonymous for fear of IRS retaliation lay the principal blame with the *United Nations Multifaith Reconciliation Treaty*, asserting that the proliferation of Muslim mosques throughout the United States enabled Al Qaeda operatives to organize on a scale never before heard of on U.S. soil, accelerating Al Qaeda's completion date by at least three years.

Hostess: Our country's First Mostly Nonwhite President scoffs at this criticism. When confronted with the overwhelming evidence of Al Qaeda involvement in the Noble tragedy, he said, "That's crazy talk. Everybody knows it's all in how you react to things. If there is anything my eight years at this country's realm taught me, it's that if you ignore problems and threats, they eventually become somebody else's problem." Preston?

Host: I'm not sure what happened to our feed, but it appears the swearing-in ceremony is already over, and President Olm is about to deliver his speech.

Hostess: Let's listen in.

Seeing Mojo and Bindi emerge from the treeline, Ani shuts off the television. In their tow is Melissa, who has been borne for a quarter mile on Rita's capacious shoulders from the outer edge of Ani's property, having gained entry through an abandoned building that was once a munitions shed for the adjoining oilfield. Every committee member has struck a pact with at least one other to protect his or her loved ones in case of an emergency. When Rita first held Melissa just hours after her birth, their rapport was so instantaneous that Jarry did not even have to ask – Rita insisted that she be Lissy's contingency plan. When Jarry failed to retrieve her from her violin lesson two days ago, Rita was there within minutes, and the contrastive duo has been on the road in Rita's rig ever since.

Rita sets her charge down onto her feet.

"Uncle Ani!"

The suddenness of Melissa's sprint takes even the dogs by surprise.

"It is wonderful to see you again, Lissy. I missed you. Tell me now, in what new way has Aunt Rita corrupted you?"

"It's a scientific fact that Petro Truck Stop pizza rolls … what's that word, Aunt Rita?"

"Optimize, darlin'."

"They optimize one's mental acuity."

"Ms. Baynes, you are indeed a renaissance woman. Lissy, let us thank our dear friend for entertaining you with a cup of coffee and a cinnamon roll."

Though she revels in Melissa's company, these last forty-eight hours have sucked Rita's emotional tanks dry. Having grown up with the Stearns boys, she assumed an elder sister role for Jarry after his beating. Though she understood it from a tactical standpoint, she took it hard when Ani assigned Jarry's protection to Eldon and Connie rather than her. For Melissa's sake, she has had to defer her own grief over Jarry's demise.

"Love one, Ani, but I gotta go see about a valve job on the pickup. Then momma needs some fried chicken livers and peach pie. But I'll be here before daybreak tomorrow to take my little cohort on an Albuquerque run."

Stealing another hug from Melissa, Rita plants a thoughtful kiss on Ani's forehead, slaps the dogs on their rumps and lumbers with them toward the trees. Ani carries Melissa to the kitchen, where he deposits both her and Tarbaby on the counter.

"What is your pleasure this morning, Lissy – pancakes or eggs?"

"Eggs, sunny side up, cooked in shortening not fru-fru oil, and hold the girly attitude."

"And with what unfortunate person does Rita take that tone?"

"There's a short-order cook in Abilene who makes faces at her because she told him once that he cooked steaks like a West Hollywood Nancy-boy. I think she likes him."

"I think you are correct. Well then, sunny side up it is."

Ani would like nothing better than to lose himself in the meal preparation ritual of which countless mates and parents have availed themselves over the centuries as a means of avoidance. Yet his compassion for the prim urchin who is thus far the only human Tarbaby has permitted to scratch her stomach is goaded by Maura's last request – *Protect her from the ugliness of this world, yes, but do not hide it from her. The sheltered child grows into a defenseless pawn. Do not suffer this little girl to become a stooge.* Alas, before the burner has begun to melt the *Crisco*, sweet Melissa takes the decision out of his hands.

"I know something bad happened to Daddy. I acted like I didn't know, because I didn't want to make Aunt Rita sadder than she already is. You look sad, too, Uncle Ani. And that makes me sad, so you might as well tell me so I'll know why we're all sad."

As he turns the stove off, a surge of regret mixed with panic and veneration shocks him from throat to groin like a gunshot. He acquires a barstool at the counter and pulls Melissa round to face him. Stroking her hair, for an instant he can see his cherished Maura in her eyes and cheeks.

"My precious, intuitive Lissy. How I wish your mother could have known you."

Melissa hugs Tarbaby close to her chest and rests her forehead against Ani's to brace herself. The only other time her uncle reminisced openly about her mother was the night Grandpa Frank died.

"Uncle Ani, no."

"Your father was killed three nights ago."

"Why would anyone kill Daddy?"

"People kill for any of innumerable reasons. And there are some who need no justification at all. I do not know what the motivation was. I can surmise, but that would be counterproductive. Remember, we have discussed the dangers with which the question *Why* is fraught? More often than not –"

"*Why* has no answer."

"That is right. And when we fabricate a solution to assuage our distress at the arbitrary chaos of this life, unduly oppressive laws are passed and entire segments of society become pariahs on a whim. That which we call tragic is the order of the day in this existence. Though we can not avert it, we can control our reaction to it. For now, you and I need not concern ourselves with the how or the why. You have forever lost your father, and I my brother. This event has wounded us. We are in a safe, private place, and I propose that we take this opportunity to cleanse those wounds lest we needlessly transfer our pain onto others."

Like a cadet dismissed for long coveted leave, Melissa lets loose her every muscle, collapsing into her uncle's chest. Ani scoops her up and carries her to his oversize easy chair in the den where they weep for Jarry. At deluge's wane, Melissa reclaims her unbound curiosity.

"What happens when we die?"

"That is one mystery whose pursuit has spawned a vast array of misdoing. A great many believe we have an invisible essence called a soul or spirit, which floats to an immaterial dimension of existence where it is either rewarded or punished for its behavior in the corporeal realm.

One's acts and omissions are judged by one of a thousand divergent standards depending largely upon one's culture. Once adjudicated, that soul is either rewarded by being admitted into paradise or punished in various ways, be it burning in an underworld for eternity or returning to Earth as a lower form of life."

"Death sounds complicated."

"Mind you, these are wholly unsupported theories."

"If we have rules, someone had to make them up. If we're judged, someone has to be the judge. It seems silly to make the rules so confusing. Someone should have a talk with the rulemaker."

"You have hit upon a very salient point, Lissy. In all of history, both recorded and anecdotal, not once has this alleged ethereal lawgiver shown its face in a verifiable fashion. Every last regulation has been communicated to human beings in the first instance by another human being. In my line of work, we call this hearsay."

"What's hearsay?"

"Were I to tell you Aunt Rita wants you to eat live crickets, would you believe me?"

"Ich, no!"

"And if I stubbornly maintained that she had told me so, how would you settle the argument?"

"I'd call Aunt Rita."

"Why?"

"Because she's the best person to know what she told you."

"Exactly. Unless and until you verify it with Aunt Rita, my claim about what she told me is no more reliable than a U.S. Treasury Bill. Likewise, the ideologies and moral schemes purveyed by the various religious officials, unsubstantiated by their purported divine authors, offer no more relevant authority on the subject than a Saturday morning cartoon. All we know is that human life ends. We have no proof anyone survives that end."

"So what are ghosts?"

"In my opinion, ghosts are nothing more than self-fulfilling prophecies conjured up from the unfettered human imagination by people who are so desperate to find proof of an alternate existence that they see things which are not there."

"My civics tutor says they're real. Why would she lie?"

"I would be very surprised if she were lying."

"If she's not lying and you're not lying, what do I believe?"

"You should not take either of our statements as true merely because we made them. It is not our duty as your elders to teach you what to think; only how. Ultimately, the decision is yours alone."

"So how do I decide?"

"I submit, my dear, that you already have. Many centuries ago, a Franciscan friar named William of Ockham proposed a system of logic that has been termed Occam's Razor. It holds that, when we undertake to determine the unknown cause of an event, the most probable explanation is the simplest. For instance, you have dreamt of Grandpa Frank since his death."

"Lots of times."

"In those dreams, he speaks and laughs and kisses you just as he so often did while he lived?"

"Sometimes, I can even smell his yucky tobacco spit."

"Do you remember last February when you caught the flu, and you would sometimes hear his voice even though you were awake?"

"Yeah, that was spooky."

"Did you conclude that your grandpa was actually visiting you from beyond the grave?"

"No, silly!"

"Why not?"

"Because dreams aren't real."

"You see, even though your body was so overtaxed that your conscious mind hovered just a step away from somnolence, you were percipient enough to distinguish between fantasy and fact. You opted for the simplest and, therefore, the most rational explanation. Scientists still can not begin to grasp the human brain's full potential. I suspect your civics tutor has had at least one similar dream experience in a semiconscious or emotionally charged state, but she interpreted the voice or vision as something generated, not from within her mind but from without. She chooses to call it a ghost."

"With multiplication tables and sentence structure and comprehension tests, it's hard enough to keep up with life. Why do people make it more confusing by imagining stuff?"

"A great many people simply do not grasp the difference between imagination and reality. And some, due to fear or lethargy, are content to let others define reality for them. Misconceiving the unreal for objective fact can take on uncounted forms along the spectrum of a phenomenon called schizophrenia."

"What's that?"

"There are two general kinds. Clinical schizophrenia is an advanced medical condition in which the patient's inability to separate fact from figment is so debilitating that he becomes a threat to himself and/or others. Your cousin Simony suffers from that disease."

"Is that why she covers herself in mud and hides in the root cellar when she doesn't take her medicine?"

"It is. Social, or existential, schizophrenia is a far subtler condition which manifests itself in many diverse forms. It connotes behavior that is self-contradictory, such as speaking or acting diametrical to our inner thoughts and values, or believing in the irrational and the unproven."

"So people who believe in ghosts and gods are schizophrenics?"

"To draw that conclusion is to presume the impossible – that one can decipher the mind of another. While the belief itself may be seen in isolation as wrongheaded, sweeping labels are irresponsible and unkind. For example, your average observer would call me an atheist because I do not subscribe to any known religion. But to level such a charge is to betray one's own ignorance of the fact that the original definition of atheism has been so perverted that, today, it has become synonymous with its diametric opposite, socialism."

"What's socialism?"

"Socialism advocates governmental ownership and administration of the means of production and distribution of goods. It is a mindset which seeks to abolish private property, to confiscate from the courageous and the innovative the rewards of their industry and bestow them upon the idle and the faint of heart. Psychologically, the socialist worldview stems from a pathological distrust of oneself and all of humanity. Sugarcoated by various despots as fascism, communism, Bolshevism, Leninism, Fabianism, Maoism and Marxism, from the death camps of Hitler to the purges of Stalin to Pol Pot's killing fields, socialism is the bane of a free society, a subversion of truth, the nemesis of self-actualization. In short, socialism epitomizes emotional poverty and cowardice. Classically, the term *atheist* described a staunch individualist who would neither have a king nor be one, whose credo was *I will not follow the crowd; nor do I seek to have the crowd follow me. I will live and die of my own efforts, and I expect no more or less from my neighbor.* Thus, the prototypical atheist endorsed the free market principle in every human affair. Unlike today's so-called atheist, the genuine atheist did not take the arrogant, illogical and unscientific position that there never was, nor can there ever be, a conscious power unknown in the observable universe.

"Sadly for a linguistic purist such as I, archetypal atheism has become so irretrievably intertwined with socialism that the stamp *atheist* is a slap in the face. So I call myself simply a realist. On the one hand, I reject extant religious practices because I have found no empirical proof to support their various claims; on the other, I acknowledge the patent reality that, in a universal and historical context, scientific knowledge is now and perhaps will ever be incomplete. So, while I refuse to place my utmost hopes in the improbable, I do not rule out – and therefore remain receptive to – that which is possible, mundane or otherwise; nevertheless, I am resolved to resist any intelligence or other volitional force that will not treat me fairly. Many can not stomach the anguish of that mental position, so they draw solace from the lullaby of mythology. I consider such believers, not enemies, but comrades in the endless search to give life meaning, who merely have a lower pain threshold than I. But they come by it innocently enough, as the natural human tendency is to seek acceptance from the crowd. I am of the opinion that those who sermonize from the pulpit, however, are cut from a more perfidious cloth. It is they, after all, who perpetuate the myth for their own gain."

"Are you saying preachers know they're spreading a lie?"

"Absent a medical condition, if they do not know, they are censurable just the same because they are in a position to know."

"Why would sane people want to make others insane?"

"Control, sweetie. Death is unpleasant. I know I do not savor the prospect of my own. When civilization as we know it was in its infancy, an unprincipled element of society realized that, if they could make unsuspecting individuals believe in an afterlife, they could wield tremendous power over them. It is not unlike the Santa Claus delusion your schoolmates will endure for a few years more. When you convince people their deeds will result in everlasting reward or punishment, you can manipulate their behavior by defining for them what is good and what is bad. This is why religion and government have been so incestuously aligned throughout history."

"But my political science tutor says church and State should be separate."

"That is not quite accurate. What our Constitution provides is that government must not support or endorse one religious denomination, such as Buddhism or Christianity, over another, such as Protestantism or Catholicism. But, as a Roman magistrate named Seneca the Younger observed two thousand years ago, despots and tyrants will always find religion in the generic sense an indispensable tool of oppression."

"Why?"

"In what situation are you more nervous when you play your violin – a rehearsal or a recital?"

"Recital."

"Why is that?"

"Rehearsals don't count. If I mess up at a recital, everybody hears it and I don't get a do-over."

"The concept of an afterlife has the same psychological effect as that of the rehearsal. So long as the bulk of voters believe this life is merely a dry run, they will more readily turn a blind eye to intrusions upon their freedoms they would not otherwise tolerate. And those who believe that an eleventh-hour gesture of repentance washes away a mountain of sin will be more likely to overlook their own misdeeds so long as death seems a distant eventuality. Thus, religious belief intrinsically cultivates immorality."

"But without laws, how do we know right from wrong?"

"To a great extent, you already do. When you play with your friends, your natural instinct is to treat them fairly and honestly because that is how you hope they will treat you. But let us not be led astray by judgmental terms such as *right* and *wrong.* These words conjure up the image of a universal yardstick which in all probability does not exist. A large part of what we call moral conduct is simply the inevitable outcome of individuals learning how to live together. So let us replace the artificial concepts *right* and *wrong* with the practical values *acceptable* and *unacceptable*. The relationship between one individual and another is an ongoing act of give and take. For example, I like to smoke my cigars, but you do not like their smell. Because I enjoy your company, I only smoke them outside when you are here, and I installed a sophisticated ventilation system so that you are not now assaulted with the stench of the one I smoked in the study last night when you were not here. I voluntarily restrict my activities in relation to you, because a happy Lissy makes Uncle Ani smile. In this way, my purely selfish concern inures to our mutual benefit."

"If morality's so simple, why do we have police and judges and lawmakers?"

"Common to every known species is the craving for routines and patterns. For good or ill, we cling to that which is familiar. This is why so many of us obsess over nostalgia. The past is friendly because it is fixed and poses no surprises. The present is messy; the future unpredictable and therefore dismaying. Our penchant for repetition creates habitual behavior. Over time, habits take on a separate existence, becoming what we call institutions and traditions. Eventually, the original impetus for the tradition fades into obscurity and it becomes an empty ritual. Successive generations dare not question these customs because they are familiar, and familiarity lends the illusion of security, culminating in what some have called the tyranny of tradition. The morality I just described requires self-reliance and a willingness to stand alone against the conventions of the day. As a general rule, human beings do not like being alone. It is not comfortable to disagree with the majority, especially when one's misgivings are directed at longstanding practice. So our natural tendency is to conform to the conventions of the day. Consider the Halloween parties you attend. What do you find so intriguing about them?"

"We get to pretend we're something else."

"Society is much like the costume party. We spend the bulk of our energy analyzing our teachers or employers, our classmates or coworkers, and adapting our speech and behavior to mirror theirs. Even the so-called rebel is careful to not deviate too wide of the norm: though he may buck the trend by dressing differently than the crowd, he still wears clothing. As communities have grown and populations condensed, the function of the individual in society has shrunk. Thanks to the syndication of farming and advanced distribution systems, the average person is spared the ordeals of foraging for vegetables and slaughtering wild game for meat. As the generational distance expands between the old days and the new, we come to expect that the dirty jobs be performed by others. Meting out justice to wrongdoers can be a very nasty business. So I don my *lawyer* mask and tell the judge to handle it. From behind his *judge* mask, he tells the jailer to take care of it. The jailer, in turn, palms the job off onto the executioner. In foisting upon others the responsibility for enforcing the morality of the day, we avoid having to remove our masks of conformity, and we can enjoy the party while others do our dirty work."

"Is conformity a bad thing?"

"To the contrary, it is a necessity in any society. It is part of the give-and-take process I mentioned. When Aunt Rita drives on the highway, she observes traffic laws, not because the laws themselves boast inherent clout, but because doing so keeps that multiaxle colossus of hers from colliding with other motor vehicles. Should I make up my own language, choosing to call a jackal an opossum or a banana a chair, I would quickly become useless to, and therefore isolated from, society. But conformity can be taken too far. Ritual and tradition foster knee-jerk behavior. The act of obeying a rule or following a fad entails the surrender of one's independent judgment. So we must be careful in deciding just how many masks of conformity we are willing to adopt, lest amongst them we permit others to so dilute our identities that we lose them altogether, because the first step toward enslavement is homogenization."

"How's conformity different from schizophrenia?"

"The common denominator is consciousness. Consider the stage actor. To play his role, he spends hours memorizing and rehearsing until the script and stage directions become so internalized that, when the curtain rises, he can perform his role without even having to think about it. From the day we draw our first breath, our parents and teachers and various other figures to whom we look for guidance add lines and stage directions to the silent script inside us which we refer to as the psyche. Our every decision – whether to have children and how many, what career path to take, whom we choose to love, which candidate to back – is thereafter influenced by this script. As adults, our ultimate fulfillment is determined by the degree to which we learn to detect that script and act independently of it. The schizophrenic stumbles through life so unmindful of his psychic script that he is incapable of differentiating the thoughts and views of others from his own. Thus, what separates the schizophrenic from you and me is that the schizophrenic is to a greater or lesser extent unaware of the conflict inside him."

"So all those people in prisons are there because they didn't wear the right mask?"

"In many instances, that is true. A great many activities labeled as crimes harm either no one at all or only their participants. Some would argue, and I am one, that such people do not deserve to be punished by the state. On the other hand, there are individuals who intentionally harm others. Let us refer to them as bullies. Be it a physical defect in their brains or faulty scriptwriting in their childhood, bullies hate themselves; therefore, they have no ability to love others or respect their rights. It is the bully whom society rightfully seeks to expel from the general population."

"Does jail teach them how to be nice?"

"I am afraid jail has the opposite effect. You see, technology and job specialization have so removed us from the cardinal tasks of survival that the typical American suffers the delusion that we can rehabilitate a twenty-eight-year-old misanthrope – who slew his wife and infant son with a machete because his wife complained once too often about his infidelity – by giving him timeout in an institutional corner. Modern life's conveniences have deluded us into thinking we need not stoop to the level of a savage to deter a savage. So we house rapists and murderers and even terrorists in climate controlled cottages with exercise facilities, televisions and computers. We feed and clothe them, and we provide doctors and medications for their ailments. Then we set them free after serving but a fraction of their intended terms, largely because prisons are overcrowded with people whose so-called crimes harmed no one. By forcing the bully to spend his every waking hour in the company of other bullies, we have only made him a stronger and meaner bully."

"So how do you get rid of a bully?"

"By first ascertaining whether or not he is, indeed, a bully. So overprotective have parents of recent generations become that, by forbidding their children to participate in so-called *violent* sports until they are in high school or college, if ever, they have denied them the opportunity to develop crucial physical and mental coping skills which can only take root in those early years. As a result, society has become so inundated with weaklings that the bar for the label *bully* has been drastically lowered, indicting as oppressive behavior a host of innocent deeds and attitudes which everyone – recipients included – once shrugged off as idle mischief. The mollycoddlers of society have so broadened the ambit of unacceptable behavior that far too many sincere and fair-minded people are scapegoated as bullies by parents or other loved ones who are too frail or biased to admit, for example, that it was a mental or emotional flaw that drove their loved one to suicide."

"So who's a bully and who isn't?"

"There is no hard and fast definition, but I would offer this guideline. If, after you have unequivocally told him to not do it again, another person proceeds to cause you bodily pain or harm, steal your possessions, or physically prevent you from carrying out your ethical activities and obligations, then that person is more likely than not a bully, and you have both the right and the responsibility to neutralize him. The same guideline applies to business entities and government organizations."

"Then what?"

"Next, you must accept the fact that the concept of *humane warfare* is the most fatuous of oxymorons. The only way to both repel a bully and deter him from future attacks is to communicate with him on a level he understands – the primitive language of indiscriminate physical violence. You hurt him by any means possible. Even if he is bigger and stronger than you, you inflict so much damage to him on your way to the ground that he will think twice before pursuing you. You see, no matter how scary they may look and act, even bullies fear pain. This is why they only pick on those who appear weaker than they. And however much he loathes his life, no bully wants to have his life or freedom taken from him, especially in an undignified manner. This is why the most successful crime deterrents in history were the stocks, the public hanging and the electric chair."

Melissa ponders an emerging Tarbaby, in awe of the fact that she has survived being wedged between her belly and her uncle's for all this time.

"When will my sadness go away?"

"Though, in time, your father's memory will not hurt nearly as much as today, it will never completely vanish."

"What will happen to the people who killed him?"

"What would you wish upon them?"

"I'd sic Mojo and Bindi on them."

"Granted, that would certainly hone the skills of the canines, but what would it do for you?"

"It would make me not so mad."

"Do you think it would alleviate your sadness?"

"I guess not."

"This is a trap people too often fall into. They think that if a jury imposes the death penalty or a life sentence on a killer, or if a deal can be negotiated with that killer in exchange for the return of their loved one's remains, they will obtain something called *closure*. But it is pure folly to pin one's internal wellbeing to external circumstances over which he has absolutely no control. Your father could just as easily have been stricken with an incurable disease or whisked away by a tornado. How does one seek satisfaction from a funnel cloud that has long since dissipated? More often than not, avengement merely deepens and festers a wound that would have healed far sooner had the victim's survivors merely asserted exclusive ownership over their emotions. That is what you and I are doing right now."

"Remember that day in the park when the skateboarder knocked me down?"

"I do."

"What did you say to his boss to make him apologize?"

"I opened a negotiation with the young man."

"What did you put on the table?"

"I offered him an opportunity to walk away a hero to those he most cherishes in this life."

She rolls her head and sighs.

"It was a simple, direct question, Uncle Ani. Don't make me tickle you."

"I told him that if he did not make things right with you, I would skin his mother alive, shave his girlfriend's … private parts with an unsharpened bowie knife – all before his very eyes – and, finally, I would smother him to death with his own … manhood."

"And he believed you?"

"He did."

"Why?"

"Because I meant every last word."

"Why would you do those things?"

"I try my best to live a life of circumspection. But I am weak where you are concerned, Lissy. If indeed I have a soul, I would barter it to preserve your innocence. And I would have repudiated it to save your father's life."

IN SPORTING EVENTS AND CASUAL COMPETITIONS, IT IS PREFERABLE THAT THE CONTEST END IN A TIE. IF VICTORY CAN NOT BE AVOIDED, THE IMPENDING WINNER SHOULD USE ANY MEANS NECESSARY, INCLUDING FORFEIT, TO LIMIT HIS OR HER MARGIN TO NOTHING GREATER THAN 3%.

This public service announcement is brought to you by the First First Gentleman and First Ex-President to Serve as First Gentleman and Only Ex-President to Service as First First Gentleman's Anti-Bullying Committee.

Chapter Sixteen

Color Human

A glint of dawn ricochets off the IV stand, stirring Peter from a dreamless slumber – the first he can recall in months. He tries to sit up, but pain like a brain-freeze slams him back to the pillow. Smoothing the bandage on his forehead, he reviews the brief glimpse he stole of the spacious suite, but finds no one there. Then he hears a faint nasal emanation to the right. Turning his head in leery increments, he finds Mira sitting upright in a chair next to his bed. With her splayed feet still clad in office heels, a notebook computer covering her bare knees and a pen-stylus clenched between her teeth, it appears she fought Morpheus with her last ounce of defiance the way so many preschoolers resist being still at naptime.

Though barely more perceptible than those of a kitten, the rhythm of her breaths ensnares him. Never in all these years has he stopped to consider how felicitously her chin-length, salted auburn hair nudges her bashful nose when her head hangs aslant. And only in her repose can he appreciate how subtle are those lips through which he has heard her outshout the rowdiest of deacons at budget meetings. Of her many facets he finds himself studying for the first time, it is the tawny freckle on her left breast that whispers through a gap in her blouse which snaps him out of his hypnotic fixation. Evocative of a similar blemish on Deanna's lower back, it reminds Peter of the man he has become.

You don't deserve her. You don't even deserve a cheap peek.

"Mira?"

She rouses as seamlessly as he imagines she dozed off.

"Oh my stars, you're awake!"

Beaming, she tosses the computer onto the endtable as though it held no more value than an hour-old newspaper, scrambles to her feet, leans over to kiss his cheek, embarrassedly removes the stylus and tucks a drool soaked tress behind her ear, kisses his cheek, then pulls the chair closer to the bed with her shin before reclaiming it.

"Don't you worry yourself about a thing, we're going to get to the bottom of these mental escapades of yours and, until we do, I will be right here taking care of you."

She caresses his closest hand in both of hers.

Mira has never so much as hugged me. And I've never thought of her as I did just now. But it can't be Athene pulling my chain ... there is a crispness here ... a substance ... no wind-no-wind. Still, why would Mira kiss me? Could it be that she feels ... no, no one could love me. No one should. That leaves only one reason.

He yanks his hand away. The effort stings his temples. He watches Mira fold her hands in her lap, contemplates her shuddering knees. Afraid to look at her any longer, Peter closes his eyes as if to stave the pain that has already subsided.

"Ms. Bonham, what are you hiding from me?"

"It's nothing urgent, Mr. Mott, and there's nothing to be done about it anyway. You should just rest and recuperate."

Though he remains motionless, his head throbs again, this time as a visceral reaction to the cruelty he means to inflict upon a friend whose loyalty eclipses that of Julia. He has never spoken harshly to Mira because she has never given him the scantest cause. But a turmoil he hasn't sensed in many years has begun to churn within him, and he is determined to quell it before it swallows up yet another person he holds dear.

"Ms. Bonham, if it involves my church, it is urgent. No employee of mine withholds information from me about my church for any reason. Is that understood?"

"Yes, Mr. Mott." She defeatedly retrieves her notebook, shuts it off and packs it in her carrycase. "The imam at the mosque next door –"

"Hosaam?"

"Yes, sir. I found some glitches on our server, and I've had three of our tech guys confirm this. The imam has been hacking our system and downloading information on our members for four years."

"All of them?"

"Just the ones with ties to the town of Noble."

"I negotiated his son's release from a Somali prison."

"And he used you to help him murder five thousand eight hundred thirty-one innocent mothers, fathers, sons and daughters." She stands, drapes her purse over one shoulder and her briefcase over the other, and relinquishes a terminal sigh. "You may consider this my two weeks' notice, Mr. Mott. I do wish you all the best."

Unable to bear the sight of her exit, Peter lets his head fall away toward the window through which the sunrise assaults his lidded eyes like an old fashioned flashbulb. But he does not hear the customary clatter of heels.

Nobody walks that softly, not even a ghost. Five thousand eight hundred ... again, I've managed to kill without even knowing it. 'Neco in absentia.' Neco, necas, necat, necamus, necatis, necant. Hosaam was my friend.

"Who is Hosaam, again?"

In his haste to ascertain that the voice he just heard was, indeed, that of Dr. Kelner, Peter jerks his head round before considering the agony such sudden exertion will invite. But, to his confusion and delight, there was no hint of discomfort. And there sits his shrink in the chair to the right of his bed the same way he takes to any chair – as though he were molded to fit it.

"He's the imam at … did you touch up your beard?"

"Why would I do such a thing? Don't lose your focus, Peter, we're making progress. For instance, I dusted off some old references this morning. This imam of yours, Hosaam ibn Abisali – his name translates into modern English usage as *Sword son of Warrior*. Coincidentally, the name of your terrorist kingpin – Muhannad ibn Saheim – bears exactly the same meaning. What does that tell you?"

Something is wrong with the sunbeam. Curious to know if the sky has become overcast, Peter turns to see that the window is now encased in heavy wire mesh. And a dirty, solid wall has replaced the accordion partition which, moments ago, separated him from a plush sitting room with a big screen television and an adjoining dinette.

"Where am I?"

"Where do you think you are?"

"Why is my ankle chained to the bedrail?"

"You do realize, do you not, that if all we do is ask questions, we'll never find any answers?"

"Isn't that illogical, Doc'?"

"Is it?"

"I just had a dream. I fired Mira, but I can't remember why."

"Dream … dream … define *dream*."

"A series of false trails and allegorical images based to a greater or lesser extent on real facts. Why aren't you taking notes?"

"Peter, Peter – we've fallen far beneath the notational phase. Or would the preposition be *behind*? I assume that by *notational* you mean jotting down thoughts and impressions in written form. If, on the other hand, you refer to the general use of specialized graphic symbols, well, one might have hoped to see the species evolve far beyond it by now."

"I didn't use the word; you did."

Dr. Kelner uncrosses his legs and scoots to the edge of his chair, a look of rapt intrigue beneath his nappy brow.

"Did I?"

"You said *we've fallen.* Have I been institutionalized?"

"Yes."

"I *have*?"

"No."

"Well, which is it?"

"It's all a matter of perspective, Peter. Perception? Perspective, yes."

"Why won't you give me a straight answer?"

"That query is best addressed in pantomime. Permit me?"

Dr. Kelner leaps to the foot of the bed and proceeds to imitate what Peter interprets as a teetering lamp post, a defecating orangutan and a spastic hula dancer. He then rushes back to his chair and eyes Peter with ardent expectation.

"Well? Well?"

"I'm sorry, Doc', I was never any good at parlor games."

"The reason I won't give you a straight answer is that I'm a fucking psychiatrist! How does any creature more advanced than a paramecium misapprehend such an expert rendition?"

"But you're not a psychiatrist."

"I'm not?"

A dispassionate nurse dressed in a starched skirt and pointed hat hearkening back to the 1930s marches in and, seemingly unaware of the doctor's presence, takes Peter's blood pressure and temperature. She then deposits a glass syringe with silver case and plunger on the endtable, replaces the glass IV bottle on the bedside tree and exits without retrieving the syringe.

"Rotten damned luck for Archduke Ferdinand, eh?"

"Excuse me?"

"The assassination that eventuated this big war?"

"You're twenty-one years off, Doc'."

"Details, details. By some measures, such a span is but a hiccup of time. And when one delves into cause and effect with fearless abandon, the lines of demarcation fade, and one understands that humankind has been at war since its birth and will remain so to the very hour of its extinction."

"Doctor, please. Why am I here? How did I come to be here? What's to be done with me?"

"I'm afraid our time is up. Allow me to offer one little nugget before I go, hm?" Dr. Kelner nods decisively at the syringe. "Therein lies the solution to your weltschmerz."

"My what?"

"You don't read enough, Peter. Weltschmerz: confusion, pain. Now then, I must go see someone about a … something or other."

Peter hears a resonant snort to his left just before the fetid air of droppings assaults him like a blast from a superheated furnace. He turns to see the four horses that have so beleaguered him.

"They don't stop for shit, you know."

To his right, Johnny Cash reclines cross-legged in an invisible chair, cleaning his fingernails with a rusty pitchfork and staring Peter down as though he had just slapped Johnny's mother.

"Mr. Mott?"

Peter is once more in the friendly hospital suite, alone but for Mira, who approaches from the dinette chewing a spoonful of gumbo. His head wound has also returned.

"Aha, oh, ow!"

"How many times do I have to tell you, Mr. Mott? Slow, easy movements. Don't make me tie your butt to that bed."

She plops nonchalantly into the chair next to him and shovels another spoonful.

"Didn't you quit?"

"Why the hell would I do that? I get more drama in your square-mile circus than I would in Congress. Wanna bite? Extra spicy!"

"No, thanks. Hosaam … the church rolls."

"I never … nifty lemon … stubble."

"Excuse me?"

She sets aside the bowl, holds up a *pause* finger and wipes a dribble of soup from her chin.

"I said I never trusted that shifty little man. Didn't I tell you he was trouble?"

Reaching for a paper tissue, she bumps the endtable with her knee, jostling a plastic syringe to the floor. She retrieves it and gingerly deposits it on the tray next to the ewer.

"Good thing that needle has a cap on it, huh, Mr. Mott?"

"What is that?"

"The neurologist said it's morphine sulfate. He injected a wee little bit an hour ago, and told the nurse to be stingy with it. That's funny, come to think of it. I thought I read somewhere that you're not supposed to administer morphine to someone with a head wound. It's probably best we don't touch it until I can find you a non-government doctor who knows what the hell he's doing."

"Dr. Kelner said it would solve all my problems."

"Which one is he?"

"The shrink."

"No, no, his name is … I wrote it down … something to do with shoulders … Schraug. That's it, Schraug."

"Impatient guy? Full, gray beard? Unruly eyebrows?"

"Hardly – this one doesn't even look old enough to shave. Kelner, you said?"

"Kelner. He's in private practice. Mira, you're the one who scheduled all my appointments."

"And I'm telling you, Mr. Mott, that I've never heard of the man. But names are funny. And you gave yourself one doozey of a concussion. I'm surprised you even remember your own name."

"Peter Shroyer Mott! Who is this little hussy?!"

IN ALL HUMAN INTERACTIONS, ONE SHOULD STRIVE TO AVOID ADJECTIVES AND RESTRICT NOUNS TO THE MOST GENERIC OF FORMS, BECAUSE THE RESPONSIBILITY FOR THE LISTENER'S INTERPRETATION LIES EXCLUSIVELY WITH THE SPEAKER.

This public service announcement is brought to you by First Bushleague-Language Tsar Ryan A. Gardner, and the First Female President and First First Lady to Become President and Only Former First Lady to Become the First Female President's Bureau of Unoffensive Speech.

Chapter Seventeen

Home the Hard Way

January 21

"Okay, gentlemen, though no one would know it from your faces, it appears we have ourselves a deal."

Though she has never been seen in her conference room wearing anything other than a brown or gray pantsuit, even her gay assistant Burnice staggered when he saw Julia waft to table's head clad in a black-on-crimson split skirt and jacket over a tantalizingly sheer, cream colored blouse. Her quarry for today are five gentlemen who represent a consortium of countries bordering the Bay of Bengal. What stuns them even more than her attire is what this woman whose reputation for unbridled greed which spans five continents has chosen to leave on the table. Most bewildered is the crotchety gentleman from Sri Lanka.

"Begging very much your pardon, but you have purchased surface rights to the exclusion of what underlies?"

"What more can I say, Mr. Vacasya? Oil is gooey and grimy, and green is the going trend. If you insist on throwing them in the package as a bonus, far be it for me to make you leave here unhappy, but I won't waste so much as a dime on mineral rights because oil is just … so yesterday."

Papers signed, her guests file out of the room as dazed as if they had escaped a murder charge for the price of a parking violation. Gathering the various transfer and security agreements, Burnice pauses in mid-collate and slumps into one of the newly vacant chairs.

"Julia Bross, I don't even know you anymore. This is fiscal suicide, what I see here. And that oafish ensemble! What has gotten into you?"

Still sitting at the head of the table, Julia stamps her feet and giggles.

"Don't you get it, Burnie?"

"I most definitely do not."

"Finance 101 – no negotiation occurs in a vacuum. Did you not see President Olm's inaugural address? Petroleum prices in Eurasia and the Middle East are about to take a 1929 nosedive. Tourism and agriculture will then soar for six to eighteen months while the world oil market sorts itself out. To boot, I've capitalized on age and culture – those chauvinistic grampuses think I'm the dizziest ditz this side of the Pacific. So, at the crest of the agricultural boom, I'll be able to trade all the land I just bought right back to those idiots for triple the inland mineral shares I could have purchased today."

"All the available offshore drilling sites were snatched up years ago. What makes you so sure there's onshore oil in that region?"

"The cleverest fraud of the industrial age – *fossil fuel.* The atmospheres of Jupiter and Saturn are overrun with hydrocarbons, and there are hydrocarbon lakes on Saturn's moon Titan. Astronomers have been finding hydrocarbon signatures on comets since the 1990s. I think it's a safe assumption no dinosaur ever lived on a comet. The universe is brimming with the building blocks of petroleum based energy, and the steady production in the Middle East for over a century suggests that Earth's core generates that miraculous gunk every time it circles the sun."

His faith restored, Burnice rises and recommences his colligative duties, lingering only to impart a final barb.

"Fair enough, but that blouse is positively vulgar. Do go and put on something that shows more self-respect."

Ever vigilant for an opportunity to goad her second most stalwart staffer, Julia stows her stilettos in hand, sprints and stops in Burnice's path and, thrusting her shoulders forward to accentuate her abounding bust, bats her eyes.

"What? You mean this old thing?"

On the cusp of losing his battle against a spate of laughter, he raps her on the head with the loose papers.

"Go now, you shameless whore, or as God is my witness I'll quit!"

Suffused with the exhilaration of having hoodwinked yet another brood of paternalists, Julia bounds her private stairs two at a time. The hidden passage was not her idea, but Burnice's. So loath is Julia of the constraints of formal clothing that, at meeting's end, it is not uncommon for her to have torn away all but her smallclothes by the time she arrives at her office door. Bristling at the frequent complaints about the lunatic often seen on the elevator in varying stages of undress, Burnice wearied of lecturing his boss on the "discretion commensurate with the dignity of our corporate mission," which Julia would always counter with a wry variation on how he might rid his dorsal orifice of the stick that had been lodged there.

No sooner has she fluttered through the side door than the sight of a messenger's pouch stops her cold. She approaches with the guardedness of a bomb defuser. When she sees it is from Stearns Law Firm, her every molecule of exuberance bleeds away. Just a foot from the ominous package, she lets fall her vesture and kneels. Twice she reaches, twice she recoils. Then, with a growl and a grimace, she seizes and tears the envelope in one spasmodic burst. The inner pocket yields a one and one half-page handwritten letter.

Dear Julia,

Please forgive the informality of my address. I trust you will soon understand that it befits the plea contained herein. I lament the rancor with which our last meeting concluded, but my line of questioning was motivated by an urgent need to evaluate your character. I will now afford you the courtesy of coming straight to the point.

Fraught as life is with uncertainty and misfortune, a man must periodically contemplate his inevitable extinction. Now that her father is gone, weighing heavily on my mind is the fact that my own eventual demise will leave my niece Melissa without the mentor I have aspired to be since she was born. Between Connie, whom you already know, and Rita, whose acquaintance I hope you will make, her physical wellbeing will never be in doubt. But she needs more than even these truest of my confidants can offer.

In the guardianship papers I drew up years ago for her father, I named Rita as my successor with strict instructions that Melissa have regular social contact with a small group of individuals whose formative influence I hope will enrich her personality and broaden her ambitions. I have added you to that list. It is my sincerest hope that you will accept what I guarantee you will find a rare honor.

It would be remiss of me not to confide that you are the only woman other than my darling Maura to whom I have felt instinctively and uniquely drawn. Had events not transpired as they have, I might have courted you. Alas, my topmost priority at this moment is Melissa. Your assent to this arrangement will complete a most solemn promise I made to her mother. With my every ambition, and with humblest respect, I ask this of you.

Unable to budge her eyes from the page, she probes the carpeting behind for her discarded skirt as pulses of indignance and gratification scrap like territorial hummingbirds about the base of her throat. Laying hold the skirt, she manages to squirm it to her knees before Connie bolts through the door, snatches the letter from her and scans it, then drops it in Julia's lap, raises her fists and stomps an erratic circle to the computer table and back.

She yanks Julia to her feet.

"Come on, we gotta go!"

She pushes her back down.

"No, you gotta stay here, I gotta go find that stupid sonofabitch!"

As Connie hurries out the door, Julia scrambles to her feet, snags her blouse and sprints after her.

"Don't you dare go without me!"

Emerging from his own office halfway between Julia's and the elevators, Burnice watches in dismay as his shoeless boss parades past him, her blouse streaming from her naked shoulders and her skirt unzipped like those of so many stoned sorority girls. Connie rushes into the first available car. Julia converges just in time to slip through the closing doors. The gangly orthodontist from two floors above was not one of the complainers who inspired the secret stairway. In fact, he has lamented the cessation of the occasional striptease once afforded by his fellow lessee, a fact that is evident in his lingering gaze. Connie stares him down, then hastens to tuck, zip and button Julia's accoutrements.

"Jule, this is a bad idea."

"Thank you, Ms. Plachette, you've told me what I didn't want to hear. Now take me to your psycho leader!"

"You don't have the first clue where we're going. The only world you see through your plasma monitors consists of numbers and probabilities and antiseptic news reports. The world you and I grew up in no longer exists."

"I have eyeballs, Connie. And I'm not a hermit. It's not that bad out there."

"Because Burnie and I have been insulating you, you moron! When was the last time you didn't leave your home or office with an armed chauffer?"

The orthodontist lays his gaunt hand on Julia's shoulder.

"Your friend is right, you know. You must always valet. Never park yourself."

Connie bats his hand away with a ferocity that frightens even her friend.

"But that's not my point, Jule. Ani and I, we changed along with that world. I don't know what kind of man you think you're going to meet, but I know you both and I don't think you should be in the same room together!"

"I'm not afraid of that creep."

"That's not my point –"

Before Connie can finish her thought, the elevator opens at the lower level parking garage and Julia slips past her. Connie catches up and guides Julia to her car. Julia stops to admire the lines and the paint job, nowise familiar with the machine's cultural significance.

"Well, isn't this a cute little thing? Cherry red … I just adore that color."

"Get your ass in and buckle up, I'm in a hurry."

As Connie backs out and crawls up two flights to the gate, Julia feels a galling vibration, a roughness she's never experienced in a motor vehicle.

"I didn't know they were resurfacing the garage. So where do we find Stearns?"

"All I can tell you is where we won't – the courthouse. You had lunch yet?"

"I hardly think this is the time –"

"C'mon, yes or no!"

"No."

"Good, because you're sitting in a 1967 Boss 305 Mustang, and I'm not gentle with her."

"A boss what?"

No sooner does a throaty rumble tickle Julia's bare feet than it crescendos into a brain-joggling roar as the four-wheeled beast explodes sideways into the wispiest of gaps in the crisscrossing traffic. Julia's ninth birthday marked her first and last roller coaster ride. More frightful than the tingle in the pit of her stomach was the sound of her own involuntary screeching that accompanied it. Before the Pirellis have stopped smoking, she has resolved that, should she survive her current trek, she will never again set foot in this *305-whatsie-whosit*. Despite the terror that moils up and down her spine, she retains the presence of mind to marvel at how elegantly Connie maneuvers the impetuous monster, darting into unoccupied left-turn lanes and commandeering side streets to bypass traffic lights, weaving her way through snarls with the precision of a slalom skier.

The automotive maelstrom finally relents when they cross the intersection of Hill St. and Olie Ave. As they prowl past the potpourri of emergency vehicles, Julia spies patrolmen conveying pill-like shapes down a right-angled stairway like a giant white centipede with blue legs. When a red trailer blocks her view, her gaze wafts to an olive toned man with a bushy mustache and clothing so undersized that it mystifies her how he can swallow that yogurt without popping his every shirt button. Recognizing the emblematic rumble of the 305, he jams his teeming spoon back into the cup and captures Connie's stare with that hue of contempt typically displayed by residents of internment camps. Though she is not the mainspring of his animosity, the mere sight of her stirs it.

Perennial archenemies though they had always been, the *Safer Community Initiative* ushered in a new era of cooperation between city and county law enforcement. But Capt. Villanueva was unable to enjoy this camaraderie, because he had volunteered to be the Compliance Bureau Liaison for the local FBI office. He learned how leprous this had made him in the local law enforcement community when one of his own federally commissioned investigators was detained in the county jail. After leaving a handful of unrequited messages, Villanueva sped to the Sheriff's office to demand her immediate release. While his underlings stood off against their county equivalents, he burst through the inner office door to find he had interrupted a meeting between the Sheriff and seven guests which included Connie Plachette and Anthony Stearns. Though no one in his chain of command has officially confirmed it, he has since heard enough rumors from the right snitches to convince him there is some sort of hit squad operating under color of authority. No less than eight times in as many months, the Chief has countermanded a missing persons investigation due to either "budgeting" or "manpower" issues. The subject of each inquiry was a newly released felon. Familiar with the reputations of Plachette and Stearns, Villanueva initiated a probe into each. Near week's end, two vulturous Internal Affairs agents escorted him to the Chief's office, where he received a gruff ultimatum.

"Chick, I promoted you to Captain because you were among my most trusted detectives. The day you took that oath for the feds, you lost all my confidence. Either you don't see the big picture or you're trying to play both sides. Because I hope to almighty Jesus you're just uninformed, let me clue you in. The battle lines are forming out there. If something doesn't change in D.C. pronto, this federal/State rivalry will erupt into armed conflict, and our streets won't look any different than those of Egypt did in the summer of 2013. I've tolerated your little g-man masquerade because it hasn't threatened to compromise my assets for that showdown. But I can't allow this latest inquiry of yours to go any farther, so listen close. You *will* stop harassing this department's most generous benefactor and his associates or (1) you *will* lose your job and pension (2) you *will* have your reputation permanently stained and (3) you *will* serve time with the same degenerates you've put away during your most impressive career!"

When Villanueva indignantly replied that he had nothing to hide from IA, the Chief traded a vulpine smirk with Villanueva's convoyers.

"Let me put it this way, Chick. Any average investigator can find what's there. It takes a great investigator to find what was never there to begin with. My IA team is the cream of the crop."

Though the Chief proceeded to explain at some length how the recent bombardment of federal laws had bifurcated the public service pathway into opposing lanes called *moral* and *legal*, he failed to convince Villanueva that the mere concept of commingling justice with underground mercenaries did not spurn every principle his father swore to uphold when he became a naturalized U.S. citizen in 1961. Villanueva's pragmatism ultimately edged out his utopian misgivings. But while he abides the official hands-off policy regarding his department's curious "benefactors," whenever he comes face-to-face with one, his hypocrisy yields to the same raw antipathy with which his father boiled when he told Villanueva of a chance meeting he'd had in 1954 with Ernesto "Che" Guevara – to whom he referred as *aquélla carniceria socialista* ("that socialist butcher").

Connie nods.

"Detective?"

"Ms. Plachette?"

"You losing weight?"

"From what phantasm did you divine the false impression that you could successfully flatter me?"

"What's cooking at the Last Stand?"

"Who should be asking whom?"

"Seen anybody I know?"

"Who in particular, and why?"

"You always this snippy with taxpayers?"

Hoisting a defiant chin, he throws the remnants of his makeshift lunch into a patrolman's open trunk and galumphs away.

"What an ass –"

Before Julia can say *hole*, the grumbling machine lurches again, and any semblance of rational thought buckles to the fuss of parking meters and trees and cars and the occasional outraged pedestrian that streak by her window until this leg of their journey comes to an equally abrupt halt in the mouth of an alley cater-cornered from the restaurant at which she celebrated her birthday last year. As Connie revs the engine and retrieves a savage looking knife from somewhere beneath the steering column, Julia spies a motionless figure sitting on the ground, his back against a dumpster, his head and right arm hanging unnaturally. A black SUV stops alongside him, from whose front passenger door emerges the biggest, darkest man Julia has ever seen. The recumbent figure does not react as he approaches. Julia can detect not a single breath in his crumpled frame.

"Is that man dead?"

"Jule, get out."

Julia covets nothing more than to feel the soles of her feet on fixed pavement. But the starkness of this moment will not permit her to move as she fixates on the lifeless bundle in the distance.

"He is, isn't he? Nobody sits like that."

"Get the fuck out!"

Gunning the engine again, Connie pops free the passenger seatbelt with the knife hilt, uses its ample blade to nudge open the passenger door and shoves Julia to freedom before she and her rambunctious steed peel away. Squinting through the tumult of gravel and dirt, Julia looks on in awe as Connie throws the car into a broadside skid and leaps from the open window just as it comes to a stop. An eye-blink later, Connie has somehow tackled the tower of a man. No sooner do they hit the ground together than the driver and rear passenger of the SUV emerge with boxlike guns and train them on Connie, who shields herself behind her quarry's head and torso while she presses her ominous blade against his meaty gullet. Yet another gunman materializes behind the SUV driver, who keeps his gun on Connie while the rear passenger turns his on the driver's new assailant. As the antagonists dial in their aim and wait for the legendary pin to drop, Julia crawls behind a nearby stack of empty fruit crates for cover from the bloodbath she expects to erupt at any second. As more debris settles, she recognizes the third triggerman as the valet from the restaurant.

Julia's father occasionally took her to a friend's farm, where he taught her how to shoot a .38 caliber handgun. Though she became marginally proficient with it, no matter how many hundreds of bullets she shot, the anticipation of the recoil from the hammer's fall on the first few rounds always made her shake so badly that she didn't even bother to aim at the target until she had emptied the first cylinder. The fact that none of the participants in this standoff evinces the slightest trepidation about either killing or being killed so unnerves her that she hasn't the mindfulness to stanch the flow of urine that streams down her left ankle like an anesthetic. Entranced, she studies every aspect of the waterloo before her, from the faintest twitch of the driver's brow as he weighs his accuracy against distance and target size to the quaking of the big man's trachea every time Connie regrips the hilt and presses its steel more firmly with the persistence of a boa constrictor.

Don't move, please, please, please, don't anybody move!

In the midst of her internal mantra, she sees the valet's free hand emerge just enough from his jacket to reveal another handgun hidden from the backseat gunman's view. In one fluent motion, he cocks its hammer, grins ever so slightly and winks at the man.

Oh no, no, Christ no …

From the dumpster emanates a lone gagging sound. Then another. Or was it a cough? Six incredulous pairs of eyeballs fix upon the crumpled heap of humanity who rises from the ground then doubles over in, not pain but a fit of laughter.

"Stearns?! You sonofabitch!"

No one is more startled at Julia's outburst than she. And it only intensifies Ani's mirth, which crescendos when the big man grouses, "When you done jacking off over there, come and get this bony little banshee off me!" When his convulsions finally subside, Ani surveys the scene, taking care to lock eyes with each individual on his ocular hike, then extends his arms.

"Ladies, gentlemen, your weapons are unnecessary. As you return them to their respective places of portage, I ask that you ponder the concept *absurdity.* Lucio, what is the cardinal rule of urban conflict?"

"Take no drastic action without first ascertaining all attendant facts, Señor."

"Correct, my good friend. And the corollary is that rash assumptions result in needless bloodshed. Connie Plachette, permit me the honor of introducing to you my longtime associate and friend, Ossie Pryne."

Connie peels herself from Ossie, but keeps her blade at the ready as he trains a wary eye back at her.

"You best keep this she-devil on a leash, man. Just look at the gash on my arm!"

"You're lucky that's the only thing I cut, crybaby!"

More than twice her size, though Ossie aches to give her the wallop he thinks she deserves, he wants nothing to do with that bolo she wields as comfortably, precisely, as if she were born with it. Ani steps between them.

"Connie's first assumption, Ossie, was that you meant to do me harm."

"And I ain't yet decided against that."

"Let us table that conversation for now. Her second assumption: that I was as debilitated as I appeared. The reason, Connie, I was resting against that receptacle was because moments earlier I had availed myself of it to force my dislocated shoulder back into socket. Lucio, is the bar open?"

Lucio extends a guardedly cordial hand to Ossie's cortege.

"Always for you and your associates, Señor. May I suggest the auxiliary access?"

"Splendid. Friends, follow me."

Ossie steps aside, orders his henchmen to move and secure the SUV, and gestures to Connie.

"After you."

Connie scowls as she navigates a wide berth past him. "Aren't you the fucking gentleman?"

"Gentleman, hell, I just don't want to lose no limbs today."

As drivers return to their respective modes of transportation, Julia waves Connie off with both hands.

"Never again, thank you."

Ani starts for the restaurant as Lucio lingers to keep an eye on his new acquaintances. When Ani stops to greet Julia, she squares off and pelts him in the jaw with clenched fist.

"Keep walking, Stearns." She then marches to a bewildered Lucio and laces her arm through his.

Ani leads the assemblage to the rear of Abuelita Rosa's, where the turn of Lucio's key in a metal box atop a pylon summons a freight elevator from beneath two metal doors labeled *Storm Sewer Access*. Because the platform can barely accommodate the entire party, Julia is forced to ride with her nose mere millimeters from Ani's sweat encrusted neck, whose gamey odor coalesces with that of the blood weeping from Ossie's forearm to create a pungency evocative of her inaugural menstruation. Ani turns aside to address Lucio.

"It was irresponsible of you to intercede on my behalf. You have your own life and loves and, for all you know, I may have deserved whatever fate awaited me in that alley. For that matter, you were foolish to even search for me."

Lucio claps a reverent hand on Ani's shoulder, but Ossie preempts his response.

"By rights, you should be dead."

"Ossie, I am unarmed and suffering a tremendous electrolyte deficit! If you want to kill me, this is an opportune time. Otherwise, shut your –"

Before he can finish his taunt, the jolt of the hydraulics at journey's end buckles Ani's knees. Ossie catches him and helps him stagger to a chair at the closest end of the Utility Committee conference table. While Connie helps Lucio remove Ani's coat and clothing to assess damage, Julia stops alongside Ossie's soldiers to marvel at the fleetness with which three waiters supply the buffet with the restaurant's select appetizers and entrees while the hostess demurely canvases the guests for their drink preferences.

"Lucio, I will need the blue bag."

"Right away, Señor Stearns."

Lucio disappears behind the bar and just as suddenly reemerges carrying a clear plastic bag containing fluid of a cerulean tincture, a small leather duffel and a wire coat tree with metal clothespins protruding from its branches. Ossie, too, follows the commotion with the wonderment of a child on his first visit to Disney World.

"The hell is that, an IV?"

Ani's voice fades with each word he excavates.

"This … one of Rita's signature recipes. Combination of saline … B-12 … natural opiate from … wild tree root whose name … take to her grave … close relationship with … Sac and Fox … trades for … steroid more potent than … conventional … pharma ... ceuticals."

IV threaded and secured, Ani draws a contented sigh and drifts to sleep. Lucio retrieves from the satchel an arciform needle and sutures. He approaches Ossie, who retreats step for step. Still occupied with Ani, Connie slaps her palm on the table to get Ossie's attention.

"Sit down, Bigfoot, so he can treat your sissy scratch."

"I'll heal up just fine."

"If you like, I can inject a local, Señor."

"You ain't sticking nothing in me!"

Without looking up, Connie grabs one of Ani's empty boots and hurls it at Ossie's head with astounding accuracy.

"Damn you, woman, if you don't –"

"It's not *your* health we're concerned about, numbnuts! I don't know what your personal habits are or where you've been. You could have AIDS or Hep-C. Until you're disinfected and stitched up, you're a walking biohazard."

Hearing this, Ossie's aides, who have closed ranks between him and Lucio, eye their boss in reproof and sidle away. Ossie plops in the first available chair and relinquishes his lacerated limb.

"So tell me, Sasquatch. Why are you here?"

"To do what I do."

"Piss people off?"

"Mediate."

"You? Fill me in; I need a good laugh."

"Some years ago, when State governments started legalizing marijuana and the more benign opioids, the street gangs didn't go away quiet when they trade dried up. To try and fend off the same street wars among the more sophisticated organizations who didn't win contracts, before they started sanctioning vigilantism on account of the *Criminal Rehabilitation and Reform Act*, a commission of governors appointed me the official, unofficial arbiter of disputes."

"What's so special about you?"

"I been with the Guardian Angels since I was fourteen. I got a rep that gives me influence with both the government-backed and private outfits. I called Ani yesterday. Offered to arbitrate a sit-down with him and the Millands."

"How'd you know they killed Jarry?"

"The way they did it – a fatal dose of the anesthesia propofol shot into his jugular by one of them high-tech walking sticks with a needle in the end, like you read about in spy stories. He'd have felt nothing more painful than a mosquito bite, if anything at all. Then, in case they was any doubt, they dressed him up in his best suit. Anyway, when Ani put on this air that he understood why they killed Jarry, I knew he was lying. I just didn't think he'd act so fast. I set up the meet with the Millands, thinking at least I could convince them to reach out to the man. We was supposed to convene a half hour ago."

"Hell of a mediator you are."

When Connie prepares to examine Ani for signs of internal injury, the snap of her surgical gloves draws Julia's attention to his bare torso which, at first glance, appears to be bloodstained. A closer inspection reveals crimson tinged bruising from his chest to his navel. Her gasp distracts Connie.

"What you see is the biological fallout of extreme exertion. Most people see similar patterns on a boxer and think they were caused by his opponent, but they're wrong. Muscles and tendons can only operate at their maximum capacity for a short time before they need rest and refueling. When you push them past that limit, blood vessels rupture. Granted, Ani took his share of hits, but most of what you see is the natural result of the punishment he dished out."

"Punishment? I don't understand, Con. What happened to him?"

"You have the same information as I, Jule. You know what happened."

Finished prodding his front side, Connie pulls Ani forward to inspect his back but finds her arms too short for the task.

"Hey, stop gawking like a tourist, get over here and be useful!"

Julia kneels and cups her arms under Ani's. Connie finds a series of long, irregular welts near his shoulder blades. This indicates that one of his oppugners managed to wrest his khukuri but, unpracticed with its use, was unable to inflict any appreciable damage with it.

"Damn you, Ani!"

"What's wrong?"

"I showed him a hundred times the best way to hold a knife so it wouldn't get taken away, but he never pays attention. Thank you, sweetie."

The hostess has brought a basin of warm soapy water, rags and isopropyl alcohol. As Connie treats and bathes her patient, Julia studies his countenance in a desperate attempt to reconcile his contradictions.

"Con, what do you know about his family?"

"What's there to know? Shift him a little that way."

"Was his dad a drunk?"

"Teetotaler."

"A physical abuser?"

"Franklin lived a long, fulfilling life and died a natural death with his sons and granddaughter at his bedside. And you know the kind of man Ani is. How's your theory jive with those facts?"

"Then it had to be his mother. Sexual molestation fits."

"What are you going on about?"

"Or maybe she didn't breastfeed him. Just last month, the New England Journal of Medicine published a compelling study relating maternal neglect with antisocial behavior."

"Stop it, Julie."

"Well, there has to be a reason."

"For what?"

"For him."

"Lie him back now. Why does there have to be a reason for anyone?"

"How can a man with so much love inside him be capable of so much hatred?"

Though it complicates Lucio's task, Ossie indulges in a spate of chuckling that brings him to tears.

"Oh, mercy! Plachette, what fairyland did you drag her out of? Talking about love and hate like they was opposing teams in a zero-sum game. That's gibberish, lady – a false distinction. These arbitrary labels *love* and *hate* ain't nothing more than extreme expressions of the same undercurrent of emotion. In the end, it's all love. What you and your other Sadie Silver Spoons ain't got the hair to admit is love ain't always fun. Sometimes, love beckons from the vile pit, and if you don't answer the call, you nothing but a coward. Let me tell you something, pixie, only love can give a man the strength and resolve to do what that man did today, what he's been doing for near thirty years."

Julia springs to her feet, spins to snarl at Ossie and punches her finger in Ani's direction.

"Love does not massacre people on a whim! And normal people don't preside over common street gangs!"

With only a few stitches left to lace, Lucio braces Ossie's arm for another tirade.

"Normal people? Lady, look around you. The social criterion *normality* is a fool's paradise, because its definition is more elusory than sincerity in the mouth of sorority trash. And I'll tell you something about love. You got any kids?"

"No."

"Brothers? Sisters?"

"No."

"So who the hell have you ever loved?"

"My pop."

"Now we're talking. I got a scenario for you. Your poppa's got his back against a wall and he's being stalked by a wild dog. What do you do?"

"Yell, shoo it away."

"So he ain't scared of your poppa, but he'll run 'cause a froufrou thing like you hollers at him?"

"I'd call for help."

"You in the wilderness, woman. Ain't nobody else, no animal control, no *po*lice. It's just you, your pop and a vicious dog looking for his next meal."

His sewing complete, Lucio douses the wound in alcohol and slaps an adhesive compress on it with such dispatch that he is standing clear by the time Ossie reacts to the sting.

"You can't just change the parameters to stump me. First it's a wall, then we're in the boondocks. If Daddy climbs a tree, I suppose the dog'll sprout opposable thumbs?"

"You ain't getting the point, pixie."

"Maybe that's because you ain't communicating, Rosey!"

Her allusion to this legendary member of the Los Angeles Rams' *Fearsome Foursome* elicits guffaws from Ossie's gun-toting contingent who are grazing at the buffet. His dominant arm now free, Ossie uses its meaty index finger to scold his disputant.

"Jesus had a name for sisters like you. But I ain't petty, so I'll move on. You alone, yeah, but you got the means to kill that mongrel. Say you got a big gun and you a crack shot. You'd kill a mangy dog for your pop, right?"

"Is this a trick question?"

"So you and your daddy walk off into the sunset, leaving the dog to die?"

"What choice do I have?"

"Dog never did nothing to you, did he?"

"I suppose now you'll tell me I'm lugging a magical bag of *Gravy Train*?"

"You just shot a dog based on what you *thought* he was gonna do, not what you *knew* he was gonna do. In them touchy-tickle seminars I attend to keep up my creds, we call that fear-based behavior."

"You don't impress me with your cryptic jargon. I can cite you a truckload of examples proving that fear is one of the essential emotions that have assured the survival of the human race."

"Follow the ball, pixie. Fear chooses to eliminate the threat from afar, so don't nobody get they hands dirty. I submit that love can save you, your pop and the dog. But it ain't easy, and it ain't pretty."

"What's up your sleeve this time, a tandem witch's broom?"

"No more hypotheticals. I'm talking about a real, live event. I was there to witness it myself."

Flexing his throbbing wing, Ossie kneels to assist Connie in togging Ani with the clean attire Lucio has brought from an anteroom. Folding defiant arms, Julia cocks her head and sets her hips in the classic pose struck by women the world over as a *put up or shut up* ultimatum.

"Just four years ago, Ani come out to see the family and me. He and my wife Tetene was discussing them highbrow books like they do. I was stoking the grill. The boys weren't there, probably at this camp or that. Anyhow, this big dog busted through some rotted out fence slats into my yard. I'd heard a rumor that the man on the adjoining acreage ran a dog fighting ring, but I never gave it credence. One look at this dog changed my mind. Not even six months old, judging from the size of his paws, he was already a foot and a half tall. His ribs was about to burst through his coat, and them teeth of his was open for business.

"We'd had our run-ins with wildlife. Before I even heard the dog growl, Tetene was on a beeline for my twelve-gauge. Just as I drew down, Ani stepped right into my fireline. He said, 'Don't you harm that animal unless he gets past me.' I asked him what the hell he was gonna do. 'Train the pup,' he said.

"Before I knew it, ole Ani had squared off with that dog, and he was snarling and gnashing like he himself was a dog, and just when that mongrel bit down on his arm, Ani bit down on its muzzle, and he didn't let go of that snout until he'd brought that mess of muscle to the dirt. Next thing I hear is a whimper of submission. Ani lets him go, but he stay hunched over him, dominant. That hound just rolled over on his back with his feet in the air. Ani snatched my potato scallops and, by the time the steaks was cooked and served, he'd taught that dog to heel and to sit and to stay.

"Well, morning next, Animal Control swarmed the neighbor's property. They found a dozen more dogs and rounded 'em up to be euthanized. Said they was lost causes. Ole boy swore to high heaven one dog was missing, but by then Ani done smuggled that pup right out the State on a private jet. Dog's still with him today."

In an epiphanous fit, Connie grabs Ossie's shoulder.

"Mojo?"

"Damn right, sister."

If anything galls Julia more than restrictive clothing, it is having a conversation stolen from her. So she pokes the hulking man in the back of the neck.

"What's a Mojo?"

"A 135-pound Rottweiler that stands thirty inches at the shoulder and lets little Lissy ride him like a pony but will chomp your jelly white ass clean off at the snap of Ani's finger."

"So he reformed a mean dog. Old news. The world already has a dog whisperer."

"Is everything a joke to you, woman? You talk about this man like he's out of his mind. They killed his brother. Might've been one or all of them, he had no way to know. Little Lissy could have been next. It was love drove him to kill for her, and love prepared him to die for her."

"What do you mean *die*?"

"He took on fourteen grown men alone. And them dudes weren't no cupcakes. Those are stiff odds, even for him. And nobody goes for a casual stroll after a melee like that. The man knew cops would be all over that place, but he didn't arrange no transportation. He expected to die up there."

Julia stomps to the chair Ossie just vacated and slumps there like a sullen brat, clenching her jaw to stave the uninvited throe of compassion welling in her throat.

"Your logic is flawed, Pryne. If he had enough love to save the dog, why didn't he have enough to make peace with his brother's killers?"

"You ever own a dog?"

"No."

"Cat?"

"No."

"Rabbit? Goldfish? Mongoose? Anything?"

"Mom was allergic."

"Why ain't I surprised? A bad dog can be salvaged because a dog don't have the mental capacity to sit around rationalizing and conniving. His conscious memory is only as long as he been awake. At day's end, all a dog wants is food, water and shelter. Beyond that, he ain't got no intentions. Human beings, we full of greed and lust and disappointments and resentments and irrational fears that bind us up in a thousand different tangles by the time we old enough to vote, and they fester for the rest of our lives. Some people get so twisted that they ain't enough love in the world to save 'em."

"If he loved Melissa as much as you say, he wouldn't desert her."

Still on his knees, Ossie pauses, then turns to Julia.

"Who said anything about desertion? Now I see where you coming from. Spare me the sad saga of whatever you lost, pixie – me and everyone in this room had our own childhood to live down. And since you ain't never had a kid, let me clue you in. Any father with any hair would rather die young a hero than grow old a coward."

"I can cite you a dozen sources right now confirming the fact that it takes bravery to grow old."

"This ain't no high school debate, where you argue for argument's sake. I'm talking about one do-or-die moment, a crossroads that defines you for the rest of your days."

"In a civilized society, you call the police."

Ossie bounds to his feet and throws up his hands.

"Child, have you even read a history book? All through the ages, back to them caveman days, ain't no society ever been civilized. In an ideal world, you could count on the government and the *po*lice. But in an ideal world there would be no crime or the like, so those bodies would be obsolete. Let's stick with reality. You want an explanation for this man? You want to know how my friend here fits into this world?"

"Please enlighten me."

"Turn of the century, was a professional cyclist name of Armstrong. Won seven consecutive Tours of France. We're talking about two weeks with your butt stuck on top of one of them flimsy bicycles, racing some hundred miles a day and going up and down them long mountain roads."

"I know Armstrong. I met him in Spain in 2004. He's an ass."

"Of course he is. So is just about every top echelon athlete in the world. If they wasn't all backstabbing narcissists, they wouldn't have gotten very far in sports. But the man's personality got no relevance to my analogy. Some years ago, the regulating bodies stripped him of all them titles when he admitted to using performance enhancers."

"An admission that proved him a liar and a hypocrite and disheartened millions of little boys who emulated him."

"You jumping on that *role model* bandwagon, are you?"

"We don't live in the wild west. Celebrities have a responsibility to the youth of society."

"That's a damned copout, lady. And the Old West was far tamer than them movies paint it. You know why? The instinct for self-preservation: when everybody and his grandmama packed a gun, people was a lot more polite than today. And as for them youngins we call *our future* to make us feel squishy inside, parents who ask pro athletes to be role models are abdicating they own responsibility to teach they own kids how to tell the real from the unreal. The only role models in my family are my wife and me. I don't trust that job to nobody, and that keeps me on my toes. You show me a dad who expects a complete stranger half his age to be his boy's mentor, and I'll show you a lazy, good-for-nothing punk oughta have that kid taken away and put in a real home.

"Anyhow, them rulemakers placed Armstrong and all his teammates and opponents in an impossible situation. It didn't take no genius to figure out that just as soon as blood and urine tests was developed to expose what them self-loathing moralists thought was the latest doping method, the dope suppliers was already three steps ahead cooking up a better recipe. So logic instructs that ain't no testing gonna catch everything or everybody. So long as just one out of two hundred athletes uses and escapes detection, his one hundred ninety-nine competitors are at a disadvantage. Their choice is simple: follow the rules and be virtually guaranteed a loss or break 'em and have a chance to win."

"But once you inject performance enhancers into the equation, nobody knows if a win is really a win because nothing is genuine!"

"Okay, pixie. Go and get yourself a state-of-the-art bike tomorrow. Find yourself a local racing club, they all over. I'll give you six months – hell, I'll give you six years to get your jiggly tush in shape. Then take yourself on an underground shopping spree. Get yourself the strongest performance enhancers that's out there, sign yourself up for a semipro race and see if you can even hang with them twenty-something dudes who practically live on two wheels."

"Your point?"

"I don't care what Armstrong took. I don't care what none of 'em did, be it Ullrich in 1997, Mercxx back in my younger days or Garin way back in 1903. You don't even get to ride in that race unless you got natural talent oozing out your pores and you train that talent like ain't no tomorrow. Like I said, you don't know who that one in two hundred is. So logic counsels the savvy contender – that ain't accurate, because the typical pro athlete don't have the brainpower to reason that far ahead. Logic counsels the savvy *coach* to presume his contender's every opponent is doping and to follow suit. By the time that starting gun gets fired, ain't no serious contender got an improper advantage because they all doped up. The playing field is even.

"As performance enhancers leveled the playing field for Armstrong, Anthony Wayne Stearns gives you and all your wisecracking friends a fighting chance to enjoy your self-righteous lives without worrying your cocktail hour will be the last thing you ever enjoy before you gangraped and tortured to death."

"Rationalize it all you want to. Armstrong was a hypocrite, and so are you for defending anarchy."

"Let's talk about hypocrisy. You a working girl, are you?"

"International investments, acquisitions, mergers."

"You get to where you are by opening your legs or using your brain?"

"I won't dignify that question."

"I take it, then, that you ain't a fan of sexism."

"I don't cater to cavemen."

"You work this morning?"

"I negotiated a real estate deal with some nice gentlemen from the greater Calcutta region."

"So you a carpetbagger."

"No one at that table was at a disadvantage, Mr. Pryne."

"All men? Not one skirt among 'em?"

"Which fact worked against me, not in my favor."

"Did you wear the same thing you wearing now?"

"What are you now, a fashion advisor?"

"I'm not a chump, lady. I know that culture. In the last ten years, I've spent half my time in the Philippines working with their Angels chapter. If you sashayed into that meeting dressed like that, with your delicates hanging here and your intimates puckering there, them poor fellas didn't have a chance. The young ones would have sold you they kids under a libidinal spell while the old ones would have peddled they grandkids in despair for the whole of humanity. Now then, what's that you was saying about hypocrisy?"

"That was strategy, not hypocrisy. And you're one to talk – you aid and abet a racist."

"What makes him a racist?"

"He named his cat Tarbaby!"

"He didn't name that cat; I did. Do you know why?"

"I'm all ears."

"Name comes from a series of animal stories published by a man name of Joel Chandler Harris, most of 'em penned in the late nineteenth century. Maybe you've heard of the fictional narrator, Uncle Remus? No? Anyhow, Harris used them books to recount stories he'd heard directly from slaves at a plantation he apprenticed at during the Civil War. That series is one of the richest and most accurate depictions of both the wisdom of my ancestors and the position of authority and respect many of them earned in white family structures – an aspect of that era don't nobody talk about anymore, because a lot of folks with political agendas have cut it out the history books. Anyhow, in one story, Br'er Fox makes a doll out of tar and dresses it up to trick Br'er Rabbit. Rabbit comes along and tries to make conversation with the Tar Baby, and gets mad when it don't respond. Rabbit slaps the Tar Baby, and his paw gets stuck. The more Rabbit strikes and struggles, the more entangled he gets in the tar. The Tar Baby represents a sticky situation that only gets worse the longer you grapple with it. Book critics and tenured professors, who ain't got nothing worthwhile to do anyhow, have dreamed up all kinds of racial overtones over the years, and their meddling has befouled the moral of the original story. But I don't put any stock in what idle minds have to say. And if you ever met that cantankerous feline, you'd damn sure understand her name."

"But you can't deny that, by today's standards, it's tantamount to calling it a … you know."

"I don't know. Spit it out."

"The *n-word*."

"They's a lot of words start with that letter."

"I will not let you bait me into saying that word."

"Does it rhyme with jigger?"

"You're an ass."

"I ain't baiting you; I'm impressing on you how foolish it is to accuse someone of racism before you know all the facts. Like them deaf, dumb and blind monkeys from the old stories, we so afraid of being accused of this prejudice or that insensitivity that we brown-bag more and more of what we say in childish jabber like *the b-word*, *the c-word* and *the f-word* to the point that communication between accomplished and educated adults ain't no more intelligible than a schoolyard spat. Connotation is all in the context. Couple of fools been using so-called racism for a half-century to make a fortune – you know 'em, but I don't want to promote 'em, so I made up emblematic names for 'em – Reverends Charlatan and Quackson. Neither one of them punks had the brains or the attention span to understand Martin's message, and they can't pull they heads out the 1960s, so they've brainwashed generation after generation of blacks to adhere to the myth of relational slavery – a self-fulfilling prophecy whereby the black man so strongly believes you whites got it in for him that he sees hatred where they ain't none. Thirty years before the oldest of them clowns was even born – 1911 to be exact – my man Booker T. Washington exposed they ilk. I memorized the passage when I was twelve:

> There is another class of colored people who make a business of keeping the troubles, the wrongs, and the hardships of the Negro race before the public. Having learned that they are able to make a living out of their troubles, they have grown into the settled habit of advertising their wrongs — partly because they want sympathy and partly because it pays. Some of these people do not want the Negro to lose his grievances, because they do not want to lose their jobs.

"Reality is, you white folk don't hold a corner on the market of prejudice or even slavery. It's a cultural fact. In their haste to coin a term for the black man that sounded rich and noble, politically correct idiots like Charlatan and Quackson came up with a phrase just as offensive to the honest student of history as that nasty little word that rhymes with snigger: *African American.* You ever wonder how the white slave traders found they merchandise? They sure as hell didn't dock they boats on a random African coast and go hunting for 'em, 'cause they'd have never got back alive. No, no, the first-line-ground-zero enablers of the entire slave trade were Africans black as me, who captured and sold the strongest members of rival tribes so they own tribe could dominate the region. Today, we denounce that practice as *ethnic cleansing.* Think about that irony, pixie: the ultimate blame for the historical snippet of slavery we all been up in arms about for two centuries rests, not with the white man, but with the indigenous African.

"And I got more recent examples for you. Back in the 90s when they had all them riots in Simi Valley over the Rodney King imbroglio, a reporter asked a black man why he was looting and burning Vietnamese stores. He said so they'd go back where they came from. You probably think my presence here today illustrates some pinnacle of interracial *rainbow* solidarity, but Ani Stearns is the only close friend I have who's white. Yeah, sister, I prefer the company of my own kind. Don't mean I hate your kind. Don't mean there ain't elements of my kind I don't shun. And it ain't bigotry because I exercise my choice without moral judgment. It's just a fact of human nature most of us don't have the hair to admit.

"As for that word you and I been tiptoeing around, they's a big ole gulf between using it as an aspersion and citing it in a descriptive way. In all my traveling and schooling, I ain't yet seen anyone get roughed up by rhetoric or maimed by a metaphor. You and I, we having an analytical conversation, so I won't take offense. Now then, say the word."

"No."

"Just say it."

"I'll not! And I don't see why that's funny to you."

"I'm laughing at myself as much as you. Even when a black man say it's okay, you can't articulate a piddling six-letter word because you been slapped in the head day after day for your entire life by the likes of Charlatan and Quackson. My own sense of fairness don't allow me to say it either, because I'm sensitive to the unmitigated guilt it would cause you, a browbeaten white lady, just to hear me say it. But I'm also a man of integrity and self-respect, and I do not suffer the Charlatan/Quackson delusion that different rules apply to me, because to believe that tripe is to tell myself *I am inferior on account of my skin color.* So, unless and until we blacks start acting like adults and admit that even that word is capable of more than one meaning in the mouth of the white man, I don't abide folks my own color using it among themselves. And let me tell you, if any brother ever use that term on me – or its affrontive twin *African American*, either one – that hip-hop punk will get a mouthful of fist."

Ossie gestures toward the tallest of his bodyguards.

"My man over there can testify to that with his corrective orthodonture."

"Rationalize him all you want to; he should have called the police."

Julia folds her arms and swivels aside to pout. Ossie marches to the bar, grunting and shaking his head.

"Ain't no talking sense to that one. Damn whiskey is what I need. Maybe ten. Lord, have mercy!"

The hostess deposits a conservative glass of merlot on the table next to Julia. Lucio rushes over with a magnum and fills it to the brim, instructing his younger cousin:

"Señor Stearns was explicit on this matter – we must never let her see the bottom of the stemware."

Wrenching the bottle from Lucio, Julia swigs the glass dry to drown a pesky pang of empathy. Refilling it, she watches Connie check

Ani's pulse, gauge his pupillary reaction with a penlight, then assess his blood pressure with an old fashioned stethoscope and sphygmomanometer. She glugs down another glassful to feed the tickly euphoria that dances about her hair like so many phrenetic pinpricks. Another gulp, another pour. In the periphery, she spies three Lucios exit to return to their restaurant duties upstairs, the door falling to behind them in a dizzying flutter. With another gulp, she squints anew at the most vivid iteration of Connie she can capture.

"Level with me, Ms. Con … conundrumum. Are you doing Stearns? If so, I respect that. But if not … I'll be damned … I'm in love with a wild rabid who wrestles mongeese …"

The shattering goblet beckons everyone's attention as Julia crumples into a most unladylike stupor – her shirt still only half-buttoned and her bra askew, the leather chair holds her skirt in place as she slips floorward like spent bathwater, exposing threadbare cotton panties so effluvious of urea that male prurience gives way to revulsion in even Ossie's youngest aide who just turned twenty-two.

As the hostess scurries to the mop closet, Connie turns her ablutionary attention to her sodden confidant. Ossie swigs a peevish shot of whiskey and ambles to her side, lifting Julia back into her chair and kneeling to hold the frothy tub for Connie.

"Thanks, Bigfoot. Your men suck, by the way. The tall one had a strong bead on me for a full second and a half, but he hesitated. And the short one might as well have shot his own head off, because Lucio was about to do him the favor."

"My sons, Keemon and Monroe. Got damned *iPods* for brains, but what you gonna do? Their momma says *Take 'em to work*, so I take 'em to work."

He nods toward her facial scar.

"You do time?"

"Nine years."

"Where?"

"A seventeen hundred square-foot ranch style house in subtopia with a two-point-five car garage, a redwood back deck with built-in hot tub and a Jenn-Air in the gazebo."

"Where you learn how to use a blade like that?"

"What's it to you?"

"I reckon the same place you learned your social skills. Why you fussing over this pixie? By rights, her kind should be extinct by now."

"Her *kind*?"

"She naïve and arrogant. If that ain't a bad enough combination, girl ain't got a lick of fashion sense."

"All true. But she restored my dignity once. I owe her this favor."

When she has cleaned Julia and secured her appendages in the appropriate garb, Connie ushers Ossie to the bar where she pours herself a glass of the most accessible wine while he refills his snifter. For the next few hours, Connie instinctually avoids revealing even the most innocuous of details about herself while Ossie regales her with stories about his role in bringing the Bronx gang wars of the 1970s to a relatively bloodless end, his romance with Tetene and his utter disillusionment with the pseudo liberals of his youth.

Behind them Julia stirs, stretching her arms and lingering for a moment in that corduroy realm between repose and wakefulness. It was not the wine that knocked her out so much as her body's natural reaction to the stress of the incident in the alley. Studying the face of Ani, who dozes tranquilly but a few feet away, she struggles to reconcile such a chivalrous man with her dawning acceptance of the fact that he is a mass killer. His left thumb twitches. She imagines those hands enwrapping a little girl she does not know. She ponders how soothing their strokes might have been to the aching muscles of a pregnant woman she'll never meet. She contemplates the rage that coursed through them mere hours ago.

Ani opens his eyes and straightens himself in his chair, jostling her from her reverie so abruptly that she belches out a reflexive yelp. Connie and Ossie bolt from their stools, but Ani waves them off.

"No more fussing, please. I am much better. That Rita is one fine cook."

Ani peels the tape from his forearm and removes the IV needle. Julia walks her chair closer to him and tears open an adhesive bandage. Her restorative doze has tempered her animosity for the man's various deeds with compassion for the man himself, lending a distinct sincerity to her next question.

"How do you feel?"

Ani stares askance as he considers the query, turns his attention to applying the bandage, then contemplates her anew.

"I have just dispatched some of my oldest friends. I know not how to codify that sensation."

"Did you take any shots to the head?"

"Why?"

"Because you're talking like a nineteenth century poet, and it's damned annoying."

They study each other like chess opponents, he groping for the appropriate words, she trying desperately to keep her own from spewing forth.

"Julia, you will please forgive me. I did not expect to see you, or anyone, ever again. Dare I take comfort in the slimmest possibility that you have not yet read my letter?"

"Do you regret sending it?"

"Only because it places us in a thorny predicament."

"Are you retracting everything you said because now you have to live it down?"

"No. I am simply observing the fact that the revelation of one's testamentary intent forever changes him in the eyes of his survivors. This is one of the countless reasons the typical Will is kept under lock and key until its author has expelled his crowning breath. I fear my letter has cast upon you an undue feeling of obligation."

"Well, let me put your mind at ease. I thought you were a strange and scary man the last time we spoke, and I still do. So you needn't look for me to fall into your arms and declare my undying devotion any time soon."

"Yet here you are … dressed like a strumpet from 1982."

Julia reaches to pull her jacket across her diaphanous blouse, only to discover she left it in the office, so she folds her forearms to cover her spilt cleavage, but this blushful act first startles then disgusts her because never before has she felt the least bit modest about her attire or anything beneath it, so she uncrosses her arms but, keenly aware that Ani's attention is now riveted to those arms and curious about where they will finally alight, she doesn't know what to do with them, so she grabs the magnum of wine from the tabletop, but she doesn't want Ani to know she's drafted it as a prop, so she hoists it to take a swig but, never having drunk wine straight from the bottle, she misjudges the circumference of the nozzle and the crimson nectar cascades from her nose to her crotch.

Without a word, Ani retrieves a handkerchief from his pants pocket. She snatches it spitefully, as if he were the cause of the spill, and frantically daubs at her sopping garments.

"Stop staring at me!"

"And miss this minstrel show? Not on your life."

"Well, make up your mind then. One minute, you think I'm such a hot commodity that you ask me to befriend your niece, you compare me to your late wife, and the next minute you call me a harlot." She clenches a vexed fist at chin level. The gesture spatters her cheeks with purplish droplets from the sodden hanky. "Do you want me or not?"

"She's not his niece, Jule."

Connie's outburst draws the bewildered attention of Julia and Ossie, and a reproachful glare from Ani.

"Don't give me that look. Your exact words were *full disclosure*. I'm surprised she didn't figure that one out on her own."

Julia thrusts her cavernous glare back upon Ani.

"Melissa's your daughter?"

"This is not some Sunday afternoon coffee klatch – I owe no one an explanation of my private affairs. I need a taco."

Ani rises and turns toward the buffet. Julia bounces to her feet and blocks his path, jabbing his chest with that implacable index finger of hers.

"Just how callous are you?! I nearly watched Connie and Ossie and, and those sneaky looking guys over there, die today on account of you. And you" poke "made" poke "Melissa" poke "*my* affair" poke "when you" poke "delivered" poke "that" poke "letter. You don't get a taco until I get an explanation."

Ani swats her hand aside and closes the distance between them.

"Are you threatening me, Ms. Bross?"

"I said you were scary; I didn't say you scared me."

He clutches her chin with such swiftness and command that his associates fear he is on the verge of either striking or kissing her. Instead, he gingerly tilts her head to whisper into her ear.

"That is mighty tough talk for a woman who can not seem to keep track of her underthings."

With a gamesome grin and a wink of the eye, Ani retreats to the bar where he pours a self-congratulatory beer while a mortified Julia gropes her seamless backside then, leery as an eight-year-old opening a dusty attic trunk, pulls the elastic front of her skirt out to peer beneath. She then takes indignant stock of her rapt audience.

"All right, which one of you creeps did it? I've seen depravity in my day, but to take liberties with a defenseless woman –"

"Julie!"

Connie hurries to her side, spins her out of earshot and hushfully informs her how the undergarment at issue disappeared and why she will never see it again.

"Was he still asleep?"

"He didn't come around until after you did."

"So he doesn't know I peed myself?"

"Not unless you and I screw around over here long enough to give Pryne a chance to tell him."

"Excellent point."

Though she still feels flushed, Julia dons her coolest boardroom smirk and leads Connie barward with a purposeful strut – not an easy task when one's shoes rest precipitously atop a stairstep two and a half miles away. Commandeering the stool next to Ossie, she clears her throat.

"Mr. Stearns, I believe we were about to probe the dubious lineage of one Melissa Stearns."

Ani indulges in a lingering gulp of his beloved amber quaff, studies the gaze of each of his companions in turn, lays aside the mug and takes the bar edge in hand as though it were a lectern.

"Until today, only Connie was privy to the fact I am about to divulge. It will surprise neither of you, I am sure, that I could not begrudge my own curiosity in the face of my brother's … imprudence. I had a nurse draw a sample of my blood right after they wheeled Maura into the operating room. Melissa is indeed my biological daughter."

Julia shakes her head like a drowning philosophy student.

"How could you just give away your own baby?"

"Actually, I did not get the results until some ten hours after I had told Jarry she was his. But consanguinity was a mere technicality, thus irrelative to my decision. In Melissa I saw the ideal emotional anchor for Jarry, an incentive to focus his life. And it worked. You saw the transformation."

Ossie nods in accord.

"And I knew empirically that I would be far more available to her as an uncle than a father."

Now it is Ossie's turn to tread water.

"How the hell did you pull it off?"

"Judge Yamane oversaw the legalities."

"I'm talking about family and friends and newsfolk. It was one thing to fool 'Tene and me fifteen hundred miles away, but Maura was a conspicuous public figure in this town. How'd you avert a scandal?"

With a dry smirk, Ani opens his wallet to show Ossie his driver license.

"Why am I looking at this?"

"It is the answer to your uncharacteristically inane question. It confirms I am not an impostor – that I am, indeed, the same Anthony Wayne Stearns you have known for thirty-seven years."

Julia's eyes drift, her chin quivers, as she stares vacantly down a melancholic tunnel at whose small end she watches her father's El Camino dissolve into shimmers of mid-August heat on Highway 81.

"Know-it-all sonsofbitches!"

"Who you talking about, pixie?"

"You. Him. All you self-absorbed pricks, deciding on a whim it's best to leave your most loyal friend behind. A little girl doesn't care if you're a coward or a hero, an idiot or a sage; she just wants a dad."

"There you go again. Try this abandonment on for size."

Ossie shoves his snifter aside and lumbers to the buffet. Connie pats Ani's hand.

"I'll go check in with Rita."

When Ani returns his attention to Julia, he finds himself preempted by the palm of her right hand. With her left, she pokes an agitated finger at the receding mountain of Ossie.

"That caustic … jackass is a mediator?!"

"Let us not forget the particular demographic he serves."

He takes her hands in his.

"Julia, you give us pricks far too much credit. Circumstance promises nothing. However brave or wise, no man can fathom a fair child's heart. I do not pretend that my decisions regarding Melissa have necessarily been right. Thanks to Jarry's compromised mental condition, I did not deem myself at liberty to be selfish with her. But my generosity pales in comparison to that of your father."

When her eyes lock onto his, he spies the panicked adolescent who has lingered there like a festering boil for all these years.

"Nothing was in the news. All I heard were rumors about mafiosi and prostitution and embezzlement. What do you know about my dad?"

"First and foremost, he never did anything illegal or unethical in his life. I don't know how privy you were to the political climate of the time but, as President Reagan's second term drew to a close, interest began to surge in alternative political parties, primarily because no establishment candidate who could hold a candle to Reagan was anywhere to be found. Having predicted this quandary years earlier, Reagan had tried to restyle Republicanism in the image of the Libertarians, who had gained tremendous political traction despite having been founded as late as 1971. But even the Great Communicator's peerless charisma proved no match for the recalcitrance of the GOP's upper crust. When his vice president then committed electioneering heresy by making *no new taxes* a major theme of his campaign, party bosses for both the Democrats and the Republicans decided it was time to take extraordinary action. Because the scheme never came to fruition, and because it was hatched at such a high level, even the conspirators can only speculate regarding its final form. What I have confirmed is that the Big Two spent three years planting false evidence and recruiting phony witnesses to create a scandal they meant to pin on the 1992 Libertarian candidate which would cripple third parties for generations to come. Your father –"

"Was a died-in-the-wool Democrat who despised third parties, so how is this story relevant?"

"He was also one of the shrewdest investigative reporters of that era. It was your father to whom the cabal leaked the bogus evidence, which at first blush suggested that the candidate had scheduled a secret meeting with a Vegas mob boss and one Lelina Frahley, a former showgirl who allegedly ran an escort service. But the Big Two operatives underestimated your father's resourcefulness. He quickly discovered that the purported mob boss was merely a rough looking obstetrician from Seattle who made twice as much money from the DNC as from his day job, Lelina was a speech therapist with two left feet from Odessa, Texas, married to an RNC bigshot, and the candidate had been duped into thinking these hoaxers were local advisors from his own party.

"Your father counted among the truest of believers in the Constitution. Recall, this was decades before the Boxheim Papers were revealed. When he considered the magnitude of the operation, the depth of the collusion between the Republicans and the Democrats, he understood that merely reporting the true facts would destroy him and everyone he held dear. He had to cut the legs off this story before it could take root in the media feeds, and he had to do it in such a way that no one suspected he had anything to do with it."

"What did he do?"

"His solution was quite cunning. Thanks to Giuliani, so many New York mobsters were hiding out in Nevada back then that you could not draw a curtain without bumping into one. The candidate's meeting was set for September 6, 1991. Two days earlier, your father presented his evidence to some mid-level goon with just enough intelligence to comprehend how unfortunate it would be for his organization to be implicated in the impending news blitz. On the sixth, the candidate's limousine was diverted to a Shriners parade. In his stead at the meeting appeared five very grouchy goombahs with a message for the employers of Lelina and her companion, which each was required to deliver in the form of a severed pinky finger."

Julia yanks her hands away.

"Liar!"

"What possible motivation would I have to fabricate such a story?"

"It's not him to just turn his back on a lifetime of loyalty. He couldn't talk about Truman without misting up."

"His own party was using him as a pawn to subvert the electoral process. What would you have him do?"

"Daddy was a gentle man."

"The lengths to which a father will go to protect his little girl would turn your stomach."

"He wouldn't put those people in danger."

"It was them or you, kiddo."

"Where is he now?"

"No one knows. On September 5, he boarded a private ten-passenger charter at McCarran International. When the plane landed seven hours later in Quito, Ecuador, he was not on it."

She clasps the edge of the bar to weather the ripples of shame and anger and pride and regret that percolate in her throat, but they threaten to consume her, so she embraces the one emotion with which she feels most at home, thrusting her finger in his face with a sneer.

"If it hadn't been for people like you, he'd have never had to leave."

"If you would indict me for what I do, madam, you may as well denounce humanity itself."

"At day's end you're just a paid killer. Violence does not resolve violence!"

"You can not throw reason out the window to pigeonhole me into a worldview you should have outgrown by now. Plutocrats with unbridled and immoral ambition did your father in. Common sense and logic do not hold the surgeon responsible for backstreet stabbings just because he uses similar tools and methods in the operating theatre."

"Look me in the eye, Stearns, and deny that you're just another gangster."

"I fail to see why I should be the least bit ashamed of that fact when, after all, our own federal government is nothing more than a legitimated mob."

"Rita's drugs have scrambled your brain!"

"How is an income withholding tax any different than *protection*? In what way is a corporate tax not *a piece of the action*? An IRS audit bears all the hallmarks of a shakedown, a government program is tantamount to hush money, and if you do not see the stark similarities between lobbying and bribery, you, madam, are delusional."

She swats his chin.

"You're grotesque!"

His retort proves she is not the only one who knows how to wield an authoritative finger.

"That is no surprise, because I am the one who cleans your sewers! And that is why only I am equipped to permanently resolve the problem of Mr. Mott."

Ani's sand drains away when his mention of her oldest friend elicits, not the protective tirade he expected but quiescent resignation. With the caution of a snake handler, he cups her shoulder.

"I must tend to some matters which my unanticipated survival has made all the more urgent. Stay as long as you need. Eat as much as you like. I will have Lucio see you back to your office, or wherever you need to go."

He turns to leave, but she pulls him back.

"I have to know. Why did you kill those men today?"

"Why does it matter to you?"

"I'm trying to decide if you're a sociopath! Was it to save Connie and your crew?"

"If you think that, you know neither Connie nor my crew."

"Were they coming for you next?"

"They were hardly that foolish."

"Melissa?"

"They were not that depraved."

"Was it a government assignment?"

"No."

"Were you sending a message to another gang?"

"No."

"Repaying an obligation?"

"No."

"Eliminating your competition?"

"No."

"Making a political statement?"

"No."

"Relieving stress?!"

"No … but that was a welcome byproduct."

"Did you have any … remotely sane reason whatsoever?!"

"Yes."

"What was it?"

"They killed my brother."

IF YOU ARE A WHITE, HETEROSEXUAL MALE AND LESS THAN 43% OF YOUR FRIENDS ARE OF AN ETHNICITY, SEX OR SEXUAL PROCLIVITY DIFFERENT FROM YOUR OWN, YOU ARE A RACIST, A MISOGYNIST AND/OR A HOMOPHOBE. YOU SHOULD SEEK IMMEDIATE COUNSELING FROM A FEDERALLY CERTIFIED DIVERSITY AND TOLERANCE ADVISOR.

This public service announcement is brought to you by the First Female President and First First Lady to Become President and Only Former First Lady to Become the First Female President's Panel on Homogeneity, the Secretary of the European & Native American Reeducation Board, the First Daughter to Serve under a Female President and Only First Daughter to Serve Under the First Female President's Respectful Couture & Coiffure Initiative, the First First Gentleman and First Ex-President to Serve as First Gentleman and Only Ex-President to Service as First First Gentleman's Anti-Bullying Committee, First Bushleague-Language Tsar Ryan A. Gardner, the First Female President and First First Lady to Become President and Only Former First Lady to Become the First Female President's Bureau of Unoffensive Speech, the Department of Housing and Urban Redevelopment, the First Female President and First First Lady to Become President and Only Former First Lady to Become the First Female President's Task Force on Equality of Outcome, the First First Gentleman and First Ex-President to Serve as First Gentleman and Only Ex-President to Service as First First Gentleman's Campaign to Perpetuate the Delusion that the First Black (Well, Not Completely, But Moreso than Her Husband) First Lady Is Relevant and to Deemphasize the First Mostly Black First Lady's Posterior Immensity, the First Female President and First First Lady to Become President and Only Former First Lady to Become the First Female President's Committee for Equal Time and Fair Play, and the First First First Ferret.

Chapter Eighteen

Petting Zoo Voodoo

"Peter Shroyer Mott! Who is this little hussy?!"

Peter follows the familiar voice to the adumbral dinette. The first feature to materialize is that lazy chin which so mesmerized him a lifetime ago. He then spies the beefy legs he'd have found unappealing on any other woman.

"Deanna?"

"No, Mr. Mott, it's still me. Oh my stars, are you hallucinating again?"

When Peter turns toward Mira to disclaim any illusions, she is no longer sitting in the chair. Gone, too, is the bowl of gumbo in which he could swear he just heard the clanking of a spoon. He finds her standing dispirited at the foot of his bed, her shoulders adrape with carryall and purse, her tumescent eyes cast toeward.

"I do wish you the best, Mr. Mott. But I can't … I won't apologize for loving you."

Gasping for air, she trundles out the door.

Mira, don't go. Say it out loud, you idiot!

A fierce thump on his left ear steals his attention back to Deanna.

"Forget the slut, Peter Shroyer, and start worrying about me. I want my children."

"Just who are you calling a slut, you squat-legged dyke?"

Mira reappears, standing to his right and pointing her gumbo spoon at Deanna like a dagger.

"Keep out of this, you twiggy little hooker!"

"I don't know who you are, but there's a skinny line between being a strong woman and just plain being a bitch, and I'm guessing you'd already plowed past it by the time you sprouted your first pubic hair!"

Deanna knocks Mira's spoon away. The second Mira retaliates with the gumbo bowl, Johnny Cash pops in at the foot of the bed decked out in gaudy jewelry, a yellow evening gown and matching elbow length gloves. He addresses Mira with an Old South accent.

"Is that any way for a lady to comport herself?"

For Deanna, he adopts the inflection and mannerisms of the stereotypical chicana.

"Damn, sister, whachoo do to your hair?!"

While the women unleash a salvo of vitriol on the transvestite Cash, another Cash fitted out like Jesus clomps into the room atop a donkey, which leaps across Peter's stomach, stopping and hovering over him in mid-hurdle. The messianic Cash erupts into flames.

"Tell me, son. You hear the one about the camel and the needle's eye?"

Donkey and rider proceed to the window, where they dissolve. Another boxed ear directs Peter's attention back to Deanna.

"Where are my kids, Peter?"

"You're not real!"

Dr. Kelner removes his glasses, cranes his neck to study Deanna, then turns to Peter.

"She is not real."

Mira slaps the doctor on the back of his head.

"She's about as imaginary as you, gramps."

"My dear woman, I was neither addressing nor referring to you."

"So you're one of those *don't speak until spoken to* pigs, are you? Define reality, smartypants."

"Now see here."

"Dylan and Millie. What have you done with my babies?"

"Define it, you old fart."

"Reality: that which exists independent of human awareness."

"But everything a human experiences is filtered through his awareness, so nothing exists for him independent of his awareness."

"Thus proving my point that the woman with the big legs is a fiction, because it's impossible to prove her independent existence."

"No, no, it proves just the opposite; if you weren't aware of her, you wouldn't have said anything about her, which makes her real to you, and my awareness of the both of you makes you, sir, a big, fat liar."

"But what if I can prove she and I are but dreams to you?"

"Pipe down, pops – objective reality is a farce and you know it."

Cash reappears, clad again as Death in dirt-caked work boots, bluejeans speckled with grass and manure, torn double-ply shirt and shearling coat. He glides to the head of Peter's bed, opposite Deanna, and leans so close that Peter can smell his words before he hears them.

"Fear. Fear in a handful of dust."

"I want them back. Do you hear me?"

"Step to, son."

"My little boy and girl, Peter!"

"Tempus fugit."

"What did you do?!"

"The lady asked you a question, worm dirt."

Kelner and Mira converge, and all four echo the *What did you do* mantra. Peter closes his eyes in an effort to evade his inquisitors, but there he finds Mira again, standing primly against the wall with hands clasped and eyelids aflood.

"Goodbye, Mr. Mott."

Seeing only one avenue of escape, Peter gropes for the morphine syringe, but just as he yanks the cap off the needle with his teeth, a severe looking man in a smart suit emerges from the clamor. Taking Peter's wrist in his ineluctable grip, the man produces his own syringe and inserts it into the IV port.

"There is time enough for death, Mr. Mott."

A numbness meanders from his forearm to his neck, then his head tingles the way his nose did so many years ago when he drank his first glass of champagne. As his consciousness bleeds away like aerosol from a ruptured spraycan, he tries to speak. But catalepsy takes him unawares.

Peter stirs to the reassuring texture of his leather office chair, still clad in his hospital gown. The dressing on his forehead has been changed, and the wound has lost its sting. The office floor and waist-high cabinetry have been covered with black Visqueen plastic from his desk to the back wall, and his funerary suit is draped over the valet next to the lavatory. His grim new acquaintance from the hospital room sits on the other side of his desk twirling an unlit cigar in his right hand.

"Peter Shroyer Mott, my name is Anthony Wayne Stearns."

Peter surveys the office, not because he particularly cares to see the same old tomes and paintings, but as a pretense to work his head and eyes. Something is amiss. He is not himself. He is still Peter, to be sure, but he is not the Peter of late. It is as though a sliver of his personality whose absence he did not detect has returned. His movements are more determinant than before. Gone is the translucent cloud through which he has experienced the world these many years. He feels he has slipped the confines of something he can not conceptualize, emerging on the outside of himself for the first time since ….

"Stearns, is it?"

"It is."

"You gave me a shot. What was in it?"

"The cure for what ailed you."

"If I have a problem, it's psychological. No shot can cure that. Are you a medical doctor?"

"I hold no such conventionally recognized certification."

"You're not a physician, but you injected something into my arm without my consent? That's assault and battery at the very least."

"Whom are you calling?"

"The police."

In one explosive motion, Ani deposits the cigar on the desk, swipes Peter's hand aside and flings the telephone against the wall.

"I can not allow that, Mr. Mott."

"Why?"

"You are beyond their help."

"Who the hell are you?"

"All you need to know is that I am a man who, given the choice between monomaniacal belief and naked fact, will choose unadorned reality without batting an eye."

"What is it you want from me?"

"The truth, Mr. Mott, about August 7, 2006."

Amid the torrent of self-contempt that erupts from his inguina, Peter averts his eyes and slumps in his chair, expecting to disappear into its tufts and folds, to descend to some psychotropic plane as he usually does at the mere mention of that night. But no horses materialize, no wind-no-wind issues forth. So swiftly is it delivered that Peter's jaw is already on the rebound before he feels the sting of Ani's backhand.

"You can not flee, Mr. Mott; I have disabled your neural escape hatch. You and I are engaged, and we will remain so until you give me that for which I came. I can see your pulse rate has increased. You think yourself too faint of heart, but the drug I gave you produces a lingering opiate effect which numbs raw nerves, as it were, and removes normal inhibitions. Let us call it a truth facilitator."

Ani retrieves his cigar and begins pacing the office as though he were cross-examining Peter in a courtroom.

"Let us begin with *Excelerate*, a program you and your ex-wife founded in 2003 with a laudable, albeit timeworn, mission. Rather than relegate ex-convicts to the menial government jobs typically available to them, you forged a consortium of private businesses to give these *unfortunate* men and women constructive employment with which to build a meaningful résumé and, thus, steer them away from old patterns of behavior."

"I'll grant you, it wasn't the freshest of ideas –"

"But old concepts repackaged often find success. Yes, I am familiar with that marketing rigmarole, Mr. Mott, but the efficacy of the program is immaterial to our discussion. If you keep interrupting me with these irrelative digressions, we will be here for a very long time. On May 17, 2006, one Freddie Herzog was paroled into your program, and you decided to teach the wayward lad how to be a businessman."

"My goal wasn't so lofty – I sought only to give my pupils a grasp of the rudiments of accounting and recordkeeping."

"But you paid special attention to Mr. Herzog, did you not?"

"Self-perception is either a doorway or a cage, and we don't have a meaningful say in its construction in those crucial, early years. Though Freddie was buried under a mountain of subliminal iron gates, I could still see promise in him. My heart went out to the young man."

"Along with your cash."

"I went through all of this in the Circuit Court of Oregon for the Twenty-Fifth Judicial District, and the jury found me not guilty."

"Yet you have lived like a fugitive ever since. Do you not find that curious, Mr. Mott?"

"My doctor says my condition –"

When Ani spins to face him, Peter instinctively covers his throbbing jaw. But rather than accost him again, Ani raises that mercurial hand of his toward Peter's bookshelf.

"The jury said this. Your shrink says that. You have eight versions of one iconic storybook over there along with over thirty-five commentaries regarding the same, tired legend. Have you completely forgotten how to turn the flywheels of your brain to formulate a thought of your own? You are not a common idiot, Mr. Mott, so it should come as no surprise to you that a lack of consensus among twelve human beings is often the poorest barometer of guilt. My question was put to you and you alone, *Reverend*."

Unlike every other self-contained glob of organic matter on our planet, the human socialization process has imposed a multitude of sinister connotations upon the fixed gaze. Thus, the typical individual finds it unnerving when another holds his stare for more than a second or two. Were it not for the fact that Peter, too, is curious to delve into his own mental processes after all these years, his every pore would be shuddering under Ani's relentless eye. Instead, like cornered game weary of the chase, Peter finds serenity in capitulation. Sensing his surrender, Ani resumes his circuitous journey.

"Though the merchants contributed to a nominal stipend for each early release, I did give Freddie … a little something extra out of my pocket."

"A *little* something, Mr. Mott?"

"At first, yes."

"And a few bucks every now and then culminated in a fifteen hundred dollar outlay on August 7, did it not?"

"I never gave that money to Freddie."

"Yet two hundred thereof was in his front left pants pocket the day he was arrested."

Bristling at the tedium of Ani's piecemeal interrogation, Peter lurches forward, plants his elbows on his desk and thrusts open palms in Ani's direction to underscore his frustration.

"You have to understand, Stearns, self-imposed though it was, I had a duty to maximize this man's chances for rehabilitation. That's a tall task for a white, privateschool kid who was raised on violin lessons and tennis tournaments. A requirement of the program was group drug counseling twice a week. I was supervising a session when I heard a parolee describe the euphoria she derived from just one hit of what she called *white lady*. I knew then and there that I would never reach Freddie unless I dipped my toe in his world. So I asked him to put me in touch with an old contact of his. On the afternoon of August 7, I acquired three tablets of methamphetamine. The man called it *yaba*."

Ani works his jaw, restive with the tack this confession has taken.

"You purchased three hits for $1,500?"

"He said it was a rare formulation."

"Oh, I suspect they all are, Mr. Mott. And what did you do with this *yaba*?"

"It's all … sketchy. I know my intention was to check into a hotel … to be cautious and take just one tablet at first. But I don't remember a front desk or a keycard or … then Freddie and I were in my car … he was driving and we were all happy … Millie and Dylan especially so, tickling each other and roughhousing in the back seat … then … there was a loud noise … and I came to on a dirt and gravel road, beneath me the mangled bodies of my … Freddie was angry … he tried to hold me back … even *yaba man* tried to stop me, but I chased them away … and … as if my mind had left my body, I watched myself thrash that knife up and down and back and forth … all the while wondering why my left sock always scrunches up and the right one doesn't, and making a mental note to scrunch the other one as soon as my hand was free … and I could hear the wind, I could see the blood, but I couldn't *feel* either."

Peter's tears hit his desk blotter in the aimless rhythm of a roof leak in a soft rain.

Pit ...

Pit pat ...

Pat ... pat pit ...

Pat ... pit ...

Ani remains in the position he assumed when Peter began his story, poised on his fists at the opposite edge of the desk, his restless eyes probing every last molecule of his mark.

"*Yaba*, did you say?"

"That's what he called it."

"In tablets?"

"Yes."

"So, your altruistic attempt to forge an avuncular bond with Mr. Herzog triggered a psychotic rage that caused you to stab your children to death?"

"Think what you want. It's what I remember."

"I doubt not your honesty, because your conscious mind is incapable of the alternative right now. The culprit here is your own memory."

"Come again?"

"Revisionist history is not always penned knowingly. Research has proved over and again that the unconscious mind is always at work restructuring one's perception of reality to fit his underlying worldview. The scientific record is replete with examples of how the subconscious insinuates into our wakeful thought processes nonsensical platitudes and otherworldly reassurances so that we can close our eyes and sleep at night despite the thousand perils that threaten from beyond the bedroom door.

Some call it selective amnesia. Catastrophe survivors suppress the most horrific aspects of the event to maintain mental stability. And murderers disguise grisly scenes with allegory to convince themselves they are not bad people after all. Your undersense is lying to us both, Mr. Mott, and my patience is running thin."

Ani retrieves a brown satchel from the foot of the guest chair and deposits it, unopened, on the desk.

"What's in there?"

"Implements of truth, Mr. Mott."

"*Implements*?"

"We shall delve into the briefcase in due time. For now, let us consider testimony which refutes your version of events. August 7, 2006 was a Monday. No less than nine witnesses place you at the job site meeting with contractors who were building your recreation center from 7:15 to 10:30 that morning. You then joined your wife at a Lions Club luncheon, which you left promptly at 1:00 so you could make court appearances to report on the progress of various parolees in your charge. The security log shows you entering the courthouse at 1:14 and exiting at 4:55. Your brother-in-law corroborates Mrs. Mott's account that you arrived at your home twelve minutes later, which corresponds with a direct, nonstop route from the courthouse. You proceeded to shower and shave. You then joined your brother-in-law for a bracing glass of lemonade while Deanna corralled the children for *Daddy's Night*, and she watched the three of you buckle up and motor away for dinner and a movie at 6:30. These are the salient facts, Mr. Mott. You had neither the time nor an opportunity to meet with this elusive *yaba man*, and you were as sober as Billy Sunday when you left that house."

There was a place to which Peter frequently fled during his trial when he heard lawyers and witnesses relate similar inconsistencies. In that headspace, the pitch of each voice would merge into an unobtrusive hum. Though he desperately wants to return there now, he has lost his way. Panic subsumes him like the chill of a fever.

"I want you to go now, Stearns."

"Things were done to that little boy and girl before they were stabbed."

"Get out of my office."

"Inhuman things, Mr. Mott."

Peter stands and points at the door.

"Leave this holy place!"

"This, for instance."

Ani yanks from the bag a cattle prod, pokes it between Peter's third and fourth ribs and activates it. The shock throws Peter into his chair, the momentum toppling both chair and occupant over backwards. Before Peter can begin to parse what just happened, Ani yanks them both aright. Holding the prod inches from Peter's nose, Ani activates it again. Peter recoils, but Ani's unremitting grip prevents his retreat.

"You will have a nasty bruise on your torso from that single charge. Between them, your children suffered thirty-one. Some were internal, Mr. Mott."

Ani fires the prod again. Peter closes his eyes and turns aside.

"That's a lie! I'll thank you to stop bearing false witness in the house of God!"

Another savage handstrike both frightens and enrages Peter. He opens his eyes to find that his desk has been arrayed with the pictures and typed narratives from the Medical Examiner's report for each child. Ani jerks him to his feet.

"Behold, Mr. Mott."

The coroner's every description coincides with a vague snapshot from one of Peter's thousand hauntings. Each picture evokes long buried sounds from that night. Aloof and jumbled at first, the elements slowly congeal, forming one coherent memory so vivid that he can discern the balm of his own perspiration from other odors few fathers ever imagine, let alone encounter. Seeing the telltale tremor, Ani releases his grip. Peter stumbles to the remotest corner of the office, collapses to his knees and commences to heave.

At convulsions' end, Peter has precious little time to catch his breath before Ani tosses him back into his chair, flings a cupful of old coffee in his face and thrusts a towel into his flailing hands.

"Now, Mr. Mott. Right now."

"Leave me alone."

"Embrace the fabled road to emancipation."

"Fuck you!"

"Tell me the truth about August 7, twenty-aught-six!"

When Ani yanks the towel away, his eyes ensnare Peter's and, under that plumbless gaze, Peter recalls the entire ordeal in a flash. This triggers another seizure, this one producing only plaintive tears.

"Please, Stearns. I can't … bear it."

This plea only intensifies Ani's glare.

"Then I will tell you what happened. You never bought anything from *yaba man*."

Peter shuts his eyes and turns aside.

"Please, no."

"You withdrew the cash because Freddie told you it would clear his last outstanding debt from his so-called old life."

"Please."

"You sent your kids into the pizza parlor ahead of you so word would not get back to Deanna, because she had always been suspicious of Freddie."

"What's done is done."

"Freddie arrived moments later."

"What's the use in reliving it?"

Ani slaps Peter's eyes open and clutches his shoulders.

"Because I am here to save your life!"

Stupefied, Peter follows Ani as he resumes his march.

"How in God's name do I deserve that?"

"You handed Freddie the money. So effusive was his gratitude that, rather than merely take your outstretched hand, he embraced you. This was no token gesture. He put his whole body into that hug. And then you felt something, Mr. Mott."

"It doesn't matter. I killed my babies."

"Believe me, Mr. Mott, you do not have that capability. You felt something."

"But the blood …"

"Focus, Mr. Mott. You felt something."

"The knife ..."

"Mr. Mott."

"The tire track ..."

"You felt something!"

"My right leg … a spider bite …"

"Freddie was not demonstrating his affection; he was immobilizing you so that his friend – whom you recall as *yaba man* – could inject you with ketamine, a clinical sedative which has been adopted by recreational users because it induces dissociative anesthesia akin to phencyclidine, or PCP."

"Dissociative …?"

"A trancelike state of mind in which your perceptions of sight and sound are detached from both you and your surroundings. Any losses of consciousness you experienced would have been sporadic and momentary. Freddie wanted you awake, but he also wanted you compliant. Ketamine is not the best tool for such a job, but it will work in a pinch. What is your next memory?"

"Freddie driving and … laughing. Millie and Dylan in the back seat …"

"But they were not alone, were they?"

"*Yaba man*!"

"And what you saw was not innocent horseplay, was it?"

Helpless to stem the onrush of his now unrestrained memory, Peter watches from above as *yaba man* kicks Dylan to the floorboard and rips his shirt away. He sees Millie spring to her brother's aid, tugging at the man's ear and biting his forearm before getting flung aside and zapped with a cattle prod. Peter can smell her flesh burn as she cries *Daddy, help us*, observes his younger self cavorting in the passenger seat like a drunken music conductor, oblivious to the terror unfolding behind his headrest. Hearing Millie scream again, he turns to find her naked on the quarry road and writhing beneath Freddie. No longer lost in his drug-induced dream, Peter sits against the front wheel of his car, cursing and crying and straining to free himself from the chain that binds his torso to the axle. When none but Peter's wails can be heard, *yaba man* thrusts a blood- and dirt-caked knife into his palm and secures it there with duck tape, joins Freddie to laugh and taunt him as he tries to shake it free, then runs to Freddie's waiting car and starts it up. With one last kick to Peter's groin, Freddie unhitches the chain and flees.

The caress of a familiar hand frees Peter from his reminiscence. Lying now in a fetal position on the floor next to his desk, he gazes up at Mira.

"Shhhh, it's okay, Mr. Mott. You're okay."

When he moves his knees to sit up, he detects a dampness, whiffs a feculent air and realizes he has soiled himself. He pushes her away.

"No, don't see me, don't … smell me."

Though Mira's backhand hasn't the same force, its swiftness rivals that of Ani.

"Damn it, Mr. Mott, shut up and let me help you, because I know a thing or two about where you are! Can you stand? Good, walk that way, I drew you a bath."

"Just no more hitting, okay?"

"Don't act like a juvenile, and I won't have to smack you."

She closes the door behind them. Outside, Ani jaws his cigar, dons surgical gloves, and proceeds to gather and dispose of the groundsheet. From the cursing and groaning that emanate from the washroom, it is evident that most of the cleansing afoot is internal. When the door opens again little more than two hours later, Peter emerges in his suit, Mira soaked head to toe in bathwater. They find Ani sitting patiently on the other side of the desk, a fresh, unlit cigar in his hand. Mira nudges Peter down into his posh chair.

"Now then, I need to get some dry clothes, and you need some food. I'll find you something in the kitchen. Mr. Stearns, can I get you anything?"

"A beer would certainly make this soap opera more palatable."

"In a Southern Baptist church, are you kidding?"

"Especially in a Southern Baptist church, madam, inasmuch as I have heard more than one Catholic priest describe your denomination as a collection of closet tipplers and dry drunks."

"Domestic or import?"

"Anything dark and hoppy, my dear."

As Mira hustles away, Peter peers at Ani with renewed curiosity.

"Why have you done this?"

"It needed to be done."

"Why should you care about a complete stranger?"

"Sharing the human condition as we all do, no man is a stranger to me."

"I don't mean to sound ingracious, but you went to a lot of trouble to help me. What's in this for you?"

"Justice."

"The detectives laughed in my face when I told them about *yaba man*. They had my prints all over the car and the knife. They never even drew my blood, so the prosecutor didn't know I was drugged. After the verdict, my lawyer cornered me in the Men's room. He said it was my reputation alone that beat the charges, that the verdict reeked of O.J.

Syndrome, and I should never call him again. I've always been convinced he was right."

"Do not ignore a most fundamental component of that decision process, Peter. From an emotional standpoint, it is preferable to believe you snapped and killed your children, that you exerted control over the situation, than to live with the fact that you were forced to witness others violate them in unspeakable ways, helpless to intervene."

"But the physical and circumstantial evidence –"

"It is a vexatious reality of this life that facts are too often susceptible to more than one interpretation."

"So how did you know which was right?"

"I have *yaba man's* DNA, and I have his confession – each obtained mere days ago, as a matter of fact."

"*Yaba man*? Who … how …"

"The coroner retrieved from your son a sequence of foreign DNA that did not belong to you, Freddie, Millie or Deanna. When the police could not find a match in the State or federal databases, they simply abandoned the search. You see, *yaba man*, whose given name is Darian Massenet, had never been arrested before August 7, 2006. Nor would he be introduced to the system until five years hence, when he was convicted of raping and dismembering his grandmother."

"You say he confessed? To whom?"

"To me, of course."

"Just like that? You walked into his cell, introduced yourself, he felt contrite and told you everything?"

"For his sake, that would have been the wiser course of action. As it happens, Mr. Massenet will never again be able to smell … or to urinate without experiencing acute pain in his left eye. Do not be misled by the politicians and the pundits and the filmmakers. While torture is, indeed, useless in the hands of the inept, it is an invaluable truthfinding tool when effected by a man who has perfected his craft."

"How did you know to even look for him?"

"Our friend Slinky Sam told me."

Peter's face drains pallid. He bounds from his chair and shuts the window blinds.

"You mean to tell me Freddie's out? How?"

"Do you not follow the news?"

"Just when have I had the time between these debilitating blackouts?"

"You may rest assured that he will never harm another human being."

"How do you know?"

"Because I killed the poor, feckless bastard."

Peter approaches his chair with heed, uncertain as yet whether he wishes to make use of it.

"Why doesn't it distress me more that you speak so casually about torture and death?"

"Because, as the events of these last few hours are testament, neither is in the offing where you are concerned. Begging your pardon for that incidental pun, I would clarify that, on the contrary, I stand in awe of both life and death. And from this reverence emanates my keen appreciation for the whimsical irony of each."

Peter opens the blinds, drinks in the sunbeam and returns to his faithful chair.

"Mr. Stearns –"

"Call me Ani, please."

"Annie?"

"Watch and listen – *Ahhhnee*."

"How about Tony?"

"How about Ani?"

"There's nothing wrong with Tony."

"Nothing at all, provided you are a discotheque gigolo."

"I feel funny calling you a girl's name."

"What is the least bit girlish about Ani?"

"How about Wayne? That's a masculine name."

"How about I give you another bruise approximately one foot lower?"

"Fine, Anthony then."

"I presume now you fancy yourself my mother?"

"It's no different than you calling me Peter instead of Pete."

"Have we regressed to preschool?"

"You're the one being persnickety about his name."

Ani slams his cigar down beside the cattle prod.

"Stearns, then. Just plain Stearns. Pose your question, please."

"Why did Freddie do it? I had bent over backwards for the man. We never had a cross word. I was showing him a way out of drugs and violence, a road to self-sufficiency."

"The answer is as old as time, Peter. You can not help those who can not or will not help themselves. He detested you simply because you were not him. You had been spared the pain and humiliation and confusion of his tender years, so you had to be destroyed. Just as a wild animal can never be completely tamed, Freddie was incapable of being assimilated into society. Men such as he are abjectly afraid of autonomy at the same time autonomy is what they most covet. That is neither his fault nor yours, but it is a fact nonetheless."

"So it was my naïveté that destroyed my family, my life."

"Only you can sort that out. While there is no guarantee you will succeed, I can assure you that you are now capable of bringing all of your faculties to bear upon the task."

"And when this drug wears off?"

"Your command of this situation is a product of your own survival mechanisms. You have been under the influence of nothing but your own mind and emotions since you awoke in that chair. You do not give that profound intellect of yours enough credit, my friend."

"But you said –"

"I lied."

"Why?"

"You did not believe yourself capable of facing the past, so I had to convince you I had given you artificial assistance."

"So your injecting me … I dreamt that?"

"Oh no, I injected you, but with a dosage measured precisely to do nothing more than reverse a biochemical process which began mere moments into the brutal spectacle you were forced to witness on that tragic night. As a matter of fact, I was equipped with a variety of … let us say elixirs."

"How did you know which one to use … assuming you did?"

"I observed you in hospital for quite some time. At one point, I counted nine separate conversations you were having with some eminently colorful, though nonexistent, characters. From this, I deduced that you were suffering from Temporal Lobe Epilepsy, commonly referred to by the acronym TLE. TLE has any number of causes including genetics, physical injury, disease and severe emotional trauma. In this condition, neurons misfire and their signals become amplified, resulting in an electrical storm that can affect many other areas of the brain. The manifestations mirror schizophrenic behavior and include existential anxiety, deterioration of the line between dreams and reality, a new or intensified interest in philosophy and spiritualism, and the tendency to ascribe objective clout upon subjective experience.

"Common treatments are to magnetically stimulate the temporal lobe, and/or prescribe months or years of psychotherapy. Developed by a dear friend of mine, the particular pharmacon I gave you consisted of conventional anticonvulsants and a rare strain of the ergot fungus known in certain circles as lysergic acid diethylamide."

"You shot me up with LSD?!"

"Indeed."

"Are you insane?"

"I could tell you I am not, because that is my subjective and wholly biased belief. But I can not account for the unnumbered definitions of *sanity* which the fucking psychiatrists and other self-appointed authorities bandy about these days. In any event, my choice of treatment was neither rash nor ill informed. Though political bugbears will never permit mainstream medicine to openly acknowledge the fact, it has been known for millennia that the same catalyst which induces aberrant behavior can also inhibit and even permanently eradicate it. My research has shown that certain hallucinogens are not only reliable stop-gap measures; the immediacy and potency of their effect most often prevents the brewing of another epileptic storm long enough for the trauma victim to accurately and thoroughly process the event which triggered the original disturbance."

"So I *am* under its influence."

"No, you *were*."

"Until when?"

"Have you an auditory deficiency I should know about?"

"No."

"*As I said*, the drug had completely worn off by the time you became fully alert in that chair on this very day."

"But my memory didn't come back until after I was awake, and you saw what it did to me. How can you be so sure I'm not about to have another seizure?"

"Peter, you have been reliving the unvarnished events of August 7, 2006 for thirty-eight hours. Consciousness has many strata. You have been functioning at the uppermost tier for only the last five hours and, trust me, you would not have wished wakefulness on your most reviled enemy during those first thirty-three. When you opened your eyes, the peril had long since passed."

Peter purses his lips to ask a most probing question, but he can not find the appropriate clothing for this budding stripe of curiosity. He stands and turns his inquisitory countenance upon the bromidic bookshelf, oblivious as yet to the aroma of the chopped steak and coleslaw Mira has deposited on his desk.

"Sorry about the plastic cups, Mr. Stearns, but we don't have pint glasses around here, and one wouldn't hold the whole bottle."

"Bless you just the same, my dear. Might you indulge my curiosity as to where you found it and how you located it so quickly?"

"I have keys to all the offices. Deacon Whitehurst keeps a half-fridge in his armoire. It's no secret what he stocks in it."

"Whitehurst, yes. I passed by his door on my way to the refuse bin. I did not catch his title."

"Abstinence Counselor for Youth and Young Adults."

Mira takes Peter by the arm. Groping in yet a new undertow of disarray, he follows her like a zombie back to the desk, where he deliberates blankly over his fare. Ani brings another chair from the outer office and deposits it next to Peter's. Like a trained ape, Peter imitates Mira as she sits down, follows her gaze to the plastic fork, which she attentively places in his palm.

"Please eat. I've not seen you finish a meal since the day we met. And you'll need your strength for …."

Mira's words are squelched by the ingestive furor that commences the moment Peter's nostrils detect their first unveiled whiff of food in over a decade.

"Do you mind?"

Plate empty, Peter confiscates the overflow beer cup without awaiting permission as an amused Ani lights his cigar. The sound of the lighter distracts Mira.

"I'm sorry, Mr. Stearns, there's no smoking here."

"Why not?"

The question came from, not Ani but Peter.

"My dad smoked cigars. Deanna couldn't stand them. Is it possible …?"

Ani produces a fresh cigar from his breast pocket. As he holds the flame for Peter, Mira punches his arm.

"What have you done to this poor man?"

"I have merely returned to him his true self."

Surveying the office in a panic, Mira spots an offering plate on the credenza next to the bathroom, races to retrieve it and slaps it on the desk between the men.

Like an addict just off a months-long wagon, Peter takes a protracted, euphoric pull from the cigar and lets his head fall back against the chair, exhaling the smoke in measured increments so that he can revel in its velvety fog. Eyes closed, he recites from Matthew 26:22.

"Lord, is it I?"

Mira punches Ani's arm again.

"You said he wouldn't hallucinate anymore!"

Ani peers intently as Peter rocks his head, chanting the same question underbreath.

"Bear with him, Mira. That verse is from the fabled Last Supper, during which the messiah has predicted that one of his disciples will betray him."

Peter drops his gaze to the empty plate before him.

"And Jesus answered unto Judas: *Thou hast said.* The temporal lobe … temporal ... it's associated with sound and speech recognition, memory …. Back in the 80s, a Canadian published some groundbreaking research. I read his book. What was his name? He was a neuroscience guy."

Ani juts forward with the anticipation of a schoolmaster whose pupil is on the verge of a watershed discovery.

"Persinger, Michael A., Ph.D."

"That's the guy! He cobbled together some Rube Goldberg helmet that stimulated the temporal lobes of human volunteers. He reproduced voices and visions of angels and gods and an afterlife. His theory was that the spiritual experience is a biological relic of human evolution, a lullaby our brain sings to us to ... sugarcoat reality so we can maintain some semblance of sanity in the face of chaos. The selective memory phenomenon you spoke of. Religious devotion is a misinterpretation of that inner monologue."

"And in your case?"

"My inner monologue ran amok … like a stylus stuck in a groove on an old phonograph record."

Mira rolls her eyes.

"Big fat news that is. An American published a similar theory ten years earlier."

Peter tosses his cigar into the offering plate and trudges back to the rear wall, next to whose window hangs an aerial photo of *The Miracle Mile*.

"What the hell have I done?!"

Mira commandeers Ani's beer and takes a swig before approaching him and taking his arm.

"A world of good, that's what you've done."

"No. No. Contraptions and linguistic postulates don't erase the fact that I didn't have the strength of will to cope with the death of my children, so I buried my head in the myth of a celestial Santa Claus. I chose sides in a perennial, sandbox feud and, thanks in large part to me, nearly six thousand people were murdered in their sleep."

He turns, takes her by the shoulders and scrutinizes her like a lab rat.

"Has Stearns stuck you with any needles?"

"Of course not."

"So you have been you this whole time?"

"I certainly hope so."

"Then why didn't you stop me?!"

"How could I?! And why would I? I'll grant you that I've never been that fanatical about religious stuff, but I was a believer and I felt a calling to come here. Yet all the while we've built this church, I've been changing. Those scientific treatises, once just compulsory reading for my degree, have begun to make new and deeper sense to me. I have supported your mission, Peter, because I believe in *you*, not a bunch of hocus-pocus. People come to places like this because they've resigned their inborn ability to think for themselves to others with cloaks of authority like the military veteran, the teacher, the preacher … anybody with accepted credentials of expertise, giving no regard to how inapt and misleading those credentials are. And whatever disguise you think you have to wear to get it done, even if you don't wear one at all, I think you have a lot more good to do."

He hangs his head and saunters back to his chair.

"I'm sorry, Mira. My faith in humanity just hightailed it, right on Jesus' heels."

Ani retrieves an envelope from his attaché.

"Perhaps I can assist you there. Mira, you will not want to see the contents of this package."

"I think we need more beer, anyway."

"That will require more cups than you –"

"Fuck cups."

Ani deposits his cigar, then sets aside the offering plate.

"Yes, humans cause problems. Some wreak inconceivable havoc. When that happens, only humans can even the score because we have no heavenly hitman to do that for us. I am telling you nothing you do not already know. Messrs. Herzog and Massenet committed unforgivable offenses that night. They did so without provocation, absent any rational impetus. They did things that would shake anyone's confidence in his fellow man."

Ani produces photographs he took of Freddie in various stages of punishment, depositing them in sequence as he continues.

"Every generation is unique unto itself. From the day we are born to the moment we issue our terminal outbreath, we are stuck, for good or ill, with our contemporaries. It is as though the greater cosmos were a colossal prison, and you and I cellmates therein. Like colliding atoms, we shape each other as we grow and learn. What one man lacks, another provides. You were caught off guard, Peter. You were overpowered by men with flawed mental processes whose behavior you could not predict. That does not make you weak. It neither makes you any less a man. Macrocosmic events then placed a man with my particular skillset in Freddie's path. Fear not that I am about to burst into a schmaltzy Streisand song about the luckiest people. I am simply illustrating the fact that when individuals conduct their lives with integrity as their bellwether, they do good things for each other ofttimes by sheer coincidence. This is the remarkable byproduct, if you will, of self-determination. This is humankind at work. Humans build roads and bridges. Humans do the mind-numbing research that leads to pivotal vaccines. Humans excise cancers from society's midst. You seek reprieve from the guilt you have harbored since that night? *I give you retribution.*"

Studying depictions that would cause the typical man to lose control of one or more bodily functions, Peter feels neither bitterness nor lascivious satisfaction. He detects a pressure lifting from his sternum, as his throat brims with … compassion … for his children … for Deanna … for himself … for even Freddie … on account of the existential tightrope every human must walk.

"Massenet?"

"He shall get his due."

Peter extends his hand.

"Thank you, Ani."

To see Ani smile is an intriguing first for Peter.

"It has been my distinct privilege, Peter Shroyer Mott."

Startled by the clunk of a handtruck against the outer door, both men scurry to scoop the photos back into the valise. Mira dollies Whitehurst's refrigerator to the bookcase, plugs it in, pulls three fresh bottles from its door and slaps a churchkey down beside the offering plate. The men watch in raptness as she removes a shoe, rests the bottle against the appliance's top edge and hammers it with her heel to pop the cap.

"What are you two staring at? With the changes I see coming, that gladhanding hayseed won't have an office here much longer, anyway."

She hijacks Peter's cigar and takes a few tugs.

"I suggest you gentlemen commence to drinking, because *Reverend* Mott has a funeral to officiate in one little hour. A funeral, hah! That'll be a hoot in a half!"

Peter opens his beer and steals his cigar back.

"A funeral? For whom?"

"Two brothers. Arnold and Bartholomew Milland."

Ani deposits his capped beer on the desk.

"If that is the case, prudence instructs that I reconnoiter your guest list."

Mira's response is motivated by compassion, Peter's by sarcasm.

"I'm so sorry. Were they friends of yours?"

"Or enemies?"

Ani stands, smooths his tie and pensively closes his satchel.

"Both."

"In what order?"

"Suffice it to say that, should I remain here one minute longer, I will cease being a facilitator of, and fast become a hindrance to, your recovery."

With a hearty clasp of Peter's shoulder, he turns to Mira, takes her puzzled hand and kisses it, then addresses them both.

"Now that we have slain Ludwig's rhinoceros, I suggest you two stop dancing around the elephant which lurks in the corner."

As Ani exits, Peter stares at his empty chair in forlorn reverie.

"Ludwig Wittgenstein's mentor, Bertrand Russell, tried to get him to admit the absence of a rhinoceros in the room, but Wittgenstein refused because he considered the existence or nonexistence of an empirical object a false dichotomy … the classic argument between what the one mistook as agnosticism and the other misconstrued as atheism. I first read Wittgenstein's *Tractatus* when I was sixteen. It was my introduction to philosophy. Those were heady times. No subsequent achievement compares to a youth's discovery of metaphysics. But in all my years of study, I can't recall that particular elephant metaphor."

Mira retrieves Ani's smoldering cigar, turns the chair next to Peter backwards and most immodestly straddles it.

"He was referring to you and me."

"Mira, I don't know what was real or what I imagined in that hospital room, let alone these past fourteen years. Where do I even start?"

"Which parts would you like to be true?"

"You called me *Peter*. Before you went to raid Whitehurst's office for the second time, you called me *Peter*."

"What of it?"

"You never used my first name before today."

"So?"

"Why the change?"

"After what we went through in that bathroom, *Mr. Mott* seemed a wee bit formal."

"Is there any other reason?"

Without manifesting so much as a tinge of acrimony, she calmly deposits her cigar, then his, slaps him once on his tender jaw, and returns each cigar to its former handhold.

"I thought we agreed to no more hitting."

"Provided you stopped acting like a child."

"Just how would you have me act?"

"There you go again, fishing for my feelings and not being man enough to say what's on your mind. I will not make this conversation easy for you, Peter Mott, because you had the cheek to fire me!"

"I did not; you quit!"

"Just when do you think I did that?"

"When I caught you lying to me about Hosaam."

"Assuming someone as wide-eyed as you could catch anybody in a lie, how did you supposedly catch me?"

"You were acting funny."

"How was I acting funny?"

"You were frail, vulnerable. You said you loved me."

"You, sir, are a common pervert!"

"A what?"

"You undressed my psyche without my permission."

"Undressed … how is that possible?"

"Besides, the computer hacking incident was the first news out of my mouth, and you said it was my fault and fired me on the spot. I never had a chance to tell you whether I loved you or hated your guts."

"I was in a compromised state, so how do I know you aren't making that up right here and now?"

"It's called *trust*. Look it up in your concordance, *man of faith*!"

"If I fired you, why are you here?"

"You tell me."

Holding his stare, Mira shotguns the last of her beer, stands up, bows her head, dangles her arms and pivots her torso side to side.

"What are you doing?"

"I can't answer you, because I don't comprehend humanspeak."

"Cut it out. I'm trying to have a serious conversation with you."

"What am I?"

"I'm not playing."

Hands clasped and still swaying, she lumbers to the desk, upturns Peter's beer to wet her fingers and, as she makes a sneezing sound, flicks a sudsy mist in his face.

"What am I?"

"Fired again?"

She cavorts to the far end of the office.

"What am I?"

"Fine, you're the elephant in the corner."

She drops the act, but remains in the corner to conceal a teardrop in its shade.

"Truth is not just a sum of facts; it's what you choose to do with those facts. Ask yourself, Peter. Why would I be here today, despite the fact that you fired me after fourteen years of being your secretary, your curriculum organizer, your press agent, your social advisor, your budgetary enforcer, your finance manager, your caretaker and your kibitzer? Then ask yourself why you care one iota about my motives."

Peter concentrates on the makeshift ashtray before him only to find a parking place for his mind as it struggles to follow a recollective cascade that streams by on its periphery. Amid the random interactions he has had with her, the countless times he has watched her corral quarrelsome deacons and curb unruly teenagers, his runaway reminiscence comes to a sudden halt on a lone image. Though he has no way of ascertaining whether it was a dream, he is captivated by the sight of her sleeping in the chair next to his hospital bed. The urges he suppressed then reemerge, the foremost of which is to protect her from life's caprice.

With the same wonderment he has oft ascribed to the fictive blind man of Bethsaida, Peter goes to her and cups her face in his hands.

"Before you open your mouth again, Peter Mott, you'd best be mindful that I'll not remold myself to fit anyone's preconceived notion of a love object or a make-do mother."

He kisses her forehead.

"That's not what I want."

She sucks back an undainty blob of phlegm, lays her palms on his chest.

"I'm listening."

"You've been a better friend to me than I deserved. Please stay. Not as my employee, but as my partner. Let me return the favor."

"Do I get a raise?"

"You can write your own paychecks."

"Deal. But only on a trial basis, you understand."

She tightens her grip on two fistfuls of his shirt.

"Peter, I know the advice columns say we're supposed to kiss now, but would you mind just holding me up for a bit? It's been one stinking bitch of a day."

OUR BEST ADVICE TO THE ASPIRING MODEL CITIZEN IS THAT YOU MOVE INTO GOVERNMENT HOUSING AND REMAIN THERE QUIETLY WITH YOUR SHADES DRAWN, CLOAKED IN A WHITE BEDSHEET, AND EATING CRACKERS AND DRINKING BOTTLED WATER. YOUR H.U.R. CASEWORKER WILL BRING SUPPLIES SOON. BY *SOON,* WE MEAN WITH EVERY GOOD INTENTION, THOUGH NO GUARANTEE, OF GETTING THERE BEFORE YOU EXPIRE FROM DEHYDRATION OR STARVATION.

This public service announcement is brought to you by everyone and everything remotely associated with your federal government – past, present and future.

Chapter Nineteen

Crass from the Past

Though some scientists have speculated that the location of a rare axe fashioned from red quartzite in a pit in Sima de los Huesos, Spain dates the first ritual burial to 600,000 years ago, skeletal remains stained with red ochre discovered in the Skhul cave at Qafzeh, Israel, as well as remnants of various plants, stone piles and bonfires in Iraq's Shanidar Cave provide stronger evidence at the 60 to 100 thousand-year mark. Though one can scarce predict the precise emotional storm which erupted in the very first hominid to witness the decease of a compatriot, it is reasonable to infer that it contained a mind-rending admixture of rueful compassion for the newly departed and a stark resentment of him for being the harbinger of mortality.

Over time, a kaleidoscopic array of funerary customs has evolved. It was not uncommon in ancient Rome for the eldest male relative to inhale a loved one's crowning sigh. Until 1981 C.E., Indian Hindus cremated the still living wife alongside her deceased husband. Called *Sati*, this ritual was intended to purify the widow and secure her passage to heaven. While some African tribes consume the ground bones of their dead, others fire spears, arrows or guns into the air to ward off evil spirits. Tibetan Buddhists perform the *Sky Ritual*, or *Excarnation*, by which they dismember the body of the dear departed and feed it to the vultures. Because certain cultures in China believe the wellbeing of one's survivors is directly proportional to the number of funeral attendees, strippers are now featured at many requiems.

Though we thumb our noses and pretend that our western conventions are more sensible, they are just as steeped in mindless compulsion as their exotic analogues. But what sets the typical American funeral apart is that, despite a recent upsurge in both the number of commemorative events and their attendance, the focus of the occasion is rarely, if ever, upon the honoree. The reasons for this are both sociological and psychological. The ageless axiom the *Multifaith Reconciliation Treaty* ignored was that every "ism" is a rank ideology except, of course, for one's own. Hence, the clash of such divergent religious traditions in close proximity has, contrary to the treaty's stated purpose of engendering interfaith tolerance, reinforced the *home team* mentality of every denomination. For the more militant dogmatists such as the Muslims and the Southern Baptists, this renewed sense of competition has amplified the *mine's bigger than yours* disposition. The for-profit church model has added to the frenzy by turning absolution into a commodity, attracting droves of existential schizophrenics such as the Milland brothers, who are happy to pay an exorbitant fee for one last blessing to hedge their existential bets.

The sheer size of today's funeral has led to logistical difficulties which the free market quickly resolved in the form of fee-based overflow parking lots skirted by food and beverage merchants, soon joined by vendors of religious memorabilia. Because no red-blooded American can long resist a spectacle, the funeral has fast become as chic a social gathering as high school football.

Midst the tailgaters and hobnobbers is a core element of the church membership which attends memorials as faithfully as it does Sunday sermons. Though more somber about the affair than their co-attendees, their interest is not wholly morbid. As humans age, we grow ever fonder of the many archetypal experiences of our youth, too often forsaking the wisdom of the intervening years in our quest to reclaim the bliss of innocence. For the vast majority of us it was during those formative years, whose impressions and experiences have the most vivid and enduring impact on our psyches, that we first encountered both the terror of death and the banal assurance from a trusted adult that a blanch-skinned middle eastern carpenter who bears a striking resemblance to the 1970s likeness of American singer/songwriter Kenny Loggins has conquered death and awaits us on the B-side of reality. Thus, for the steadfast congregant, every observance of death reinforces the promise of a hereafter.

Having exhausted her repertoire of traditional religious songs, the frolicsome organist has segued from *Just a Closer Walk with Thee* into Debussy's *Reverie* when Peter finally ascends the stage. Close at his side, Mira settles into one of the high backed chairs at the base of the choir loft as he proceeds to the lectern. He peers at the regulars who occupy the forwardmost rows of the floor pews, pores over each countenance as if they were fifty-year reunioners. Glancing back to Mira for one last nod of support, for the first time since his ordination he wheels the podium aside. He then descends to the main floor and lays a hand on each closed casket.

"Who knew these men?"

It has become customary among the protestant camps for the preacher to bestow a special blessing upon the family and close friends of the deceased.

From a folding chair beside the last pew at the rear of the auditorium, a lone gentleman stands.

"Anyone else? Anyone at all? Very well. If you will, sir, please join me."

When the man emerges from the obscurity of the balcony, Peter recognizes him as Ani. Exasperated by his wry grin, Peter flips the toggle switch to mute his lapel microphone. Though Ani stops within mere inches of him, Peter leans even closer to keep the congregation out of earshot.

"The rotting piles of flesh in those rapaciously priced boxes may not be any more consequential to you than week-old road-kill, but I will not have you make a mockery of this ceremony!"

Peter has learned to heed the clearing of Mira's throat, for that means something is woefully amiss. Ani's finger to his lips confirms it.

"Am I still on?"

All eyes follow Peter's as they scale the balcony, where the sound engineer sits in an open booth, his tinny voice in the overhead speakers barely loud enough to drown the giggles emanating from the foyer.

"Yes, Reverend Mott."

"But the switch is off, Howie."

"Try cycling it again, sir."

"Testing ..."

"It's still hot, sir."

"And testing ..."

"I think I've figured it out, sir. Please cycle it once more."

"And testing ..."

"Yes, and once more for confirmation, please, sir."

"And testing ..."

"Thank you, sir."

Laughter now invades the outermost pews as Peter's leer grows ever more imperative.

"Well?"

"Sir?"

"Have you fixed the problem?"

"Oh, I can't, sir."

"Why?"

"Because your selector switch is broken ... more or less."

"More or less?"

"You see, sir, though it won't turn the feed off, it obviously turns it on ... and with awesome fidelity, don't you think, sir?"

"Howie."

"Yes, sir?"

"I want to have a private conversation with this gentleman."

"Well, sir, okay. With that particular model, I think stowing it on the back row of the choir loft under a hymnal will defeat its reception. To be sure, you could, of course, leave the auditorium."

Mira's heels pierce the air like a jackhammer as she stomps to the edge of the stage.

"Howie!"

Silence befalls even the foyer titterers as they marvel at how her pocketsize frame can muster such volume.

"Yes, Ms. Bonham, ma'am?"

"You are sitting at a sound board, son! When Reverend Mott gestures like this, pot him down!"

"Pot, ma'am?"

"You have little knobs that slide up and down. This mike should feed into number seven. All the way down is mute."

"Oh … wow ... okeydokey."

Mira turns to reclaim her chair.

"Um, Ms. Bonham, ma'am?"

"What, Howie?"

"Now that his volume is off, how will I know when to turn it up?"

She whips back around like an irate drill sergeant and beelines toward the balcony stairway, mumbling underbreath.

"Because I'll swat you on the back of your obtuse head!"

Though a flurry of finger taps indicates his mike is now dead, Peter motions for Ani to follow him up the steps and to the rear of the stage for good measure. He then adopts the classic pastoral posture, taking Ani's right hand in his and draping his left arm around Ani's shoulder.

"Shall we dance now, Reverend?"

"Just pretend I'm ministering to you."

"Why?"

"Because you're supposed to be mourning these men."

"But I am. Bart and Arnie counted among my closest friends. I had known them since elementary school."

"Yet you killed them. Didn't you?"

"Oh, most definitely."

"Why?"

"They had it coming."

"That isn't friendship; it's sociopathy."

"That statement reveals how little you know about friendship. I certainly hope we need not rehash the euthanasia debate which long predates Hippocrates."

"The rumor's afloat that these guys were hacked to bits. That goes a little beyond giving a dying man a painkiller overdose to end his suffering."

"My friends were suffering just the same, ethically."

"Just what did they do?"

"How is that relevant?"

"They killed somebody, didn't they? At least I hope they did something that egregious to deserve what you did to them. Don't get me wrong when I say I hope they killed; you see, I'm having difficulty relating to the man who butchered the guests of honor at a funeral in my church!"

"Arnie's high school sweetheart took another man, an underclassman, to the senior prom."

"So he never forgave the guy for stealing his girlfriend?"

"Oh, he did not steal her. There was not even a breakup. She married Arnie that summer, and they remained happily so until his recent demise."

"Why did she go to the prom with the other guy?"

"She pitied him. He was mentally challenged."

"What rational man holds a lifelong grudge over something like that?"

"That is precisely my point. Arnie was a perceptive man. He knew the hatred he had harbored for so many decades was unreasonable. He also knew how I would respond if he surrendered to it. Because I loved Arnie, I endeavored to show him another path. Powerless beneath the sway of his long engrained behavior patterns, he rejected my offer.

Like the terminally ill patient who faces an excruciating decline, Arnie's act was a plea to be released from his compulsions."

"And Bart?"

"He did not stop his brother."

"It's protocol that I escort you to the place of honor and … bless you."

"Rules be damned, sir."

"Fair enough. I *am* sorry for your loss, Ani."

"Thank you, Peter."

Ani descends the steps, kisses his fingers and lays them on each coffin in turn, then disappears in the shade of the foyer.

Peter plods to the edge of the stage and folds his hands. Just before they entered the auditorium, he and Mira promised each other they would never again so much as patronize, let alone mislead, their followers.

"Let us pray. Dear Lord. When I was a boy, Halloween lost its allure the moment I began to suspect ghosts did not exist. So with the Christmas season when I was told Santa Claus wasn't real. But in the same breath, I was assured that you and Jesus *were* real. Though, as with goblins and Saint Nicholas, no one could produce solid evidence of your existence, I was persuaded to have faith that you were somewhere out there, that you loved me, that you would look out for me and mine.

"But then I studied history. And it struck me that, over the centuries, human beings who worship you under one name have slaughtered scores of other human beings who call you by another. Though all of the killing, and all of the dying, have been done in your name, not once have you intervened to settle the argument.

"Just last May, three F5 tornadoes plowed through our city, laying waste homes, hospitals, nurseries and schools, taking hundreds of innocent lives and leaving as many homeless. In umpteen churches like this one, we sang hymns of thanks to you for sparing the survivors. We paid no mind to the logical precept that, if you had the power to spare tens of thousands, you certainly could have saved hundreds. This fact can sustain only two conclusions: that you are less than omnipotent or that you are a homicidal maniac."

He retrieves his well worn scripture from the lectern and retakes stagefront.

"Either way, whatever your true name – be it Jehovah, Allah, the Prime Mover, the First Cause, Shang Ti, El Shaddai or Rabb al-Alameen – I renounce you, sir, and I demand that you prove yourself to me, to everyone here, right now!"

Peter throws the leatherbound volume to the floor. The impact sends a tremor up Old Man Harlen's cane. Peter himself is nonplussed as the echo emanates to the balcony, then turns on itself and, as the feedback builds to a rumble, columns of blinding light materialize, one before each and every patron. The columns take on various human forms, and the churchgoers begin carrying on frantic conversations with their phantasmal counterparts. Toting heels in hand, Mira dashes to the stage and clutches Peter from behind.

"What did you do?! What is the matter with these people?!"

"See Mrs. Paff in the eighth row? She's talking to her grandmother, who's been dead for nearly twenty-four years. Francine over there is doing the softshoe with Ben Vereen."

"You mean to tell me you see what they see?"

"You don't?"

"Garland Wertz is nodding his melon head like a whipped schoolboy. Who's talking to him?"

"Comedienne Ruth Buzzie."

"Peter, what is that infernal noise?"

"Some sort of engine. Sounds angry. This is curious."

"What do you see?"

"The ghosts have shrunk into … pinpricks of light. They're all converging in the baptistery."

"Oh my stars, Peter, it's coming right at us!"

"You see it, too?"

The mysterious lights have congealed into a 1940 Indian Chief motorcycle, which explodes from the baptistery, soars over the floor sections, turns about in mid air, and lands just in front of the foyer. The olive drab fog that enshrouds the rider gradually dissipates from the ground up when the kickstand is engaged. First to emerge are camel hued knickerbocker style pants tucked into full-calf leather boots. Soon a hip holster materializes. It carries an ivory-grip Colt .45, behind which a custom tailored WWII era Class A dresscoat boasts an august array of pins, ribbons and medals from nine sovereign countries and the Vatican. Finally, beneath the glistening, four-star emblazoned M1 helmet emerges the calculating visage of General George Smith Patton, Jr. So vigorously does he raise and aim his riding crop at Peter and Mira that even Howie can hear the *pop* of the warrior's coat sleeve and sashes.

"Step aside, son. You, too, miss. I don't have all day, move your ass!"

They comply. The General takes the stage, turns and surveys the stunned onlookers with no less displeasure than a sorority girl casts upon off-brand clothing.

"Ladies, gentlemen, crumb snatchers. The individual human being, provided with the appropriate method and level of discipline in childhood, is one shrewd sonofabitch. He will see through the most sophisticated scams. He will debunk the most convoluted hoaxes. He is not given to phobia or panic. A community of humans, however, is a gullible gaggle of monkeys who don't know any better than to play in their own shit, and who will blindly follow the alpha male, even at their own peril, because they are deathly afraid of being ostracized.

"This has been the grand paradox of our existence. As man advances society, society in turn molds the man. The technological revolution of late has demanded ever increasing specialization. Specialization is an insidious trap. It requires that we focus our energies upon subjects of ever finer detail, creating the illusion that we are smarter when, in reality, our endeavors have so much more blinded us to the big picture."

Old Man Harlen rises from his front-and-center perch. Patton stabs the imperious crop in his direction.

"You there, speak up."

"See here, young man. I don't know what you're trying to pull, but Old Blood and Guts died three quarters of a century ago. I was only six, but I remember my papa reading that headline and weeping. I will thank you to stop this tomfoolery, as we have a remembrance at hand."

"Your father was a perceptive man. I will overlook your charge that I fail to grasp the solemnity of this occasion because the inattentive one here is you, Mr. Harlen. Still, you're right about one thing. These corpses are a distraction. I therefore order all persons who have died within the last calendar week to vacate the premises!"

The casket lids fly open. Like extras from a 1980s slasher movie, the former Milland brothers lumber from their places of rest, their gaping and jagged wounds visible through their burial garb, and begin to saunter up the center aisle. Patton flourishes his crop in Bart's direction.

"Hold it! You there. Bartholomew P. Milland, Sergeant, First Battalion, Seventy-Fifth Ranger Regiment, Granada, 1983. Have you forgotten your protocol, son? Salute your superior officer."

The ambulatory cadaver which was once Bart snaps to attention, plants its foot and pivots to face the General.

"Well, boy? What have I got to do to get a salute out of you, ram this crop up your insolent ass?!"

Still at attention, the creature stares forlornly with its only remaining eyeball at the stump where its right arm once was. Patton slaps his knees and guffaws like an adolescent prankster.

"Well, then, if you can't salute, at least have the decorum to dance the Lindy for me!"

The brothers turn to each other and gyrate in the disjointed fashion of deranged marionettes – Bart with only one arm and foot, Arnold with his left femur bent at a 30-degree angle and his head split down the middle. His laughter building, Patton stutters down the stagesteps and throws his arm around Old Man Harlen's neck.

"Sorry, ole boy, but I'm an avid fan of *humour macabre*. Death bites us all in the ass sooner or later, so why not have a little fun with the bastard? Dismissed!"

Still dancing, the morbid siblings resume their teetering gait down the aisle until they vanish into the foyer.

Patton slaps Harlen on the shoulder.

"Bear with me, my dubious friend; I'll get to the punch line in quick order."

"Hey, mister!"

Before Patton can reacquire the stage, Krissy Canaught plants herself halfway up the steps to block his path.

"What the hell do you want?"

"Show us another miracle."

"I'm not a circus barker, kid."

"People have been telling me about you all my life. I'm seven and a half now, and you haven't answered one of my prayers. So pay up."

Mounting the step just below hers, Patton peers down at her like a menacing oak. Yet she remains defiant.

"Well, then? What do you want?"

She looks down at her fidgety hands and, when she reengages his stare, her effrontery has melted away.

"Will you make me pretty?"

Patton kneels down beside her, sizes up her parents, then smiles at her.

"Don't you worry, little one. That pasty, cocksucking potatohead over there isn't your real dad. You come from Columbian stock, complements of the sous chef at the country club. Fifty years from now, when all your friends start to sag and droop like so many sea lions, you'll still have the skin of a twenty-year-old."

Krissy's ersatz father erupts at this revelation. Patton gives the girl a hair-tousle, stalks to the now bickering couple and removes his gloves.

"That will be enough out of you. On your feet, mister."

An indignant Mr. Canaught hesitantly rises.

"You, too, miss."

No sooner has a sniffling Mrs. Canaught joined her husband than Patton treats them each to a slap in the face so concussive that it makes even Howie shudder.

"I will not have my address interrupted by a pair of goddamned crybabies! *Boohoohoo, my wife cheated on me*. If you were a real man, she wouldn't have. *Poor, pitiful me, I was driven into the arms of another man*. I'm sure it was pure hell for you, honey, wrapping your thighs around an exotic beef bayonet seventeen years your junior. Sit!"

As the Canaughts huddle together in shock, Patton regloves and retakes the stage. Peter and Mira have not budged from their spot halfway between the dais mark and the choir loft, Peter staring like a blinded deer, Mira crouching behind him and peeking around his shoulder. Patton studies the pair the way a dog responds to a perplexing noise, then taps Peter's free shoulder with his crop.

"Don't you turn yellow on me. I have a job for you, and I won't have you shirking your duty."

He points his crop slowly so their eyes will follow it.

"You see those chairs, there? Fill 'em."

So cautious is their retreat that Peter and Mira hold their pose, not separating until Mira detects a chair leg with her calf. Patton touches an approving crop to his helmet, then turns again to the attendees.

"You may be wondering just who I am. Am I the supreme being known by various cultures as Jehovah, Allah, the Prime Mover, the First Cause, Shang Ti, El Shaddai and Rabb al-Alameen? Am I, indeed, this magnificent specimen of a soldier and commander, that son of a goddamned bitch Georgie Patton, who stands before you now? Or am I something else altogether? The answer, ladies, gentlemen and curtain climbers, embraces some four thousand years of human history.

"In his 1976 book titled *The Origin of Consciousness in the Breakdown of the Bicameral Mind*, American scholar Julian Jaynes, made a poignant observation which embodies the story I am about to tell: *Poems are rafts clutched at by men drowning in inadequate minds.* Now what in hell does that mean? It took Jaynes over four hundred pages to explain it. A brilliant man, Dr. Jaynes, but he didn't have Georgie's gift for concision. Here's the pith of what he said, with a little polish here, a dash of extrapolation there.

"Prior to the second millennium before the common era, human beings did not have the ability to think subjectively. They had no mental mirror, as it were, to consider themselves in relation to their surroundings – what we call introspection – the process Rene Descartes referred to as *cogito ergo sum*. This is because our ancestors' very own brains were deceiving them.

"Nowadays, we use the left hemisphere of our brain to determine what we want to say and order the mouth to say it, while our right brain remains, in many pertinent respects, asleep. When we remember events from the past or talk to ourselves, the sounds we generate internally are muted. The great majority of us who do not suffer from a mental defect have no trouble at all distinguishing this inner voice from audible speech.

"Until four thousand years ago, the right hemisphere of the human brain was far more active, equally so to our left. This condition is what Dr. Jaynes referred to as bicamerality. As countless case studies of modernday schizophrenics demonstrate, the inner voice of the right brain is as robust and distinct as was Charlton Heston's stage voice. Imagine your shadow speaking to you as loudly as I am now. These poor schmucks didn't understand the brain any better than a goldfish understands nuclear physics, so when they heard their right brain comfort them in a time of crisis or tell them how to solve a problem, they wrongly assumed this wisdom was coming from some invisible being greater than they.

"Gods, ladies, gentlemen and carpet rats. At this critical time in history, our comparatively ignorant ancestors were conned by their own minds into concocting a doggone brigade of unseeable authority figures. Our most precious attributes, the abilities that distinguish us from every other species – reason, abstract problem solving, morality – our forebears ascribed to otherworldly sprites. Well, when you give someone else the credit for your virtues and accomplishments, two things happen. Your self-concept goes right down the shitter, and you become consumed by the idolization of others whom you perceive to be smarter, stronger or better looking than you.

"As the end of the precommon era approached, our presumption that the voices were external to us forced the right brain to fall silent as its counterpart became more dominant; hence, the breakdown of bicamerality. We see evidence of this progression when we compare the vocabulary of the Greek epic *Iliad* to that in its sequel, *Odyssey*. In the *Iliad*, the characters merely saw and did. Nothing at all happened in the mind between perception and response. Likewise, all extreme emotions were the sole province of the gods. A century later, the *Odyssey* adds mental deliberation to the decisionmaking process, depicting the internalization of rationality, ethics and emotion. For the first time in history, man had become aware of his inner self, and ole Rene's *I think therefore I am* was born.

"But without the benefit of presentday scientific knowledge, our dumb-schmuck forefathers interpreted the silence of the right brain as an abandonment by the gods. Because the emergence of our own inner chatter coincided with the silence of what we had perceived to be external instruction, we blamed ourselves for the retreat of our presumed protectors, casting a pall of suspicion on our unique creativity, rejecting our every innocent appetite and urge as an abomination, a weakness, a *sin* against our chimerical superiors.

"Any idiot today knows that mindless repetition lulls the conscious mind to sleep and, when the left brain isn't watching, the right brain wanders into our field of awareness. Our progenitors associated this sporadic right brain activity with a return of the gods, so they developed redundant rituals of ever increasing complexity to appease their long lost moral authorities, spreading the various practices from culture to culture faster than the goddamned Black Death that ravaged Europe in the fourteenth century. Religion, my friends. That creed of bigotry which turns neighbor against neighbor and father against son, and which is, historically speaking, the number one cause of death."

Old Man Harlen whacks the pew with his cane and hobbles up the stage steps. Stopping an arm's length from Patton, he upends the cane and raps its cleat against the warhorse's chest.

"That will be quite enough of that, you blaspheming agitator! I read that book you speak of. It's a nifty thesis, I'll grant you that. But it's just one of a hundred theories out there, and leaving aside whatever first inspired the faith we share, we came by it honestly."

Patton raises his crop like a dueling sword, rests the business end against his detractor's chin.

"I'll thank you to get to the point."

"What's the harm, young man? Whether they did it in the name of Jehovah or Knute Rockney, look at the many extraordinary, humanitarian accomplishments so many great men and women have wrought in the name of their idol."

"To that, sir, I reply: All of that good would have been done with or without the pretense of some grand marionetteer in the sky, a pretense which only denigrates the inbuilt generosity of the human heart. You speak of fortunate accidents. You stand on coincidence. I call your bluff, sir, with an appeal to individual self-worth."

Old Man Harlen raises his cane until it hovers but a rumor from Patton's left nostril.

"My pa was the wisest man I ever met. He was a devout Christian. So was my grandpa, like his papa before him. My line goes back to the settlers of Roanoke, sonny. Longsuffering disciples of The Almighty, every one, and I allow that all them generations can't be wrong."

Patton lowers his crop until it nudges the codger's jugular.

"I don't give a hoot in hell for tradition. From the dawn of recorded history until just a few centuries ago, it was a customary practice, sanctioned by governments the world over without exception, to buy and sell human beings like so many goddamned cattle. For the last century and a half, the conventional wisdom was that a vote for a Republican would provide the storied check and balance to the totalitarian policies of the Democrats. But that was exposed as a truckload of hooey just one year ago, when ...?"

"The feds turned over them infernal Boxheim Papers."

"Goddamn right. That's tradition for you, right up the ass."

Old Man Harlen holds his opponent's stare as he considers his rebuttal, then lowers his cane.

"I'll concede on that one, sir, but there's still something I don't like about you."

Patton grins and touches his crop to his helmet.

"I wouldn't have it any other way."

Ever the magnanimous victor, Patton remains attentive to Old Man Harlen until he has clomped down the steps and resumed his perennial post. Then, with a precise tug at his dresscoat to maintain a flawless presentation of his every glistening accolade, he resumes his lecture.

"The bottom line is that our ill informed predecessors jumped to a false conclusion which caused a temporary evolutionary relapse and, ever since, humanity has been chasing the rumor of a mirage. Because mores are imprinted socially, it took only a few people in influential positions to set the societal tone; everyone else gladly adopted the bandwagon mentality. Because we naturally assume our forerunners and elders know what the hell they're doing, every generation who advances the baton of religion adds another coat to the patina of legitimacy surrounding the childish endeavor. At the same time, deep in the recesses of our minds, on a cellular level, we know our reverence for the extramundane contradicts logic and degrades the whole of humanity. This fundamental conflict has turned us into a race of semiconscious schizophrenics. Not the kind who eat pocket lint and carry on conversations with their belly buttons, but the subtler, more insidious manifestation that is truer to the term's original meaning. *Schizophrenia* derives from two Greek words: *skhizein* meaning *to split* and *phren* which denotes *mind*. Because I haven't the patience to recount the entire laundry list of the thousand ways this society exhibits its split mind, I will submit for your consideration the silliest.

"My all time favorite is the blur on the television screen. Your censors have no compunction about permitting virtually every millimeter of the nude female form to be splashed across the primetime networks, but there will be hell to pay if just one eight-year-old boy catches glimpse of a nipple. Your censors are quite content to allow the most graphic portrayals of violence and gore, but let one actor say the word *fuck* and hordes of you blushing biddies will swarm the networks screaming for his head. You can't understand why your children nonchalantly mistreat animals or steal a gun and massacre their classmates. This is because you have so compartmentalized the facts and circumstances associated with death and dying that little Johnnie and Jennie see it as nothing more than the end of a cartoon game on their *Xbox*. You have abdicated your conscience to such an unwieldy list of statutes and regulations that you have lost the ability and incentive to formulate your own moral judgments, in the process forsaking all notions of self-control. Your societal head is so far up its ass that you people can't even call a goddamned elephant a goddamned elephant anymore! You toss around the words *freedom* and *independence*, but you don't have the faintest fucking idea what they mean, let alone the sacrifice they require. So brimming are you with redundant euphemism, reality for you has been preempted by a crude approximation thereof.

"You've become the prisoners chained to a rock in Plato's cave, content to accept as reality the shadows your captors cast on the wall opposite the only source of light in the cave – the entrance to which your backs are turned. Who are your jailers? The pop stars and the preachers and the politicians who, to enrich themselves and their cronies on your backs, exploit your penchant for hero-worship – a vestige of that ancient practice of looking outside oneself for answers. You're unhappy with the stress and monotony of your life but, rather than improve it, you go to a convention center or a ballpark, where you spend your precious free time and hard-earned money living vicariously through an athlete who couldn't care less about you, and a few hours later he waltzes home to the mansion schmucks like you built for him while you shuffle back to your miserable little hovel. Death scares the living shit of you but, rather than wring all the fun you can out of life while you have it, you come to a place like this to wallow in a fantasy that won't change the fact that someday you will go toes up. You're too lazy to be bothered with the messy issues that arise when you live in a community, so you fob off your haggling and rulemaking responsibilities onto a conclave of bluebloods in whose minds you are but a nameless, indentured goose on a golden egg plantation.

"But that disgraceful chapter in the story of humanity is coming to an end, because you are, as I speak, in the midst of a quantum developmental leap. And this very city is the epicenter of that awakening. Now that you've had forty centuries to grow up and develop the mental tools to use it responsibly, your right brain is coming back to life. Yes, ladies, gentlemen and rug apes, you are on the road to complete right-left brain integration. Your generation will be the first in human history to achieve full consciousness. But there will be a steep learning curve. You've been having some queer dreams, haven't you? Outlandish, disturbing dreams that seem more vivid, more real, than even your wakeful lives? Don't go trotting off to a fucking psychiatrist to try and figure it out, because that dumb bastard is even more confused than you. Just be patient. Remain vigilant. Those dreams reflect your right brain learning to walk again after all this time. As it stretches its muscles, you will experience a revival of self-sufficiency, self-responsibility, overall integrity.

"These qualities are so foreign to you people that, when your right brain has driven you in the direction of unqualified sincerity, you've been oblivious to it. You don't believe me, do you? Consider the national election of this last November. Recall how surprised you were during the campaign to hear old-guard politicians abandon the cover stories of their respective parties and reveal what their true motives were. Do you think they intended to do that? Ponder, if you dare, the odds that 100% of the voting populace would agree on anything, let alone what amounts to a bloodless revolution. Yes, you. And you. Every goddamned last one of you told the two most powerful political machines on the planet to kiss your ass on the rail out of town. And whom did you elect, unanimously I remind you, to preside over your new crop of administrators? A rogue. A convicted felon. A wiseass and a brawler whose brand of so-called cowboy diplomacy makes Dutch Reagan look like a sissy-missy.

"And this brings us back to my original question. Who am I? I, ladies, gentlemen and shin kickers, am your collective hallucination. Indeed, I am perhaps the last hallucination your right brain will produce. When the good Reverend Mott defied the delusion of the ages moments ago, your emergent right hemispheres scrambled to assume the likeness of a familiar historical figure with both the credibility and the brass to keep your left brains from scampering away to unconsciousness. And I commend you for making a damned fine selection. But I am merely a crutch, a temporary bridge spanning the chasm that is quickly filling with axons and dendrites and muscle fibers. One moment, if you please."

The General pivots a precise one hundred eighty degrees and marches to the rear of the stage, where Peter and Mira, having gained a fuller appreciation for what is happening, rise confidently to receive him. The General beams.

"Sly bastard, the human brain – dredging up the ghost of the greatest strategic mind in the history of warfare so you can carry on an honest conversation with yourselves. You both made this evolutionary jump years ago. Your new friend Stearns? His integration happened in the goddamned womb. Unfortunately, Mr. Mott, you backslid some because of that little episode with Herzog and Massenet. Now what should that tell you? That these billions of new connections now being forged between the two hemispheres will be frail for some time. Human beings despise change, and old habits are ornery sons of bitches. Though you have advanced far ahead of your compatriots, you have managed to keep one foot in their semi-conscious world, retaining the ability to see what they have seen today. You have, this very hour, watched your flock cast aside Plato's shackles. This lone event has changed the world forever. The question is which of two pathways humanity will take. The captors have sounded the alarm. Whoever doesn't escape will be punished and, if only a few succeed, the efficacy of any future escape will decrease exponentially. This is an all-or-nothing proposition. As we speak, many of your charges have discovered the entrance, but they fear what lies beyond. If they don't step outside, if their more cowardly companions lure them back to the perceived safety of ignorance and dependency, they may never get another chance, because humanity's right hemisphere will retreat again, most likely atrophy and die altogether, and with it will perish every last notion of personal ambition or civil liberty. It will be as if the *Magna Carta* were never written. Mr. Mott, Ms. Bonham, it is up to you to use your extraordinary gifts to lead these people across the threshold into full consciousness. If you fail, the abuses and atrocities of the Dark and Middle Ages will seem like a beach party in contrast to what the statists will mete out for centuries to come."

Stowing his crop in an armpit, he places a vicelike grip on the forearm of each.

"So, you see, your task is really very simple: Don't fucking fail."

Crop in hand again, the General straightens his jacket and turns to face the awestruck congregation. With a shrill whistle, he calls out, "Here, boy!" The motorcycle obediently ascends the steps and stops by his side.

"I now leave you in the capable hands of Peter Mott and Mira Bonham, your spiritual shepherd and shepherdess of these many years. To those of you who still think I am Georgie Patton resurrected, I can assure you that he died on December 21, 1945 in Heidelberg, Germany and, most regrettably, he has not been reborn. To the stubborn few of you who cling to the fading notion that I am the God of your childhood fables, I have only this to say: I'm not really here. I never was."

Turning aside to mount his bike, the General hears little Krissy weep. Retracing his earlier path to her pew, he removes his glove and raises her chin ever so gently.

"Don't despair, little one. This doesn't mean you're all alone. Having rid yourself of the fables, you have cleared a new pathway in your quest to answer the Primordial Why. Twelve years ago, a geophysicist with the Ph.D. in philosophy named Stephen C. Meyer published a little tome called 'Signature in the Cell: DNA and the Evidence for Intelligent Design.' Contextualizing cellular biology with the science of probabilities, Meyer not only offered empirical proof for the hypothesis of intelligent design; he methodically disproved the leading evolutionary theories. Read the book, kid. Has Uncle Georgie steered you wrong yet?"

With a wink and a pat on her grinning cheek, the General returns to his bike, stows his crop across the handlebars and revs the engine.

"As you were."

In a deafening 1200cc roar, the General and his Indian rocket from the stage to the foyer, where they dematerialize in a spectacular burst of light.

"DON'T YOU GET IT BY NOW? THIS CAMPAIGN ISN'T ... NO POLITICAL CAMPAIGN IN AMERICAN HISTORY HAS EVER BEEN ABOUT THE PEOPLE'S WELFARE OR PROSPERITY. IT'S A CONTEST FOR BRAGGING RIGHTS BETWEEN MY TEAM AND THOSE SONOFABITCH REPUBLICANS TO SEE WHO CAN HIGHJACK THE MOST SECTORS OF THE ECONOMY FROM YOU IDIOTS. WHAT THE RICH AND POWERFUL DID WITH ARMIES AND SIEGE MACHINES IN OLDEN TIMES, WE IN THE CIVILIZED ERA DO WITH ADVERTISING AND TALK-SHOW PARTY-STRATEGISTS. SO GET OUT OF MY FACE, YOU SNIVELING LITTLE MORLOCK!"

The First Female President and First First Lady to Become President and Only Former First Lady to Become the First Female President's involuntarily honest response, induced by her emerging right brain, on September 28, 2020 (her last public appearance before she secluded herself in abject shame), to a question from the press about the devastating economic effect of the mass expatriation of retirement accounts spurred by her Social Security Act of 2017.

Chapter Twenty

The Taunted Beast Stirs

February 1

A glimmer of morning sun ricochets off Ani's coffee cup as he trades tabletalk with the owner of the downtown corner café, then swivels his stool to exit the establishment. Just as he stands, Capt. Villanueva clumps through the door. The proprietor's daughter hands Villanueva a courthouse flyer, which he rips in two and flings to the floor in disgust. When their eyes meet, Ani reaches inside his overcoat. Villanueva instinctively tosses his coat aside and prepares to draw his .45. Ani measures his motion, not out of caution, but to toy with his sullen adversary, who now unsnaps his holster and assumes the Weaver stance on the vain expectation that turning his torso perpendicular will in the slightest way streamline his epic profile. As Ani's hand gradually emerges, Villanueva tightens his grip and begins easing the pistol from its cradle.

Ani's production of a cigar only compounds Villanueva's umbrage. Ani approaches and offers his hand. Villanueva scowls at it, keeping a defiant grip on his holstered weapon.

"Oh, come now. The dispute between us ended a lifetime ago. You surely know after all this time that fostering a grudge can be a deadly business."

"Is that a threat, Stearns?"

"It is a statement of psychosocial fact. I bear you no ill will, Chick."

"You may address me as Captain or Detective."

"That would be a discourtesy. Regardless of who did what to whom in that alley, the contest forged between us an indelible bond."

"You delude yourself and insult me with that nonsense. The only lasting results of that incident are a thirty percent hearing loss in the ear you did not chew off, persistent tinnitus in what is left of the one you did, and the alienation of my only child."

"I did not recruit Lucio; he came to me. I merely trained the lad."

"The skills you taught him, no boy should know."

"You would have preferred that he learn from the dead-enders on the streets, like his father did?"

"You made him a mercenary."

"I taught him discipline he did not have. I instilled in him fundamental respect for all human life."

"Strip away the embellishments and the rationalizations, and a killer is just a killer."

"Cops and soldiers restrain, maim and kill at the behest of their superiors, having ceded their capacity for moral judgment to a rulebook. Your son *chooses* to place his life and possessions in jeopardy to protect the defenseless. Your son earns your undying respect every day he wakes up and decides to *own* his life."

"He is no son of mine."

"It breaks my heart that you have learned so little from your own struggles and accomplishments."

"I came here for a mocha latte, not to trade philosophical barbs with the likes of you."

"Chick, we need not be enemies."

"I will tell you once more, and once more only. You may address me as Captain or Detective."

"And if I don't?"

"Thanks to these puerile political games that will cast us back to the Stone Age, I have no official authority here."

"To the contrary, I see a bright and bold era adawn, and I find it invigorating."

"An era that will spell the extinction of us both."

"Unlike the modernday soldier, my very existence is not contingent upon a state of war." Ani snatches a flyer from the greeter's pregnant stack and brandishes it under Villanueva's nose. "My loved ones and I shall adapt handily to the metamorphosis unfolding around us. If you have lost a son, Chick, you have only yourself to blame."

Ani stalks closer. Villanueva circles ever so carefully to clear a path but keep a wary eye on the man who still bedevils his dreams, backpedaling as Ani pursues at a measured pace.

"My offer of friendship remains open, *Captain.* But do not misapprehend or abuse my generosity."

"What the hell does that mean?"

When his heel collides with a barstool, Villanueva realizes he has no route of escape. Ani converges until their noses almost touch.

"Ask Eldra Frye."

Villanueva scours his inner landscape for the feeblest of justifications to cling to the lifelong presumptions Ani's utterance threatens to crush. Ms. Frye has been in protective custody ever since the butchery at Custard's Last Stand ten days ago, and the media have honored Villanueva's plea to keep the incident quiet until he can find the scantest of leads – a trace of DNA, a murder weapon, a motive – to put him on the trail of multiple assailants. Here, the man who maimed him a lifetime ago has both corroborated Frye's outlandish claim that a lone assailant killed fourteen grown men and confessed to being that assaulter. *Impossible! No one man can be so potent.* But the connection between the tomahawk/khukuri and the roofer's axe/awl from over forty years past can not be discounted in the face of his antagonist's inexorable, denuding stare. This realization amplifies the ordinarily tolerable hum in his left ear into a clangorous rumble as Ani strides away.

"What'll it be today, Officer?"

The owner's astringent voice robs Villanueva of his last fading notion of self-restraint.

"What do I want? You're asking me what do I want?! I have been coming to this bistro every Monday morning for how many years, and I always order the same large mocha latte to go. In the entire universe of facts, which one makes you think I would order anything different today?"

Matching his indignant glare, the owner points emphatically to the television above the breakfast buffet, where an urgent news bulletin has preempted the local weather.

Hostess: Are we live? Ladies and gentlemen, we're getting reports ... I ... I can't ... Preston?

Host: Devastating news, folks, from all over the Middle East. Why don't we ... do you have that clip on four? Cue that. Ladies, gentlemen, you no doubt recall the ominous threats our new President made on Inauguration Day. We're still trying to verify some of this information so, while we work on that, and in case ... I don't know ... one or two of you were in a coma and missed President Olm's inauguration speech, we're going to play that now to set the stage for our report. This is our coverage from January 21. Roll the tape.

Olm: *A funny thing happened on my way to this rostrum. On November 4 of this last year, five hundred thirty-five lawmakers awoke to find that their jobs had been terminated. So it took no persuasion on my part to call an emergency session of Congress three days ago. I will share the results of that session in a moment.*

In his 1982 book of the same title, legendary economist Milton Friedman discussed the tyranny of the status quo. To illustrate what he meant, I'll borrow an unattributed analogy that's been circulating for a great many years. You catch a herd of wild pigs by spreading corn in a clearing. Once the pigs grow accustomed to eating it, you place a fence panel on one side of the clearing. When they overcome their fear of that panel and begin eating the corn again, you install another panel, then another and, in the last, you install a narrow gate. By now, the pigs are so used to getting free corn that they don't hesitate to enter through the gate. Once they're all inside, you close the gate. So long as you feed them a steady diet of free corn, they don't even notice they've been captured until the day you stop doling out the free corn. But by then they're doomed, because they've forgotten how to forage for themselves.

I promised you from the day I announced my candidacy that I was going to tell you, not what I thought you wanted to hear, but what I gathered from history and current events that you needed to hear. It appears I was right, not because I'm all that smart, but because your support demonstrates that you and I understand how far this nation has fallen and what must be done to recapture its grandeur. Your votes confirmed my suspicion that the American populace is not a herd of carping freeloaders. We are a proud nation. We don't need a warehouse full of laws to tell us what is right and wrong. We don't need a brood of pretentious millionaires to dictate how we spend our hard-earned money. We are also a charitable nation. We are eager to assist those who are truly in need. But a government which confiscates our wages to create an annuity for those who are unwilling to work only diminishes our ability to help our neighbors who are unable to work.

We have outgrown the partisan political model of centuries past. I have said many times that the Republicans and Democrats are two faces of the same evil. A prime example of this took place a mere four years ago, when two bills flew through both chambers with virtually zero opposition, bills which disarmed you while they freed rapists and murderers and gave them the right to vote alongside you. On the very day that U.N. treaty was signed, many of us woke up to the fact that the war to preserve States' rights did not end in 1865.

But some remained unconvinced until just two years ago, when the governors of forty-seven States held their own convention, as was their right under Article V of the Constitution.

They presented to Congress a series of constitutional amendments aimed at reversing or revising various forced wealth redistribution measures going all the way back to 1935, which have worked in concert to debilitate our economy and erode the American Dream beneath an ever growing tax burden. Rather than obey the Constitution, our elected representatives ignored the amendments, prompting a flurry of lawsuits. It was during the discovery phase of that litigation that the government was forced to turn over the now infamous Boxheim Papers: that collection of letters and memos written by various top echelon Democrat party operatives dating to as far back as 1817, which reveal that the Republican party was never anything more than a strawman – originally conceived, structured and populated by the Democrat party – which has, ever since, functioned covertly as a subsidiary of the Democrat party.

Let me reassure you, I owe no loyalty to any political party. The one I used to acquire this podium is merely my ticket onto the runaway train of federal government, which you and I will now bring into the station for a long belated overhaul.

In a world which has collapsed into a pitched battle between deadbeats and producers, and in a United States of America whose taxpayers last year were forced to shell out over one trillion dollars in matching funds to Medicaid alone, you and I have opted to stand with the producers. We reject the federal government's free corn, choosing to live consciously, passionately and conscientiously, preferring the hardships of such a life to the robotic existence of freeloaders. We choose the chaos of local policy decisions and the discomfort of face-to-face debate over the mock security of a distant lawgiver. Your votes in this election, my good friends, proved that the apathy of the American citizen has come to an end.

In keeping with the spirit of personal responsibility which motivated all of you to lend me this office, let me put some rumors to rest right now. I will not be granting any preemptive pardon to the outgoing President, I will revoke the one she issued for her predecessor, and I hereby declare myself ineligible for any such amnesty.

I thank each and every one of you for the confidence you have demonstrated, not just in me, but in your country and its political system. Congress and I will do our damnedest to prove worthy of your trust.

To honor that pledge, I must now address the thugs who are sitting in a hut or a cave or a penthouse suite in a ritzy hotel, celebrating the biggest massacre of innocents since nine-eleven-aught-one.

My meeting with the outgoing Congress was by far the most productive since the Second Continental Congress of 1776, and here is why. With nothing to lose, these fine ladies and gentlemen were free to do something unprecedented in modern American politics – vote their conscience. I was informed hours ago that the last of our embassies in the greater Middle East has been closed and its personnel evacuated. Furthermore, because the charity/welfare distinction I alluded to earlier also pertains to foreign policy, at the unanimous behest of Congress all foreign aid has been suspended indefinitely. You in the Gulf Cooperative Region have scoffed at the carrots we have offered by the shipload for over half a century. Now you will see just how heavily the American stick can strike. Until someone delivers you to me alive, the new Congress and I will authorize the random obliteration of cities and towns in your suspected countries of origin. While your act of mass murder was quiet and clean, our retaliation will be loud and bloody. Your men will suffer. Your women will be shamed. Your children will burn alive. Your places of worship will be defaced, desecrated, demolished. The only reward we offer for your surrender or capture is a cessation of the carnage which will commence very soon.

You demand that non-Muslims respect your religion. Yet you are so bigoted that you riot, maim and kill just because someone utters the name of your icon in a way which you perceive is the least bit irreverent. It defies rationality for you to expect us to tolerate a religion you use to justify indiscriminate slaughter and genocide.

Hostess: *Is that what I think it is?*

Host: *It looks to be a Muhammad doll.*

Olm: *I hold in my hand a child's toy made of a quarter pound of burlap, bunting and plastic. It is one of roughly eight hundred produced last week at an Indonesian factory.*

Hostess: *For any of you who are unable to see the visual feed, President Olm has just pulled out a scary looking switchblade, sliced the head off the doll and stuck its body to the Presidential seal with that knife.*

***Host**:* *You know that'll go viral.*

***Olm**:* *If I have offended Allah, let Allah come out of hiding and face me like a man. Short of that, so long as you persist in behaving like a rabid pack of hyenas, my fellow Americans and I will treat you in kind. We care nothing about your religion, your personal or national creed, or your sexual persuasion. The United States of America is, at heart, a peaceable nation. But peace is too often the terminus of a long and bloody pathway. As my predecessor Ronald Wilson Reagan observed, true peace is enjoyed only by those who demonstrate their strength. And we will usher in a new age of American peace, just as soon as we annihilate every last one of you sons of bitches. You heard me right. You will not be housed indefinitely at Guantanamo, only to be released by a successive administration. You will definitely never see the inside of a civilian U.S. courtroom. Your guilt will be confirmed by a military tribunal, then you will be promptly and publicly executed. We aim to kill you for the simple reason that you have killed our American brothers and sisters. You have been warned.*

Host: Many expected Armageddon to erupt the very next day, but nothing happened, no targets of any kind were struck, for two weeks. Some were beginning to wonder if the President's speech were a bluff.

Hostess: Well, it was no bluff. Beginning shortly after midnight this last Friday, the U.S. military unleashed a fierce display of munitions, including JDAMS, or bunker busters, fuel-air bombs, even land- and sea-launched nuclear missiles of varying sizes. Reports of damage and loss of life are pouring in from cities, towns and villages in all parts of the globe, including such unlikely targets as North Korea, China, Russia ... Mexico?

Host: Sherry, we just received confirmation that Iran took the brunt of the attack and Tehran, if you'll forgive the expression, has been reduced to a ghost town.

Hostess: Do I see Canada on this list? Canada?! Just a shocking turn of events. Shocking.

Host: We will, of course, keep you updated on these events. In other breaking news, the last of the deathrow releases is set to take place just minutes from now. The new President and Congress have worked at lightning speed these two weeks, and one of the first pieces of legislation they repealed was the *Criminal Rehabilitation and Reform Act.*

Hostess: Though reversing the slated releases was more of an administrative rollback than anything else, easily handled by federal and State authorities, the President issued a statement days ago in which he said the release of deathrow inmate Darian Massenet would proceed as planned to "serve as a cautionary example of what awaits all previously released felons who do not report to the nearest law enforcement outpost in a timely fashion."

Host: The administration then disseminated to news outlets and law enforcement officials a graphic description of the brutal double murder he was involved in back in the summer of 2006, along with a rundown of the evidence against him.

Hostess: And beginning Tuesday of this week, flyers with that information have been supplied to businesses surrounding the downtown Oklahoma City courthouse where Massenet is being processed.

Host: I guess it doesn't take a fortuneteller to predict the fate awaiting Massenet.

Hostess: You are not smiling about that, Preston, tell me you are not smiling at the prospect of mob justice! The man hasn't even been tried for the '06 crimes!

Host: Oh, pull the stick out of your ass, you plastic prude. The evidence is overwhelming that he helped rape, torture and murder two kids. You know it, I know it, my pet iguana knows it.

Hostess: You are so fired!

Host: You can't fire me.

Hostess: How much you wanna bet I can get you fired?

Host: Don't bother. I'm moving to Oklahoma.

Hostess: Don't you walk away, he's walking off set. You have man-boobs! He does; I've seen them.

Host: Wish I could say you had woman-boobs!

Hostess: Are we still on? Why are we still on?

Outside, Darian Massenet smooths his lapels as the deputies usher him through the courthouse door. When the deputies break formation, he struts to the topmost of the eighteen steps that will carry him to street level and pauses to drink in the adulation of what the bailiff told him was a record turnout. For as far as he can see, the street teems with men and women of all ages and origins, each cheering and flourishing an identical flyer with his image emblazoned on the front. When he has danced halfway down the steps, three meaty cowboys rush up to greet him. He takes their smiles to mean he is about to be hoisted in place for a shoulder-borne parade.

They heft him sure enough, but not in the direction he anticipates. He soon emerges from a vortex of denim and leather and spurs to find himself lying prone at the top of the steps, hogtied and gagged. A frantic glance to the left finds the courthouse door falling to behind the last of the departing deputies. Looking back to his right, he sees that the mood of the throng has taken a frightful tack. What he mistook for ovation he now understands to be invective. The moiling assemblage forms a single-file line, which patiently mounts the steps. At its head is Sonja Gavula, the four-foot-seven manager of the downtown library who personifies demureness – from the muted tones of her jacket and ankle-length skirt to the cameo brooch that covers the top button of her taffeta blouse. Halting one step below Massenet, Sonja examines him through her schoolmarm glasses. She then draws a meat tenderizer from her handbag, delivers a savage blow to his ear, returns the mallet to its designated purse pocket, primly descends the steps and wends her way toward the library as though it were any other workday.

Next in line, the auto mechanic from Reno St. crushes Massenet's forefinger with a wrench. Behind him, seven-year-old Ben Hesch unzips his dresscode khakis and urinates on his bloody ear. Massenet's panic intensifies when he scans the length of the meandering posse to find a beastly assortment of weapons. His imagination comes unhinged when, among the general population of cattle prods and hammers, he spies such curious implements as a battery-operated curling iron, an apple corer and a turkey baster filled with liquid the tinge of antifreeze.

Across the street, Ani exits the café and stops to relish in a lungful of brisk morning air. A stocky man rushing to preserve his place in what has been christened the Reckoning Line knocks Ani's cigar to the ground with a grappling hook. Thinking nothing of the inadvertent collision in light of the surrounding hubbub, Ani turns to find it. To his surprise, the passerby has jostled his way back upstream, retrieved the cigar and is inspecting it for damage.

"I apologize, sir, I'm such a klutz. Let me buy you another stogie."

Ani accepts his rescued cigar and unwraps it.

"Thank you, but that is hardly necessary. I see not a blemish on it."

Tucking the hook underarm, the burly man fishes cash from his hunting vest.

"Are you sure? I feel awful."

Ani claps the man's shoulder and gestures toward the main event.

"No harm has been done here, my friend. On the other hand, Mr. Massenet's consciousness may fade sooner than you think. I suggest you get in line before it is too late."

The two engage in a handclasp which dispels the myth that only women can speak volumes without saying a word.

"Good point you got there. Tell you what, I'll give the sumbitch a poke for you."

"You don't find that at all ironic?"

As the broad man hurries away, Ani turns to see Julia approach, hand in hand with a buoyant Melissa.

"Ironic you say?"

"A man who is racing against the clock to inflict excruciating pain on a complete stranger takes the time to make amends with another complete stranger over a seven-dollar cigar."

Ani furls his brow at Julia, then Melissa, folds his arms and gives the matter some seconds of somber thought.

"To the contrary, I submit that my new acquaintance has just displayed uncommon decency and a degree of self-awareness heretofore rarely exercised by the human species. The man has his priorities in order. Perhaps humanity is not doomed after all."

Julia kisses his neck and laces her arm through his.

"We two spent breakfast wrestling with the contingencies and hashing out the possibilities, and we've come to a consensus."

"Consensus? About what?"

"Tell him, Lissy."

"You need a vacation, old man."

"And why do you think that, miss moppet?"

"This is the third morning in a row you've scrambled our eggs. You, sir, are in a rut."

"Then a holiday we shall take."

He kisses each lady's hand, and the three embark upon a leisurely stroll mid the ruckus all about them.

"The time away will prove opportune for this old man to restructure his vocation now that the calves have, at long last, grown their horns."

One block to the east, another colossal mass of downtowners commences a quieter, though no less methodical, protest. One by one, they approach the open cell of the revolving entry door to the IRS office and deposit on its floor all of their incomplete 2021 tax forms. Identical revolts, having begun an hour earlier on America's Atlantic extremity, sweep west as the mountain of discarded returns in Oklahoma City advances toward the street.

HELLO? IS ANYBODY LISTENING?

This desperate plea was voiced by an archaic political monopoly.

Finale

Leaving Catatonia

Sean Hogan once lived in the Tudor City apartment building at First Avenue and East 40th St. in Manhattan. Every morning just after dawn, he would take his dogs for a walk to 49th, then over to Second and back home. Long familiar with the sights, sounds and odors of the neighborhood, so ingrained was their sunup ritual that, were it not for the strict leash laws, Sean often swore he could let them walk the circuit on their own and they would always return at the same time.

But on this Thursday, February 4, 2021 something was amiss. As they approached 43rd, the dogs began to whine and yelp, trying to pull Sean off course with them toward the East River. Bracing himself to restrain two hundred pounds of agitated canine, Sean peered to the west where, at the United Nations complex, he spied an unusual amount of activity for this time of day. The driveway swarmed with city cabs as ambassadors of all nationalities scurried to load suitcases and vacate the premises. Beyond the vehicular commotion, Sean detected the eerie absence of a long familiar sound. As the rising sun peeled another veneer of night from the world, he followed the smoldering stare of a stationary jogger to the flagpole a block to the south where, in place of the flag of Zimbabwe, a human body had been hung upside down. Scanning back northward, he calculated that roughly three-quarters of the other flags had met the same fate.

He tapped the jogger on the shoulder, and she removed an ear bud.

"I'm sorry, but do you know what the hell happened here?"

She pointed to her ear bud, then to the gruesome display. "It just came across the AP. Those bodies are the Noble terrorists. Two hours ago, President Olm sent a communiqué to each delegate whose country either directly sponsored or indirectly enabled one or more of the terrorists, along with a copy of the corresponding intelligence file. He told them their immunity has been rescinded and, if they don't blow town by end of business today, they'll be arrested for espionage. Look at them all, running like rats. I guess we killed the right motherfuckers this time."

"And exposed our true enemies."

"Right here in our own fucking borough."

Though religious and political dictators of various nations denounced the United States for its attacks of days earlier and insisted upon reparations, no such demands were met. But not a single army, terrorist force or splinter group retaliated because, as our government proceeded to withdraw its multifarious tentacles from around the globe, lookers on saw neither the weakness of retreat nor the bluster of a wounded animal, either of which would have whetted their appetites for more American blood. Instead, they detected the instantaneous reawakening of a quiet confidence unknown to our shores since the eighteenth century – that rare brand of serene intrepidity born of a genuine partnership among the populace and its governing bodies.

President Olm had concluded his victory speech of November 3, 2020:

> In his book *Capitalism and Freedom*, Milton Friedman observed over half a century ago: "Freedom is a rare and delicate plant. Our minds tell us, and history confirms, that the great threat to freedom is the concentration of power. Even though the men who wield this power initially be of good will, and even though they be not corrupted by the power they exercise, the power will both attract and form men of a different stamp." The solution to a despotic government is simple. If you want to change the makeup of the typical politician, you must change the nature of the office to which he aspires. So tonight, ladies and gentlemen of America, I renew my pledge to:
>
> - Repeal the federal income tax;
>
> - Revoke our country's assent to the *Enlightened Society* and *Multifaith Reconciliation* treaties, and quash the enabling legislation for each;
>
> - Dismantle the party system;
>
> - Institute strict term limits upon every public office, including the Supreme Court, because the surest path toward corruption is to make public service a lucrative career;

- Bar political action committees and other lobbyists from the political process;

- Reduce the federal work force by two thirds;

- Transition infrastructure and personnel from the Immigration and Customs Enforcement Agency to the States, ceding all federal authority therewith so that the States, which are far better equipped to do so, will be free to detect and deport illegal aliens, including their children, regardless of where they were born;

- Pass legislation to overhaul the federal election process, including the institution of voter identification, and remove all federal roadblocks to State equivalents;

- Repeal the Social Security Acts of 1935, 1965 and 2017, while systematically privatizing their various disability and retirement programs;

- Revive the Monroe Doctrine on foreign policy; and

- Because recent events have proved we have precious few allies, slash foreign aid expenditures.

Though my proposed reforms will have the ancillary effect of reducing waste and achieving a balanced budget, their primary purpose is to relegate national government to the subservient role it should have played from the start. If I fail to make good on any one of these promises after four years, you won't have to fire me – I'll quit.

President Olm and the new Congress brought all of his covenants to fruition. Contrary to the chicken-little campaign predictions of the old-guard politicians and their collaborators in the traditional media, our economy did not collapse when a multitude of federal services were either relinquished to State management or scrapped altogether. With the dismantling of the Big Two and the imposition of single-term limits, a new and fresh breed of lawmakers and executives and judges, liberated from the manacles of ideology and job preservation which had so crippled their forebears' ability to make pragmatic and rational decisions, resurrected from the ash heap of oligarchy our founders' dream of a nation in which regulative power originates in, and is never more than one electoral step removed from, the very people upon whom it is exerted. Within a mere decade, strict adherence to this paradigm by a fully conscious society wrought an extraordinary transformation – a phenomenal chain reaction triggered by the single act of repealing the federal income tax.

In its wake, a slew of federal and State regulatory taxes were abolished, and all were replaced with a six-penny sales tax split between the two levels of government per a 30/70 ratio, respectively. The resultant economic upturn saw an explosion of both job opportunities and product development. As entry level openings overspread the landscape in rural and industrial communities alike, millions of people theretofore abandoned as a permanent underclass of government dependents rejoiced in their first taste of the rewards of an honest day's work: autonomy and bona fide property ownership. With their newfound stake in society, these initiates into the fellowship of competitive capitalism developed a new sense of responsibility to their neighborhoods. Crime plummeted at a historic rate. Juvenile delinquency took a similar nosedive as former welfare parents derived from their productivity pride and self-respect, which in turn lent them credibility and authority in the eyes of the youth. Child neglect and abuse became things of the past as a burgeoning number of young adults, comprehending the breadth of the responsibility that comes with childbearing, either (a) took a proactive role in postponing conception until they became financially and emotionally stable enough to be effective and devoted parents or (b) cognizant of their personal predilections or limitations, compassionately decided to forego accouchement, opting to fulfill their reproductive urges by adopting a carefully selected pet. Dead weight was culled from the administrations and faculties of the public education system. Outcome-based education with its unmindful reliance on standardized testing was scrapped in favor of Peter Mott's tried and true holistic model, which offered a greater emphasis on linguistics, logic and conceptual analysis. Because this method entailed subjective evaluation, it spawned a wiser and more practically functional breed of educator, tolling the death knell for the parasitic career academician of yore and opening the gates of schools and universities to competent instructors with cogent and useful information – a transition reified by a popular recruiting slogan of the '20s: *Those who would teach must first do.* The Mott technique, which challenged students to thresh out *why* an answer is A and not C, so transformed the fundamental fabric of our youth that the succeeding generation grew to exhibit that long lost Benjamin Franklinesque versatility which can at once contemplate the forest and its every constituent tree.

The linguistic core of The Mott Method both stimulated and reinforced right/left brain integration. As this process elevated our awareness, preserving the dignity of self and others emerged as our cardinal motivation in all activities. At the same time, we developed a vicious intolerance for those who would in the slightest way violate that dignity. The former value further reduced crime; the latter spawned severe penalties whose deterrent effect shrank criminal court dockets and drastically depopulated prisons.

Meanwhile, a new passion for relevance triggered the *Constructive Entertainment* movement, whose revival of interest in documentary studies, historical research and intelligent comedies eradicated escapism and gratuitous sensory exploitation from the film and television industries. Quintessential cloister of incestuous self-absorption that it ever was, Hollywood, having long since forgotten there was a world beyond its studios, continued to produce tabloid swill for its own consumption, the circulation for its films shrinking to a two-mile radius known as *The Vanity Circuit.* As Hollywood faded into obscurity beneath our burgeoning distaste for propaganda, dogma and the heedless celebration of rank conjecture on the whole, we retasked churches, mosques and temples, which we found perfectly tailored and situated for far more generative uses such as community recreation facilities and town hall meeting venues.

Rather than stifle the quest to unriddle the *Primordial Why*, society's wholesale discard of religion delivered our minds from the quicksand of prejudgment, kindling a renaissance of unconstrained metaphysical study and space exploration, and resurrecting the long stagnant alliance between philosophical theory and the so-called *hard sciences.* Having cast away the childish bickering between the theist (whose consternation in the face of life's chaos drove him to pin his deepest hopes upon the supernatural father figure of lore) and the mainstream atheist (who, thanks to an abundance of arrogance and, in most cases, a deep-seated and irrational snit against the very entity whose existence he denied, presumed he alone had the power to understand the infinite universe), our openness to possibilities in the realm of the unknown engendered by our newfound self-reliance hatched revolutionary breakthroughs in the workaday sphere, from roadway gridlock to disease and even world hunger.

The new America was certainly not without its strife. Disagreements and even fistfights were as common as ever, especially at the town hall discussions. But, unlike those of recent generations, the newly enlightened debaters and combatants possessed a sense of honor which would not permit them to stray from the overarching goal of cultivating the common good. Among other things, this focus gave them a pronounced aversion to allowing the controversy to cross the line where spirited deliberation regresses into fighting for the sake of fighting. This attitude extended to the civil justice system. At the same time tort-reform constraints against product liability and professional malpractice lawsuits were removed, the rapid and widespread upsurge in fiscal prosperity counseled would-be plaintiffs to forsake the jackpot mentality of myopic years past. Thus, as had happened in the realms of politics, celebrity and religion, the elemental complexion of jurisprudence underwent a revolutionary shift: at long last, the search for truth slew the juggernaut of agenda.

Among the countless hoaxes that foundered before this new touchstone was the *manmade global warming* ploy conceived at the turn of the century to defraud U.S. taxpayers, which had quickly festered into the multinational economic extortion scheme touted as *manmade climate change.* As elevated consciousness renewed our interest in Earth sciences, the uncolored study thereof exposed the hubris of militant environmentalism. As various regulatory agencies were since pared down to size or excised like tumors from the body politic, and as the Federal Register was culled by eighty-five percent, the economic boom originally sparked by the taxation overhaul kicked into overdrive.

The administration of 2028 wasted no time in passing an Amendment to dissolve both Congress and the Presidency, replacing them with a panel that consists of one elected delegate from each State entitled *Governor's Liaison.* An annex was constructed at each State capitol, where the delegates meet to confer and vote on issues strictly confined to (a) standardizing State laws to promote interstate commerce and travel (b) repealing old laws in recognition of the truism that a cast left on after a broken bone has healed will only weaken that bone and (c) coordinating border protection with the State militias into which the national military branches were assimilated. The venue for the New Congress, whose procedures are based on *Robert's Rules of Order*, now rotates among the States at three-year intervals.

Now, a mere eighteen years from that portentous day, the United States of America has burst forth from its socioeconomic cocoon to become the true superpower its architects envisioned three centuries ago – one that leads by, not force or bribery, but inspiration.

Demagoguery in its myriad forms is dead.

Long live the United States of America.

Anthony Wayne Stearns retired from law and spent the remainder of his working life teaching English at a local university. During their long and rambling conversation on his deathbed at age ninety-six, he bestowed three nuggets of parting wisdom upon his grandson:

- "The world has plenty asses, but too few smart ones."
- "When fact opposes belief, the latter must always yield."
- "The puritan's bane is almost always the pragmatist's boon."

Julia Bross soon outgrew her quest for pecuniary patricide, so she gave Connie and Burnice a generous final bonus, sold her company, and devoted her time and resources to animal welfare. Though they seldom agreed on anything beyond their preferred brand of dental floss, she never left Ani's side, and they shared one last cocktail in his final hour, their forty-year argument about the proper complexion of a civilized society ending in a draw. When she emerged from the bedroom long minutes after his passing, she directed Melissa to the wine cellar for *the good stuff*, admonishing: "Death laughs loudest at a sober funeral." She then jabbed her intransigent finger at her grandson and barked: "Don't just sit there, boy; fire up the backhoe and make yourself useful!"

Peter and Mira transformed the Miracle Mile into a sprawling university campus dubbed *Academiae Utilis*. They lived happily ever after, primarily because they agreed to never again share a bathroom.

Following an unsuccessful attempt to sell knife fighting to the Olympics Committee, **Connie Plachette** devoted herself to the study of the Stamenphone – a free-hanging, pendulum shaped instrument with sixteen strings played with a cello bow. After five seasons with the Boston Pops, she wearied of orchestra life and took up abalone diving. In 2037, she wrote a bestselling autobiography with the help of Ani, who dabbled as Editor-at-Large for a major book publisher. The title: *If Love Is a Shiv, Cut Me*.

Soaring to overnight prominence in 2025 for her *Hustler Magazine* feature *Hauling Ass*, **Rita Baynes** sold her rig and moved to Chile to take up Alpaca ranching, where she had a chance meeting with newly divorced **Chick Barceno Villanueva**. She slimmed him down with a mystical tonic and took him with her to Albuquerque, where they opened a hybrid ballroom dance studio and naturopathy clinic. Rumor has it that Villanueva commissioned his own Pinocchio tattoo soon thereafter.

By 2026, it became painfully apparent that actors **Tom Cruise** and **Charlie Sheen** had missed the evolutionary boat when, though promised an Academy Award if they refrained from making boneheaded public statements, each failed miserably because he was unable to distinguish the rational from the daft. In 2028, their cronies lowered the bar by asking that they make no public statements whatsoever. Neither could muster the self-restraint. They eked out the remainder of their careers as regulars on *The Vanity Circuit*, their shared soundstage regarded by the general populace as Hollywood's equivalent of the padded cell.

Melissa Vivena Stearns ... well, what do you think?

Printed in the United States
by Baker & Taylor Publisher Services